RUNNING SCARED

RUNNING SCARED

Mandasue Heller

MACMILLAN

First published 2022 by Macmillan
an imprint of Pan Macmillan
The Smithson, 6 Briset Street, London EC1M 5NR
EU representative: Macmillan Publishers Ireland Ltd,
1st Floor, The Liffey Trust Centre, 117–126 Sheriff Street Upper,
Dublin 1, D01 YC43
Associated companies throughout the world
www.panmacmillan.com

ISBN 978-1-5290-2431-9

1 3 5 7 9 8 6 4 2

A CIP catalogue record for this book is available from the British Library.

Typeset by Palimpsest Book Production Ltd, Falkirk, Stirlingshire
Printed and bound by CPI Group (UK) Ltd, Croydon, CR0 4YY

Visit **www.panmacmillan.com** to read more about all our books
and to buy them. You will also find features, author interviews and
news of any author events, and you can sign up for e-newsletters
so that you're always first to hear about our new releases.

For my beautiful mum, with eternal love x

Acknowledgements

All my love as ever to my beautiful family: Win, Michael, Andrew, Azzura, Marissa, Lariah, Antonio, Marlowe, Ava, Amber, Martin, Jade, Reece, Kyro, Diaz, Azariah, Silvia, Paul, Marvin, Joseph, Daniel, Natalie, Amari, Aziah, Elle, Auntie Doreen, Peter, Lorna, Cliff, Chris, Glen, Julie and co. – and the rest of our loved ones, past and present.

Love to my friends: Liz Paton, Norman Brown, Katy and John, Amanda Jayne, Betty and Ronnie Schwartz, Trixy, Jo Mitchell, Tasha Rea, Louis Emerick, Steve Evets, Joe Gill, Jodie Prenger, Neil Hurst, Brian and Jac Capron, Sean Ward, Angela Lonsdale, Laney, all my old Hulme friends, Carolyn Caughey, Rick, Chris, Dr Sue.

Special thanks to Sheila Crowley, Wayne Brookes, and everyone involved in getting this book into readers' hands.

Gratitude to everyone who buys, sells, or lends them out, and to my lovely friends and supporters on social media.

And, lastly, a special mention to Adelweiss for your help with the detective stuff – you're a star! Also, Brenda Farrugia – for your kindness; and Rachel Thomas, who won the competition to have a character in this book named after her. Hope you like your namesakes, ladies x

PART ONE

1

Bored with the book her English teacher had ordered the class to read, Lexi James tossed it aside and flopped back against her pillows. She didn't know why the stupid cow thought any teenager in this day and age would be remotely interested in a load of plum-in-gob Victorian women whose lives revolved around pleasing their controlling, womanizing husbands, but she refused to waste one more second of her life on it. And if Ms Matthews threw one of her spot-tests later in the week, well . . . that's what Google was for.

Suddenly aware it was getting dark outside, she glanced at the alarm clock on her bedside table and shuffled off the bed to draw her curtains when she saw that it was almost 7 p.m. She'd started on her homework as soon as she got home and hadn't even changed out of her school uniform yet, never mind eaten.

Belly rumbling at the thought of food, she headed into the kitchen to heat a bowl of stew from the pan her mum had left on the stove before setting off for work that afternoon. The air

3

in there was icy, and she hugged herself when goosebumps sprang up all over her body as she waited for the microwave to ping. Seconds before it did, she heard a key scraping the lock of the front door, and her heart sank when her stepdad, Tony Lawson, stumbled inside muttering drunken curses under his breath. He didn't usually leave the pub until last orders, so he must have run out of money – or run *into* someone he owed money to. Either way, her plan to eat dinner in front of the TV was wrecked, because there was no way she was going to sit in the front room playing happy families with that fat pig.

'Beth?' Tony called out as he staggered up the hallway. 'Where are ya? I need some dosh.' He fell against the kitchen door frame in a fug of booze fumes, BO and stale smoke, and narrowed his glazed eyes when he spotted Lexi. 'Where's your mam?'

'Work,' Lexi said, eyeing him warily. She didn't like being alone with him at the best of times, but she especially didn't like being anywhere near him when he was pissed. Changing her mind about the stew, she tried to edge around him, but he put his hand on the door frame to prevent her from getting past.

'Not rushing off and leaving me on me own, are you?'

'I need to revise for my exams,' she lied, folding her arms when his gaze slid down to her breasts, which were straining against the buttons of her too-tight school shirt.

'Why bother with all that shit when you can lie back and let a man take care of you?' he said, grinning as he lowered his

4

face to within inches of hers. 'You're a pretty girl and you need someone to show you the ropes before the lads start sniffin' round – know what I mean?'

Nauseated by his boozy breath and the leery glint in his eyes, Lexi jerked her head back when he tried to stroke her cheek with a nicotine-stained finger.

'Like that, is it?' he chuckled. 'Gonna make me work for it, are ya?'

'Get lost!' she hissed, ducking under his arm and running to her room.

'Cock teaser,' Tony called after her.

Heart pounding, Lexi closed her door and pressed her ear to the wood, praying that he wouldn't follow and try to force his way in. He'd never done so before. But then he'd never looked at her like that before, either; and that remark he'd made about teaching her the ropes had totally creeped her out.

Relieved to hear the TV go on in the living room a few seconds later, Lexi pulled her jacket on and stuffed her feet into her trainers, then slid the window with the broken catch open and climbed out onto the communal landing outside, quietly sliding the window shut again.

It was dark and raining and she cursed Tony for coming home early and chasing her out as she jogged along the landing and down the stairs. The wind was howling through a broken windowpane when she reached the bottom of the stairwell, and she paused to zip her jacket and pull up her hood before pushing out through the heavy door. Hurrying up the path, she hesitated when she heard her name being called, and looked round to see little Jamie Holland from the second floor waving to her from the concrete play-area in the centre of the estate. Alone, as usual, wearing pants that were a good inch too short and a Christmas-patterned jumper that had seen far better days, the boy scooped up the half-flat football he'd been kicking against the wall and ran over to her.

'Where y'off?' he asked, his nose a bright red button in the middle of his pasty face.

'To my mate's,' she said, trying not to grimace at the odour of stale piss that always emanated from him. 'What you doing out in the rain without a coat?'

'Some lads chucked it in the canal after school,' he told her. 'Said it were covered in fleas and they needed to drown 'em.'

Incensed that he was being bullied because of the crappy clothes his junkie mother made him wear, Lexi said, 'Who were they? I'll chuck the little shits in and make them get it back for you.'

'Dunno.' Jamie shrugged. 'They was from the big school. But it don't matter; me jumper's warm.'

'It's soaked,' Lexi countered. 'And you'll catch your death if you stay out too much longer, so why don't you go home and dry off?'

'Can't,' he sniffed, wiping his nose on his sleeve. 'Me mam and her fella was scrapping over a wrap of gear, and she told me not to come back till she called for me.'

Lexi shook her head in disgust. He was only ten, and he

ought to be safe and warm at home, not left out here to get soaked while his mother and her latest shag got high. But he was a tough nut who knew no different, so her pity was wasted on him.

'That your dad?' Jamie jerked his chin up at the flats behind her.

Lexi followed his gaze up to the fourth floor and clenched her teeth when she saw Tony standing on the landing, the tip of his roll-up glowing red in the dark. Skin crawling when she realized he must have gone into her room and seen that she had sneaked out, she muttered, 'No it ain't. It's just the fat, useless dickhead my mum married.'

'Want me to do 'im in?' Jamie offered. 'I've been learning karate from a book I nicked out the library, and I'm dead good. Look . . .'

Trying not to laugh when he dropped the ball and started chopping and kicking at the air with a deadly serious expression on his thin face, Lexi said, 'Pack it in before you slip on the mud and break your neck. And *no*, I don't want you to do him in – he'll only sit on you and squash you to death.'

'I'll get our Mark to shoot 'im then.'

'I thought he was in prison?'

'Yeah, he is. But he's got mates on the outside who'll do it if he tells 'em.'

Touched that he wanted to help her, Lexi smiled and shook her head. He might look a mess and stink to high heaven, but he was a good kid and she had a real soft spot for him.

'I've got to go,' she said, reaching out to ruffle his wet hair. 'Don't stay out too long. And if those big lads bother you again, karate chop their balls. OK?'

Jamie wiped his nose on his sleeve again as he watched Lexi walk away. He wished he was older so she could be his girlfriend, because no one ever spoke to him as nice as she did. Everyone else treated him like shit – even his mam, who was more inter- ested in drugs and men than she was in him. But Lexi acted like she really cared about him, and he loved her for that.

As Lexi disappeared into the shadows of the alleyway leading off the estate, Jamie heard angry shouts coming from the flats and turned his head in time to see his mother's boyfriend stumble out onto the landing and puke over the balcony. Seconds later Jamie's mam came out and started punching him. Guessing that the man must have necked the wrap of smack they'd been fighting over, Jamie scooped his sodden football up off the grass and went back to his solitary game.

It was a two-mile, half-hour walk to her best friend Nicole Harvey's house, and Lexi was soaked to the bone by the time she got there. When she and Nic had first started hanging round together, the Harveys had lived on the next block along from her on the Kingston estate, so neither of them had had to walk too far to meet up. But since Nic's dad, Danny, had got rich and bought them this big house on the much posher Riverside estate, it was a slog and a half to reach her; hence she preferred to meet up at the park or the indoor market outside of school hours.

Shivering now, her teeth chattering loudly, Lexi rang the bell and stamped her frozen feet as she waited for an answer. The porch light came on a few seconds later and Nicole peered out at her.

'Oh, it's you,' Nicole said, a tinge of disappointment in her voice as she glanced over Lexi's shoulder and did a quick scan of the road. 'I was hoping it might be Ryan.'

'Are you expecting him?' Lexi asked, praying that her friend would say no, because they wouldn't want her hanging around if he came over, and she had nowhere else to go.

'He said he'd try to call round if he got the chance, but he must be busy,' Nicole said, sighing when she saw that the road was deserted. 'What you doing here at this time, anyway? I don't usually see you for dust after dark.'

'Dickhead came home early and started acting weird, so I had to get out of there,' Lexi told her. 'Can I stop here till my mum finishes work?'

'Can't you wait for her at the pub?' Nicole asked, glancing back over her shoulder and lowering her voice, before adding, 'Mine's in a bit of a funny one today.'

'Kids aren't allowed in there at night,' Lexi reminded her. 'Please, Nic. I'm freezing.'

Nicole chewed on her lip for a moment. Then, nodding, she said, 'OK. But you can't stay long, and you'll have to be quiet. And take them off.' She nodded at Lexi's soaked trainers. 'The cleaner was in today and my mum'll lose her shit if you get the floor dirty.'

Lexi gratefully stepped inside and took off her trainers. As she was standing them in the corner, the living room door opened and Nicole's mum, Rachel, appeared. She was the same age as Lexi's mum, but the Botox, breast implants and hair extensions made her look closer to Nicole and Lexi's age. She dressed young, too, and Lexi thought she'd be beautiful if it wasn't for the permanent *I can smell shit* expression on her otherwise perfect face.

'What's going on?' Rachel asked, flashing a disapproving glance at the puddle of rainwater that had formed on the laminate flooring around Lexi's sodden socks.

'Lex needs some notes for a science project we're working on,' Nicole lied. 'I meant to give them to her after school this afternoon, but I forgot.'

'And it couldn't have waited till morning?' Rachel almost managed to raise an eyebrow. 'You're supposed to be doing your homework.'

'I did it when I got home, and this has got to be handed in first thing,' said Nicole. 'Don't worry, it won't take long.'

'Make sure it doesn't. And clean that up.' Rachel pointed at the puddle and gave Lexi a withering look before flouncing back into the living room.

'I'd best go,' Lexi whispered as Nicole spread the water around with the bottom of her slipper to make it look as if she'd wiped it.

'Don't be daft, you're here now,' Nicole said, gesturing for her to come upstairs. 'I told you she was in a funny one, so don't take it personal. She's been biting everyone's heads off since I got home. My aunt reckons it's the menopause, but the vain bitch'd rather die than admit she's old enough for that.'

Lexi nodded, but deep down she knew it *was* personal. She didn't know why, because she'd always been polite and respectful, but the woman had made it quite clear that she didn't like her. Even before she'd had money, Rachel had acted like her shit didn't stink; and now she'd gone up in the world and could afford to wear proper designer gear instead of the snide stuff everyone wore on the estate, she was a thousand times worse.

'Put your jacket on the radiator so you don't wet my duvet,' Nicole ordered when they entered her bedroom a few seconds later.

Doing as she was told, Lexi looked around and felt a twinge of envy in her gut. It was a while since she'd been in there and she'd forgotten how nice it was. Her own room was small, messy, and always cold, even in summer; but this was a warm, spacious haven of girly pinks that any girl would be proud to call her own. The lacquered furniture matched, as did the bedding; and a flat-screen TV that was bigger than the one in Lexi's living room was attached to the wall opposite the bed, on the screen of which a Netflix movie was currently paused.

'So what's Dickhead been up to this time?' Nicole asked, settling on the bed and stretching out her legs.

'He was pissed and he trapped me in the kitchen,' Lexi

said, flopping down beside her. 'Reckons I need someone to *show me the ropes before the lads start sniffing round.*' She mimicked the last bit while making quote marks in the air with her fingers.

'Dirty bastard,' Nicole scowled. 'He didn't touch you, did he?'

'No, I didn't give him the chance. I told him to get lost and did a runner.'

'Are you gonna tell your mum?'

'What's the point? Everything goes in one ear and straight out the other where he's concerned.'

'Maybe he's got a massive dick,' Nicole mused.

'*Ewww!*' Lexi grimaced. 'Why would you even *think* something like that?'

'Well there's got to be something special about him to make her stick with him this long,' Nicole laughed. 'And it sure ain't his looks or his charming personality.'

'You're sick,' Lexi muttered, shaking the unwelcome images out of her head as she plucked a chocolate out of a box she'd spied under a magazine on the bedside table.

'Oi!' Nicole protested. 'They were really expensive and I've only got a few left.'

'I haven't had my tea yet,' Lexi said, popping the chocolate into her mouth before Nicole could demand she put it back. 'And I'm sure your dad'll get you some more if you ask nicely. You know he can never say no to his little princess.'

'That ain't the point,' Nicole grumbled, leaning over to grab the box to stop Lexi from taking any more of them. After putting it down on her own side, she glanced at the door to make sure it was shut before saying quietly, 'Subject of me dad, it's their anniversary on Saturday and he's taking bitch-face to Paris for the weekend.'

'Nice,' Lexi said, wishing her mum had married someone like Danny Harvey instead of getting stuck with a loser like Tony. The only holiday she'd ever had was a week in a caravan in Wales when she was four or five – which she didn't even remember. And, these days, they'd be lucky to afford a day trip to Blackpool, never mind a weekend in Paris.

'Yeah, it *is* nice, 'cos we're having a party,' Nicole whispered. 'Our Adam's been organizing it in secret all week.'

'Really?' Lexi perked up at the thought of a party. 'What time's it starting?'

'Oh, sorry, babe, you're not invited,' Nicole said, instantly bursting her bubble. 'It's Adam's party, not mine, so it's gonna be all his mates. But it wouldn't be your kind of thing, anyway, 'cos there'll be loads of booze and weed, and you're more of a jelly and balloons sort of girl, aren't you?'

'No I'm not,' Lexi pouted. 'I hate jelly.'

Laughing at her expression, Nicole said, 'I'm joking, you idiot. Course you can come. But don't be telling Dawn and Hannah, 'cos they're definitely not invited.'

'How come?' Lexi asked, surprised to hear that, because those were the girls they hung out with at school.

'They're too pretty and I don't want Ryan getting his head

turned,' Nicole said. 'You're all right, 'cos I know he'd never look twice at you, but I'm not having those two flaunting themselves in front of him.'

Lexi raised an eyebrow, offended to hear that Nicole didn't consider her pretty enough to be a threat. In truth, she knew she wasn't, because she was positively mousy compared to Nicole with her big green eyes and her long blond hair. But still . . . there was no need for her to be so blunt about it.

'Hey, why don't you ask your mum if you can stay over?' Nicole suggested. 'You'll have to kip on the sofa if Ryan decides to stay as well. Or you could always bunk up with our Adam.' She gave a sly grin. 'I know you've always fancied him.'

'No I haven't,' Lexi argued, cursing herself for immediately blushing, because she knew her friend would take that as a sign that she *did* fancy him – which she didn't. Not anymore, anyway. He might be as handsome as his sister was pretty, but he didn't half know it, and she always felt like he was taking the piss out of her – if he bothered to speak to her at all.

'Whatever,' Nicole smirked, convinced that her friend *did* fancy her brother – along with every other bitch in Manchester.

Eager to change the subject, Lexi said, 'What you wearing for the party?'

'I haven't decided yet, but you can help me choose while you're here,' Nicole said, jumping up off the bed and going over to her huge built-in wardrobe. 'I was thinking about this . . .' She pulled out a pink minidress and held it up against herself. 'What d'ya think?'

'Jelly and balloons,' Lexi said, thinking it looked like something a twelve-year-old would wear.

'Yeah, you're right,' Nicole agreed, tossing it onto the bed and pulling out a long green jersey dress. 'What about this?'

'I like that,' Lexi said. 'It's classy.'

'*Classy?*' Nicole screwed up her face. 'I need sexy, not classy.' She threw that dress aside and pulled out another, and another, until there was a heap on the bed. Staring down at it in despair, she moaned, 'I've literally got *nothing* to wear.'

'Come off it, you haven't even worn some of these,' Lexi said when she noticed that some of the garments still had tags attached. 'How about this?' She picked out a lilac blouse. 'I bet it'd look great with those grey pants you got for your birthday.'

'Are you taking the piss?' Nicole scowled. 'They made my arse look huge so I binned them.'

'If your arse is huge, mine must be the size of a bleedin' bus,' Lexi laughed.

'It's all right for you; you don't care what you look like,' Nicole said, scooping the clothes up off the bed.

'Wow, cheers, Nic. Nice to know what you *really* think of me.'

'Don't get your knickers in a twist. I only meant you're not obsessed with yourself, like Dawn and Hannah.'

And you, Lexi thought as she watched her friend toss the bundle into the bottom of the wardrobe – no doubt leaving them for the cleaner to re-hang. As much as she liked Nicole, there were times when she could cheerfully strangle her for the insensitive comments she threw out.

'Right, I'll have to get some money off my dad and go shopping,' Nicole declared, sitting down again. 'We'll catch the bus into town after school on Friday and you can help me choose something hot to blow Ryan's mind.'

Unsure if she could stomach watching her friend spend a fortune on clothes she didn't need, while she herself would have to plump for whatever was cleanest out of her own shitty wardrobe, Lexi said, 'I don't know if my mum's going to let me stay yet. But even if she does, I'll need to go home and get my stuff, so I'm probably best meeting you back here.'

'I'm not going shopping on my own,' Nicole protested. Then, shrugging, she said, 'Oh, well, if you don't want to come, I'm sure Sarah Green would be happy to take your place. But then I'd have to invite her to stay over, and there isn't room for both of you, so . . .'

She left the rest unsaid, but Lexi got the message loud and clear: if she refused to go shopping, she could kiss goodbye to the party *and* the sleepover. Unwilling to miss out on the rare chance to escape the flat – and Tony – for a night, she forced a smile, and said, 'Course I'll come, stupid. But only if I can have another chocolate.'

'Don't push it,' Nicole grunted. Then, tutting when Lexi pushed out her bottom lip and batted her eyelashes, she selected a chocolate from the box and tossed it to her, saying, 'Here, have the coffee one. I hate them.'

'My favourites,' Lexi grinned, stuffing it into her mouth.

'Nicole?' Rachel's voice drifted up the stairs.

'What?' Nicole called back, rolling her eyes at Lexi.

'Don't *what* me,' Rachel snapped. 'Come here.'

'Fuck's sake,' Nicole muttered, sliding off the bed and walking out of the room.

Stomping back in a couple of minutes later, she said, 'Sorry, Lex, you've got to go. She says we're being too loud.'

'Eh?' Lexi was confused. 'But we've been dead quiet.'

'I know, but she reckons she's getting one of her *migraines*,' Nicole sneered. 'Stupid fucking bitch. I hope it's a brain tumour.'

'Don't say that,' Lexi chided, getting up and reaching for her jacket. 'You'd never forgive yourself if it was that.'

'Wanna bet?' Nicole shot back. Then, chuckling at the look of disapproval on Lexi's face, she said, 'Chill out, I was joking.'

'Not funny,' Lexi said, following her out onto the landing and down the stairs.

'See you in the morning,' Nicole said as she showed her out. 'And don't forget – not a word to Dawn and Hannah about the party. If they find out, I'll know who to blame.'

'I won't say anything,' Lexi promised.

'Make sure you don't, or you'll be off the list,' Nicole warned.

She closed the door at that, leaving Lexi in darkness when the porch light went out. It had stopped raining by then, but the wind was getting stronger, and Lexi pulled up her hood and stuffed her hands into her pockets before setting off.

2

Behind the bar at the Dog and Duck pub, Beth Lawson covered a yawn with her hand and glanced up at the clock that was hanging at an angle next to the ancient TV in the corner. It had been a busy place when she'd first started working there four years earlier, but the elderly regulars had been steadily popping their clogs ever since, and the youngsters in the area wouldn't be caught dead in the dump, so it had got really quiet in there of late.

It had been a particularly slow night tonight, and they were the ones that exhausted her the most. Not only was it boring to have nothing to do and no one to talk to, but standing in one spot for so long had made her ankles swell up like balloons. Desperate to get home and put her feet up, she made short work of shooing out the last three customers as soon as the clock hit eleven. Bolting the door behind them, she washed their dirty glasses and gave the tables a quick wipe, then bagged the money from the till and carried it through to the back room, where Maurice, the landlord, had, as usual, spent the night watching cricket on a portable TV.

'Hundreds or thousands?' Maurice joked, bouncing the feather-light bag in his hand as if it weighed a ton when she handed it over.

'More like twenties or thirties,' Beth said, hoping that tonight wouldn't be the night he decided to face reality and admit it was time to sell up and move into the sheltered housing unit down the road. In his seventies now and riddled with arthritis, he had long ago given up any pretence of actually running the place; leaving Beth to single-handedly manage that side of things while he withered away in here. Her wages were crap, and she couldn't remember the last time anyone had left her a tip. But Maurice was barely making enough to cover his overheads, so there was no way she could ask for a raise. And there were no vacancies at any of the other pubs or shops in the area, because she regularly checked, so this would be her lot for the foreseeable.

'Here you go, love.' Maurice handed her a couple of notes out of the bag before struggling up to his feet. 'I'm off to bed so you'll have to see yourself out,' he wheezed, holding onto the back of the sofa to steady himself before hobbling out into the dingy hallway. 'Don't forget to lock up.'

'I won't,' Beth said, watching as he hauled his old bones up the narrow staircase.

Relieved when he made it all the way to the top without falling back down, as she often feared he might, she wondered if she ought to force his hand by quitting. Nobody else would do what she'd been doing for the pittance she got paid, so he would have to throw in the towel if she wasn't here to keep things ticking over.

Beth dismissed the idea as quickly as it had entered her mind, reminding herself that she needed every penny she could get while Tony was out of work and drinking her purse dry. She was pulling her coat on when she heard a noise in the back yard. Instantly wary, because several pubs in the area had recently been targeted by a gang who forced their way in after closing and trashed the place before robbing the till, she crept into the hallway and pressed her eye to the spyhole. Surprised to see her daughter on the other side, she opened up and waved her inside.

'What are you doing here? Has something happened?'

Lexi shook her head and blew on her fingers. She'd been sheltering in the stinking outside toilet in the yard since leaving Nicole's, which had saved her from the worst of the wind but not the cold, and she was absolutely freezing now.

'Why are you out this late, then?' Beth frowned. 'You know I don't like you walking around on your own at night. It's not safe.'

It was on the tip of Lexi's tongue to say that it was a damn sight safer than being stuck in the flat with Tony when he was drunk. But her mum would only demand to know what she meant by that, and she couldn't be bothered with the argument it would cause. So, instead, she repeated the lie Nicole had told *her* mum about needing notes for a project they were working on.

'You could have got them tomorrow,' Beth chided, unwittingly repeating what Nicole's mum had said as she picked up her handbag and looked around to make sure she hadn't left anything.

'It's got to be handed in first thing,' Lexi said. Then, stomach growling when she spied a stack of boxes standing against the wall beside the cellar door, she said, 'Can I get a pack of crisps, Mum? I haven't eaten since lunch.'

'Why not? I left a pan of stew on the stove.'

'Yeah, I know, but I wasn't hungry then.'

'Go on, then,' Beth said. 'But be quick,' she urged, peering up the staircase to check that Maurice wasn't eavesdropping. He was a soft touch in many ways, but not when it came to stock, and she could do without getting sacked over a stupid bag of crisps.

Ushering Lexi outside when the girl had got what she wanted, Beth locked the door and dropped the keys into her bag. 'So where are your notes?' she asked as they set off down the road.

'Eh?' Lexi gave her a blank look, too busy enjoying the crisps to remember the lie.

'For your project.'

'Oh, that . . . I, um, looked through them at Nic's and saw what I needed to see.'

'More like you made it up as an excuse to go over there,' Beth said knowingly. Sighing when Lexi shook her head, she said, 'I know you think I nag you for the sake of it, but I'm only trying to protect you, love. A girl got raped in the park the other night, and they still haven't caught the bloke.'

'I never go near the park on my own,' Lexi lied, shuddering at the thought that she might have got attacked when she took a shortcut through there earlier.

'Well, make sure you don't, 'cos he might end up killing the next one,' Beth said ominously. 'Men like that want castrating,' she went on huffily. 'But it's usually the girl who gets the blame. Shouldn't have gone out on her own at night . . . shouldn't have worn a short skirt . . . shouldn't have had a drink—'

'All right, Mum, I get it,' Lexi interrupted. 'I won't go near the park on my own.'

Lips pursed, Beth nodded and walked on.

Matching her pace, Lexi said, 'It's Nic's mum and dad's anniversary this weekend and they've invited me to their party. They said I can stay over – if it's OK with you?'

'We'll see,' Beth said. 'I'll talk to Tony.'

'What's it got to do with *him*?' Lexi scowled. 'He's not the boss.'

'Don't start, love. He's my husband, so I have to run things past him.'

'He doesn't run anything past *you*. He does whatever he wants, him.'

'That's enough,' Beth said wearily. 'You know what he's like, and I don't need you stirring the pot, so drop it.'

Lexi tipped the last of the crisps into her mouth without answering before stuffing the empty bag into a hedge. She didn't see what business it was of Tony's if she went to a party, but as usual her mum was handing the power to him, so now she would have to wait to see if the idiot gave his permission.

They walked on in silence for a few minutes, but as they neared their block, Beth said, 'If you really want to go to this party, it's fine by me. But I'll still need to run it past Tony.'

'What if he says no?' Lexi asked, refusing to get her hopes up just yet.

'You leave him to me.' Beth gave a conspiratorial smile. 'I know you think I'm a pushover, but I can still get my own way when I need to. The trick is to make him think it was his decision. But don't you dare tell him I said that.'

'As if!' Lexi said, grinning as she followed her in through the door. Now she'd had her mum's blessing, she didn't give a toss what Tony had to say about it. She was going to that party, whether he liked it or not.

Tony was slumped on the sofa snoring like a pig when Beth and Lexi entered the flat a few minutes later; a half-smoked roll-up in one hand, a can of beer in the other – some of which had spilled out onto his jogging bottoms, making it look as though he'd pissed himself.

'Tone?' Beth shook his shoulder after switching the main light on. 'Tony. Wake up.'

'Quit fuckin' shaking me,' he grunted, squinting up at her. 'Time is it?'

'Half eleven,' she told him, slipping her coat off and draping it over the back of her chair.

'Why you so late?' he demanded, sitting up and rubbing at the stain on his crotch before peering into the can to check if there was any beer left in it.

'It's the same time I always get in,' she replied as she flopped down and kicked off her shoes. 'Make us a cuppa, love,' she called to Lexi, who was taking off her jacket in the hallway. 'It's the first time I've sat down all day.'

'Fetch me a beer while you're at it,' Tony ordered as he squashed the empty can and chucked it at the overflowing wastepaper bin.

Muttering, 'Get your own beer, I'm not your slave,' Lexi was about to head into the kitchen, but hesitated when she heard Tony say: 'What the fuck are you wearing?'

'What d'you mean?' her mum replied warily.

'That top,' he snarled. 'It shows everything you've fuckin' got. You look like a right slag.'

'What you on about? I've worn it loads of times and you've never said anything.'

'Well, now I fuckin' am! Think I like knowing my wife's out there givin' every cunt on the estate an eyeful, do ya?'

The living room door suddenly slammed shut, and Lexi held her breath as she strained to hear their now-muffled voices. Jumping at the sound of a slap, followed by a cry of pain, she rushed back to the living room and burst through the door. Infuriated to see that Tony had her mum pinned to the chair with one hand around her throat and the other, fisted, raised in the air above her, she ran at him, yelling, 'Get off her you fat bastard!'

Staggering back when Lexi crashed into him, Tony let go of Beth and turned on her instead. 'What did you say?'

'You heard me,' she hissed, darting behind the sofa when he made a lunge for her. 'There's nowt wrong with her top; she looks lovely. You're just jealous 'cos you know she could do way better than you.'

'You'd best shut that mouth of yours before I give *you* a wallop, an' all,' Tony warned.

'Lay one finger on me and I'll call the police.' Lexi defiantly raised her chin. '*She* might let you get away with that shit, but *I* won't.'

'Lexi, that's enough,' Beth croaked, clutching her throat as she struggled to her feet. 'This is between me and Tony, so don't—'

'You keep out of this!' Tony pushed her roughly aside, his glare still fixed on Lexi.

'Don't you touch her,' Lexi yelled, hatred burning in her eyes as she glared right back.

'Or what? Think you're a big woman now, do ya?'

'No, but *you* obviously do. What was it you said earlier about teaching me the ropes?'

Tony faltered for a second, but quickly recovered. 'What you on about, ya lyin' cow? This is the first time I've seen you all day.'

'You're the liar, not me,' Lexi spat. 'You know exactly what you said.'

'Lexi, go to bed,' Beth interjected, pushing herself between them. 'I'll handle this.'

'But you need to hear what he said,' Lexi argued. 'That's why I really went to Nic's, 'cos *he*—'

'Alexis!' Beth used her daughter's full name as a warning to match the one in her eyes. 'I said go to bed.'

Frustrated that her mum was refusing to hear her out, and furious that Tony was smirking at her behind her mum's back, Lexi blinked back the tears that were welling in her eyes, and said, 'Fine, I'll go. But don't come crying to me when he puts you in hospital, 'cos it'll be your own fault!'

She marched out of the room at that, slamming the door as hard as she could behind her. She'd never hated anyone as much as she hated Tony, and she didn't understand why her mum couldn't see him for the fat, ugly bully he was. One beating would be enough for most women to come to their senses and kick him out, but not her mum. No matter how many times the bastard laid into her, the stupid cow always went back for more, and Lexi was sick of it.

Furious with her mum now as well as Tony, Lexi changed into her pyjamas, climbed into bed and pulled the pillow over her head to drown out the sound of her mum trying to placate Tony while the idiot blasted her for letting Lexi get away with disrespecting him.

'Nine months,' she whispered through clenched teeth. 'Nine more months and I'm out of here for good!'

And she meant every word. In nine months, when she turned sixteen, she was going to get her own flat off the council and move the hell away from her pathetic mother and that lecherous, piss-taking wife-beating husband of hers.

3

After a restless night, during which she woke several times convinced she'd heard her mum screaming, Lexi felt groggy when her alarm went off the following morning. As usual, her room was freezing, and goosebumps pimpled her arm when she reached out to silence the clock. Reluctant to leave the warmth of her bed, she grabbed her school shirt and pants off the floor where she'd dropped them and pulled them on under the quilt.

When she was dressed, she got up and shivered her way to the bathroom. The door was locked when she tried the handle and, guessing that it was her mum, because she could hear Tony's rumbling snores coming from their room, she tapped on the wood.

'Mum, are you gonna be long? I need to have a wash.'

The door opened a few seconds later and Beth shuffled out in her dressing gown. Still annoyed with her, Lexi was about to pass without speaking, but hesitated when she noticed the way her mum's slippers were dragging across the lino, as if she didn't have the energy to properly lift her feet. Following her into the kitchen, where she was able to see her face more clearly in the daylight coming through the window, she frowned when she saw the finger-shaped marks on her neck and the livid bruise around her swollen eye.

'Are you OK?' she asked, feeling guilty now for leaving her alone with Tony. 'That looks really bad.'

'I'm fine,' Beth said, averting her face as she lifted the kettle off its stand and carried it to the sink.

'You're clearly not,' Lexi argued. 'Look at the state of you. He went for you again after I went to bed, didn't he?'

'No, he didn't; this had nothing to do with him,' Beth lied. 'If you must know, I tripped over my shoes and fell onto the coffee table.'

'Why are you lying?' Lexi asked, frustrated that her mum was covering for him, as usual. 'I'm not stupid. I know it was him, and you need to kick him out before he—'

'What I *need* is for you to stop treating me like a child!' Beth slammed the kettle onto its stand. 'I know you're upset about last night, but it wasn't your business and you shouldn't have interfered.'

'But it *is* my business. You're my mum and I hate seeing you like this.'

'I told you I'm fine, so drop it. Now go to school, 'cos you're giving me a headache.'

Before Lexi could point out that Tony was the one who'd caused her headache by beating the crap out of her, the door opened and the man himself lumbered in; hair on end, reeking of stale booze and sweat, and wearing the same grubby vest from the previous night along with an equally grubby pair of pyjama bottoms. Too busy rubbing the sleep from his eyes to notice Lexi behind the door, he walked over to Beth and wrapped his arms around her waist.

'Mornin', sexy.'

Conscious of Lexi watching, Beth wriggled free, saying, 'I'm making a brew. Go back to bed; I'll fetch it through in a minute.'

'Make sure you fetch these, an' all,' Tony grunted, sliding his hands inside her dressing gown and groping her breasts.

'Oh my *God*,' Lexi muttered. 'That's so disgusting.'

Shocked, Tony snapped his head round and gaped at her. 'What are you still doing here? Shouldn't you be gone by now?'

'If anyone should be gone, it's *you*,' she replied icily.

'Eh?' He squinted at her, confusion in his eyes. 'What you on about?'

'*That!*' She pointed at her mum's bruised face. 'Proud of yourself, are you?'

'Go back to bed, love.' Beth pushed Tony toward the door. 'I'll deal with this.'

Tony started to walk out, then stopped and peered down at Lexi. 'I don't know why you hate me so much. I know we've had our ups and downs, but all I've ever done is try to be a good dad to you.'

'You ain't my dad, and you never will be,' she spat through clenched teeth.

Tony shook his head, as if he genuinely didn't get what he'd done wrong, and then sloped out of the room.

'Why did you have to go and do that?' Beth hissed at Lexi as she pushed the door shut behind him. 'I'd sorted everything out with him, and now you've gone and upset him again.'

'Don't blame *me*,' Lexi protested. 'He's the one who beat you up.'

'Look, I don't expect you to understand at your age, but that was the drink, not him,' said Beth. 'We talked about it after you went to bed and he admitted he's got a problem.'

'And that makes it all right, does it?'

'I'm not saying that, but him admitting he needs help was a big step. He's promised to see the doctor as soon as he can get an appointment, but it's not going to be easy and he's going to need our support, so all this arguing has got to stop. Do you understand?'

Lexi opened her mouth to point out that she had every right to argue with the man considering the way he treated them both. But she could tell by the look on her mum's face that she'd be wasting her breath, so she muttered, 'Whatever,' and turned to the door.

'Hang on a minute,' Beth said.

'What?' Lexi hesitated.

'Here . . .' Beth pulled one of the twenty-pound notes Maurice had given her out of her dressing gown pocket and held it out.

'I haven't got time,' Lexi said, thinking that she wanted her to nip to the corner shop before heading to school.

'No, it's for you,' Beth said. 'You probably don't deserve it after that little scene just now, but I – *we* – thought you might want to get yourself something nice to wear at the party. That's if you still want to go?'

Conflicted, Lexi bit her lip. Still angry, she wanted to tell her mum to stick the money up her arse and then flounce out with her nose in the air. But it was ages since she'd had any new clothes. And she really, *really* wanted to stay at Nic's. So, swallowing her pride, she reached for the note and murmured a grudging, 'Thanks.'

'I know you think I'm an idiot for letting Tony off the hook, but he needs me,' Beth said quietly. 'That doesn't mean I love him more than I love you, though, 'cos you mean more to me than anything or any*one* in the world. You know that, don't you?'

Feeling suddenly emotional, Lexi shrugged and dropped her gaze when tears welled in her eyes.

'Come here, you daft sod.' Beth pulled her into a hug. 'It's going to get better, I promise. You just need to back off and give Tony a chance. Can you do that? For *me*?'

Lexi doubted that anything was ever going to change where *he* was concerned, but she didn't want to make life more difficult for her mum, so she nodded her agreement.

'Thanks, love.' Beth squeezed her and kissed the top of her head before breaking the embrace. 'You'd best get going before you end up on detention for being late. I'll see you tonight. And try not to worry – OK?'

Nodding, Lexi sniffed back her tears and headed to the bathroom to finish getting ready. As much as she hated Tony, she loved her mum more, so she would honour her promise to quit arguing with him. But if he so much as *looked* at her mum in the wrong way again, all bets would be off.

Shoulders slumping when she heard the front door close behind Lexi a few minutes later, Beth listlessly stirred the teabags in the cups. She hadn't lied when she'd said that Tony had agreed to get help for his drinking, but it was one of the promises he always made after a fight – none of which he had ever followed through on. In light of that, she hated that she had effectively bribed her daughter into laying off him when the girl had every right to be angry. Hell, Beth was angry, too – with herself as much as with him, for allowing him to treat her the way he did. But the die had been cast the first time he'd laid into her and she had accepted his apology instead of reporting him to the police. She should have kicked him out then – and wished she had the strength to do so now. But Tony wasn't the kind of man to leave quietly, and she couldn't face another beating so soon after the last one, so she was left with no option but to try to keep him happy while he was in a good mood – even if that meant lying to her daughter and sacrificing what little was left of her dignity.

4

The rest of that week passed without further incident at home, and Lexi was excited when she set off for school on Friday morning with her pyjamas, her toothbrush, and the new leggings and top she'd bought with the money her mum had given her stuffed into her bag along with her books.

She'd never been particularly fond of school, but it dragged on to the point of feeling like torture that day, and she was out of her seat as if she had a rocket up her backside as soon as the home-time bell rang. As prearranged, in order to avoid Hannah and Dawn, who usually walked part of the way home with them, Nicole was waiting for her at the back of the gym block. Linking arms, they slipped out through the back gate and ran, giggling with excitement, all the way to the bus stop.

After a few hours spent traipsing from shop to shop in search of the perfect outfit for Nicole to wow Ryan with, Lexi was footsore, tired and hungry by the time Nic finally made a decision and bought the red satin dress and gold high-heeled sandals she'd tried on in the very first shop they had visited. Excitement well and truly waning, she felt like going home and climbing into bed. But she quickly perked up again when they arrived at Nicole's house and found that they had the place to themselves.

Able to relax without Rachel Harvey tossing out dirty looks and making her feel like a rat that had crept in under the door, Lexi took a shower in the main bathroom while Nicole used the one in her parents' en suite. There was only a bath with rusty taps and a deeply ingrained tidemark at the flat, so the shower was a rare luxury, and she took full advantage of the expensive body-scrubs, shampoos and conditioners on offer.

Dressed a short time later, and feeling a million dollars with her skin glowing, her usually dull brown hair hanging in glossy curls around her shoulders, and her face almost unrecognizable thanks to Nicole's make-up skills, Lexi smiled when her friend twirled round in front of her and asked how she looked.

'Gorgeous,' she said, genuinely meaning it. Nic always looked good, but tonight, with the red dress clinging to her curves and the strappy shoes making her legs look like they went on forever, Lexi thought she looked like a film star.

'I do, don't I?' Nicole agreed, preening in front of the mirror for a few seconds before heading for the door – *without*, Lexi noted, repaying the compliment.

Nicole's brother, Adam, had come home from college while they were upstairs, and the previously clear countertops were now crammed with bottles of wine, spirits and mixers. As Nicole cracked open a bottle of red wine and started pouring two glasses, Adam strolled in from the garden carrying two cases of beers. Doing a comical double-take when he saw Lexi, he looked at his sister and said, 'Who's this beauty? I thought you said that funny-looking mate of yours was the only one you'd invited?'

Blushing, Lexi self-consciously twiddled with one of her curls. On the rare occasions Adam bothered to speak to her, he usually made a sarcastic comment, so it was flattering that he'd complimented her for a change – even if he *was* only teasing.

'Pack that in!' Nicole slapped Lexi's hand down. 'It took me ages to get it looking decent, and I don't want you messing it up with your sweaty paws.'

Embarrassed, Lexi reached for her glass and glugged a mouthful of wine.

'Slow down,' Nicole chided, dropping a straw into her own glass. 'This ain't cheap shite, and I don't want you getting pissed before the party gets started and making a show of me.'

'Don't listen to her; you have as much as you want, darlin',' Adam said, winking at Lexi.

'Hadn't you best go and get a shower?' Nicole sniped, wafting a hand in front of her nose. 'You absolutely reek.'

'I've got loads of time yet,' he drawled, dropping the cases of beers onto the table.

Almost as soon as the words had left his mouth, the doorbell rang, and Nicole gave him a smug grin. 'You were saying?'

'Shit, they're early,' Adam said, glancing at his watch. 'Go let 'em in while I get changed, Nic. And I'll be seeing *you* later,' he added, pointing his finger at Lexi as if it was a loaded gun.

'He's taking the piss, so don't be getting your hopes up,' Nicole sniffed when he rushed out of the room and thundered up the stairs. 'And stop blushing every time he talks to you. It makes you look really desperate.'

'Why are you being such a bitch?' Lexi asked.

'I'm not,' Nicole said, dipping down to check her reflection in the glass of the microwave door. 'I just don't want you embarrassing me in front of Adam and his mates.'

'Oh, so now I'm embarrassing?' Lexi raised an eyebrow.

'Grow up,' Nicole tutted, flashing an irritated look at her before sashaying out of the room.

Lexi shook her head as she watched Nicole exaggeratedly swaying her hips. For someone who took the piss out of her own mother for dressing sexy and acting like God's gift to men, the stupid cow was doing a mighty fine impression of her right now.

Nicole came back a few seconds later with two boys, and Lexi smiled when one of them nodded hello to her. Noticing, Nicole immediately linked her arm through his and, turning him away from Lexi, walked him to the far end of the counter, asking, 'What can I get you to drink?'

Aware that her friend had deliberately diverted the boy's attention in order to keep the spotlight firmly on herself, Lexi grabbed a bottle of wine and retreated to a chair in the corner, from where she watched as Nicole flicked her hair around and batted her eyelashes at the boy and his friend. It was having the desired effect, because they were both grinning like Cheshire cats, but they were in for a shock if they thought they were in with a chance, because Lexi knew that Nic would drop them like hot bricks as soon as Ryan King arrived.

Thinking about Ryan, Lexi released a wistful sigh and sipped her wine. He lived by the Kingston and hung out with some of the lads off her block, so she had seen him around well before Nicole ever laid eyes on him. Mixed-race, with sexy hazel eyes, she had always got butterflies in her stomach whenever he gave her that killer smile of his, but she'd been far too shy to do anything beyond nod hello to him in return. And then Nicole had set her sights on him, and that had been that. It still pissed her off that Nicole had made a play for him without first checking if Lexi liked him, as per the girl code. But that was Nicole all over: if she wanted something, she would trample over anyone to get it – best friend, or not.

The doorbell rang again and the house was soon buzzing with the sound of music and laughter. Everyone seemed to know each other, and Lexi felt out of place as the chatter grew louder and more raucous around her. It wouldn't have been so bad if some of her own mates had been there to keep her company, but, apart from Nicole – who was flitting round playing hostess and seemed to have forgotten she was there – she didn't know a single soul.

Beginning to regret her decision to stay over as the party went on around her, Lexi steadily worked her way through the bottle of wine. Light-headed after a while, she was about to head out into the garden for some fresh air when Adam appeared in front of her. It was the first time she'd seen him since he went upstairs to get changed earlier that evening, and he was now wearing a tight white T-shirt that enhanced his gym-toned biceps and a pair of ripped jeans that hugged his muscular rugby-player thighs.

'Hey, sexy Lexi, why are you hiding over here?' he asked, his eyes glittering brightly as he gazed down at her.

Surprised that he was wasting time on her when there were older and far better-looking girls he could be talking to, Lexi self-consciously reached up to touch her hair, but immediately dropped her hand back down into her lap when she remembered Nicole's rebuke.

'I don't really know anyone,' she admitted.

'You know *me*,' he said, winking at her for the second time that night. Laughing when she blushed, he grabbed her hand and pulled her to her feet, saying, 'Come on. It's time we got you livened up.'

'Where are we going?' she asked, feeling a bit unsteady on her feet as he led her through the crowded kitchen.

'To get you in the party mood,' Adam said, pulling her on into the living room.

The music was much louder in there, and the lights were turned down so low Lexi could barely make out the faces of the people who were dotted around. Three lads were kneeling on the floor around a low table by the window, and Lexi was shocked to see they were snorting coke off the glass top when Adam led her over to them.

'Here,' he said, picking up a rolled banknote off the table and offering it to her.

'No, you're all right.' She shook her head.

'Aw, come on,' he wheedled. 'One little line ain't gonna hurt.'

'Honest, I'm OK with this,' she insisted, holding up her glass.

'That shit's for pussies,' Adam scoffed, snatching it out of her hand and tipping the wine into a plant pot before putting his own glass into her hand. 'If you won't have a line, at least have a decent bevvy.'

'What is it?' Lexi sniffed the clear liquid cautiously.

'Tequila,' he said, pushing the glass toward her lips. 'Try it.'

Lexi took a tiny sip and pulled a face. 'Eww, that's horrible.'

'You'll get used to it,' he said, putting his hand over hers and guiding the glass back to her lips. 'Come on . . . bottoms up.'

Spluttering when he tipped the glass and the liquid poured into her mouth, Lexi pushed his hand away when her throat started burning and her eyes began to water. 'Why did you do that? I could have choked.'

'Don't be such a *girl*,' Adam teased, sliding his arm around her waist and pulling her up against him. Grinning when she stiffened, he said, 'What you looking so scared for? You've dressed all sexy for me, so I'm only showing my appreciation.'

Trapped when he pushed her into an alcove and pressed himself up against her, Lexi twisted her head when he tried to kiss her, so his lips landed on her cheek instead of her mouth. Totally out of her depth, she said, 'Adam, stop it. I'm only fifteen.'

'So?' He licked her neck.

'Pack it in!' she squealed, trying to wriggle free. 'I thought you had a girlfriend?'

'She ain't here, so fuck her,' Adam said, grasping her chin in his hand to force her to keep her head still.

Lexi tried to push him off, but he was too strong for her, and she winced when he mashed his lips down on hers and started forcing his tongue into her mouth. Unlike Nicole, who had been with at least ten lads that Lexi knew of before hooking up with Ryan, Lexi had only ever been kissed a couple of times. She hadn't particularly enjoyed either of them, but neither had been as sloppy as Adam's was, and she feared she might throw up when his alcohol-laced saliva pooled in her mouth and she was forced to swallow.

On the verge of passing out from lack of air, Lexi sucked in a sharp breath when someone called Adam's name from across the room and he pulled his head back to see who it was.

'Stay there,' he ordered when he spotted a mate waving to him from the doorway. 'I'll be back in a minute.'

Seizing the chance to escape when he left her, Lexi stumbled back into the kitchen. A rowdy group of lads had cleared the table in the middle of the room and were playing a noisy game that seemed to involve one of them lying on it while the others poured a variety of neat spirits down their throat. Already queasy from the wine and the tequila Adam had forced her to drink, Lexi felt her stomach churn when the latest victim rolled over and puked on the floor as she was passing. Quickly detouring into the hallway, she clamped a hand over her mouth when a thick cloud of smoke coming from a spliff another group were sharing by the open front door hit her in the face. Aware that she was about to throw up, she clambered over a couple who were having a full-on necking session at the bottom of the stairs and ran to the bathroom.

After emptying the booze out of her stomach, Lexi splashed cold water onto her face and patted it dry with one of the big fluffy towels she'd earlier admired. Instantly feeling guilty when she saw that some of her make-up had transferred onto it, she stuffed it into the laundry basket in the corner before going out onto the landing. Still feeling iffy, and in no mood to go back to the party, she went to Nicole's room and tapped on the door to make sure no one was in there before opening it. About to go in when she got no reply, she cried out in alarm when someone crept up behind her and clamped a strong arm around her stomach.

'Gotcha!' a voice whispered into her ear.

'Adam, put me down!' she squawked, struggling to get free when he lifted off her feet and carried her into the bedroom, kicking the door shut behind him. 'What are you doing?'

'Finishing what we started,' he said, tossing her face down onto the bed and falling heavily on top of her.

'I can't breathe!' she wheezed.

'Sshhh,' he purred, his breath tickling her ear as he tugged at the waistband of her leggings. 'You know you want it.'

'I don't!' she cried, trying to wriggle out from under him when he slid a hand inside her top and squeezed her breast. 'Stop it!'

'Relax, my little virgin,' he said huskily as he unzipped his fly. 'I'll be gentle, I promise.'

Lexi clamped her thighs together, but he easily forced them apart, and she cried out when he thrust his hand inside her knickers.

'*Shhhh!*' he hissed, using his free hand to push her face into the duvet.

Unable to move or breathe properly, Lexi let out a squeal of fear and pain when he jabbed the tip of his erect penis into her. Behind them, the door opened and a shaft of light filtered in from the hallway, and the weight was suddenly lifted off her.

'Get the fuck off me!' Adam yelled.

'What the hell are you doing, man?' another voice hissed.

Mortified when she realized that it was Ryan, Lexi sobbed with shame as she scrambled to pull up her leggings and knickers.

'What's it fuckin' look like I'm doing?' Adam snarled. 'And I don't need an audience, so get out.'

'Bro, you're wasted,' Ryan replied evenly. 'And she don't look like she was enjoying whatever this was, so let's get you out of here and sobered up, eh?'

'Screwing my sister don't make you my *bro*,' Adam hissed, slamming his hands onto Ryan's chest in an effort to force him out of the room. 'And the bitch was well up for it before you stuck your oar in, so fuck off and let me get on with it.'

Unable to get past because they were blocking her path to the door, Lexi pressed herself up against the wall when Adam started throwing sloppy punches. Easily dodging them, Ryan pushed him away, and she threw a hand over her mouth when he fell backwards and smacked his head on the side of the dresser.

'Is – is he OK?' she asked when he didn't get up again.

'He'll live,' Ryan said, leaning over to check on him. 'Probably have a massive hangover when he wakes up, but that's his problem. What about you?' He turned to face her with concern in his eyes. 'Are *you* OK?'

Unable to meet his gaze, Lexi hugged herself and bit her lip as her tears continued to spill.

'Hey, come on, don't cry,' he said, putting his arms around her and stroking her back. 'He's pissed, so I doubt he meant any harm.'

'He really scared me,' she whimpered.

'Well, he won't be bothering you again tonight, so why don't you go get yourself cleaned up, then—'

'What the *fuck* . . . ?' Nicole appeared in the doorway at that exact moment and glared at them. 'What's going on?'

Instantly feeling guilty, even though she'd done nothing wrong, Lexi pulled herself free, and said, 'Nothing. I was just—'

'Just *what*?' Nicole cut in nastily as she marched over and pushed Lexi further away from Ryan. 'Just trying it on with my man 'cos you can't get one of your own, you skanky bitch?'

'No, it's not like that.'

'Well it fuckin' *looks* like that to me!'

'Nic, stop it, you've got it all wrong,' Lexi cried when Nicole started tearing at her hair. 'Adam attacked me and Ryan came in and pulled him off. That's all this is, I swear.'

'*Liar!*' Nicole spat, teeth bared as she twisted the hair around her hands. 'Our Adam can get any girl he wants, so why would he go after an ugly tramp like *you*?'

'Nic, pack it in,' Ryan hissed, trying to pull them apart when some of the guests began to congregate in the doorway to watch the fight. 'You're making a show of yourself.'

'You stay out of this,' Nicole roared. 'This is between me and her!'

'But I haven't done anything,' Lexi cried, holding onto Nicole's wrists to prevent the girl from tearing the hair right out of her scalp. 'I *wouldn't*. I'm your best mate.'

'No you're not, you're a *snake*, and I should've known I couldn't trust you! I've seen the way you look at my Ryan with your tongue hanging out, but you're thicker than you look if you think he'd ever choose *you* over *me*!'

'That's enough,' Ryan said, wrapping his arms around Nicole and pulling her off.

'Leave 'em to it, man,' one of the onlookers complained.

'Fight!' another chanted, punching the air with his fist. 'Fight, fight, fight . . .'

'Shut your fuckin' mouths!' Nicole bellowed, turning on the crowd when the rest of them joined in. 'And get the fuck out of my house!'

'You heard her,' Ryan said, his fierce glare shutting the chant down as quickly as it had started. Kicking the door to when the crowd moved back, he tightened his grip on Nicole when she made to lunge at Lexi again and ordered her to calm down.

'Why are you defending her?' Nicole twisted round and slammed her fist into his chest. '*I'm* your girlfriend, not *her*! If you've been fucking her behind my back, I swear to God—'

'What?' Ryan screwed up his face. 'Don't be so stupid.'

'I *caught* you!' she screeched.

Seizing her wrists to prevent her from hitting him again, Ryan peered down into her wild eyes, and said, 'What are you on? This ain't just booze.'

'Get off me, you're not my fuckin' dad!' she spat, pulling her hands free. 'And why are *you* still here, you shameless bitch?' she yelled at Lexi over his shoulder. 'Get out!'

'I can't,' Lexi argued. 'My mum thinks I'm staying the night.'

'I don't give a flying *fuck* what she thinks! GET *OUUUT*!'

In tears, Lexi gathered her things together and rushed out of the room and down the stairs. Pushing through the jeering crowd in the hallway, she stumbled out through the front door. The freezing early morning air took her breath away and she hugged the bag to her chest as she walked to the gate. Hesitating there, she looked both ways along the road. No lights were showing in the windows of the other houses, and the dull orange glow of the widely spaced street lamps made the shadowed areas look sinister.

Unsure how she was going to explain coming home at this

time if her mum caught her sneaking in, she cast a longing glance back at the house. The door was now closed, so she opened the gate and stepped nervously out onto the pavement. Remembering the rapist her mum had said was still on the loose, she scanned the shadows as she set off down the road.

She'd been walking for five minutes when she heard footsteps pounding the pavement behind her. Terrified that Adam had woken up and was coming after her, she glanced back over her shoulder and was relieved to see that it was only Ryan.

'Yo, Lex, wait up,' he called out when she carried on walking.

'What?' She hesitated.

'Are you OK?' he asked, breathing heavily when he caught up with her.

'I'm fine,' she lied, swiping the tears off her cheeks. 'Don't worry about me. Go back to the party.'

'Nah, I've had enough,' he said, stuffing his hands into his pockets. 'Come on, I'll walk you home.'

'You don't have to do that. I'll be all right on my own.'

'We're going the same way, so it's no problem.'

Hanging back when he set off, Lexi bit her lip. She and Nicole had fallen out many times over the years, but the girl had never physically attacked her before, and she knew there would be hell to pay if she allowed Ryan to walk her home and Nicole found out. But none of this was her fault, and she knew she would feel a lot safer walking with Ryan than continuing on alone. So, pushing her misgivings aside, she hurried after him.

'So all that with Adam,' Ryan said, glancing down at her when she fell into step beside him. 'That was all him, yeah?'

Ashamed and embarrassed, Lexi clutched her bag tighter and gave a tiny nod.

'I only asked 'cos Nic reckons you've always had a thing for him,' Ryan went on. 'Is that right?'

'No it's not!' she spat. 'I *hate* him.'

'Whoa, chill.' He held up his hands. 'I believe you.'

'Sorry,' she apologized, feeling bad for biting his head off when he was as innocent in this as she was. 'And I'm sorry if I caused trouble with you and Nic,' she added quietly.

'She caused it, not you,' he said. 'But she ain't my problem anymore, so don't stress about it.'

'What do you mean?' Lexi frowned.

'I'm done with her.' Ryan shrugged. 'Too much drama, man.'

'But she really likes you,' Lexi said, feeling guilty all over again, because none of this would be happening if she hadn't got drunk and given Adam the impression that she wanted him – although she genuinely didn't think she had. Not intentionally, anyway.

'She should've thought about that before she started accusing me of shit I haven't done,' said Ryan. 'It ain't just you. She goes off on one every time I speak to another girl, and I'm sick of it.'

'I know she can get a bit jealous, but it's only 'cos she's scared of losing you,' Lexi said loyally.

'Why are you sticking up for her after she went for you like

47

that?' Ryan asked. 'If one of my mates pulled that shit on me, I'd lay 'em out cold.'

'She's my best friend,' Lexi said. '*Was,*' she corrected herself.

'Her loss,' Ryan said.

Glancing up at him, Lexi quickly dropped her gaze again when he smiled at her. This was the first time they had ever been alone together and, apart from when he'd held her in Nic's room, the physically closest they had ever been. And he smelled really good – unlike Adam, whose aftershave had been so over-powering she had almost been able to taste it when he'd . . .

Shuddering at the memory of what he'd done to her, she squeezed her eyes shut in an effort to clear the visions of his leering face out of her mind.

'Careful,' Ryan said, reaching out to steady her when she bumped into him and almost tripped over.

'Sorry,' she mumbled, recoiling from his touch. 'Just felt a bit dizzy.'

'You didn't take anything back there, did you?' he asked.

'Like what?' She frowned.

'I dunno?' He shrugged. 'There was a lot of shit getting passed around when I got there – coke and tabs, an' that. It can mess you up if you're not used to it.'

'I didn't take anything,' Lexi said. 'I'm not into drugs.'

'I didn't think so, but thought I'd best ask in case you collapsed and I had to call an ambulance,' Ryan said. 'Nic was off her box, and I know you two usually do everything together.'

'Not that,' Lexi said, thinking that she obviously didn't know

Nicole as well as she'd thought if drugs was the cause of her behaviour tonight. Spliffs wouldn't have sent her off her head like that, but if Nic had taken something else on top of the weed and the booze it would explain how crazy she'd acted.

They walked on in silence until they reached the path that led onto the estate. Stopping when the blocks of flats came into view, Lexi said, 'I'll be all right from here.'

'Are you sure?' Ryan asked. 'I don't mind walking you to your door if you're still feeling iffy.'

'No, I'll be fine,' she insisted, dreading to think what her mum and Tony would say if they caught her not only coming home this late, but also with a boy.

'Before you go,' Ryan said. 'I was wondering . . . do you fancy hanging out sometime? Nothing heavy. Maybe go see a film, or bowling, or whatever.'

'What?' Lexi stared at him in confusion. 'You can't be serious. You're my best mate's boyfriend.'

'Not anymore,' he reminded her. 'And now you and her aren't speaking, I thought . . .' He tailed off and shrugged. 'Well, I wouldn't mind getting to know you a bit better.'

'This has got to be a joke,' Lexi spluttered, unable to believe what she was hearing. 'Me and Nic might have fallen out, but she's crazy about you so I'd never do that to her. And how could you even think I'd be interested in you or *any* boy after what Adam did?'

'Lexi, wait,' Ryan said, going after her when she started walking away. 'I'm sorry if you think I was out of line.'

'You were, and I'm not interested,' Lexi said, jerking away from him when he reached out to touch her arm. 'Now get lost and leave me alone.'

'I'm sorry,' he said again. But she walked on without looking back.

5

Beth woke early on Saturday morning and slid quietly out of bed. As usual when he'd been on a bender the night before, Tony was sprawled out like a starfish, snoring his head off, and she wrinkled her nose in disgust at the stench of stale alcohol coming from his gaping mouth. He'd had all week to make an appointment with the doctor, but – surprise, surprise – he still hadn't done it. For the first couple of days when she'd asked, he'd insisted that he had been trying to ring the surgery but couldn't get through. After that, he'd started to get narky whenever she raised the subject, so she'd been forced to back off. Now it was clear that he'd never had any intention of doing it, and she was annoyed that she had allowed herself to hope that he might actually have meant it this time. She was only glad that Lexi hadn't been here to witness him crashing through the door at just gone midnight in a foul temper, because she wouldn't have been able to look the girl in the eye after persuading her to give him another chance.

After getting dressed, Beth tiptoed out of the room and quietly closed the door. In the bathroom, she stood in front of the mirror and lifted her blouse. Tony had been too far gone to do much damage, but the punch he'd managed to land before flaking out had left a huge bruise on her side. Fortunately, none of her ribs appeared to be broken. And, better yet, he hadn't touched her face, so she wouldn't need to plaster herself in make-up before heading out to work – another excuse for him to accuse her of putting it on to attract other men, seeming to forget that she wouldn't even need it if it wasn't for him and his fists.

Sighing at the irony of it, Beth straightened her blouse and had a quick wash before heading to the kitchen to make a cup of tea. Almost there, she hesitated when she heard a noise coming from Lexi's room. Hoping to God that it wasn't a rat, because she'd seen a couple of the buggers scuttling in and out of the bin cupboards during the week, and they were *huge*, she cautiously opened Lexi's door and peeped inside. The curtains were closed so she didn't immediately notice Lexi lying in the bed, and she almost jumped out of her skin when the girl rolled over. Curious to know why her daughter was home when she should still be at Nicole's, Beth went over and gently touched her shoulder.

'Lexi?'

Jolted awake, Lexi's eyes shot open and she let out a little cry of fear.

'It's only me, love,' Beth said, guessing that she must have been having a bad dream. 'When did you get home? I didn't hear you coming in.'

'This morning,' Lexi croaked, hoping her mum didn't ask what time, because she'd go mad if she knew it had been in the early hours – *and* that she'd had to climb in through the window because she'd realized her key wasn't in her bag when she got back.

'Why?' Beth asked. 'I'd have thought you'd want to spend the day with Nic.'

'I had a headache.'

'Well, I hope you helped to clear up before you left? I wouldn't want them to think you were rude after they invited you to their party.'

'They've got a cleaner.'

'Now why doesn't that surprise me?' Beth tutted. Then, tilting her head to one side when she noticed Lexi's swollen eyes, she said, 'Have you been crying?'

'No.' Lexi pulled the quilt up a little higher.

'You look like you have. Is it the headache, or did something happen to upset you over there? You and Nic haven't fallen out, have you?'

Lexi shook her head again, but Beth saw a tell-tale tear trickling down her nose and sat down on the edge of the bed. 'Oh, love, what's the matter?' she asked, reaching out to stroke her hair. Hesitating when Lexi flinched, she narrowed her eyes when she spotted a clump on the pillow. 'What's this?' She picked it up. 'Have you been fighting?'

'It wasn't me, it was Nic,' Lexi sobbed, unable to hold in the tears any longer. 'She thought I was trying to get off with her boyfriend and went for me – but I wasn't, I swear. I tried telling her he was only pulling Adam off me, but she—'

'Whoa, back up a minute,' Beth cut in. 'What d'you mean he was pulling Adam off you? And have you been drinking?' she added, picking up the scent of alcohol.

'A bit.'

'Well, I'll be having words with Nicole's mum and dad about that. But right now I'm more concerned about what you and Adam were up to – and, more importantly, how far you went. The pharmacy shuts early today, so if we need to get you the morning-after pill—'

'He didn't do *that*,' Lexi spluttered, her cheeks on fire. 'Not all the way, anyway.'

Instincts prickling when she realized Lexi had said *he* not *we*, Beth said, 'But he tried?' Frowning when Lexi nodded, she said, 'And did you want him to?'

'No,' Lexi whimpered. 'I told him to stop, but he wouldn't.'

'Right, get dressed,' Beth ordered. 'I'm calling the police.'

'You can't!' Lexi yelped, sitting bolt upright. 'Please, Mum. They'll say it was my fault for drinking.'

'No, they'll say it was his parents' fault for *letting* you drink. I should've known they couldn't be trusted to look after you. That Rachel's always looked down her nose at us, and as for that husband of hers—'

'They weren't there,' Lexi interrupted.

'You what?' Beth was confused. 'You mean they took off from their own party and left a load of kids around booze?'

'They went to Paris for their anniversary,' Lexi explained guiltily, unable to meet her mum's gaze. 'They didn't even know about the party. Adam organized it behind their backs.'

'So let me get this straight...' Beth's eyebrows knitted together as she started to put the pieces together. 'If they're not there and didn't know about the party, they couldn't have invited you to stay over, which means you lied to me.'

'I'm sorry, Mum. It was Nic's idea.'

'Are you lying about Adam as well?'

'No, that's true, I swear. I was drunk and got sick, so I went for a lie-down. He came up behind me and pushed me onto the bed. I told him to get off, but he . . .' Unable to carry on, she pulled up her knees and buried her face in them.

'Lexi, this is serious, so I need you to be completely honest with me,' Beth said. 'Have you and Adam ever done anything in the past that would make him think you wanted him? Have you ever kissed him or slept with him?'

'No, never,' Lexi said truthfully. 'I always thought he was good-looking, but he's not very nice to me, so I don't like him like that. But last night . . .'

'Last night what?' Beth prompted when she tailed off. 'Did he say something to make you think he liked you?'

Lexi nodded and wiped her nose on her hand. 'Nic had done my hair and make-up really nice, and he said I looked beautiful.'

'And you were flattered?'

'Kind of. But that was before the party started, and I didn't see him again for ages, 'cos I was sat by myself all night.'

'Why were you on your own? Where was Nic?'

'I don't know. She'd gone a bit funny with me earlier on and then disappeared. I didn't know anyone else, so I sat in the corner. But then Adam came over and . . .'

'*And?*' Beth pressed, struggling to curb her rising anger at the thought of her daughter being abandoned in a room full of strangers by her so-called best friend.

'He pushed me up against the wall and kissed me, and he didn't care when I told him I'm only fifteen,' Lexi said quietly. 'One of his friends called him and I got away, but he must have seen me go upstairs and followed me.'

'Did he touch you?' Beth asked, softening her tone when she saw fresh tears glistening in her daughter's eyes.

Lexi nodded and bit her quivering lip.

'Where?' Beth asked. Blood boiling when Lexi pointed at her breasts and then between her legs, she hissed, 'Little bastard! Wait till I get my hands on him.'

'I think it might have been my fault,' Lexi gulped. 'He – he told Ryan I'd been up for it before he came in, so I must have done something to make him think I wanted it.'

'Now you listen to me,' Beth said, gently cupping Lexi's cheeks in her hands and forcing her to look up. 'I don't care if you'd been dancing naked in front of him before that, if you said no he should have stopped. Do you understand?'

Tears streaming again, Lexi nodded.

'Good girl.' Beth hugged her. 'Now tell me exactly what happened from the beginning, then we'll decide what we're going to do about it.'

Tony woke to the sound of voices in the hallway, and he muttered a curse under his breath when he squinted at the clock and saw that it was only 9 a.m.

'Beth?' he yelled. '*BEEEETH!*'

'Stop shouting,' Beth hissed, slipping into the room and closing the door. 'The police are here.'

'What?' His face paled. '*Why?*'

Immediately guessing that he thought she'd reported him for hitting her the previous night, Beth wished she could string it out and make him sweat – payback for all the times he'd got away with abusing her in the past. But her daughter needed her, so she had no choice but to let him off the hook.

'They're here to see Lexi.'

'Why?' Tony looked no less worried. 'I haven't spoken to her all week, so if she's saying I've done something, she's lying.'

'What are you talking about?' Beth frowned.

'Nothing.' He shiftily averted his gaze. 'So what's she done?'

Annoyed that he'd immediately assumed Lexi was at fault, Beth said, 'She hasn't done anything. If you must know, she was nearly raped last night.'

'You what?' Tony scowled. 'By who? I'll skin the fucker alive.'

'It was Nicole's brother, and you'll do no such thing,' said Beth. 'The police will deal with it.'

Bravado disappearing as fast as it had appeared, Tony said, 'Hang on . . . you're not talking about Danny Harvey's lad, are you?'

'Yeah, why?'

'And you've called the police?'

'I just told you the boy tried to rape her, so why wouldn't I?'

'Because Harvey's a fuckin' nutter,' Tony said as he sat up and shoved the quilt off his legs. 'How could you be so stupid?'

'Where are you going?' Beth asked when he started getting dressed. 'You can't go in there while she's giving her statement.'

'Don't worry, I ain't getting involved in that shit,' Tony assured her. 'I'm out of here before Harvey turns up and caves my head in.'

'He's in Paris, so that's not going to happen. And his son's the one who caused this, so *he's* the one he'll be mad at, not us.'

'Get a grip. Harvey ain't gonna give a toss about two kids having a fumble; all he'll care about is *you* grassing him up.'

'A *fumble*?' Beth repeated incredulously.

'There's certain things you don't do, and sending the pigs to a dealer's house is one of them,' said Tony. 'What d'ya think'll happen if they search his gaff and find a shitload of gear? Who do you think he'll blame?'

'That's his problem, not mine,' Beth said stiffly, turning to the door. 'I've got to do what's best for my daughter.'

'Beth, this ain't a joke,' Tony hissed, grabbing her arm before she could leave. 'If Harvey gets us in his sights, we're fucked. Did his lad actually – *you* know?'

'He started to, but he got pulled off.'

'That's good then, isn't it?' Tony said. 'I mean, it ain't *good*, obviously, but at least it wasn't like proper rape.'

'Are you serious?' Beth scowled, unable to believe he was trying to downplay what the boy had done.

'I'm deadly serious,' said Tony. 'Tell her to say she made it up before this goes any further, I'm begging you.'

Wincing when his knuckles grazed her bruised ribs, Beth clenched her teeth. 'No chance! And get your hands off me before I report *you* as well.'

Tony stared down at her for a few more seconds, his blazing eyes telling her that he was battling the urge to punch her. Then, abruptly releasing her, he said, 'Do what you want, you stupid cow. But don't say I didn't warn you when it comes on top.'

Beth scuttled out and closed the door. Shaking all over, she wondered if she ought to do as he'd said and call this off before Lexi made her statement. But if she let Adam Harvey get away with what he'd done, who knew how many more girls he would attack before somebody decided to take a stand?

Terrified at the thought of the potential repercussions, but convinced that she was doing the right thing by her daughter, Beth raised her chin and walked into the living room.

6

Danny Harvey was in a foul mood. He'd spent a fortune on plane tickets and a suite at a swanky hotel within walking distance of the Eiffel Tower and all the designer shops Rachel had set her heart on visiting. But now, less than twenty-four hours after leaving, they'd been forced to fly back to sort out the mess their fuckwit son had got himself into while they were away.

Fresh off the phone with his solicitor, who had assured him that the police would probably drop the investigation unless the as-yet-unnamed witness verified Lexi James's account of the assault, Danny poured a glass of neat whisky and slammed the bottle down on the kitchen table.

'So what happened?' He scowled at his son, who was slouched in the chair facing his. 'And don't be giving me any of your bullshit, boy. This is serious and I need the truth.'

'I didn't do anything,' Adam muttered, a hard-done-by expression on his handsome face.

'Then why were you in the bedroom with her?' Rachel asked

curtly, equally as furious as her husband – if not more so, after coming home to find her beautiful house trashed.

'I was pissed; I don't remember anything,' Adam replied sullenly. 'But I *deffo* know I didn't do what she said. Why would I? I've got a girlfriend.'

'He was out cold when I got there, so he couldn't have done it even if he'd wanted to,' Nicole added in her brother's defence. 'If you ask me, she's doing this for revenge.'

'Revenge for what?' Danny switched his glare onto her. 'Did something happen between them before last night?'

'Only in her dreams,' Nicole sneered. 'She's always fancied him, and she wouldn't listen when I told her she stood no chance. She was proper embarrassing last night; following him round like a little dog. I wish I hadn't invited her now.'

'But you did,' snapped Rachel. 'Even though I've told you a million times I don't want her in my house. God only knows what the neighbours think of us when they see slum-rats like her at the door.'

'Well, it won't be happening again,' Nicole huffed. 'I'll kill her if she comes anywhere near me after this. And she's *double* dead if she goes near Ryan again.'

'Who's Ryan?' Danny asked.

'Her boyfriend,' Rachel told him as she got up to open a fresh bottle of wine.

'Since when?' Danny glowered. 'And how come this is the first I'm hearing about it?'

'If you stayed home more often instead of spending all your

time with your *crew*, you might know what your children were getting up to,' Rachel sniped as she topped up her glass.

'And if *your* kids hadn't pulled a fast one and thrown a fuckin' party behind our backs, we'd still be in Paris and I wouldn't have wasted a shitload of dosh,' Danny shot back. 'So think on before you start having a go at me.'

Satisfied that he'd made his point when his wife came back to the table without replying, Danny turned back to Nicole. 'So what's this Ryan boy got to do with this?'

'He was there,' she said, her eyes narrowing in anger as she recalled the moment she'd walked into her bedroom. 'She was crying and clinging onto him, but I could tell she was putting it on, 'cos she looked dead guilty when she saw me. I asked what was going on, and that's when she came out with that bullshit about Adam attacking her. But Ad was out cold, so I knew she was lying.'

'I don't get it.' Danny was confused. 'Why would she be crying if nothing had happened?'

'To get Ryan to feel sorry for her, obviously,' said Nicole. 'She's always fancied *him*, an' all, so when our Adam knocked her back, I reckon she made up that story about him attacking her so she could try it on with Ryan instead.'

'I need to speak to him,' Danny said. 'Call him and tell him to come over.'

'He won't answer,' Nicole said miserably. 'I've been trying all day and he's ignoring my calls.'

'Give me his number.' Danny pulled out his phone.

Scared now, because she knew how angry her father could get if he thought someone was taking the piss out of one of his kids, Nicole said, 'Please don't hurt him, Dad. I really like him, and I know we'll be OK when I've had a chance to talk to him. This is her fault, not his.'

'This isn't about you, it's about your brother,' Danny replied sharply. 'Now hurry up and give me the number.'

'If he's grassed me up, he's dead,' Adam muttered as Nicole scrolled through her phone.

'Shut your mouth!' Danny barked, slamming his fist down on the tabletop and making them all jump. 'You caused this, and I don't want to hear another word out of you until I ask you to speak. Have you got that?'

'What you shouting at *him* for?' Rachel snapped. 'He's the victim here, don't forget.'

'So what was that crack about the lad grassing him up?' Danny asked. 'Only the way I see it, you don't worry about shit like that unless you're guilty. And, let's face it, this ain't the first time, is it?'

'And that little slut was lying, as well,' Rachel hissed, her anger about the ruined holiday and trashed house momentarily forgotten as the habitual urge to defend her son rose to the fore.

'I didn't even mean it the way you took it, Dad,' Adam interjected, giving his father a wounded look.

'So what did you mean?' Danny glowered.

'Ryan's a prick and he knows I can't stand him, so I only

meant I wouldn't put it past him to try and drop me in it out of spite.'

'He'd never do that,' Nicole protested.

'You're screwing him, so you're bound to say that,' Adam sniped.

'No I'm not!' Nicole's face turned as red as a beetroot. 'Don't listen to him, Dad. He's only trying to make you mad at me so you'll lay off him.'

'It don't even matter what Ryan says, anyhow,' Adam sighed. 'If my own dad doesn't believe me, I'm fucked.'

'Of course he believes you,' said Rachel.

'It's all right, Mum,' Adam said, scraping his chair back and standing up. 'I know he's ashamed of me 'cos I'm not a thug like the lads on his crew. He'll probably be glad if I get sent down for this.'

'You can get that nonsense out of your head right now,' Rachel said firmly. 'We're both very proud of you. *Aren't* we, Danny?' She glared at her husband.

Sighing, Danny raked a hand through his hair before looking up at his son. 'I ain't ashamed of you, son. I'm just sick of you getting yourself into these situations.'

'But I didn't *do* anything.'

'It won't matter what you did or didn't do if it gets round that you tried to rape a fifteen-year-old,' said Danny. 'You'll be labelled a nonce and every fucker in Manchester will be gunning for you. And shit like that sticks for life, so you'll be a dead man walking.'

64

Adam's shoulders sagged, and the sickly look on his face told Danny that he was finally beginning to grasp the seriousness of the situation.

'You need to go and see her,' Rachel said. 'The other one dropped it after you had a word, so you can make this one drop it too.'

'The other one hadn't been to the police yet,' Danny reminded her. 'But this one has, so I can't go near. If it looks like I'm trying to intimidate her, I'll get nicked.'

'So what are we going to do?'

'If this Ryan boy is the only so-called witness, I need to talk to him before the pigs get to him,' Danny said. 'But this shit had better not happen again – *ever*,' he added, giving his son a fierce look. 'Are we clear on that?'

'Yes.' Adam nodded his agreement.

'Right, make yourself scarce, 'cos I don't really wanna look at you right now,' Danny said dismissively. 'And don't go putting any nonsense online slagging her off, 'cos you ain't in the clear yet. Keep your head down and your gob shut till it's sorted. Right?'

'Right,' Adam muttered, sloping out of the room.

7

Ryan was nervous as he approached Nicole's house later that evening. She'd been calling him all day and bombarding him with messages threatening to kill herself if he didn't speak to her. He hadn't for one minute thought she would go through with it, so when her father had called out of the blue and ordered him to go round there, his stomach had dropped like a brick. The man hadn't said *why* he wanted to see him, but Ryan figured it had to be pretty serious to make the couple come home early from Paris, so the relief, when Nicole answered the door, washed over him like a tidal wave.

'Thank fuck you're OK,' he said, releasing the breath he'd been holding. 'I've been thinking all sorts since your old man called.'

'Have the police been to see you yet?' she whispered, waving for him to come inside.

'The police? No. Why?'

'That bitch has accused Adam of trying to rape her, and we think she's named you as a witness.'

'Who, Lexi?'

Teeth clenching at the sound of *that* name coming out of his mouth, Nicole said, 'My dad's waiting for you in the kitchen so you'd best hurry up. And don't worry,' she added ominously. 'He's promised not to hurt you.'

Unnerved by that comment, Ryan was on edge as he followed her into the kitchen, where her parents were sitting at the table, each with a glass of booze in their hands. He'd seen Rachel a couple of times in the past, but this was the first time he'd ever come face to face with Danny Harvey – although he'd heard plenty about him and knew that he was well-respected among the dealers on and around the estate, most of whom either worked for him or got their gear off him. He'd also heard that the man had a rep for extreme violence if crossed, and he hoped to God that him dumping Nicole wouldn't be considered a 'cross'.

'Dad, this is Ryan,' Nicole introduced them. 'He hasn't spoken to the police yet.'

'Take a seat.' Danny gestured to the chair facing his.

Ryan sat stiffly down and tried not to fidget when the man stared at him for several seconds without speaking. Nicole and Adam were fair-haired and green-eyed like their mother, but Danny Harvey had the look of a traveller with his dark hair and intense blue eyes, and Ryan felt a trickle of nervous sweat snake down his back.

'Have we met?' Danny spoke at last. 'You look familiar.'

'I, er, don't think so,' Ryan said, clearing his throat nervously.

'But I hang out with some of the lads who work for you on the Kingston, so you might have seen me there.'

'That's probably it.' Eyes never leaving Ryan, Danny sat back and took a swig of his drink. 'So what happened last night?'

'With Adam and Lexi?' Ryan flashed a hooded glance at Nicole, who was leaning against the counter behind her parents, chewing on her thumbnail. Continuing when she gave a tiny nod, he said, 'I was going to the loo and heard noises in one of the bedrooms. It sounded like a girl crying, so I looked in to check she was OK.'

'And?' Danny waved his hand in a circular motion to speed him up.

'I could see two people on the bed, but it was too dark to make out who it was,' Ryan went on. 'Like I said, the girl was crying, so I went in and pulled the lad off her. That's when I realized it was your Adam and Lexi.'

'Were they having sex?' Rachel asked bluntly.

'I, um, don't think they'd got that far,' Ryan replied.

'But it looked like they were about to?' Danny asked.

About to say yes, Ryan changed his mind when Nicole made a cutting motion across her throat with her finger. Instead, diplomatically, he said, 'To be honest, he was so wasted I'm not sure he knew what he was doing.'

'Nicole said he was out cold when she walked in,' said Danny. 'How did that happen?'

'That was an accident,' Ryan said warily, hoping he wasn't about to get hammered for knocking the man's son out. 'Like

I say, he was mad drunk, and he took a swing at me so I pushed him away. He smacked his head on the dresser, but he wasn't bleeding when I checked on him, so I figured he'd sleep it off.'

'And what did *she* say?' Rachel asked.

'She'd been drinking as well, so she wasn't making much sense,' Ryan lied. 'I told her Adam wouldn't have meant her any harm, and she'd calmed down by the time she got home, so—'

'What do you mean by that?' Nicole blurted out before he could go on. 'How would you know what she was like when she got home?'

Cursing himself for slipping up when he felt Rachel's glare boring into him, Ryan said, 'I passed her when I was walking back to mine and asked if she was OK – after the fight, and that. She said she was, and she looked it, so I left her to it.'

'That'd better be the truth,' Rachel said. 'Because if we find out you've been messing with that little bitch behind Nicole's back . . .'

She left the rest unsaid, but Ryan got the point loud and clear. 'I'd never do that,' he insisted, hoping that Lexi never decided to tell them what had really happened. He did like her, because she was the complete opposite of Nicole in that she wasn't flashy or mouthy; and she was also way prettier than she gave herself credit for. But he'd acted like a knob when he'd asked her out straight after finishing with her best mate, not to mention how she must have felt, given what had happened with Adam, so he didn't blame her for turning him down flat. But she had, so now he had to forget about her and look out for himself.

'And how do things stand with you and Nic now?' Danny changed the subject. 'She says you've been ignoring her calls all day.'

'I've been playing Xbox at my mate's and my phone was on silent,' Ryan explained. 'I didn't even know she'd been trying to get hold of me till I looked at it just before you rang.'

'So it's still on, then? You and her?'

'I, um, guess so,' Ryan said, feeling totally cornered. 'She got the wrong end of the stick last night, but I swear nothing went down with me and Lexi.'

Danny peered at him thoughtfully for a moment and then nodded. 'OK, I believe you.'

'So do I,' Nicole said, a sheepish look on her face as she rushed over and sat next to Ryan. 'I'm so sorry for kicking off, babe. I flipped when I saw you and her together, but I know you'd never cheat on me.'

'As if.' Ryan forced a smile.

'Careful, son,' Danny teased. 'You'll have her checking out wedding dresses if you carry on with that soppy shit.'

'*Dad!*' Nicole giggled, her cheeks flushing as she slipped her hand into Ryan's.

'Well, now that's sorted, here's what we're gonna do, son.' Danny rested his elbows on the tabletop. 'If you're with my girl, you're one of us – and we stick together no matter what. So when the police ask, you saw nothing. Understood?'

Aware that it was an order not a request, Ryan nodded.

'Good lad.' Danny smiled. 'Now let's me and you go and have a little chat, man to man.'

'Is that it?' Rachel asked when they both stood up. 'Think you've got it all sorted now, do you?'

'I reckon so,' Danny said, unscrewing the lid off the whisky bottle to top up his glass. 'Without a witness, it'll be her word against Adam's and the pigs'll have to drop it.'

'Maybe so, but that won't stop her from spreading lies about him and giving him a bad reputation,' Rachel snapped. 'But don't you worry about that,' she went on sarcastically as she got up and yanked her jacket off the back of the chair. 'You go and have your little chat and leave me to deal with it.'

'Don't be going round there kicking off,' Danny warned when he saw the icy glint in her eyes.

'I'm not stupid,' she replied curtly, snatching her handbag up off the floor and checking that her car keys were in it. Then, turning on Nicole, who was still mooning over Ryan, she said, 'You'd better not still be sitting there with that gormless look on your face when I get back, lady. I want this place cleaned up.'

'Why do I have to do it?' Nicole whined. 'It was Adam's party, not mine.'

'Don't argue with me,' Rachel snapped. 'Get it done!'

8

Beth had been on edge all day, waiting for the inevitable visit from the Harveys, who she had guessed would fly home as soon as they heard the news. Aware that she would have to face whatever was coming on her own because Tony still hadn't shown his face after doing a runner that morning, she had called her boss and told him she had a stomach bug and wouldn't be coming in. Then, wanting her daughter out of harm's way in case things took a nasty turn, she had asked her old friend Mary Murphy from four doors down if Lexi could spend the night there. She'd felt a bit cheeky asking, because she and Mary hadn't really spoken since Tony moved in. But, thankfully, Mary had agreed without hesitation; and Lexi, who had been close friends with Mary's daughter, Ann-Marie, when they were younger, had been more than happy to go.

Alone, Beth had tried to keep her mind off the approaching shitstorm by giving the flat a long overdue spring clean. The place was now spotless, but she still couldn't settle, and her nerves jangled like livewires every time a car pulled into the parking area below or somebody walked past the door. When, at last, the doorbell rang that evening, she wasn't surprised to see Rachel Harvey standing outside when she peeped through the spyhole – although she *was* surprised that Rachel was alone, because she'd expected the woman's husband to come as well. Checking that her phone was in her pocket so she could call the police if the man was hiding out of sight waiting to jump her, Beth took a deep breath before opening the door.

'Where is she?' Rachel demanded without preamble.

'If you're talking about my daughter, it's none of your business,' Beth replied coolly, flicking a hooded glance both ways along the landing.

'None of my *business*? That lying bitch has accused my son of trying to rape her, so of *course* it's my fucking business.'

'She's not lying. And I'd keep my voice down, if I was you – unless you want the whole block to know what he's done?'

'That's rich coming from the woman who turns a blind eye to her pervert husband touching her daughter up every chance he gets!'

'*Excuse* me?'

'You heard me,' Rachel hissed, stepping closer. 'And don't act like you didn't know, because our Nic reckons she's tried to tell you loads of times. But you're obviously too busy trying to stop the bastard from beating the crap out of *you* to care what he's doing to *her*, eh?' Sneering when Beth's face paled, she said, 'Yeah, I know about that an' all, because, unlike you, our Nic *does* listen to her.'

'Whatever goes on between me and my husband, it's got absolutely nothing to do with this,' Beth said, raising her chin proudly.

Staring at her in disbelief, Rachel said, 'Are you actually stupid or just playing dumb? It's got *everything* to do with this, you thick bitch. If you ask me, it was probably *him* who tried to rape her, and she only said it was our Adam because she was scared he'd beat the shit out of her if she grassed him up.'

'He's never laid a finger on her,' Beth replied angrily. 'And you're forgetting it happened at *your* house, so don't try and turn this on us, because facts are facts.'

Losing patience, Rachel said, 'Fetch the little bitch out. I'll soon get the truth out of her.'

'She's not here,' said Beth. 'But even if she was, I wouldn't let you anywhere near her. Now go home or I'll call the police.'

'Go ahead. And I'll tell them what a barefaced liar your daughter really is, starting with when she told you we'd invited her to stay over knowing full well we'd be in Paris.'

'That was your Nic's idea, not hers.'

'And she went along with it, because she couldn't wait to get away from this dump. But it was still a lie – just like this nonsense about my Adam attacking her is. She's the one who tried it on with him, and when he knocked her back she cried rape out of spite. That's the truth of it, and we both know it.'

'So why did your Nic's boyfriend have to pull him off her? Or didn't they tell you he saw it all?'

Rather than look shocked, as Beth had expected, Rachel gave a pitying smile.

'Oh dear . . . you think he's going to back up Lexi's story, don't you? Sorry to burst your bubble, sweetheart, but his loyalty lies with us, not her.'

'That's not what I heard,' Beth sniffed. 'He told Lexi he was done with her.'

'And yet they're together at my house right now, talking about getting engaged,' said Rachel. 'Starting to get the picture yet?' she went on smugly. 'There's no witness and no evidence, because it's all in Lexi's silly little head, and the only one who's going to end up getting charged is *her* for making false accusations. So if I was you, I'd get her to admit she's lying before she gets hurt.'

'Is that a threat?'

'Take it any way you like, darlin'. All I'm saying is, she'd best keep her trap shut or I guarantee she'll regret it. And so will *you* when I tell the police what that nonce has been doing to her under your nose, because they'll have her in care faster than you can blink. Oh, and in case you think I'm bluffing, Nic's still got Lexi's messages on her phone telling her all about it, which I'm sure the police will be *extremely* interested to read.'

Rachel walked away at that with her nose in the air, and Beth retreated inside and closed the door. Head spinning, sick to her stomach, she stumbled into the living room and sank down onto her chair. She knew Lexi didn't like Tony, but she'd assumed it was because of the way he treated *her*, not because of something he'd done to Lexi. But her daughter had never been scared to voice her opinions where he was concerned, so she would have told Beth if he'd done something untoward.

Wouldn't she?

Chewing on her nails as she tried to think if there had been any signs she'd missed, Beth frowned when she recalled the night Lexi had met her at the pub and walked home with her. Tony had kicked off that night and Lexi had got mad and blurted out something that he'd supposedly said to her earlier that day. She hadn't really listened at the time, because she'd been desperate to get Lexi out of the way, but she now wondered if the girl had been trying to tell her that Tony had abused her?

Unable to believe that, Beth shook her head. As nasty and as violent as Tony could be, even in his worst fit of anger he had never tried to force himself on her, and she couldn't see him doing it to a child. But *something* must have happened to make Lexi tell Nicole those things.

Unless that bitch had made it up to cast doubt on Lexi's version of events?

That had to be it, Beth decided. Rachel Harvey had intimated that Nicole's boyfriend would deny he'd seen anything if questioned, which meant it would be Lexi's word against Adam's. And once the police heard that Lexi had supposedly confided to Nicole that she was being abused, their focus would immediately shift onto Tony – which would open up a whole new can of worms. Beth wasn't stupid. As hard as she tried to cover the bruises, she knew her neighbours had seen them at various times in the past, because she'd seen their pitying looks. If one of them mentioned it to the police, they'd be bound to think that Tony was a danger to Lexi as well as her. And if they also believed Rachel Harvey's claim that Beth had known about the supposed abuse and turned a blind eye, Lexi would be taken into care and Beth would be in just as much trouble as Tony.

Unable to see a positive outcome for any of them if this case was allowed to go ahead, Beth knew that she was going to have to tell Lexi to retract her statement – and that made her feel like the worst mother in the world. Lexi hadn't even wanted to report the assault in the first place, but now, because Beth had insisted, she'd not only been subjected to the humiliation of being questioned and physically examined, she was also at risk of being labelled a liar and potentially charged with making false allegations. But the alternative was unthinkable, so it had to be done.

Not tonight, though. Lexi had been through enough today already, so Beth would leave her to enjoy her sleepover with Ann-Marie before breaking the bad news. And, even though she genuinely couldn't see Tony doing what he'd been accused of, the way he'd reacted when she told him that the police had come to speak to Lexi that morning told her that he was hiding *something*, so she would take this opportunity to confront him. He would undoubtedly deny it, but if she detected the slightest hint of deception, he was gone. And this time, if he tried any of his usual tricks, she would call the police and have him removed – for good.

Too exhausted to think about it anymore, she took a hot bath to ease the tension in her muscles, and then changed into her nightclothes and lay on the sofa to watch TV while she waited for him to come home.

9

Lexi had really enjoyed her sleepover with Ann-Marie. When their mums had been friends – in the carefree days before Tony wormed his way in and ruined everything – she and Ann-Marie had been really close, too, and she'd forgotten how nice the girl was. Unlike self-obsessed Nicole, who always wanted to be the centre of attention and got narky whenever the spotlight wasn't on her, Ann-Marie was laidback and funny; and she didn't give a toss about fashion and labels, and all that other superficial shit Nicole was into.

She hadn't told Ann-Marie about Adam assaulting her, because her mum had warned her not to mention it in case it got back to the Harveys. But that, followed by the fight with Nicole and the embarrassing encounter with Ryan, and then being railroaded into giving a statement to the police, had left her feeling pretty traumatized, so it had felt good to immerse herself in the noisy world of the Murphys again – although, seeing how close Ann-Marie and Mary were had highlighted how little she saw of her own mum and made her yearn for the days when it had just been the two of them.

Determined to start spending more time with her, Lexi went home straight after breakfast in the hope of catching her on her own while Tony was still sleeping. She didn't care what they did or where they went; even a simple walk in the park every now and then would be good. *Anything*, as long as it didn't involve him.

Using the spare key her mum had given her, Lexi stepped inside just as Tony walked out of the living room, and the shock on his deathly white face when he saw her matched the shock on her own face when she noticed the blood on his T-shirt. Instantly fearing that Nicole's dad had been round and kicked off, she said, 'What's happened? Where's my mum?'

'It wasn't me,' Tony croaked. 'I swear to God it wasn't.'

'What wasn't you?' Lexi asked, her mouth going bone dry as a wave of sheer dread washed over her. 'Where is she, Tony?'

'I – I stayed out last night,' he said, holding out his hand as he took a faltering step toward her. 'I just got back and found her like that, I swear.'

Head spinning when she saw the blood on his fingers, Lexi placed her hand on the wall to steady herself, and called, 'Mum, where are you? *MUUUUMMMM?*'

'Keep your voice down,' Tony hissed, lurching forward. 'The neighbours'll hear you.'

A rush of adrenaline surged through Lexi's veins and she dodged around him and ran up the hall. After checking her mum's bedroom and the bathroom, she moved on to the living room. At first she thought the room was empty. But then she saw the blood-soaked slipper sticking out from behind the sofa, and the room went into a sickening spin when she realized it was still attached to her mum's foot.

A scream rose into her throat, but Tony ran up behind her and clamped a hand over her mouth, trapping it inside. Feeling as if she might pass out, Lexi wasn't aware that she had sunk her teeth into his flesh until he cried out in pain and she tasted blood. Unsure if it was his or her mum's, she tore herself free of his grip and raced to the front door. Heart pounding when she heard him coming after her, she fumbled with the lock and stumbled out onto the communal landing just as he reached out to grab her.

'HEEEELP!' she screamed, running away from the flat. 'SOMEBODY HELP ME! HE'S KILLED MY MUM!'

Doors began to open along the landing and confused neighbours stepped outside. Mary was one of them and, guessing that Tony had been getting handy with his fists again, because it was no secret on the estate that he regularly laid into Beth, she said, 'What's happened, love? Is it your mam?'

Too scared to stop in case Tony was coming after her, Lexi ran on; but as she reached the stairwell, she collided with Mary's husband, Len, on his way home from the shops.

'Whoa, what's the hurry?' he asked, grabbing her arm to steady her when she almost fell head first down the stairs.

'She says someone's killed her mam,' Lexi's next-door-but-one neighbour, Linda Jarvis, called out from the other end of the landing. 'I've called the police.'

Lexi's front door suddenly opened and Tony, now wearing a jacket to cover his blood-soaked T-shirt, careered out of the flat and barged past Linda before racing for the stairs at the other end of the landing.

'Len, stop him!' Mary yelled. 'He's getting away!'

As Len dropped his shopping bags and charged after Tony, Mary rushed to Lexi and put an arm around her shoulder, saying, 'Come on, pet, let's get you out of the cold.'

A moment later, Linda, who'd slipped inside Lexi's flat the moment she saw that Tony had left the front door ajar, came staggering out onto the landing with her hand over her mouth and her eyes bulging. 'Oh my God,' she cried. 'He's stabbed her! There's blood everywhere!'

Furious that the woman had said such an insensitive thing within earshot of Lexi, Mary gave her a filthy look before grabbing the shopping bags her husband had dropped and hustling Lexi inside.

The police turned up in a blaze of blue lights and sirens, and the curious neighbours, who had all been ordered to stay indoors, watched through their windows as the landing was taped off at both ends. When the forensics team arrived and set to work, a detective and a policewoman called round at Mary's hoping to question Lexi; but she'd gone into shock by then and they couldn't get any sense out of her, so they called in the paramedics.

Following them to the door when they pushed Lexi out in

a wheelchair, Mary and Ann-Marie watched until they disappeared into the lift at the opposite end of the balcony from her flat.

'Is she going to be OK, Mum?' Ann-Marie fretted. 'She looked awful.'

'She'll be fine,' Mary said, ushering her girl inside when she glanced the other way and saw a man in a white suit walk out of Beth's flat carrying a clear plastic bag containing a large, bloodstained knife. 'I need to get dinner started, so go peel the spuds while I ring your dad.'

When Ann-Marie did as she'd been told, Mary pulled her phone out of her pocket and tried to ring her husband. In the two hours since he took off in pursuit of Tony, she hadn't seen or heard from him. She had no clue if he'd managed to catch up with the murdering bastard, but if he had, she hoped he'd beaten him to a pulp.

Superstitiously crossing herself as soon as the thought entered her mind, Mary said a silent prayer asking for forgiveness for thinking such wicked things. Then, releasing her tension on a sigh when she got no reply, she joined Ann-Marie in the kitchen and set about preparing the lamb joint for the oven.

As always happened when the police turned up on the estate en masse, residents from the surrounding blocks of flats had gathered on the grass to watch – and film – the goings-on. Among them, Jamie Holland's heart leapt into his scrawny throat when he saw Lexi being wheeled out through the main door. Desperate to see her, he pushed his way through the crowd and ran over to her.

'What's happened, Lex? Are you OK?'

Staring straight ahead, her gaze blank, Lexi didn't respond. Concerned, Jamie asked the paramedic what was wrong with her.

'Are you related?' the man asked.

'No, she's me friend,' Jamie told him. 'She's not hurt, is she?'

'Don't worry, son, we'll take good care of her,' the man said kindly. 'But you'd best go back over there.'

'Love you, Lex,' Jamie called out as they wheeled her on.

Lexi didn't hear him, and nor did she see the concern etched on his peaky face as, still rooted to the spot, he watched her being bundled into the back of the ambulance.

10

The next few weeks passed in a haze of grief for Lexi. Taken to a children's home after being discharged from hospital, she stayed in the tiny room she'd been allocated; refusing to eat any of the food the staff sent up for her at mealtimes, and crying herself to sleep. Her life had been torn to shreds and she prayed each night that she would wake up to find it had all been a bad dream. But every morning brought the fresh realization that her mum was gone and she was never going to see her again, and it broke her heart into a million pieces.

Hilary, the social worker who was assigned to her, asked if she knew of any relatives who might be willing to take her in, but Lexi had never met any of them and didn't know their names. She had a vague memory of once hearing her mum tell someone that she'd cut all ties with her family, but she couldn't remember who her mum had been talking to. And her mum had never discussed it with her, so she had no clue why it had happened. As for her father, all she'd ever been told about him was that he had died in a work-related accident before she was born, and his family had subsequently turned their backs on her and her mum, so they had never figured in her life, either.

It was five weeks before Beth's body was released and a council-funded funeral was arranged. Absolutely dreading it, but determined to say her last goodbyes, Lexi sat stiffly beside Hilary in the back of the limo following the hearse to the crematorium. As Hilary had warned might happen, because her mum had been murdered, several photographers and what looked like a TV news crew had set up their equipment a short distance away from the chapel, and she ducked her head and quickly followed Hilary inside when flashes started going off as she stepped out of the car.

A handful of mourners were already seated in the small chapel, and Lexi felt the sting of tears in her eyes when she spotted Mary and Len Murphy among them. She instinctively began to move toward them, but Hilary took her arm and led her to the front row instead. Seconds after they had taken their seats, the coffin was carried in and placed on a stand in front of them. Tears streaming at the sight of it, Lexi didn't take her gaze off it throughout the short service that followed – not one word of which she heard.

Breaking down when the curtains began to close, Lexi collapsed into Mary's arms when the woman jumped up and rushed over to comfort her.

'Shush now, pet,' Mary soothed, stroking her back. 'She's in the Lord's hands now.'

'I'm sorry, but we need to leave,' Hilary interrupted after a few seconds.

'Give her a minute, for pity's sake,' Mary replied sharply, holding Lexi tighter. 'Can't you see she's upset?'

'I need to get her back to the home,' Hilary insisted.

'Have a heart, love,' Len chipped in, walking over. 'We've known her since she was a bairn, and we're the closest thing she's got to family.'

'Yeah, she's one of us,' another neighbour piped up. 'And we look after our own, so wind your neck in and give 'em some time.'

'They'd have had all the time in the world if they'd offered to take her in when they had the chance,' Hilary shot back.

'You wicked bugger,' Mary gasped, covering Lexi's exposed ear with her hand. 'How could you say such a thing at a time like this? We only said no because we haven't got the room.'

Furious with herself for overstepping the mark, Hilary opened her mouth to apologize. But Lexi had already pulled herself free of Mary's embrace and was heading for the door.

As a confused-looking Hilary went after the girl, Mary called out: 'You know where we are if you need us, pet.' But Lexi didn't reply or even look back.

In the limo, Lexi slouched low in her seat as the driver drove slowly past the photographers. Jolted by the sight of a familiar figure standing between the trees on the perimeter of the grounds as they neared the gates, she twisted her head to take another look, but there was nobody there. Convinced that she must have imagined it, she hugged herself and rested her cheek against the cool glass of the window.

'I'm sorry for what happened in there,' Hilary said quietly as they turned onto the road and picked up speed. 'I shouldn't have said that.'

'It doesn't matter,' Lexi murmured. And she truly meant it, because *nothing* mattered anymore. For those few brief moments when she had been held in Mary's arms, she had felt safe again. But after hearing that the Murphys had been offered the chance to take her in and had refused, citing lack of room as an excuse when she could easily have bunked in with Ann-Marie, she knew there was nothing and nobody left for her in Manchester.

PART TWO

Ten Years Later

11

The train slowed on its approach to Piccadilly Station, and Lexi felt a flutter of apprehension in her stomach as the familiar landmarks of her youth came into view. She hadn't set foot in Manchester since the day of her mum's funeral – and hadn't ever intended to come back. But losing her job, her boyfriend and her flat in quick succession had forced her hand, so here she was.

Rising from her seat when the train squealed to a stop, she took a deep breath to steady her nerves before lifting her rucksack down from the overhead rack and retrieving her suitcase from the luggage compartment by the door. The job she was starting in three days' time might not have been her first choice, but it was the only one she'd been offered from the hundreds of applications she had submitted after losing her previous position; and it came with cheap accommodation, which was a bonus, so she would have to make the best of it for now.

The smells and sounds of the city hit her in the face with the force of a sledgehammer when she stepped onto the platform, and she swallowed the sickly taste that flooded her mouth as memories she had long ago buried tried to resurface. Determinedly pushing them back down, she walked briskly out through the exit and hopped into the back of one of the taxis that were queued outside.

After a twenty-minute drive, the taxi pulled up in front of a scruffy mid-terraced house on a backstreet in Chorlton, and Lexi's heart sank when she gazed out at the peeling paintwork, the grubby nets and mismatched curtains at the windows, and the overflowing wheelie bins cluttering the tiny, weed-choked front garden. It looked nothing like the neat, clean house shown in the photographs on the agency's website, and she asked, 'Are you sure this is the right place?'

'It's the address you gave me.' The driver shrugged.

Conscious that the meter was still running, Lexi pulled out her phone to double-check. Dismayed to see that it was the right place, she handed over the fare and climbed out. Alone on the pavement when the man dumped her suitcase and ruck-sack beside her and drove away, she looked up when a window on the first floor of the house next door opened and loud music filled the air. Two heavily tattooed men were staring down at her, each of them swigging a can of Special Brew, despite it not yet being noon.

'All right, love?' One of them grinned, flashing a row of silver-capped teeth at her. 'Need a hand?'

Forcing a smile because she didn't want to make enemies of the neighbours if she was going to be stuck there for the next year, which was the length of the tenancy she'd signed, Lexi shook her head. 'No, I'm OK, thanks.'

'Knock on if you ever want owt.' Silver-Teeth winked. 'Tea, sugar—'

'Smack,' his mate chipped in, earning himself a sharp elbow dig.

'Ignore this dickhead,' Silver-Teeth said. 'He's got Tourette's.'

'Have I fuck!'

'See what I mean?' Silver-Teeth grinned. 'The name's Billy, by the way.'

'Billy big balls,' his mate added. ''Ung like a donkey.'

'Shut yer fuckin' mouth, man,' Billy scowled. 'You can't be talkin' shit like that to ladies.'

Leaving them to it when they started squabbling, Lexi carried her luggage past the foul-smelling bins and let herself into the house with the keys she'd received in the post a few days earlier. The hallway was dark, narrow and stank of mildew and stale piss. Squeezing past a couple of old bicycle frames minus wheels that were propped against the wall, she climbed the stairs to the first floor, where she'd been told room number four was situated. Unlocking the door, she hesitated and peered around in confusion. It looked as if somebody was still living there – a *dirty* somebody, at that. The air reeked of stale smoke and sweat, the rumpled bedding was filthy, and there were used cups, plates, take-away boxes, overflowing ashtrays and clothes every-where she looked.

Backing out, she tapped on the door across the landing. A

hacking cough came from the other side, and then the door opened a crack and a woman's pale face peered out at her.

'Yeah?'

'Sorry to disturb you,' Lexi said. 'I'm supposed to be moving into room four, but there's a load of stuff in there. Do you know if someone's still living there?'

'No, she left a couple of weeks back,' the woman said, coughing into her hand. 'Chest infection,' she explained when she saw the alarm on Lexi's face. 'Don't worry, I'm past the infectious stage.'

'Have you tried a hot toddy?' Lexi asked. 'Lemon, honey and whisky usually does it for me.'

'Ugh, can't stand the stuff.' The woman pulled a face. Then, smiling, she held out her hand. 'I'm Debs.'

'Lexi. But it's probably best if we don't,' Lexi said, keeping her own hands firmly to herself. 'I start work at a care home on Monday morning, and I can't risk taking germs in. Sorry.'

'No, you're right; I wasn't thinking.' Debs rolled her eyes and withdrew the hand. 'I'm mornings, too, so we'll be working together.'

'Oh, you work at the home?'

'Most of us do. The owners have got a special-rate contract with the landlord. That's why it's so cheap.'

Concerned when the woman went into another coughing fit which made her eyes bulge and her face turn beetroot, Lexi said, 'I'd best let you get back to bed.'

'I'm all right,' Debs insisted, thumping her chest after spitting into a tissue she'd pulled out of her dressing gown pocket. 'Sooner it's out, sooner it'll be over with, an' all that. Anyhow, chuck that shit out.' She nodded to the open door behind Lexi. 'Best put some rubber gloves on before you touch anything though, 'cos Stinky Stella wasn't the most hygienic of people.'

'I kind of gathered that,' Lexi said, casting a dismayed glance at the mess.

'By rights, the agency should have cleared it out before you got here, but I doubt anyone will come out till next week now. I'd give you a hand, but I'm not sure I'd be much use.'

'It's OK, I'll manage. Anyway, you go get yourself settled.'

'Catch you later.' Debs waggled her fingers goodbye and, coughing again, closed the door.

Sighing, Lexi pulled her suitcase into her room and parked it behind the door. Then, dropping her rucksack, she tiptoed through the debris and opened the curtains with her fingertips before unlatching the window to air out the room. Unwilling to touch anything else, she headed out to find the local shops to stock up on bin bags, disinfectant and rubber gloves.

After a full day and most of the night spent clearing out the previous tenant's crap, Lexi was so exhausted by the time she dumped the last bag outside, she fell asleep as soon as her head hit one of the cheap new pillows she'd bought at the local pound shop. There was still a ton of cleaning to be done, but she had planned to have a lie-in before tackling it, so she wasn't happy to be woken by the sound of a jackhammer pounding concrete the following morning. Aware that she would never get back to sleep with that racket going on, she dragged herself out of bed and slammed the window shut before heading into her tiny en-suite bathroom.

Feeling a little more human after a lukewarm shower, she decided to go for a walk to escape the horrendous noise and explore the area. As she reached the foot of the stairs, the door of room number one opened and a skinny older woman came out with an ancient dog on a lead.

'Morning.' Lexi smiled. 'I'm—'

'I know who you are,' the woman rudely cut her off. 'You're the one who dumped all that rubbish under my window last night.'

'Sorry, there was nowhere else to put it,' Lexi apologized, thrown by the animosity in her new neighbour's tone. 'I rang the agency and left a message asking them to come and move it, so it shouldn't be there too long.'

'It'd better not be, or I'll be putting in a complaint about you,' the woman snapped.

'Wow! Nice to meet you, too,' Lexi spluttered when the woman abruptly marched out, dragging the poor dog along behind her.

'Take no notice of her,' someone said from the other end of the hallway. 'She ain't happy unless she's making someone else miserable, that one.'

Turning, Lexi saw a man with long red hair and a bushy beard coming out of the kitchen carrying a steaming mug of tea. He was wearing ripped jeans, a T-shirt bearing the logo of an old heavy metal band she'd vaguely heard of, and a leather waistcoat, and looked exactly as she'd always imagined a Hell's Angel would look.

'Six.' He held out his free hand when he reached her. 'Welcome to the madhouse.'

'Thanks,' Lexi said, shaking it. 'I'm Lexi.'

'No, you're Four,' he said, his blue eyes crinkling at the corners when he smiled. 'I've got a shit memory for names, so I call everyone by their room number instead.'

'Ah, right. So I take it your name's not really Six?'

'Nah, it's Jim – but if you tell anyone, I'll have to kill you.' Chuckling softly when her eyebrows rose, he took a noisy swig of tea before asking, 'So are you days or nights?'

'Days,' she said, guessing that he was referring to the care home since she'd been told that most of the residents worked there.

'Ah, that's a shame; I could've shown you round if you'd been on nights. Now you'll be stuck with Five.' He pulled a face.

'Debs?' Lexi ventured.

'That's her,' he said, grinning as he added, 'I'm only messing, by the way; she's one of the good 'uns. One's a cow, as you already know, and Two's a bit of a dick, so you might want to give him a wide berth; but Three's OK.'

'Good to know,' Lexi said.

Six was about to say more when his phone beeped. He pulled it out of his back pocket and read the message on the screen.

'Sorry, I need to make a call,' he said. 'Pop up for a chat some-time,' he added as he edged past her to get to the stairs. 'I'm in number—'

'Six?' Lexi said.

'You got it.' He winked at her before heading up the stairs, taking them two at a time and sloshing tea out of his cup as he went.

Glad that at least two of her new neighbours seemed nice, Lexi opened the front door and stepped outside. It was a warm day and the foul odours coming from the wheelie bins and the bags she'd stashed under the rude woman's window had attracted a swarm of flies. Batting them away as she rushed out onto the pavement, she couldn't help but smile when one of the crew of shirtless workmen who were digging a hole on the other side of the road gave her a wolf-whistle. The stresses of the last few months had robbed her of the motivation to make any sort of effort with her appearance, so it felt nice to get a bit of male attention – even if the man *did* look old enough to be her father.

Despite growing up only a few miles away, Lexi and her friends had never ventured over to this side of Manchester before, and she made mental notes of the locations of the laun-derette, the chip shop and the local GP's surgery as she walked. Eventually she came across a small park, wandered inside and took a seat on a bench by a pond that was tucked away between the trees. Two ducks were gliding between the handles of a shopping trolley, a bicycle frame and various other bits of debris that were sticking out of the murky water, and she smiled when it occurred to her that they were in pretty much the same boat as she was: living in a shit-pit, with no choice but to make the best of it.

She watched the ducks for a little while, but decided to make a move when she heard male voices and laughter and looked up to see four men – her neighbour, Billy, among them – entering through the gate with cans of beer in their hands. Quickly walking away from the pond before the men spotted her, she made her way back to the house.

Glad to find that the workmen had gone by the time she returned, she reopened her window and ate a Pot Noodle before getting stuck into the rest of the cleaning.

Later that night, every muscle complaining after a day spent on her hands and knees scrubbing the skirting boards and the filthy carpet, Lexi made a cup of instant chocolate and lay on her bed. With no TV or radio to amuse her or drown out the sounds of music, flushing toilets, conversations and coughing from the other residents' rooms, she scrolled through the photos on her phone.

Homesickness washed over her as she gazed at the faces of her old friends chilling out at a festival in Hebden Bridge the previous year. But then a shot of her ex, Kyle, came up on the screen, and her stomach clenched. She had thought she'd deleted all the photos of him, but she had obviously missed this one, and the sight of his smiling, handsome face filled her with mixed emotions. Four years she had wasted on him. Four long years of working her arse off to pay the rent, the bills, and fork out for the booze and weed he couldn't function without while he played at writing the next great novel.

What a fucking joke that had turned out to be!

The only thing he had ever created was the persona of a charming, brooding creative type – and she had fallen for it hook, line and sinker. So hard, in fact, that she had turned her back on all the friends who had tried to warn her about him, believing his assertion that they were only interfering because they were jealous. The only one who hadn't had anything bad to say about him was her best friend and upstairs neighbour, Violet, and Lexi had loved her for that. But her rose-tinted spectacles had been shattered on the morning she came home early after being told that the company she worked for had gone into liquidation, only to catch the pair of them having sex in her bed.

It was only after she had kicked them both out that she began to realize the true depth of Kyle's duplicity. Not only had he been screwing Violet for months behind her back, he'd also been siphoning money out of her bank account and charging all sorts of shit to a credit card he'd taken out in her name. Jobless, almost broke, and forced to listen to the two people who had betrayed her having sex in the flat directly above hers night after night, it hadn't been long before the rest of her life had unravelled. With no job vacancies anywhere nearby, and the benefits she had applied for taking way longer to get processed than expected, she had fallen into rent arrears and been served an eviction notice – which was why she'd been forced to make a new start back here.

Annoyed with herself for reopening those old wounds by going through her photos, Lexi deleted the one of Kyle and slammed her phone screen-down on the bedside table. Then, finishing her hot chocolate, she switched off the lamp and pulled her quilt up over her head.

12

Excited to be working again and earning an honest wage, Lexi got up bright and early on Monday morning. She'd have preferred to travel in with Debs, given that it was her first day, but she hadn't seen the woman since their initial meeting on Friday, so she made her own way there.

Unlike the house, which had looked clean and well-maintained on the agency's website but was the absolute opposite in real life, Daisy Nook Residential Care Home in the heart of Didsbury was far grander than it appeared on the photos Lexi had seen. A three-storey Victorian mansion with huge windows, it was set in beautifully landscaped grounds and had a sweeping driveway with tall electronic gates at either end; one marked *Entry*, the other marked *Exit*.

The interior was even more impressive, with high ceilings, polished real-wood flooring, and numerous doors leading off the reception area. Already nervous, because she'd never done care work before and had only a vague idea of what would be expected of her, she felt like an imposter as she approached the reception desk, behind which a smartly dressed young woman with the most immaculately applied make-up Lexi had ever seen was sitting.

'Hi,' she said, hitching the strap of her handbag higher on her shoulder when the woman looked up. 'I'm starting work here today.'

'Alexis?' The woman smiled and stood up. 'I'm Katie. Come with me.'

Surprised that the girl sounded Mancunian and friendly, because she'd expected posh and standoffish, Lexi followed her through a door behind the desk and along a corridor to a door marked *Staff* at the far end. Katie pushed it open and waved Lexi inside. This room was large and had the same high ceiling as the other rooms they had passed, but the furnishings were far less grand. A long table surrounded by plastic chairs took up most of the floor space, and a row of metal lockers occupied one full wall. There was a basic kitchen area on the other side, with a sink, an oldish-looking fridge, a microwave and a kettle.

'Dress and shoe size?' Katie asked, opening a cupboard.

'Twelve and six,' Lexi said.

Katie pulled out a neatly folded pale green top and a matching pair of pants and handed them to Lexi before opening a different cupboard and taking out a pair of flat, white, lace-up shoes. 'The changing room's through there.' She gestured to another door. 'If anything doesn't fit, just go through the cupboard until you find something that does. You take your uniform home and wash it after each shift, and make sure you clean your shoes, as well. Oh, and you'll need to keep your hair tied back at all times,' she added. 'I've got spare scrunchies and clips in my drawer if you need any.'

'Thanks, but I think I've got one in my bag,' Lexi said.

Nodding, Katie walked over to the metal units and took a key out of an open locker. 'This is yours,' she said, handing it over. 'All personal belongings, including your phone, must be locked in here during work hours. Try not to lose your key, or you'll be charged twelve quid to replace it,' she added quietly.

'I'll keep it in my bra,' Lexi said.

'Most of the girls do.' Katie smiled. 'Right, I'll leave you to it. The morning staff will start arriving in the next ten minutes or so. In the meantime, make yourself at home and help yourself to tea or coffee.'

Thanking her, Lexi waited until she'd left the room before slipping into the changing room and quickly putting on her uniform. It fitted perfectly, and she smiled as she checked out her reflection in the mirror on the back of the door after tying up her hair. All she needed was a stethoscope around her neck and she would look like an actual nurse.

At the sound of voices on the other side of the door, Lexi hurriedly gathered her things together and went back into the staffroom. Several women of various ages were chattering as they took off their coats and stuffed them and their bags into lockers.

'Morning, love,' one of them said when she spotted her. 'You Alexis?'

'I prefer Lexi, but yeah,' Lexi said, smiling at the others when they turned to take a look at her.

'Coffee or tea?' asked a short, older woman who was already filling the kettle.

'Erm, tea, please,' Lexi said. 'White, one sugar.'

'I'm Julie,' the first woman said. 'Put your stuff away then I'll introduce you to everyone.'

Doing as she'd been told, Lexi wiped her clammy hands as she joined the others, who were now seated around the table. She smiled at each of the women as Julie reeled off their names, but she knew she would struggle to remember them all, so she was relieved when one of them pulled a lanyard out of her pocket and she saw her name on it.

The older woman – whose name Lexi had already forgotten – was handing out the teas when a car pulled up outside. Glancing out through the window over the sink, she said, 'It's Ada.'

'Great.' Julie rolled her eyes. 'Day super,' she explained when she glanced at Lexi and saw the question in her eyes.

'And by that she means super *bitch*,' one of the younger girls added, between puffs on an e-cigarette.

Already dreading meeting the woman since it was clear that her co-workers didn't like her, Lexi's heart sank into her flat white shoes when the back door opened a few seconds later and the rude woman from the ground-floor room in her house walked in. It was the first time she'd seen her since the rubbish-bags-under-the-window debacle, but it was obvious from the cold look the woman flashed her that she wasn't yet forgiven.

'Five minutes,' the woman barked, looking pointedly at the clock on the wall.

'We've only just got our teas, Miss Briggs,' one of them complained.

Ignoring her, Ada clicked her fingers at Lexi and said, 'Follow me.'

Eyebrows shooting up, Lexi looked at the other women in shock when Ada marched out of the room. She knew she'd upset her the other day, but there was absolutely no need for that level of rudeness.

'Welcome to Daisy Nook,' Julie chuckled.

Determined not to let Ada think she was intimidated by her, Lexi raised her chin and followed the woman out of the room and into a small office further along the corridor. Ada took a seat behind a desk and motioned for her to sit down before pushing a sheet of paper over to her.

'This is the list of clients I've assigned to you. Study their notes carefully during break times, because they all have different needs, some more complex than others. You'll be shadowing Julie for the first week, so make sure you do exactly as she tells you.'

'Of course,' Lexi agreed, relieved that she wasn't going to be thrown in at the deep end and would have someone to show her the ropes.

'As you've already demonstrated you're not the most . . . *hygienic* of people,' Ada went on snippily, 'I need to warn you that slovenly behaviour will not be tolerated here. We have exceptionally high standards, and if you fall below them you will be dismissed on the spot. Do I make myself clear?'

'Perfectly,' Lexi said through a fixed smile, thinking: *Fuck you, bitch! You live in the same shithole as me, so don't be lecturing* me *about hygiene!*

'I'll be watching you closely,' Ada said. Then, flicking her bony wrist in a gesture of dismissal, she picked up a pen and started making notes on a pad she'd taken out of the drawer.

Guessing that the introductory meeting – or whatever the hell that had been – was over, Lexi picked up the client list and, still smiling, walked out and made her way back to the staffroom, where the other women were now washing their teacups.

'You're alive!' Julie mock-gasped.

'Yeah, but *she* might not be for much longer if she talks to me like that again,' Lexi muttered. 'Who the hell does she think she is?'

'Oh, you're going to fit in here just fine,' Julie laughed.

Feeling better when she received several pats on the back from the other women as they made their way out, Lexi nodded when Julie asked if she was ready to get started.

'Keep your head down and don't let Ada get to you,' Julie advised. 'I might not like her, but she's bloody good at her job – and she's got far too much on to waste time watching you. Stick with Auntie Julie and you'll be fine.'

Hoping so, because she had a feeling she was going to like it there, Lexi pushed bitter little Ada out of her mind and followed Julie out of the staffroom.

* * *

Care work was a lot more intensive than Lexi had anticipated, and she was rushed off her feet that first day – and every day that followed. Under Julie's patient tutelage, she soon got into the swing of things and by the end of her first week had memorized not only her clients' names but also which of them needed their medication before or after breakfast, and which had special dietary needs or needed extra help with washing and dressing.

She hadn't expected to enjoy it quite as much as she did, but her joy was decidedly tempered by the fact that Ada Briggs seemed to be there every time she turned around. So far, Lexi was confident that she hadn't put a foot wrong; and Julie had told her that she had picked things up way faster than newbies usually did, so she knew she was doing all right. But she couldn't shake the feeling that she was on borrowed time, so she had already decided to spend her weekend looking for another job – just in case.

Woken by a knock at her door on Saturday morning, Lexi was surprised to find Debs on the landing.

'Morning, hon,' the woman greeted her cheerfully. 'Didn't wake you, did I?'

'No, I was just getting up,' Lexi lied.

'Could've fooled me,' Debs chuckled, taking in her bleary eyes and unbrushed hair. 'Here, you haven't got someone in there, have you?' she added in a whisper. 'I haven't interrupted *you know what*?'

'Definitely not,' Lexi laughed, rubbing the sleep from her eyes. 'You're looking a lot better than last time I saw you,' she said. 'How are you feeling?'

'Great,' said Debs. 'It actually cleared up a few days ago, but I didn't fancy going straight back to work, so I laid it on a bit. But don't you dare tell Ada.'

'Believe me, I don't speak to her unless I absolutely *have* to.' Lexi rolled her eyes.

'Julie told me she'd been giving you a hard time.'

'You can say that again. I've never met a more miserable bitch in my entire life.'

'You and me both,' Debs agreed. 'But Ju reckons you're doing fine, so don't stress about it. Anyhow, forget her. What you doing tonight?'

'Nothing much.' Lexi shrugged. 'I need to wash some clothes and catch up on the cleaning, but that's about it.'

'OK, get that out of the way early then get your glad-rags on,' Debs said. 'You're coming out with me and the girls, and the cab's booked for nine.'

Conscious that she needed to eke out her remaining money carefully until she got paid at the end of the month, Lexi said, 'I'd love to, and thanks so much for inviting me, but I can't really afford it.'

'You won't need money,' Debs assured her. 'The cabbie's a mate, so he never charges me; and women get into the club free before ten.'

'I'd still have to buy a drink, though.'

'Not with your looks, you won't. Blokes'll be falling over themselves to buy you one.'

Uncomfortable with the idea of accepting drinks from

strangers, Lexi had just opened her mouth to say as much when Debs yelped, 'Oh shit, my toast! Best go rescue it before I set the whole house on fire. Don't forget – nine on the dot. And glam up, 'cos us Daisy Nook Hotties like to make a good impression.'

When Debs rushed away, Lexi closed the door and sloped back to bed. A night out had not been on her agenda, and she wished she'd been quick enough to think up an excuse as to why she couldn't go. But she'd already admitted that she hadn't made any plans, so there was no way out of it.

13

'Whit-*woo*, missus!' Debs said, looking Lexi up and down with approval when she knocked on for her that evening.

'Do I look all right?' Lexi asked, feeling self-conscious because she hadn't had any reason to dress up in a while and it felt strange to be in a dress, heels and make-up again.

'You look fan-bloody-tastic,' Debs said. 'Now how about me?' She turned in a circle in the narrow hallway. 'Scrub up OK for a big bird, don't I?'

'You look gorgeous,' Lexi said, checking out her new friend's low-cut sequined top and stylish culottes. 'Although, I'd watch where you're putting *them*, or you'll have someone's eye out,' she quipped, nodding at Debs's huge breasts.

'As long as their cocks come out at the same time, it's all good, baby,' Debs chuckled. 'Anyhow, the cab's here, so we'd best get moving.'

'Oh my God!' Lexi laughed, almost falling over when Debs linked arms with her and marched her down the stairs.

* * *

Lexi had been too young to go clubbing when she'd lived in Manchester, and the clubs she and her friends had frequented after she'd left the care system and settled in Hebden Bridge had been more like social clubs than nightclubs, so she felt a bit nervous when their taxi pulled up outside a flashy-looking place called Zenith.

'The girls got here before us,' Debs said, nodding to a group of women who were puffing on cigarettes to the side of the smoked-glass double doors. 'Makes a change. It's usually me waiting for them.'

Lexi glanced over as she climbed out of the cab, and felt decidedly underdressed when she saw that they were all wearing sparkly clothes like Debs.

'Cheers for that, love,' Debs said, leaning in through the driver's open window and pecking him on the cheek.

'Want me to come back for you later?' he asked, his lusty gaze riveted to her breasts when she pulled back.

'Thanks, but I've arranged to stop at my mate's tonight,' she said, tapping the roof. 'Catch you later, handsome.'

Grinning, the man winked at her before taking off.

'I think he likes you,' Lexi said as she and Debs walked over to their group. 'He was checking you out in the rear-view mirror all the way here.'

'He's a sweetheart, and we did do the dirty once,' Debs said. 'But his dick was so small I didn't even realize he'd put it in until he rolled off and lit a fag. I'd been lying there for the entire two minutes thinking he was dry-humping me.'

'What's the joke?' Julie called out when Lexi started laughing.

'Wee willy winky,' Debs said, letting go of Lexi's arm to hug her friends.

'Don't be so cruel,' Julie admonished her. 'He's a good-looking lad; you could do a lot worse.'

'I don't need ornaments, I need a man,' Debs snorted, pushing her and Lexi in through the doors.

The music was so loud in the foyer, Lexi could barely hear herself think, and it was louder still in the main room.

'What you having?' Debs bellowed after using her breasts to force a path to the bar. 'The girls'll get their own, but I invited you, so I'll get yours.'

'White wine, please,' Lexi yelled back.

As Debs tried to attract the attention of one of the bar staff, a man who was standing with a group a few feet away clocked her and made his way over.

'Well, hello there,' he drawled, resting his elbow on the bar counter and staring blatantly down her top before raising his gaze to her face. 'I haven't seen you here before.'

Giving him a quick once-over, Debs gave a flirtatious smile, and said, 'You obviously weren't looking hard enough.'

'Larry.' He held out his hand.

'Delilah.' She offered hers in return.

He kissed it, then asked, 'What are you drinking?'

'White Russian,' she said. 'And my friend will have the same.'

'Four Scotches, and two White Russians for the ladies,' the man called to a barman.

'You're a gent,' Debs said, nudging Lexi with her elbow. 'Isn't he a gent, Francesca?'

Unsure what was going on, and feeling decidedly uncomfortable, Lexi nodded and faked a smile. Murmuring, 'Thanks,' when Larry handed a tall glass to her after he'd been served, she scanned the room to see where Julie and the others had gone.

'Hello, beautiful.' One of Larry's friends sidled over and gave her what he obviously considered to be a sexy smile but which she found a bit creepy. 'I'm Mack.'

Flashing a glance at Debs and frowning when the woman waggled her eyebrows as if to say *you're in there*, Lexi said, 'I'm sorry, you'll have to excuse me; I think my friends are looking for me,' before rushing off to join Julie and the other women, who she'd spotted at a table on the other side of the room.

'You OK?' Julie asked, patting the seat beside hers.

'Yeah, fine,' Lexi lied, sitting down.

'Debs copped off already, has she?' Julie gave a knowing smile as she glanced across to the bar. Clocking the troubled look on Lexi's face, she leaned closer and said, 'Don't think badly of her, love. She had a nasty break-up last year and it really knocked her confidence, so this is her way of giving that wanker ex of hers the finger.'

'Oh, I didn't know that,' Lexi said guiltily.

'You haven't known her long, so how would you?' said Julie. 'She might go a bit wild when she lets her hair down, but she'd give you the shirt off her back if you needed it – *and* the spare buttons to go with it.'

Lexi nodded and sipped her drink. She did like Debs, but they had very different ideas about what constituted a good night out.

A couple of hours and several drinks later – most of which were top-ups from the various bottles Julie and the other women had smuggled into the club in their handbags – Lexi cited sore feet as an excuse to stay put when they tried to persuade her to join them on the dance floor. Sure that they must think she was a boring cow as she watched them strutting their glittery stuff, she covered a yawn with her hand when Julie popped over to check on her a few songs later.

'I'm getting a bit tired, so I might head off in a minute,' she said. 'Do you think Debs will be all right getting home?'

'She'll be fine,' Julie assured her, glancing across at their friend, who appeared to be slow-dancing with Larry; her arms around his neck, his hands on her arse. 'I'll check him out before we leave and make sure he's not a serial killer.' Laughing when she saw the alarm on Lexi's face, she said, 'I'm joking, love. She's almost forty and more than capable of looking after herself so don't you be worrying about her. Just drop me a text to let me know you got home OK.'

Promising that she would, Lexi exchanged numbers with her and then finished her drink before making her way to the ladies. She'd just sat down when the toilet in the adjoining cubicle flushed and she heard heels clipping across the tiled floor. Smoothing her dress down, she opened the door and saw a woman standing by the sinks wearing a red fitted jacket and skin-tight shiny black trousers tucked into thigh-length high-heeled boots. But it was the platinum-blond hair that caught her attention, and her heart started pounding in her chest when she switched her gaze to the woman's reflection in the mirror. It had been a long time, and the woman had larger breasts and very obvious lip and cheek fillers. But there was no mistaking those emerald-green eyes.

'What you looking at?' the woman suddenly snapped, glaring at her in the mirror. 'I'm not into pussy, so do one if that's what you're after.'

'Still got the same hot temper, I see,' Lexi said.

'You what?' Nicole turned round and looked her up and down. 'Do I know you?'

'You should,' said Lexi. 'We used to be best mates.'

Narrowing her eyes – which was no mean feat considering how tight her skin looked – Nicole's mouth fell open after a moment, and she gasped, '*Lexi?*'

'That's my name, don't wear it out,' Lexi said, the old phrase falling easily off her tongue, as if they were still those fifteen-year-old girls who had thought they were super-cool for saying it.

'Oh my God, I haven't seen you in forever,' Nicole said, rushing over to give her a hug. 'Why didn't you call me?'

'My phone got lost when I went into care and I couldn't remember your number,' Lexi said, feeling a little awkward. She'd thought about Nicole many times over the years, but she had never dreamed the girl might actually be pleased to see her if they ran into each other again. 'To be honest, I didn't think you'd want to talk to me after everything that happened.'

'Eh?' Nicole gave her a blank look.

'Adam,' Lexi reminded her.

'Oh, that was years ago.' Nicole flapped her hand dismissively. 'And the case was dropped, so there was no harm done.'

'Seriously?' Lexi stared at her wide-eyed.

'Come on, Lex, we were all kids,' Nicole said. 'But never mind that, where the hell have you been? It was like you fell off the face of the earth. Here one day, gone the next.'

Lexi guessed that Nicole still thought her brother had done nothing wrong. But she had doubted herself that night, wondering if she had done something to make Adam think she wanted him, so she could hardly blame Nic for thinking the same.

Deciding to let it go, she said, 'My last placement was in Hebden Bridge, and I liked it there, so my social worker helped me to get my own place after I left the care system.'

'Hebden Bridge?' Nicole pulled a face. 'Isn't it full of sheep and cows?'

Amused, Lexi said, 'It's a town not a field. And it's actually really beautiful.'

'Rather you than me,' Nicole sniffed. 'So what you doing here? I never thought you'd want to come back after what happened to your mum. I couldn't believe it when I heard. But you always said Dickhead would do for her one day, didn't you?'

'Mmmm,' Lexi murmured, breathing in deeply through her nose to quell the rage that always reared up at the thought of Tony Lawson. She still hated him with a vengeance, and had cried for a full week after learning that he'd only got seventeen years for murdering her mum. Years of therapy had taught her not to grant him any headspace, so, shaking him out of her mind, she said, 'Actually, I moved back last week to start a new job.'

'Really? Where are you living?'

'I've got a room in a house in Chorlton, but it's only temporary till I find somewhere better.'

'Ah, brilliant. We'll have to meet up for lunch.'

'That'd be nice.' Lexi smiled. 'So what have you been doing with yourself? Are you married? Got any kids?'

'Yes and no.' Nicole raised her hand and flashed a whopper of a diamond. 'I got the man, but no kids. Ryan's desperate for one, but there's no way I'm ruining these babies for one of the screeching and dribbling variety.' She ran her hands over her pert breasts.

'You're still with Ryan?' Lexi was surprised to hear that.

'Of course,' Nicole said, as if it had never been in question. 'He proposed on my eighteenth and we got married on my twentieth. I wish you could have been there, 'cos it was the wedding of the century, but I didn't know where you were.'

'I'm sorry I missed it,' Lexi said, very much doubting that she'd have been invited even if she hadn't left town. Rachel Harvey had hated her even before she'd reported her precious son to the police, and Ryan had lied to them and made her look like she'd made the whole thing up – no doubt revenge for knocking him back when he'd asked her out.

'It was the best day *ever*,' Nicole went on. 'My dad paid for everything, no expense spared – and you should have seen my dress. It cost seven grand and had like a million Swarovski crystals hand-sewn onto it by that woman who makes the gypsy dresses. The train was so long I had to have six bridesmaids to hold it. And I'd just had my boobs done for the first time, so I looked *super* hot.'

'I can imagine,' Lexi said, stepping to one side when the door burst open and Debs stumbled in.

'Watch it!' Nicole snapped, brushing the arm of her jacket when Debs fell against her. 'This cost more than you probably make in a year, you stupid cow!'

'Sorry, hon,' Debs slurred, already peeling the elasticated waist of her culottes down as she staggered toward a cubicle. Hesitating when she spotted Lexi, she gave a glassy-eyed grin. 'Hey, there you are. Larry's taking me for a kebab. Wanna come? His mate's been asking for you.'

'No, you're OK, I'm going home,' Lexi said. 'Will you be all right getting back?'

'I'll be fine, my little honey bun.' Debs pinched her cheek. 'He's giving me a ride – and not just the car kind, if you get my drift?'

'Don't tell me you actually know her?' Nicole asked Lexi, watching in disgust as Debs, cackling loudly, waddled into a cubicle and fell heavily down on the toilet seat before kicking the door shut.

'She's my neighbour,' Lexi said quietly as Debs started to loudly pee.

'That doesn't mean you have to hang out with her,' Nicole replied. 'Seriously, Lex, you'll get yourself a bad reputation being seen with an old tart like her.'

'She's all right,' Lexi said, hoping that Debs hadn't heard Nicole's comments. She might not know the woman well, but she didn't want her to think she was slagging her off.

'Oh, well, each to their own,' Nicole said, pulling her phone out of her tiny handbag when it pinged and tutting when she saw the message. 'Great!'

'Everything OK?' Lexi asked.

'I was supposed to be meeting someone here to go to a party, but she's been held up and wants me to go straight there, so now I'm going to have to find a cab,' Nicole grumbled. 'Hey, why don't you come with me?' she suggested. 'We can have that catch-up on the way there.'

'I'd love to,' Lexi said. 'But I've been working all week and my feet are killing me.'

'Aw, that's a shame, but never mind. How about tomorrow? You can come over to mine for dinner. You remember where the house is, don't you?'

'You still live with your mum and dad?'

'God, no!' Nicole squawked. 'My dad needed to lay low for a while, so they buggered off to Spain a couple of years ago. It was only supposed to be temporary, but they loved it so much they decided to stay. They bought a villa and I got the house. Anyway, is eight o'clock OK? I've got an appointment in town at six, but I should be home by then.'

Daunted by the prospect of returning to *that* house, Lexi said, 'It's a bit short notice, Nic. I only moved into my room last week and I've still got a ton of cleaning to do.'

'You can do that anytime,' Nicole said dismissively. 'Give me your number and I'll text you when I'm on my way home.'

'Couldn't we meet somewhere else?' Lexi asked. 'I'm not being funny, but I really don't want to see Adam.'

'He doesn't live with us,' Nicole assured her. 'He's got his own place in town and I hardly ever see him.'

'What about Ryan?'

'He works late every night, so it'll only be us girls. Now hurry up and give me your number so I can get going. Or, better still, give me your address and I'll pick you up on my way home.'

'Thirty nine Chamberlain Road,' Debs said, coming out of the toilet at that exact moment. 'Just look out for the one with all the shit piled up outside; you can't miss it.'

Wishing that the ground would open up and swallow her, Lexi said, 'It's all right, Nic, I'll catch the bus.'

'Too late,' Nicole said, already tapping the address into her phone. 'There, it's saved. I'll pick you up at eight.' She air-kissed Lexi's cheeks then flashed a disdainful look at Debs before sashaying out, leaving a trail of expensive perfume in her wake.

'Oooh, look at me with my big fake titties and my inflatable gob,' Debs said in a mock-posh voice as she drunkenly tried to imitate Nicole's walk.

Old loyalties made Lexi want to defend her friend, but she couldn't deny that Debs had a point – even if her impression *was* more reminiscent of Mick Jagger. Nicole had always been stunning and Lexi didn't understand why she'd had so much work done. But Nicole obviously liked the way she looked, so who was Lexi to judge?

14

As happy as she was that she had seen Nicole and there had been none of the animosity she'd expected, Lexi really wasn't looking forward to going back to that house, and she cursed herself as she reluctantly got ready the following evening for not thinking to ask for Nic's number. If she'd had it, she could have rung her and made an excuse to call off their dinner date. But she didn't, so she couldn't. And thanks to Debs, Nicole now knew her address and was coming round to pick her up, so there was no way out of it.

Dressed casually in jeans and a T-shirt, and no make-up since it was only going to be her and Nicole, Lexi was leaving her room when Debs opened her door and gave her a sheepish smile.

'Hey.'

'Hi,' Lexi said, taking in the dark bags under the woman's eyes and the slight green tinge to her skin and guessing that she must have had a rough night. 'You made it home in one piece, then?'

'Yeah, Larry dropped me off,' Debs said. 'I, um, need to apologize for taking the piss out of your friend last night. I remembered it when I woke up and felt terrible. I know I was a bit tipsy, but that's no excuse for being nasty.'

'You weren't nasty,' Lexi assured her, resisting the urge to laugh at her use of the word tipsy when she'd been so drunk she could barely stand up.

'So me and you are cool?'

'Course we are.'

'Thanks, hon.' Debs looked relieved. 'You off out?'

'Yeah, Nicole's picking me up and taking me to hers for dinner,' Lexi said, glancing at her watch. 'She'll be here in a minute, so I'd best get going.'

'If she heard me last night, please tell her I didn't mean any harm.'

'She didn't hear you. Now stop feeling guilty and go get a bath, or something. No offence, but you look terrible.'

'I think the kebab was off. I've been sick as a dog all day.'

'You poor thing,' Lexi said, momentarily wondering if she could tell Nicole that she had to stay home to look after Debs in order to wriggle out of the dinner.

'Right, well, enjoy yourself; I'm off to bed,' Debs said, knocking that idea on the head. 'If I'm still alive in the morning, I'll catch the bus to work with you.'

Sighing when Debs closed her door, Lexi headed down the stairs. Glad that it was already dark outside so Nicole wouldn't see how rundown the house actually was when she arrived, she waited outside the gate. Ten minutes later, she heard the roar of a powerful engine and smiled when Nicole drew up in a silver Mercedes.

'Christ, what a dump.' Nicole wrinkled her nose as she gazed out at the house after air-kissing Lexi's cheeks. 'Why on earth would you choose to live here?'

'I needed somewhere fast and it was the cheapest I could find,' Lexi said as she fastened her seat belt.

'If I'd known you were back in town you could have stayed with us,' Nicole said, putting her foot down as she drew away from the kerb.

'It's fine for now,' Lexi said, pressing her foot down on an imaginary brake pedal when Nicole turned the corner at speed.

'Relax, I'm a really safe driver,' Nicole said, chuckling when she noticed her friend clutching the sides of her seat.

'Sorry, can't help it,' Lexi apologized. 'I was in a crash a couple of years back when my ex took his eyes off the road to read a text and I've been a nervous passenger ever since.'

'Men are such shit drivers,' Nicole scoffed. 'They swear they're better than us, but they have way more accidents.'

'Mmm hmm,' Lexi murmured, wincing when Nicole put her foot down to get through an amber light.

Relieved to still be alive and in one piece when they reached Nicole's house, Lexi unclipped her seat belt and followed her friend inside. She had always thought the house was beautiful, so the change of decor shocked her. The walls, which had previously been a cool cream throughout, were now hung with gaudy silver and purple wallpaper; and the laminate flooring had been replaced by a thick grey carpet. There were huge, elaborately framed mirrors on every wall, and most of the tables and cabinets also had mirrored edges, so the light coming from the enormous chandeliers bounced off every surface. The only room that didn't appear to have been changed was the kitchen, but it quickly became apparent that it was next on Nicole's hit list.

'These units are so old-fashioned, I hate them,' she complained as she waved for Lexi to sit at the table while she popped a frozen pizza into the microwave before taking a bottle of wine out of the rack. 'I found some gorgeous red lacquered ones online, but Ryan says they're too expensive. Like I need *his* permission,' she snorted. 'He might be running things, but it's still my dad's business so I'll ask *him* for the money when I'm ready.'

Smiling when Nicole handed a glass of wine to her, Lexi said, 'I honestly don't know why you want to change it. I always really liked this room.'

'Only 'cos yours was so shit,' Nicole replied bluntly. 'It was always freezing in there, as well. I remember when I came over once and you made me a brew, and there was actual ice on the inside of the window.'

'The whole flat was like that,' said Lexi, remembering the times she had been forced to get dressed under her quilt in the mornings, or worn her coat and gloves to do her homework.

Carrying the pizza to the table after roughly slicing it, Nicole sat down, and said, 'Right, tell me what you've been up to. This ex of yours who had the crash, where did you meet him?'

'Online,' Lexi said, taking a swig of wine before reaching for a slice of the decidedly slimy-looking pizza. 'He came across my Facebook page and started messaging me. We chatted on there for a while then he asked for my number. We'd been talking for a few weeks when he told me he was coming to Hebden for some work-related thing and suggested meeting up. We had a couple of drinks and I invited him back for coffee, and . . . that was it. He never went home.'

'You mean you let him move in with you the first time you met him?' Nicole looked horrified.

'I know it sounds stupid, but it wasn't meant to be permanent,' Lexi explained. 'He told me he was a writer and said Hebden was inspiring him. And he was really good-looking and interesting, so when he asked to stay for a couple of days I thought it would be a chance to get to know him better.'

'And then you found out he was a top shag and begged him not to leave?' Nicole teased, wiping tomato sauce off her chin with a napkin.

'Not quite,' Lexi said, rolling her eyes at the memory of the sob story Kyle had fed her. 'He kept getting phone calls that he never answered, and when I asked what was going on he told me his ex had run up a massive debt with a drug dealer and they were coming after him for it.'

'So he was using your place as a hideout?'

'I guess.' Lexi shrugged. 'He said he needed a few weeks to

sort things out and then he'd find his own place, but you know how it goes . . . a few weeks turns into a few months, and you sort of get used to having them around.'

'So who finished it?'

'Me. I lost my job and went home early, and caught him screwing my so-called best mate.'

'Bastard!'

'Oh, it gets worse. After I kicked him out, he moved in with her – in the flat above mine.'

'Jesus, no wonder you wanted out of there. Talk about rubbing salt in the wound.'

'To be honest, I'd stopped caring by then,' Lexi sighed. 'But I couldn't find another job and ended up getting into arrears with my rent, so when I was offered the job in Manchester with cheap accommodation, I decided it was time to cut my losses.'

'Good for you,' Nicole said approvingly. 'So where are you working?'

'In a residential care home in Didsbury.'

'What, like, changing shitty nappies and washing old blokes' bits?' Nicole pulled a face.

'There's more to it than that,' Lexi laughed. 'But, yeah, that's part of it.'

'*Ewww.* I'd rather die.'

'It was a bit freaky at the start, but you get used to it pretty fast. And it's keeping a roof over my head, so I can't complain.'

'You need to find yourself a rich man to take care of you,' Nicole said, reaching for the wine bottle to refill their glasses, even though Lexi's was still half full. 'Preferably one with his own place, so you can move out of that shithole. I'm not being funny, but I could smell the rat piss from the car.'

'Well I've never seen any,' Lexi said, shuddering at the thought. 'Anyway, I haven't got time for dating. But even if I did, I'd never let a man keep me,' she added, conscious as the words were leaving her mouth that Nicole had been a kept woman her entire life: first by Daddy Big Bucks, and now Ryan.

'You'll never get anywhere with that attitude,' Nicole scoffed, jiggling her breasts. 'God gave us these babies for a reason, and it sure as hell wasn't so we could work ourselves into an early grave changing shitty nappies.'

'We're not all as blessed as you in that department,' Lexi laughed, relaxing as the wine began to soak in.

After finishing the pizza, Nicole cracked open another bottle and they chatted about old times and laughed about the situations they had used to get themselves into. Both a little tipsy by 10 p.m., Lexi said, 'I'd best get going soon. I've got work in the morning, and I'll never wake up at this rate.'

'Wait, you haven't seen my wedding photos yet,' Nicole said, getting up and rushing out into the hall.

She came back with three thick albums and plonked them down on the table before opening the first. It was filled with pictures of her in various pre-wedding stages; from early morning champagne with her mum and her bridesmaids in a lavish hotel suite, all wearing snow-white dressing gowns which had their individual roles for the day embroidered across the backs in purple, to having her hair and make-up done, to descending the hotel's sweeping staircase in her dress and train before joining her dad, who was waiting by a Rolls-Royce at the foot of the hotel steps wearing tails and a beaming smile.

'You look incredible,' Lexi said, studying her friend's face in the shots and noticing that they'd been taken before she'd succumbed to the lip-fillers and Botox and was still a natural beauty. 'And how handsome and proud does your dad look?'

'If you think he looks good, wait till you see my Ryan,' Nicole said, closing that album and opening the second.

The first few pictures were of the exterior of the church and the arrival of the bridesmaids, followed by Nicole and her dad. The next were of the interior, and Lexi swallowed deeply when she caught her first glimpse of Ryan waiting at the altar for his bride. He'd always been good-looking, but he'd matured into an exceptionally handsome man in the five years between the last time she had seen him aged seventeen, to his wedding day aged twenty-two.

'The poor thing was so nervous he could barely get his words out when we had to say our vows,' Nicole said. 'My dad nearly took over at one point, but my mum made him sit back down. You'll see it all when I show you the video. It was so funny.'

Heart sinking at the idea of having to sit through a video when they still had another album to get through, Lexi said, 'It's a bit late, so maybe we'd best leave that till another time?'

'It's not that long,' Nicole said dismissively as she flicked the page.

Jaw clenching when she found herself looking at Adam's grinning face, Lexi snatched up her glass and drained it. He was still handsome, and she totally understood why he'd been so popular with the girls when they were younger. But those girls had only seen the charming face he presented to the world, whereas Lexi had seen the true ugly heart of him, and her stomach churned at the memory of him groping her breasts and forcing his fingers inside her.

Almost as stomach-churning was the realization, after seeing that Adam was standing on the other side of the altar, that he must have been the best man – a privilege usually reserved for the groom's closest friend. And the shots that followed, of Adam and Ryan with their arms around each other, clinking glasses and grinning like idiots at the reception, confirmed that Ryan was a snake who had lied to the police to get his buddy off the hook.

'State of that,' Nicole sneered, pointing out an uncomfortable-looking woman who was standing to the side in a group shot.

'Who is she?' Lexi asked, forcing herself to stop thinking about Adam.

'Ryan's mum,' Nicole said. 'Can you believe a gorgeous man like him came out of her? And she wondered why I didn't want her in the family photos. Right miserable bitch, she was – and a proper cheapskate, an' all. Know what she bought us for a wedding present? *Plates*! Can you believe that? My dad had paid for absolutely everything, and she turns up with a set of shitty plates. They went *straight* in the bin.'

'Where's his dad?' Lexi asked, realizing that the only black or mixed-race faces she'd seen so far belonged to Ryan and some of his mates and their girls off the Kingston.

'In prison,' Nicole said, with another sneer. 'He took off to Jamaica as soon as he found out Ryan's mum was pregnant, so Ryan's never even met him. But he doesn't need scum like that now he's a Harvey.'

Before Lexi could ask if Ryan had taken her surname when they married, the front door opened and a cold draught blew up the hallway and into the kitchen.

'That you, darling?' Nicole called out, jumping to her feet.

'Who else would it be?' a deep voice replied.

Seconds later, Ryan walked into the room, and Lexi's heart started pounding so hard she could barely breathe. He was even more handsome in the flesh, but his expression was unreadable, so she couldn't gauge what he was thinking as he stared at her.

'Why are you home so early?' Nicole asked, rising up onto her tiptoes to kiss him. 'I thought you said you were working late tonight?'

'I needed to pick something up,' he said – subtly moving his head, Lexi noticed, so his wife's kiss landed on his cheek instead of his lips.

'Look who I bumped into,' Nicole said, gesturing toward Lexi, as if she hadn't noticed that he'd already seen her. 'Can you guess who it is?'

'I know who it is,' he said. Then, to Lexi: 'I didn't know you were back in town. How you doing?'

'Good, thanks.' She forced a smile. 'You?'

'Can't complain.' He shrugged. 'You're looking well.'

Eyes swivelling from Ryan to Lexi and back to Ryan again, Nicole stepped in front of him, as if to block his view, and folded her arms. 'So what did you need to pick up?'

'This.' He opened a drawer and took out a thick white envelope.

'Why didn't you take it before?' Nicole frowned, watching as he slid it into the inside pocket of his jacket. 'You know I don't like you going over there at night,' she went on quietly. 'Can't you leave it till morning?'

'He wants it tonight,' Ryan replied, equally quietly. 'If you don't like it, have a go at *him*, not me.'

'You'd better not go inside.'

Ryan flashed an irritated look at her but didn't reply. Instead, sidestepping her, he nodded goodbye to Lexi, saying, 'It was good to see you.'

'You too,' she murmured, wondering what the hell was going on when he walked out into the hall with his wife on his heel. Nicole had spent the whole night banging on about what a wonderful marriage they had, but if looks could kill the woman would have dropped down dead after the one Ryan had just given her.

After a whispered but heated argument in the hallway, followed by the sound of the front door slamming, Nicole marched back into the kitchen with a face like thunder and snatched the bottle of wine off the table.

'Everything OK?' Lexi asked, watching as she poured a glassful and sank it in one before immediately refilling it.

'Does it look like it?' Nicole snapped.

'I was only asking.' Lexi held up her hands. 'No need to bite my head off.'

'Don't sit there acting like butter wouldn't melt,' Nicole hissed. 'I've got your number, lady!'

'Sorry?' Lexi was confused. 'Have I done something to upset you?'

'*Have I done something to upset you?*' Nicole mimicked, slamming the bottle down on the table. 'You think I didn't see the way you looked at him? You might as well have come right out and asked him to fuck you!'

'Don't be ridiculous,' Lexi spluttered. 'I hardly said two words to him.'

'You didn't *need* to; your eyes did all the talking for you,' Nicole shot back. 'But he didn't want you first time round, and he *definitely* doesn't want you now, so jog on and find your own man, bitch.'

Lexi opened her mouth to argue that she had done absolutely nothing wrong, but Nicole's blazing eyes told her that the woman was too far gone to listen to reason, so she snapped it shut again and stood up.

'I think I'd best go.'

'Yeah, you do that,' spat Nicole. 'But don't bother running after my husband like the desperate little dog you are, 'cos he'll be long gone by now.'

RUNNING SCARED

'I knew this was a mistake,' Lexi said, taking her jacket off the back of the chair and pulling it on. 'You always were a paranoid bitch, and you obviously haven't changed. I'm only surprised Ryan's put up with you for this long.'

'Get out,' Nicole snarled, baring her teeth.

'With pleasure,' Lexi said, snatching her bag up off the floor.

Shocked that things had deteriorated so quickly after Ryan's appearance, Lexi walked briskly away from the house without looking back. Nicole had always had a mile-wide jealous streak, and it clearly hadn't improved with age, but her reaction to Lexi and Ryan exchanging a few awkward words had been so extreme it was crazy.

Glad that it had happened tonight and not further down the line when she might have wasted time investing in a friendship that had never been all that great in the first place, Lexi continued on her way, not realizing that she was taking the same route she had used to walk as a teenager until the all-too-familiar blocks of flats and shabby houses that made up the Kingston estate came into view. Hesitating when she saw them, she contemplated turning around and finding another way home. But something was tugging at her and, before she was even aware that she had started walking again, she found herself on the path facing her old block.

It was difficult to see much in the dull orange glow of the few street lamps that were actually working, but it was clear from the odour of dog shit in the air, the broken glass glittering on the concrete, and the bags spilling out of the bin cupboards, that the area hadn't improved since she'd left. Switching her gaze to the flats, which were more brightly illuminated, she felt the prick of tears behind her eyes when she picked out her old front door. It had been green when she'd lived there and was now red, but everything else still looked the same, and she felt a physical pain in her heart when she visualized her mum coming out through the door wearing her old blue work coat.

''Scuse me, love.'

Lexi snapped her head round at the sound of the voice, and murmured, 'Sorry,' when she saw a tall thin man in a tracksuit and a baseball cap pushing a stroller in which a young child was sleeping.

The man nodded his thanks when she stepped aside to let him pass. But he'd only taken a couple of steps before he stopped and looked back. Thinking that he'd probably noticed she was close to tears and was going to ask if she was OK, Lexi started to walk away, but froze when he spoke her name.

'Sorry, do I know you?' she asked, turning back and peering at his face.

'It's Jamie,' he said. 'Jamie Holland.'

'*What?*' Her mouth fell open in shock. 'No way!'

'You remember me?'

'Of course I do.'

'Oh, wow, I don't believe this.' He grinned from ear to ear. 'I never forgot you, but I totally thought you'd have forgotten me.'

'Never,' Lexi said, staring at him in disbelief. 'But when did you get so tall? You were only up to my shoulder last time I saw you.'

'I shot up just before I started high school. Which was kind of cool, 'cos it made people think twice about trying to bully me.'

'Glad to hear it. You were a sweet kid and I used to really worry about you.'

'You were the only one who ever did,' Jamie said quietly. Then, looking embarrassed, he shuffled his feet and said, 'I couldn't believe it when I heard what had happened to your mam. I tried to talk to you when they were putting you in the ambulance, but you were out of it.'

'They reckoned I'd gone into shock,' Lexi said, remembering nothing of that day. 'But let's not talk about that, eh? Tell me about this little one.' She nodded at the sleeping child. 'Boy or girl?'

'Girl,' Jamie said proudly. 'Her name's Poppy. She's a terror for wanting to play at night, but she goes out like a light if I take her for a walk in her buggy.'

'Bless her.' Lexi smiled. 'She's beautiful. And who's her mum? Anyone I'd know?'

'I don't think you ever met her, but do you remember that mad woman off the sixth floor?'

'The one who used to do yoga in the rain at the back?' Lexi asked, frowning when she remembered that the woman had looked older than her mum, which meant she must be in her fifties or sixties by now. 'Aren't you a bit young for her?' Grimacing as soon as the words left her mouth, she said, 'I'm so sorry, that was really rude – and none of my business.'

'I'm not with *her*,' Jamie laughed. 'I'm with her daughter, Jenny. You probably wouldn't have seen her 'cos Sandra didn't let her out much. She was a bit eccentric, but she was proper protective of Jen.'

'So are you and Jenny living with her, or have you got your own place?'

'I moved in with them when me and Jen first got together, but San died last year so we took over the tenancy.'

'I'm sorry to hear that,' Lexi said, touching his arm. 'And how's *your* mum doing?'

'Couldn't tell you.' He shrugged. 'Haven't seen her in years – and couldn't care less if I ever do again. She got hooked on crack and went on the game, and I'm not having that shit round my girls.'

'Good for you,' Lexi said, glad that he'd taken the opposite path in life to his neglectful mother.

'Hey, if you're not in a rush, why don't you come up and meet Jen?' Jamie suggested. 'She's heard me talking about you loads over the years, and I know she'd love to meet you.'

Unsure if she could face stepping foot inside the block with all the memories it still held, Lexi said, 'Maybe another time. I've got work in the morning, and I'm worried I won't wake up if I don't get home soon.'

'No problem,' Jamie said. 'It's been great seeing you again.'

'You too,' Lexi said, giving him a hug. 'And your daughter's a lucky girl to have a daddy like you.'

'I do my best,' he said modestly. 'Can I, um, get your number? I won't pester you, or nothing, but I'd like to stay in touch – if that's OK?'

'Yeah, sure,' Lexi said, making a show of rooting through her bag. 'Oh damn, I must have left my phone at home, and I don't know my number off by heart. Tell you what, why don't you give me yours instead?' She took out a scrap of paper and a pen and handed them to him.

Thanking him when he'd scribbled his number down, Lexi hugged him again, and said goodbye, then watched as he pushed the pram on up the path, looking back and smiling every few steps. When he'd disappeared through the main door of the flats, she turned and walked away. As lovely as he'd undoubtedly turned out to be, she had already decided that she would never contact him. He was the third person she had met from her old life tonight, and if the shambolic ending to her catch-up with Nicole had taught her anything, it was that the past was best left well behind her.

15

Still pissed off with Nicole for going off on him in front of Lexi, Ryan slammed the door of his Range Rover harder than he'd intended to after pulling into the car park of The Danski, the seedy lap-dancing club his brother-in-law had bought the previous year, which was situated on a weed-infested lot surrounded by derelict warehouses in the bog-end of Cheetham Hill. Hissing a curse through his teeth when the door bounced open again and he saw that the clasp of his seat belt was dangling out and had made a dent in the metal, he closed it properly and then locked it before strolling to the door of the club.

He greeted the bouncer with a nod when the door clicked open, and said, 'Where is he?'

'In the back,' the man said, his slight eye-roll letting Ryan know that Adam was being his usual loud, obnoxious self.

The throbbing bass of the music coming from the club room vibrated the sticky floor beneath Ryan's feet as he walked along the red-lighted corridor, and he wrinkled his nose in disgust at the combined odours of sweat and smoke that seemed to ooze out of the peeling flock wallpaper. He knew exactly why Nicole hated him coming here at night, but if she thought for one minute that he'd be turned on by the sights that would greet him when he opened the next door, she was crazy. Unlike her brother, who, along with his so-called posse, spent most of his nights here getting high on coke, cheap pussy, and the even cheaper house-fizz the club passed off as champagne, Ryan had no interest in that scene whatsoever.

The main room was packed and Ryan had to push his way through the leering, mostly middle-aged men who were crowded around a circular stage in the centre of the floor, on which two naked, dead-eyed women were listlessly gyrating around a pole. The tables and private booths were located at the rear of the room, and he headed toward them when he heard Adam's raucous laughter ringing out above the music. As he got closer, he clocked the source of the man's amusement: a grossly overweight woman bouncing up and down on another man's lap; her enormous breasts smashing into his face with every movement.

One of the other men at the table spotted him and alerted Adam, who immediately turned his head, spraying sweat in an arc as he did so. Booming, 'About fuckin' time,' he rose to his feet.

Motioning him away from the table with a jerk of his head, Ryan took the envelope out of his pocket.

Adam snatched it out of his hand. 'Where's the rest?' he demanded after flipping through the banknotes it contained.

'Another shipment went missing,' Ryan told him. 'Your dad told me to cut your share till we get back on track.'

'So *you* cocked up again and *I've* got to suffer?' Adam scowled. 'Fuck that!'

'If you don't like it, take it up with your dad.' Ryan shrugged.

'Don't get cocky,' Adam snarled, jabbing a finger into Ryan's chest. 'You might think you're special, but you ain't shit. *I'm* his son, not you, and when I get what's mine, I'll put you back in the gutter as fast as he dragged you out of it.'

'Whatever,' Ryan said, batting Adam's hand aside when the man went to jab him again.

'Hey there, handsome,' a topless girl cooed, appearing at Ryan's side and giving him a sultry look. 'Looking for a dance?'

'Do one, bitch,' Adam barked, shoving her so hard she fell back against a table. 'In fact, get the fuck outta here,' he yelled as she slunk away. 'You're sacked!'

'Way to treat your staff,' Ryan said sarcastically. 'And you wonder why Danny didn't put *you* in charge when he went to Spain. You're a fuckin' liability, man.'

'Says the prick who crawled so far up my dad's arse he came out the colour of shit,' Adam shot back. Impressed by his off-the-cuff joke, he turned to see if his boys had heard it. 'Did youse catch that? Crawled so far up my dad's arse, he came out the colour of shit.'

Some of the men started laughing but quickly stopped when Ryan glared at them. Angered that they were bowing down to the jumped-up prick, Adam curled his lip and flapped a dismissive hand at him, saying, 'Off you go, boy. I'm done with you.'

'See you next time,' Ryan said, smiling slyly as he added, 'If you're still here, that is.'

'Meaning?' Adam scowled.

'Take a look around you,' Ryan said, casting his own gaze around the room. 'This place is heaving and you should be raking it in hand over fist, and yet you still need your *allowance* from Daddy to keep things ticking over. That tells me you're either putting the profits up your nose, or someone's on the take. Either way, you'd best get it sorted before you prove how much of a fuck-up you really are.'

Chest heaving, sweat dripping into his eyes, Adam bared his teeth and thrust his face into Ryan's. 'You'd best learn your place and start showing me the respect I deserve before I tell my sister what her precious husband gets up to behind her back.'

'And what would that be?' Ryan challenged, confident that the prick had nothing on him.

'Coming round here propositioning my girls and trying to get freebies,' Adam said, giving a snake-like grin. 'Bet she'd love that, wouldn't she?'

'Nice try,' Ryan smiled unconcernedly. 'But she'd never believe that for one minute.'

'If I send one of them round to tell her all about it in person, she would,' said Adam. 'And maybe I'll word my dad up while I'm at it; see how long it takes for him to put a bullet through your head.'

Leaning closer, Ryan lowered his voice and said, 'I'd quit with the threats, if I was you, *boy*. Unless you want your dad to find out where that five extra grand you asked for the other month to clear your debts really went?'

Twitching with rage when Ryan patted his cheek and then walked away, Adam barged past the customers who were standing around and marched into his office, slamming and locking the door behind him.

Nodding goodnight to the doorman, Ryan climbed into his car and slammed his fist down on the steering wheel. Adam had always been a prick, but at least he'd been a semi-bearable prick before his folks went into hiding. Once they were gone, the rot had set in, and Adam's true colours had come out with a vengeance. Furious that Danny had put Ryan in charge instead of him, he'd morphed into a self-pitying weasel who thought the world owed him a living. Ryan despised him. Fortunately, unlike Rachel, who was still in denial about her son's less savoury habits and would defend him to the moon and back, Danny had little time for him and was unlikely to pay any heed if he tried to feed him that bullshit story about Ryan propositioning his girls. But if Adam played on Nicole's paranoia and planted that seed in *her* mind, she'd start watching him like a hawk – and that could make things very tricky.

Aware that he'd left things on a sour note with her earlier, he decided to stop off at a garage and pick up some flowers and chocolates. It was a cheap fix for a much deeper problem, but it was exactly the kind of superficial show of affection Nicole liked and he hoped it would smooth things over. Until the next time.

Rachel Harvey sipped her cocktail and gazed out over the Mediterranean Sea. She could see the lights and hear the party music pumping out from the nightclubs further along the Golden Mile, but Jackie's – the tiny bar outside which she was sitting – only ever played country and western music, because that was what the older ex-pat criminals who congregated here seemed to prefer.

Danny loved the place, and she could hear him now, cracking jokes with his buddies and spouting shit about how bad things were back home without real geezers like them, with brains *and* brawn, to keep things running smoothly. The bastards bored the crap out of her – their wives even more so; and she resented that Danny made her come here instead of taking her to one of the more fashionable places. But he hated the hustle and bustle of Marbella Town, so she got her own back by going on solo shopping sprees during the day while he was sleeping; treating herself to expensive facials and manicures and flirting with the hot young waiters.

Making a mental note to book herself into Marianne's – the ludicrously expensive clinic where all the ex-pat wives got their Botox and fillers – in the morning, she was about to head inside to get another drink when her phone started ringing, and she smiled when she saw Adam's name on the screen.

'Hello, son . . . how are y—'

'Where's Dad?' Adam cut in. 'I've been trying to get hold of him but he's not answering.'

'Busy playing Al Capone, as usual,' Rachel sneered, fanning her face with her hand. 'Anything I can do?'

'Yeah, you can tell him to get his lapdog under control,' Adam hissed. 'I'm sick of the prick trying to lord it over me.'

'What's he done now?'

'He's dropped this month's money off and there was less than usual again. When I asked where the rest was, he said Dad told him to cut my share.'

'I see,' Rachel murmured, flashing a glance at her husband through the open door of the bar.

'It's not on, Mum. He bangs on about the family sticking together no matter what, but where's his loyalty when it come to me? I'm his son, and it should be me running things, not that cunt.'

'Darling, you know why he left Ryan in charge. But things will change when we get back, I promise.'

'It needs to change *now*,' Adam said petulantly. 'I know I fucked up a few times in the past, and I'm working my arse off to turn things around and make a success of the club; but it's gonna take time and money to get it back on its feet.'

'I know you're doing your best, but I told you from the start I had a bad feeling about that place,' Rachel said. 'And if you still need handouts to stay afloat, I was obviously right.'

'*Handouts?*' Adam squawked. 'What the actual fuck, Mum?

Nic gets whatever she asks for without doing jack shit, but I'm expected to grovel for my rightful share? It's a fucking joke!'

'You know I didn't mean it like that,' Rachel sighed. 'But that place is a money pit, and you can't keep throwing good cash after bad and expect to come up smelling of roses. If you want your dad to take you seriously, you need to stop messing about and show him you're capable of running the business at a profit.'

'Like *Ryan*, you mean?'

'I don't like this any more than you do, but if you don't step up your game and prove you can be trusted, your dad will never let you take over.'

'I don't need to prove a damn thing,' Adam shot back angrily. 'And they'd all best start watching their backs, 'cos I'm sick of being taken for a mug.'

'What do you mean by that?' Rachel asked. 'Adam? *Adam!*'

Tutting when she realized the line had gone dead, Rachel breathed in deeply as she stared at the blank screen. She understood why her son was frustrated about Danny handing the reins over to Ryan instead of him: it must have felt like the ultimate slap in the face for his father to choose an outsider over his own son. Danny insisted that he'd done it for Adam's own good, claiming that the gangsters they did business with would chop the boy into a thousand pieces if they ever got wind of the ridiculous accusations of sexual abuse that had been levelled against him in the past. Whatever his reasons, he could easily have left one of the older guys in charge instead of handing it to Ryan. But Danny was a law unto himself when it came to business. It was his way or *no* way – and to hell with what anyone thought about it.

'Ray, you out here?'

Gritting her teeth at the sound of her husband calling her by the shortened version of her name – an irritating habit he had picked up from one of his cockney bank-robber buddies – Rachel slotted her phone back into her bag and stood up. Adam had clearly been drunk, so she wasn't going to pay too much mind to what he'd said before cutting the call. But he was right about one thing: if Danny could fund his daughter's extravagant lifestyle, kit his son-in-law out with a top-of-the-range motor *and* treat his new buddies to beers and cigars every night, then he could flaming well see to it that his son got his fair share.

Nicole was curled up in bed when Ryan arrived home, and he could see in the glow of the light from the landing that her eyes were swollen. Guessing that she had cried herself to sleep, he gently touched her shoulder.

'Nic?'

'What?' she croaked.

'I'm sorry,' he said, sitting beside her and laying the flowers and chocolates on the bedside table. 'I shouldn't have stormed off earlier, but you got it all wrong. I'm not interested in Lexi.'

'So why did you tell her she was looking good?'

'I said it was good to see her,' Ryan corrected her. 'And I was only being polite. What was she doing here, anyway?'

'I bumped into her when I went to that party and invited her round,' Nicole said, shuffling into a sitting position.

'Why? I thought you hated her?'

'I don't know.' Nicole shrugged. 'I'd had a couple of drinks and forgot what had happened. I could tell she wasn't doing too well for herself, 'cos her clothes were really cheap and her shoes were shit, and I . . . well, I guess I wanted to show her how well we're doing compared to her. But then you came home early and I thought you fancied her and I got mad.'

'I was shocked to see her here after everything that went down before she left, but I didn't look at her in any kind of way that could have made you think that,' Ryan insisted.

'I know I shouldn't get so insecure,' Nicole sniffed, resting her head on his shoulder. 'But you're always leaving me by myself and I start thinking all sorts.'

'I'm working, you know that. Your dad trusted me with his business and I don't want to let him down.'

'I know, but I wish you'd take a break sometimes. I'm always asleep by the time you get home and we hardly ever have sex anymore.'

'I've been working flat out to get things back on track after those shipments went missing. And I'm the boss, so I can't just drop everything to rush home to you every time you want a bit of attention.'

'You do still love me though, don't you?' Nicole gazed up at him. 'And you swear you don't fancy Lexi?'

Sighing, Ryan said, 'How many times do I have to tell you before you believe me?'

'I'm sorry,' she apologized. 'It's just hard when I don't know where you are half the time. And I *hate* our Adam for making you go to that horrible club with all those dirty slags,' she added vehemently.

'You and me both,' said Ryan.

'You didn't look at any of them tonight, did you?'

'Didn't even go inside,' Ryan lied. 'I got the doorman to fetch him out and handed the money over on the step.'

'Good,' Nicole said, wrapping her arms around his waist.

'I got you these,' Ryan said, leaning away from her to reach for the flowers. 'Thought they might cheer you up.'

'Oh, they're lovely,' Nicole said, sniffing them. 'And my favourite chocolates, too,' she said, smiling when she spotted the box. 'I love you.'

'I know,' Ryan said, giving her a quick hug before disentangling himself. 'Sorry. Need the loo.'

When he went into their en-suite bathroom, Nicole carried the flowers downstairs. After trimming the stems and arranging them in a vase, she was disappointed to find Ryan in bed and already asleep when she went back up to their room. Sighing because she had hoped they might at least have a cuddle, if not sex, she climbed in beside him and, quietly tearing the cellophane off the box of chocolates, popped one into her mouth.

The picture she had painted for Lexi earlier of a blissful marriage was far from the truth, but she would rather die than admit it to that bitch – or anyone else. She was Ryan King's wife and Danny Harvey's daughter, and she enjoyed the perks that afforded her: the respect she was shown by some of the most hardened criminals in Manchester, and the freebies she received at whichever salon or clinic she deigned to visit. When she was a girl, she had never understood why her mum turned into a nagging, hard-drinking bitch as soon as night fell. But she totally got it now. Alone within the confines of these four walls, with nobody to admire her or fawn over her, she was invisible – and that sucked.

Glancing at Ryan when he made a noise, Nicole popped another chocolate into her mouth and narrowed her eyes thoughtfully. She hadn't been lying when she'd told Lexi she didn't want a child if it meant ruining her perfect body, but it *had* been a lie when she'd said Ryan wanted one, because he'd never once mentioned it. But she'd heard that every man secretly craved a son to carry on their family name, so why would he be any different?

Quite liking the idea now that she'd thought of it, she lay back against her pillows and let her imagination run away with her as she munched on yet another chocolate – a crunchy one, this time. If she had a baby and it came out with its father's skin tone and her green eyes, it would look stunning, and she could open up an Instagram page and get paid for advertising baby clothes and yummy-mummy products. Modelling agencies from all over the country would clamour to sign it up – and maybe her, as well, once they saw how gorgeous she was. She would be so famous she would probably be invited to film premieres and—

'Nic, I'm trying to sleep,' Ryan said, breaking into her fantasies. 'If you've got to eat the chocolates, can you at least pick soft ones?'

'Sorry,' she murmured, closing the lid on the box and snuggling up behind him. 'How do you feel about having a baby?'

Ryan stiffened. 'You're not pregnant, are you?'

'Not yet, but I soon could be if I get my implant taken out. What d'you think?'

'It's probably not the best time right now. I'm really busy with the business, so I wouldn't be much use.'

'We could get a nanny to help out until my dad comes home and takes over,' Nicole said. 'Then you'd have loads of time to do your share.'

'Has he said he's coming back?' Ryan asked, twisting his head to look back at her over his shoulder.

Unable to see his expression in the darkness, Nicole shook her head. 'No, but they're not going to stay away forever, are they? And can you imagine how happy they'll be if they find out they're going to be grandparents when they get back?'

'Don't get ahead of yourself,' Ryan cautioned, resting his head on the pillow again. 'I'm not even sure I want kids.'

'Neither was I, but I think I'm ready now. Will you at least think about it?'

'Yeah, sure. But not now, eh? I need to sleep.'

'OK, we'll talk tomorrow,' Nicole said, smiling as she slid her arm around him. He didn't sound overly enthusiastic about the idea, but he was bound to get on board once he realized how serious she was. But if he didn't, oh well . . . It was her body, and if she had the implant removed he'd have no choice but to deal with it.

16

In the weeks following her disastrous dinner date with Nicole, and her unplanned visit to the Kingston and subsequent unexpected meeting with Jamie, Lexi felt like she had finally laid some of her ghosts to rest. Immersing herself in work during the weekdays, she spent most of her evenings and weekends with Debs, watching TV, eating together, and gossiping over a bottle of wine. And their neighbour Jim – or *Six* as he still insisted on being called – would often pop in if he wasn't on a night shift, bearing beers, weed, and a ton of hilarious stories about his life as a roadie for a punk band before it disbanded and he found his calling as a care worker.

Fond of her new friends, and still thoroughly enjoying her job – especially so now her bitch neighbour and supervisor, Ada, had found a new girl to pick on; Lexi soon forgot about Nicole and threw herself into her new life. The area wasn't half as bad as she'd initially thought, and she no longer felt nervous about walking to the shops at night if she or Debs had forgotten to pick something up on their way home.

When she nipped out for a bottle of milk one evening and found the corner shop closed, she decided to go to a nearby all-night garage instead. But it turned out she wasn't quite as familiar with the neighbourhood as she'd thought, and she realized she must have taken a wrong turn when she found herself on an estate she'd never been to before. She took out her phone to ring Debs and ask for directions back to the main road, but as the screen lit up and she was about to scroll through her contact list, a shadowy figure lurched out of an alleyway between the houses, and she cried out in alarm when a strong arm was wrapped around her neck.

'Keep your mouth shut or I'll cut your throat,' a deep voice hissed into her ear.

Terrified when she felt herself being dragged into the shadows of the alley, she screamed for help, and saw stars when the man punched her in the side of the head. Clinging onto her phone when he tried to snatch it from her, she glimpsed a flash of silver in his hand and drove her heel backwards into his shin as hard as she could. When he momentarily loosened his grip, she tore free and ran out of the alleyway, stumbling into the path of an oncoming car and causing the driver to slam on his brakes.

The driver, a bald, muscular black man, leapt out, shouting, 'What the fuck? Are you crazy?' His anger evaporated in an instant when he noticed her distress, and he quickly walked round to her, asking, 'Are you OK? I didn't clip you, did I?'

'A man,' she spluttered, pointing back toward the alley. 'He – he had a knife.'

155

'Get in and lock the doors,' the driver ordered, pushing her toward the car before racing into the alley.

As she was fumbling with the door handle, a woman came out of a house across the road wearing a dressing gown.

'What's going on? I heard screaming. Has someone been knocked over?'

'I got jumped,' Lexi told her. 'Someone's gone after him.'

'I'll call the police,' the woman said.

'Don't bother, he's legged it,' the driver said, coming out from the alley in time to hear her. Then, turning to Lexi, who hadn't yet got into the car, he said, 'Did he hurt you?'

'No.' She shook her head. 'I kicked him when I saw the knife and got away before he could do anything. Thank you so much for stopping,' she added. 'I was scared he was going to come after me.'

'I doubt you'll be seeing him again in a hurry,' the man said, scanning the road through narrowed eyes. 'But I'll walk you to your door just in case. Which house is yours?'

'I don't live here,' Lexi told him. 'I got lost looking for the all-night garage and was about to ring my housemate for directions when he grabbed me. I shouldn't have taken my phone out in the street. That's what he was after.'

'Did he get it?'

'No. I held onto it.' Lexi showed him the phone.

'OK, hop in and give me your address,' the man said, walking back to the driver's side. 'I'll drive you home.'

'Thanks, but I don't want to put you out any more than I

already have,' Lexi said warily. 'I'll be fine once I find my way back to the main road.'

'If it makes you feel any safer, take a picture of my number plate and send it to your friend,' the man suggested. 'That way they can show it to the police if you don't turn up.'

Ashamed of herself for being suspicious when he'd potentially saved her life and was being so kind, Lexi erred on the side of caution and took a snap of the number plate – making sure that she also caught his face in it, just in case. After sending it to Debs, she climbed into the car and gave the man a guilty smile.

'Sorry. It's not that I don't trust you, but . . .'

'Don't worry, I get it,' he said when she tailed off. 'Theo.' He held out his hand.

'Lexi.' She shook it and then slid her hands between her knees.

'Address?'

'Chamberlain Road.'

'That's only a few streets away,' he said, turning the car round after typing the address into the satnav.

When they pulled up outside the house a few minutes later, Debs was standing by the gate with her phone in her hand and a worried look on her face.

'What's going on?' she demanded, eyeing Theo with open suspicion when he climbed out. 'If you've done something to my friend, I'll—'

'He hasn't done anything,' Lexi said as she too climbed out.

'Why did you send me that picture then?' Debs asked. 'I was about to ring the police and tell them you'd been kidnapped.'

'Theo told me to send it, so you'd be able to show it to them if I went missing,' Lexi explained. 'I got mugged, and he chased the guy off and offered me a lift.'

'You got mugged?' Debs was alarmed. 'Oh my God, are you OK?'

'I'm fine,' Lexi said, handing over the bottle of milk Theo had stopped off at the garage for on the way back. 'I'll tell you about it in a minute. Go put the kettle on.'

Turning to Theo when Debs had gone inside, Lexi said, 'Thanks again for your help. I feel a bit stupid now I know how close I was to home.'

'Hey, it's dark, and these roads all look the same at night.' He shrugged. 'I'm just glad you weren't hurt. Anyway, you'd best go see your friend; she's looking kinda worried,' he said, gesturing with a jerk of his chin to a window above, where, Lexi saw when she glanced up, Debs was standing, watching them intently.

'Thanks again,' Lexi said, smiling as he walked round the car.

'My pleasure.' He returned the smile. 'Take care.'

Waving as he drove away, Lexi went inside and made sure the door was securely locked before heading upstairs.

Debs was waiting in her doorway, with a glass of brandy in her hand. 'Here, drink this,' she ordered.

'Thanks, but tea would have been fine,' Lexi said, sinking down on her friend's tiny sofa.

'Shut up and get it drunk,' Debs said, perching beside her. 'So what happened? Did you get a look at the mugger's face?'

Lexi shook her head and took a sip of the drink before relaying the events of the night. 'It was my own fault,' she concluded. 'You and Six are always telling me not to use my phone on the street at night. I'm such an idiot.'

'Don't you dare blame yourself,' Debs berated her. 'There are some nasty fuckers out there, and he'd probably been waiting ages in that alley for someone to pass by. If it hadn't been you, it could have been some little old woman who wasn't strong enough to fight him off, so you might actually have saved someone's life.'

'Maybe,' Lexi sighed, taking another sip of her drink. 'But God knows what would have happened if Theo hadn't stopped and chased him off.'

'Shows what a cowardly prick he was,' Debs sneered. 'Targets a woman but runs at the first sight of a man. And *what* a man that Theo is, eh? Proper bit of all right, he was. I hope you got his number?' Tutting when Lexi shook her head, she said, 'Why not, you idiot?'

'I was a bit distracted by the fact that I'd just escaped having my throat cut.'

'I'd have used that to my advantage,' Debs snorted. '*Oh Theo, I was so scared,*' she said in a pathetic voice. '*Please give me your number so I can ring you if he ever comes after me again.*'

'It's not a joke. I was terrified.'

'I'm only messing, hon. But did you see the *thighs* on him?'

'You're unbelievable,' Lexi said drily. 'You say you're looking for love, but you waste so much time lusting after total strangers you can't even see what's right under your nose.'

'Eh?' Debs gave her a questioning look.

'Six. You must know he's got the hots for you.'

'*What?* Behave! He's like the brother I never had.'

'Believe me, that's not how he sees you. I've been watching him when he comes over, and he's crazy about you.'

'Nah, he's just being friendly,' Debs said dismissively. 'But even if he did fancy me, he's not my type.'

'You haven't got a type. And he's way better looking than that last bloke you brought home. Way less boring, as well.'

'Oi, I brought him home for a shag not a conversation. But if we're talking types, that Theo one is mine to a tee. There'd be none of my usual *wham, bam, there's the door fuck off* with him, I can tell you. And you can quit with the disapproving looks, 'cos I bet you wouldn't kick him out of bed.'

'I would, actually,' said Lexi. 'He's married, in case you didn't notice his wedding ring.'

'Really?' Debs frowned. 'He didn't smell married to me.'

'How on earth does someone *smell* married?'

'They just do. And he didn't.'

'Well, it doesn't make any difference either way. He's too old for me.'

'Is he buggery! He looks like he's in his late thirties, tops, and you're – what? Twenty-five? That's only fifteen or so years, and there were twenty between my mam and dad. Never bothered them.'

'Still not interested,' Lexi said, finishing the brandy and putting the glass on the table. 'Right, I'm going to bed. See you tomorrow.'

'See ya,' Debs said, smiling as she opened her phone and pulled up the photo Lexi had sent to her. 'Me and Mr Universe are going to have a bit of fun before I hit the sack.'

'Knock yourself out,' Lexi said, shaking her head bemusedly as she headed for the door.

In her own room, she locked and bolted the door and made sure the window was properly latched before getting undressed. She still felt a bit shaky, but she knew things could have been a whole lot worse if she hadn't landed that kick and got away from her attacker. Making a mental note to sign herself up for the self-defence class she'd seen advertised on the noticeboard at work, she climbed into bed and switched off the lamp.

Woken by Debs hammering on her door the next morning, Lexi was confused to find her on the landing holding a bunch of roses.

'Why have you bought me flowers?' she asked, rubbing her eyes. 'It's not my birthday.'

'They're not from me, they're from Theo,' Debs said, thrusting them into her hand. 'Read the card.'

Lexi pulled the little card out of its envelope and squinted at the spidery writing. '*Been thinking about you*,' she read it aloud. '*Hope you managed to sleep OK. Love T.*'

'You forgot the kisses,' said Debs, letting her know that she had already read it.

'That's so thoughtful,' Lexi said, sniffing the flowers.

'Thoughtful my ass. He fancies you.'

'Don't be daft.'

'Give him a ring, then,' Debs challenged, snatching the card out of Lexi's hand and turning it over to show her the mobile number written on the back.

'I'm not ringing him,' Lexi said, aware that she was blushing. 'You're the one who's got the hots for him; *you* ring him.'

'He might be as fit as fuck, but I don't waste time on men who clearly fancy someone else,' said Debs. 'Tell me to butt out if I'm overstepping the mark, but men who look like him and send expensive flowers to women they've only just met are few and far between, and the least he deserves is a thank you. So get them in a vase and ring him!'

Rolling her eyes when Debs turned and went back to her own room, calling over her shoulder that she was going to put the kettle on and to come over when she was done, Lexi closed her door and re-read the short message on the card. Then, sighing, she laid the flowers on the table and, reaching for her phone, tapped in Theo's number.

'Well?' Debs said when Lexi walked into her room a few minutes later.

'Well what?' Lexi played it cool.

'Did you speak to him?' Debs handed a cup of coffee to her. 'What did you say?'

'I thanked him for the flowers, like you told me to; and he said I was welcome.'

'Is that it?'

'Yep.' Lexi nodded. Then, pursing her lips thoughtfully, as if she'd just remembered something, she said, 'Oh, wait . . . he might have asked me to go out for dinner with him tonight, as well.'

'You bitch!' Debs grinned. 'See, I told you he fancies you. And you'd better have said yes, or I'm gonna slap the stupid right out of you.'

'I agreed to go,' Lexi confirmed. 'Oh, and he's not married, by the way.'

'Yay!' Debs clapped her hands excitedly. 'So where's he taking you?'

'To some Italian restaurant, I'm not sure where. He's picking me up at nine.'

'Ooh, a late one; I like it. Perfect for the old *wanna come back to my place for a nightcap* scenario.'

'I'll be coming straight home, so there'll be none of that,' Lexi insisted. 'Anyway, you got your way, so you can shut up about it now.'

'Shan't say another word.' Debs mimed zipping her lips.

Sipping her coffee, Lexi caught Debs flashing sly glances at her, and mock-sighed. '*What?*'

'Nothing.' Debs feigned innocence. 'I was wondering what you're going to wear, that's all. Only I'd go with that nice purple dress you had on the other week, if I was you. You look really sexy in that one.'

'I'm aiming for classy, not sexy,' said Lexi. As soon as the words left her mouth, she remembered Nicole saying the exact opposite in the run up to the fateful party and shook her head, wondering how they had ever been friends when they were so different in so many ways.

'Penny for them,' Debs said, watching the thoughts flicker in her eyes.

'I was thinking I might wear my black pants and that silver top you gave me,' Lexi lied, pushing Nicole out of her mind.

'Seriously?' Debs was unimpressed. 'Don't you think he'd prefer my choice?'

'I need to feel comfortable,' Lexi argued, glancing at her watch. 'Anyway, I've got some stuff to do so I'd best get going. I'll catch you later.'

'Off to touch your roots up?' Debs gave a knowing smirk.

'Shut your face,' Lexi laughed, standing up. 'I'll bring your cup back later.'

'Make sure you do. That's one of my Royal Doultons.'

'You got it at Aldi last week. I was with you, you daft cow.'

'Just piss off and get your hair done,' Debs smirked. 'You're starting to look greyer than Ada.'

Sticking two fingers up, Lexi was smiling as she walked out.

17

'Wow!' Theo drew his head back when Lexi came out of the house later that night. 'You look incredible.'

'Thanks,' she said, thinking he looked pretty good himself when she noticed the way his soft blue shirt was moulding itself to his muscular chest and biceps, and how his grey trousers showed off the thigh muscles Debs had drooled over.

Smiling when he opened the passenger side door for her, she tugged down the hem of her purple dress before climbing into the car, conscious of Debs spying on them from her window as Theo got behind the wheel and started the engine.

Giuseppe's was located in a rural area several miles outside the city centre, and had once been a farmhouse and then a pub before it became a restaurant. The building looked ancient, with low doors and leaded windows behind which the flicker of candlelight was visible, and Lexi guessed that it was quite an exclusive place judging by the expensive cars parked outside.

Taking Theo's hand when he came around to open her door

after pulling into a space between a Bentley and a Ferrari, she said, 'This looks so pretty. But it must be really expensive.'

'It is a bit pricey,' Theo conceded as they strolled toward the door. 'But it's worth every penny. The chef's an old Italian guy, and he uses recipes that have been handed down through his family from generation to generation, so it's the real deal. You're gonna love it.'

Inside, seated at a table in the corner, they placed their orders and thanked the waiter when he poured their wine before discreetly moving away. Sipping on hers, Lexi surreptitiously checked out the other diners who were seated around the room. The men were all suited and looked every inch as perfectly groomed as the elegant women they were sharing dinner with, and she felt like an imposter in her cheap dress and even cheaper shoes. Theo, however, looked totally at ease with his arm casually draped along the back of the banquette seat.

'So tell me about yourself,' he said, giving her his full attention.

In the habit of giving out the bare minimum after years of receiving pitying looks whenever people heard about her mum, Lexi gave him a brief rundown of her life so far, then said, 'Your turn.'

'Not much to tell, really.' He shrugged. 'I'm forty-three, and I was born and raised in Manchester, but I've been out of the country for the last few years. Secret Service stuff,' he added, lowering his voice even though none of the couples at the other tables were close enough to overhear.

'Really?' Lexi's eyes widened.

'Nah, I'm messing with you.' He grinned. 'I've got business dealings abroad so I relocated for a bit. But you know what they say: there ain't no place like home.'

'So you're back for good?' Lexi asked, thanking the waiter when he brought their starters over. 'Your family must be happy about that?'

'Don't really have any,' Theo said, reaching for his fork. 'I was an only child and my mum and dad both passed away when I was in my late twenties. I've got a few distant cousins, but they live in Birmingham so I never see them.'

'I know you told me you aren't married, but I take it you were?' Lexi asked, nodding at the gold band on his finger.

'Nah, this was my granddad's.' Theo smiled. 'He handed it down to my dad and my dad passed it on to me. When I go, my boy will get it.'

'You've got a son?'

'Yeah, but me and his mum split before he was born so I haven't seen much of him growing up. How about you?'

'No kids and never been married.'

'Any boyfriends that I need to know about?'

'Not now. I was with someone for a few years, but he cheated so I finished it.'

'Say *what*?' Theo drew his head back and gave her an incredulous look. 'A dude cheated on *you*? Was he crazy?'

'Not crazy, just selfish and narcissistic,' Lexi said, rolling her eyes. 'He claimed he was a writer and, sucker that I was, I worked my arse off to keep us both while he lounged in bed all day writing the next *Wuthering Heights*. I had to laugh when I went through his stuff after I kicked him out and found his notebooks.'

'Let me guess . . . no book?'

'Oh, there was a book, but it wasn't *his*. He'd lifted a load of passages out of one of the books on my shelf and rewritten them in his own crappy words; like he thought I wouldn't recognize the story if he changed the characters' names and shifted a few things around. Idiot.'

'A liar *and* a thief.' Theo shook his head. 'But, hey . . . his loss was most definitely my gain,' he added softly, peering deep into her eyes.

Blushing, Lexi took a swig of wine. He was older than anyone she had ever dated before, but maybe that was where she'd been going wrong? Kyle was the first man she had ever actually lived with, and his immaturity, despite being the same age as her, had seriously irritated her at times, so maybe a more mature man would suit her better. And Theo was certainly ticking a few boxes right now. Handsome, charming, and easy to talk to, he was the complete opposite of her lying scam-artist of an ex, and she reminded herself how lucky she was that Kyle was now Violet's burden and not hers.

After dinner, which was every bit as delicious as Theo had promised it would be, they chatted for an hour over Irish coffees before heading back to Lexi's. Sitting in the car outside the house, she was contemplating whether she ought to invite him in for a nightcap, when he said, 'Well, thank you for a lovely evening, Miss Alexis, but I know you've got an early start tomorrow, so I'll say goodnight.'

Relieved – if also a bit disappointed – Lexi smiled and said, 'Thank you. I really enjoyed myself.'

'Me too,' he said, winking at her as he added, 'And hopefully we can do it again soon?'

Floating up the stairs after waving him off, Lexi was glad when Debs didn't come barrelling out of her room demanding to know how it had gone. Still a little tipsy from the wine and the whisky-laced coffees, she took a quick shower and made sure her uniform was ready for morning, then climbed into bed and mentally replayed the date from start to finish before falling asleep with a smile on her lips.

18

When Theo rang the following morning to ask her out on another date, Lexi accepted without hesitation, and it quickly became a regular thing. The more time she spent with him, the more she grew to like and trust him, and it wasn't long before she started spending the occasional night at his flat in a high-rise block in Stockport.

Unlike Kyle, whose first words when she arrived home from work had usually been a variation of *What's for tea?* or *Did you get me that booze/weed/money I asked for?* Theo liked to take care of her and would tell her to sit down while he poured a drink, ran a bath, made – or, more often, ordered – dinner. He also insisted on calling her by her full name, claiming that it sounded classy, which felt a little strange, because no one ever called her Alexis unless she was in trouble or being interviewed for a job. But she gradually got used to it.

As much as she enjoyed being with someone who was as attentive and sensitive to her needs as Theo was, it was still early days in their relationship, so when he asked her to move in with him one night as they lay in his bed after making love, she turned him down flat.

'It's way too soon. And my place is more convenient for work. If I had to take the bus from here I'd be adding an extra couple of hours to my journey every day, and it'd cost me an absolute fortune.'

'I can drive you there and pick you up,' he offered.

'You've got your own business to take care of,' she reminded him.

'I'll buy you a car, then.'

'I can't drive.'

'So I'll teach you.'

'You've got an answer for everything, haven't you?' Lexi laughed.

'Is that a yes?' Theo grinned.

'No,' she said firmly. 'You know I love spending time with you, but it's only been a few months and I don't want to rush it. If I change my mind, I'll—'

'*When* you change your mind,' Theo interrupted.

'OK, if and *when* I change my mind, I'll let you know,' she continued. 'But, for now, let's just keep things as they are.'

'Whatever you say,' he sighed. 'But don't blame me if I find myself a spare wifey to fill in on the nights you're not here.'

'Go for it,' she challenged, knowing full well that he wouldn't.

'As if,' he chuckled, reaching for his phone when it started vibrating on the bedside table.

'Aren't you going to get that?' Lexi asked when he glanced at the screen before putting it back down.

'It'll keep,' he said, rolling onto his side and pulling her toward him.

'It might be important,' Lexi said when, immediately after stopping, his phone started vibrating again. 'Go on, answer it. I need the loo anyway.'

Climbing out of bed, she reached for the dressing gown she'd brought over a couple of weeks earlier and, slapping Theo's hand away when he made a grab for her, pulled it on and padded out to the bathroom.

Theo was getting dressed when she came back. 'Sorry, I need to nip out,' he said when she gave him a questioning look. 'Go back to bed. I won't be long.' He kissed her, then snatched his keys off the table and hurried out.

Lexi wandered over to the window and watched as he emerged onto the path down below a couple of minutes later and hopped into his car. No longer sleepy, she closed the blinds when he'd driven away and went to the kitchen to make a cup of tea before heading into the living room. She switched on the table lamp, then sat on the sofa and scrolled through the channels on his huge flat-screen TV. She still hadn't got around to buying a TV of her own, and Debs talked so much whenever she tried to watch anything at her place it was impossible to concentrate, so this was a rare luxury, and she intended to enjoy it while she could.

Finding an old episode of *Medium*, she settled back against the cushions to watch as Allison DuBois battled the demons in her latest dream. Half an hour in and beginning to wonder if she ought to have opted for a comedy instead when a creepy-looking man slithered out from the shadows behind an oblivious young girl who was chattering on her phone, she almost jumped out of her skin when the living room door suddenly opened and Theo walked in.

'Christ, you scared the life out of me,' she squawked.

'Sorry.' He leaned over the back of the sofa and kissed her. 'I thought you'd be asleep by now.'

'Decided to have a brew,' she said, lifting the empty cup off the table. 'Want me to make you one?'

'I need something stronger,' he said, walking over to the drinks cabinet.

'Is everything OK?' Lexi asked. Then, hearing a low voice in the hall: 'Is somebody with you?'

'My boy,' Theo said, pouring shots of Jack Daniels into three glasses. 'Someone ran a red light and smashed into his car, so I had to pick him up.'

'Oh, no. He wasn't injured, was he?'

'Nah, he's fine. The motor took the brunt of it.'

'That's good,' Lexi said, smiling when he handed one of the glasses to her. They hadn't really spoken about his son in any great detail, but Theo always called him "my boy" so she'd assumed it was a child. If he had a car he had to be at least seventeen, however, which meant she was only eight or so years older than him. The age gap between her and Theo had never bothered her, but how would the boy feel about his dad dating someone who was closer to his own age?

'Cheers for picking me up, Dad,' Theo's son said as he entered the room. 'I've arranged to have the car towed to—' He abruptly stopped speaking when he spotted Lexi, and time seemed to grind to a halt as they locked eyes.

'This is my girl, Alexis,' Theo said, handing a glass to him. 'Alexis, this is—'

'Ryan,' she said, swallowing the sickly taste that had flooded her mouth at the sight of him.

'You know each other?' Theo looked at each of them in turn.

'She used to be Nic's best mate,' Ryan told him. 'But I knew her as Lexi, so it didn't click when you mentioned Alexis.'

'*Oh . . .*' Theo said slowly.

Confused by his reaction, Lexi frowned when she caught a hooded look passing between them. 'What's going on?'

'Nothing,' Theo said, smiling again. 'I didn't realize you and Ry knew each other, that's all.'

Frown deepening when something occurred to her, she said, 'Hang on a minute . . . when Nic was showing me the wedding photos, I asked where Ryan's dad was and she told me he was in prison in Jamaica. But you told me you've been working abroad for years, so which one's true?'

The men exchanged another uneasy glance. Then, sighing, Theo held up his hands, and said, 'OK, I was in prison. But not in Jamaica, in Wakefield.'

'*What?*' Lexi stared at him open-mouthed. 'Are you kidding me?'

'I got out a couple of weeks before we met,' he said, squatting down beside her and reaching for her hand. 'I was going to tell you when the time was right, but things have been moving so fast I haven't had the chance.'

'You've had three *months*,' she argued, snatching her hand away. 'But you haven't even tried.'

'I've wanted to, loads of times. But it was going so good I didn't want you to think badly of me.'

'Well, that worked out well for you, didn't it?' she replied sarcastically. 'I can't believe you've spent the last three months telling me about all the different countries you've been to, when all the time you were in *prison*. How long were you even in there?'

Shamefaced, Theo dipped his gaze. 'Fourteen years. But I was set up, I swear. That's why me and Ry have been—'

'Dad, don't,' Ryan cautioned.

'No, let him speak,' Lexi snapped. 'I want to hear this.'

Theo ran his fingers over his shaven head as if struggling to make a decision. Then, sighing, he said, 'No, he's right. It's better you don't know.'

'*Wow!*' Lexi stared at him in disbelief. 'First you lie, and now you're blatantly hiding stuff from me? Well, fuck you, Theo!'

'Babe, wait,' he said, following when she jumped up and marched into the bedroom after slamming her glass down on the coffee table. 'I'll explain everything when I can, I promise.'

'Whatever,' she muttered, pulling her clothes on under cover of the dressing gown. 'You know what I went through with my ex and you swore you'd always be honest, but it's been nothing but a pack of lies from the start. And you know what the worst thing is? I wouldn't have even *cared* that you'd been in prison, as long as you hadn't raped or murdered someone.'

'You really think I'm capable of that?' Theo looked hurt.

'How am I supposed to know?' She threw up her hands. 'All I know is you don't get fourteen years for nothing.'

'I told you I was set up.'

'Yeah, and that's probably another lie,' she said, snatching her handbag and jacket off the chair in the corner. 'I feel like I don't even know you.'

'Don't say that,' Theo pleaded, trying to take her in his arms.

Pushing him aside, Lexi walked out into the hall.

'Please don't go,' he begged, going after her and jumping in front of the door. 'It's gone midnight. You can't be walking round on your own out there. It's not safe.'

'Move,' she ordered, folding her arms.

'OK, if you insist on going, at least let me drive you.'

'No thanks.'

'I can take you, if you want?' Ryan offered, coming out of the living room.

'And why would I go anywhere with *you* when you're as much of a liar as he is?' Lexi glared at him. 'Remember what happened at that party, do you? And how you denied you'd seen anything when the police questioned you, so they thought I'd made it up and dropped the charges? Well, I do, so, *no* . . . I don't want a fucking lift off you!'

'What's all this?' Theo asked.

'Ask your *boy*,' Lexi spat, yanking the door open and walking out before slamming it behind her.

19

The cab ride home from Stockport racked up a much higher fare than Lexi had expected, and she asked the driver if he could wait a minute while she went inside to get the rest when she spotted that Debs's lamp was on.

'Hey, what are you doing home?' Debs asked when she cracked her door open and peeped out. 'I thought you were staying at lover boy's tonight?'

'I'll tell you in a minute,' Lexi said. 'Can you lend me twenty quid for the cab? I'll pay you back first thing.'

Clocking her friend's red eyes, Debs said, 'Yeah, course; give me a sec.'

She left her door ajar, and Lexi immediately felt guilty for disturbing her when she heard a man ask who it was.

'Not your wife, if that's what you're worried about,' Debs replied curtly before coming back to the door.

'Sorry,' Lexi whispered when her friend handed over the money. 'I'd have gone to the cash machine if I'd known you had company.'

'Don't worry about it,' Debs said. 'I'm bored with him anyway, so give me a minute to get rid while you pay the cabbie and I'll make us a brew.'

Nodding, Lexi headed downstairs and paid the driver. As she was going back into the house, a balding, overweight man in his fifties or sixties, who looked like he'd dressed hastily, rushed out clutching his jacket and yelled for the cab to wait. Closing and locking the front door behind him, Lexi went upstairs and plonked herself down on Debs's sofa.

'So what happened?' Debs asked. 'I take it you and Theo had an argument?'

'If me finding out that everything he's ever told me was a lie can be classed as an argument, then yeah.'

'What d'you mean?' Debs sloshed milk into the cups of tea and carried them over.

'Remember all those countries he told me he's been working in for the last few years? Well, guess what – he was in prison.'

'You're kidding me?' Debs looked as shocked as Lexi still felt. 'What for?'

'No idea?' Lexi shrugged. 'He reckons he was set up, but you don't serve fourteen years unless you've been found guilty of something really bad.'

'Fourteen years?' Debs whistled softly through her teeth. 'Wow.'

'Exactly! Oh, and remember I told you he's got a kid he hardly ever sees?'

'What, no kid?'

'No, there is a son; I met him tonight. But he's not a kid, he's twenty-seven. And I know him.'

'Really? Who is it?'

'Nicole's husband.'

'No way! Jeez, that must have been awkward?'

'Just a bit,' Lexi said, reaching into her bag to look at her phone when she heard a ping.

'That him?'

'Yep. He's been ringing and messaging me since I left his place, but he can piss off if he thinks I'm answering.'

'So tell me exactly what happened,' Debs said. 'From the start.'

After Lexi had told her the entire story, Debs mulled it over for a few minutes, then said, 'OK, I'm not condoning him lying about the prison stuff, but I get why he was reluctant to tell you. I mean, it's not the kind of thing you'd want to broadcast at the start of a relationship, is it?'

'*I* would if I cared about them as much as Theo claimed to care about me,' Lexi huffed.

'Hon, I get why you're angry, but whatever he did or didn't do, he's served his time, so don't you think he deserves the chance to make a fresh start?'

'Yeah, but he can make it without me. He's had three months to come clean, but he never would have if Ryan hadn't turned up tonight.'

'Was it Ryan who told you?'

'No, I figured it out,' Lexi said, going on to explain about the wedding photos and how Nicole had told her that Ryan's dad was in prison and he'd never even met him. 'Turns out *that* was a lie as well,' she finished. 'Because it was obvious they've been seeing each other for a while.'

'Maybe they met up after Theo was released and sorted things out,' Debs suggested. 'Ryan was still a kid when Theo went inside, so it's only natural he'd want to see him if he got the chance.'

'I suppose so,' Lexi conceded. 'But something wasn't right.'

'In what way?'

'After Theo admitted he'd been in prison, he was going to tell me something but Ryan stopped him. Then he clammed up and said it was better I didn't know.'

'Are you sure this isn't more to do with Ryan and Nicole than you and Theo?' Debs asked. 'She's a stuck-up little bitch, so I can't see her wanting an ex-lag in her life, and Ryan was probably scared to tell her he's been meeting up with him in case she went mad. He must have got worried when he walked in and saw you there.'

'If he's too much of a wuss to tell his wife that he wants a relationship with his own father, there's something seriously wrong with him.'

'Some people will do anything for a quiet life. Especially men with ball-breaker wives.'

'That still doesn't justify Theo lying to me.'

'I agree,' said Debs. 'But why don't you sleep on it and see how you feel in the morning? I know it must have been a massive shock, but you two are good together, so don't cut him off without giving him a chance to explain.'

Nodding her agreement, although she knew she would feel the same even if she slept for a full year, Lexi said goodnight and went to her own room. Taking her phone out of her bag after changing into her pyjamas, she swiped the screen to clear off the numerous missed calls and text message notifications, then climbed into bed.

For as long as she lived, she would never understand men. They were an alien breed to her: one minute declaring their undying love, the next keeping secrets and screwing around. She had genuinely thought Theo was different, but she now realized that she hadn't really known him at all. He had spent the last three months telling her – in great detail at times – about all the exotic places he'd visited, when he hadn't even been out of the county, never mind the country, and that told her everything she needed to know about him. With the best will in the world, there was no way back from that. No way whatsoever.

Over at Theo's flat, watching his father pace the living room floor, as he'd been doing ever since Lexi walked out, Ryan said, 'Dad, sit down, for God's sake; you're making me dizzy. She doesn't know anything; we're safe.'

'You don't get it,' Theo said, slumping down on the sofa and agitatedly jiggling his leg up and down. 'I really like her. She's funny and smart, and sexy as hell. *Man*, is she sexy.'

'Yo, too much information.' Ryan held up a hand to stop him from going any further. It was one thing having these kinds of conversations with a mate, but it was downright weird discussing birds with his old man – and he felt particularly uncomfortable talking about Lexi like that. It had been a big enough shock finding her in his own house, but seeing her here tonight and realizing that she was the girl his dad had been banging on about for the last few weeks had been gut wrenching, and he was struggling to hide the jealousy that was eating away at him at the thought of his old man succeeding where he had failed.

He'd liked Lexi from the first time he ever saw her on the Kingston, but she'd been a timid little thing back then, always scuttling away before he had the chance to speak to her. And then Nicole had set her sights on him, putting paid to any chance of him and Lexi ever getting together. He'd still liked Lexi, though, and had genuinely felt guilty for throwing her under the bus when Danny Harvey had offered him a job in exchange for his silence – although it had been more of an order than an offer, because he'd sensed that Danny would probably have killed him if he'd refused. Now Lexi was back – and more beautiful than ever – he hadn't been able to stop thinking about her. But she'd made it clear tonight that she hated him, so he would just have to suck it up.

'I need to speak to her,' Theo said, interrupting his thoughts.

'There's no point calling her again,' Ryan sighed. 'She's not going to answer, so just leave her be. She'll come round in her own time.'

'OK, I'll text her then; ask her to call me when she's calmed down,' Theo said, reaching for his phone. 'Shit, my battery's dead. Where did I put my charger?'

Irritated when his dad started throwing cushions around in search of his charger, Ryan said, 'Here, use mine,' and held out his phone.

Thanking him, Theo tapped out a quick message and handed the phone back.

'Ready to get back to business now?' Ryan asked, switching the phone to silent and placing it face down on the arm of his chair so he wouldn't have to tell his dad if Lexi decided to answer.

'Sorry. Yeah, go on,' Theo said.

Across town, in his office at The Danski, Adam Harvey nodded as he listened to what his caller, Wes Caine, was telling him.

'Good,' he said, a sly smile raising his lips when Wes described the carnage. 'Maybe the fucker will start to realize what he's up against and quit prancing round like a fuckin' don. As long as no one saw you?' he added. 'They didn't, did they?'

'Nah, man, I stayed well out of the way,' Wes assured him. 'The dude was some random I met at a boozer. He don't know me, and he didn't ask any questions when I told him how much he'd be getting paid.'

'I hope you're right,' Adam said. 'I don't want him sussing out where any of this is coming from.'

'Trust me, he won't trace this back to you.'

'Any injuries?'

'His motor's a write-off, but it was a piece of shit so I'm sure he won't miss it. He looked a bit banged up, but I couldn't see much 'cos I was watching from a distance. Nowt major, though, as far as I could tell.'

'I meant the cunt not the patsy,' Adam said, guessing that Wes was talking about the man he'd paid to crash into Ryan's car, because there was no way anyone would describe a Range Rover as a piece of shit.

'Ah, right, I get you,' Wes said. 'Nah, he seemed fine when he got out; yelling about the damage to his wheels, and ripping the dude a new arsehole. Mind you, I didn't stick around too long in case someone had called the pigs, so he could've keeled over and croaked it after I left, for all I know.'

Liking the idea of that, Adam decided to pay his sister a long overdue visit in the morning. They hadn't been on the best of terms lately, but she would need the support of her big brother if her hubby was dead or in a bad way – which would earn him a few brownie points with the folks, if nothing else. But even if Ryan had managed to escape serious injury this time, one way or another, the cunt was going down. And when it was done and his brother-in-law was out of the picture, Adam's dad would have no choice but to put him in his rightful place at the head of the family business. If he didn't, he'd only have himself to blame when Adam took over anyway and ousted him.

20

Nicole was sitting up in bed with a drink in her hand and watching a film on Netflix when Ryan got home in the early hours. Scowling when he walked into the bedroom, she grabbed the remote and turned off the TV.

'Where have you been? I've been calling you all night.'

'I was busy,' Ryan said, draping his jacket over the back of a chair and pulling his T-shirt off over his head.

'Too busy to answer your wife?' she asked, the slur in her voice and the flush on her cheeks and nose telling Ryan that the drink wasn't her first by far.

He went into the en-suite without replying and tossed the T-shirt into the laundry basket.

'Who were you with?' she demanded. Getting no answer again, she slammed her glass down on the bedside table, shoved the duvet off her legs and marched after him. 'I said, who were you with?'

Ryan flashed a glance at her in the mirror over the sink as he folded his jeans and placed them on top of the basket and quickly looked away again when he saw that she was wearing one of her baby-doll nighties. She had obviously been waiting up for him, but she'd be waiting a month of Sundays if she thought he was having sex with her. They had barely spoken since she'd almost started a fight with one of his mates' girl-friends for daring to speak to him at a party a few days earlier, and he was in no mood for her nonsense tonight.

'Why won't you talk to me?' Nicole whined, changing tack when she realized that going on the offensive wasn't working.

'I'm tired,' he said.

'I'll soon wake you up,' she purred, walking over to him and sliding her hand down his stomach to his crotch.

'Leave it out, Nic.' He irritably pushed her hand away.

Eyes narrowing, she said, 'You'd best quit treating me like a piece of shit, Mr Big Shot, or my dad's going to have something to say about it. You seem to forget he only put you in charge because you're married to me.'

'No, he put me in charge because he knew your loser brother couldn't handle the business and he needed someone he could trust to hold the fort,' Ryan replied coolly.

'I could have taken over if I'd wanted to,' Nicole argued. 'But you're my husband and it's your job to take care of me, so I let you do it.'

'Whatever,' Ryan said, reaching inside the shower cubicle to turn the water on.

Instantly suspicious, Nicole said, 'Why are you taking a shower at this time of night? Trying to wash *her* smell off you?'

'There is no her, and I'm not in the mood for this,' Ryan said wearily. 'I've had a rough night and I want to get cleaned up and go to bed. If you want to talk, we'll do it in the morning.'

'If I find out you're cheating on me you won't even *be* here in the morning,' spat Nicole. 'This is my house, don't forget.'

'You want me to leave?' Ryan raised an eyebrow. 'Just say the word and I'm gone.'

'I never said that.' Nicole hastily backtracked. 'But why can't you appreciate what you've got? I'm still young and gorgeous, and plenty of men would jump at the chance to take your place.'

Biting his tongue to keep from telling her to go out and get one then, Ryan reminded himself what was at stake, and said, 'Nic, I'm tired and my head's banging, so give me a break and back off. *Please.*'

'Whatever,' she muttered, flouncing out and slamming the door behind her.

Still fuming about Ryan's rejection when she'd made a huge effort to look sexy for him, Nicole heard the shower door click shut and tiptoed over to the chair where he'd draped his jacket. Patting the pockets, she located his phone and, glancing round to make sure the en-suite door was still shut, carefully lifted it out. He had changed his password a few weeks earlier after he'd caught her checking up on him, but she had spied him entering his new one a few days ago and had memorized it. Hoping that he hadn't changed it again since then, she tapped in the six digits and, casting another nervous glance at the en-suite door when the phone opened, clicked into his call log. He'd made several calls throughout the day, most to guys who worked for him whose names she knew. There was only one name she didn't recognize: someone called *Django*. It sounded male, and the call had lasted for less than a minute, so she dismissed it and switched to his messages instead.

When she saw the most recent message he had sent, her blood ran cold.

Baby, I know you're mad at me and I don't blame you, but we got something good and I don't want to lose you. Please call me xx

Heart pounding, she read and re-read the message. She'd been right all along. Ryan *was* cheating. The bastard . . . the absolute fucking bastard! How could he do this to her? She was way hotter than any of the bitches his mates were shackled to, and she knew they all envied him and wished they could have a piece of her, so why would he want someone else? It didn't make sense.

Snapping out of her daze when she heard the shower go off, Nicole quickly jotted down the number connected to the message in the notepad she kept in her drawer before slipping Ryan's phone back into his pocket. In bed when he came out of the bathroom with a towel wrapped around his waist a few seconds later, she peeped at him through her lashes and felt physically sick at the thought of him screwing another woman. She wanted to scream and shout and demand to know who the bitch was, but she didn't want to risk pushing him into the woman's arms and face the humiliation of everyone knowing he'd chosen someone else over her. So, staying quiet, she breathed deeply in and out to calm herself down and clarify her thoughts.

She had two options, she realized. One, she could let Ryan know that she was on to him and give him a chance to break it off; or, two, she could tackle the woman and warn her off.

Much preferring the second option, she decided that she would ring that number in the morning and put an end to whatever was going on – and God help the bitch if it turned out to be someone she knew!

The bed suddenly dipped on Ryan's side, and he said, 'You still awake?'

'Why?' she replied coolly, guessing that he was about to apologize and wanting to string it out.

'I was looking for painkillers in the bathroom cabinet but I couldn't find any. Have you got any in your drawer? I think I might have whiplash.'

'Whiplash?' Nicole sat up at that and turned to face him. 'How d'you get that?'

'A car ran into me when I was on my way home. That's why I was late – 'cos I had to wait for the police and arrange to get the motor towed.'

'Are you serious?' Nicole asked, momentarily forgetting all the other stuff. 'Is it badly damaged? My dad'll go mad if it's written off. It cost him a fortune.'

'Can you forget about your dad for one fucking minute?' Ryan snapped, twisting his head round to glare at her.

Immediately regretting it when the muscle in his shoulder spasmed, he muttered, '*Fuck!*' and started rubbing it.

'Here,' Nicole said, reaching into her drawer and pushing the notepad aside to get at a strip of paracetamol tablets that were under it. 'Do you want a glass of water?'

'No, I'll have whatever you were drinking when I came in.'

Nicole handed her glass to him and tentatively touched his shoulder. 'Want me to massage it for you?'

'Thanks, but these should do the trick,' he said, popping two tablets out of the strip and washing them down with the last of her drink. 'Christ, that's strong. How many of them have you had?'

Not nearly enough, she thought, clenching her teeth when unwelcome images of the unknown woman touching his skin leapt into her mind. Was that why he didn't want a massage: because he was still thinking about *her*?

Sinking back against her pillows when Ryan lay down and turned his back to her, Nicole waited until she heard his breathing grow deeper and then poured herself another drink. Whoever he'd been seeing, the fact that he was still coming home each night told her that all was not yet lost. If she could eliminate the other woman and get pregnant, it would cement their relationship and ensure that nobody ever came between them again. And tonight would have been the perfect opportunity to try, since her chart told her that she was ovulating. But she'd waited this long, so one more day wouldn't kill her.

* * *

Ryan had already left for work when Nicole woke up the next morning. Feeling sick when she remembered the text message she'd read on his phone, she sat up and held her head in her hands when a pain throbbed behind her eyes. Cursing herself for pouring that extra drink, she reached for the strip of painkillers she'd given to him and dry-swallowed two of them before gingerly getting up and pulling her dressing gown on. With the sheet of paper on which she'd written the number in her hand, she grabbed her phone and made her way downstairs.

After making a cup of coffee and lighting a cigarette, she sat at the kitchen table and tapped the number into her mobile. Blinking in confusion when *Lexi* came up on the screen, she cleared it off and typed the number in again. The same name appeared, and the room went into a spin when she realized that the number she had taken from Ryan's phone must already be in her contact list – which could only mean one thing: Lexi was the woman he'd been screwing behind her back.

Screaming, 'NOOOO!' she swiped the still-full cup off the table. *Lexi*? That ugly desperate bitch who had hung onto her coat-tails for years when they were kids ... why the fuck would Ryan want *her*?

Hands shaking with rage, she snatched the paper up off the table and compared the number written on it to Lexi's stored number. Sucking deeply on the cigarette when she saw that it was indeed the same, she slumped back in her chair. Ryan had adamantly denied that he had any interest in the bitch – and she knew she would get the same response from Lexi if she went at her all guns blazing demanding answers, because they would have already planned what to say if their secret ever came out. But had they been at it since Lexi moved back to Manchester – or was Ryan the *reason* Lexi had moved back, because it had been going on for longer than that?

Unable to believe that they could have been seeing each other for any great length of time without her suspecting a thing, Nicole decided it must have started after she'd invited Lexi round for dinner that night. The mistake she'd made was kicking Lexi out straight after arguing with Ryan, because the whore had probably caught up with him and wormed her way in with him out of spite.

Sure that she was right, and determined to stop them in their tracks, Nicole brought up Lexi's number and rang it.

Lexi answered a few seconds later.

'Hello?'

'Weren't expecting to hear from *me*, were you?' Nicole said when she heard the question in her ex-friend's voice.

'Not really, no,' Lexi said. 'What's up?'

'You tell me,' Nicole replied coolly.

'Nic, I'm not in the mood for games,' Lexi sighed. 'I hardly slept last night, and I've got a banging headache, so if you're ringing to apologize, great, I accept. But I need to go now.'

'*Me* apologize?' Nicole squawked. 'Are you fuckin' kidding me? You screw my husband then expect *me* to apologize? I've met some barefaced people in my time, but you take the—'

'Whoa! Hang on a minute,' Lexi cut in, sounding confused. 'What you talking about? I've not been anywhere near Ryan.'

'Oh, really?' spat Nicole. 'So how do you explain him sending you that text message last night? And don't bother denying it, because I saw it. *Baby I know you're mad at me, but we've got something good . . .* You dirty fucking slag!'

'Nic, listen, you've got it all wrong,' Lexi said. 'I—'

'No, *you're* the only one who's got it wrong if you think I'm going to let you get away with this,' Nicole hissed. 'If you ever go near my husband again, I'll *kill* you – and that's your one and only warning!'

'The text wasn't from Ryan, it was from his dad,' Lexi said. But Nicole had already hung up, so Lexi didn't know if she'd heard her.

Furious, Nicole let out a scream and hurled her phone across the room before swiping the ashtray off the table. Then, leaping to her feet, she started throwing everything that was close to hand.

Outside, Adam had been about to ring the bell when he heard screams and the sound of breaking glass coming from inside. Remembering that he still had his key, he quickly let himself in. It was almost a year since he'd stepped foot in there and the garish pattern on the new wallpaper made his eyes go funny. Averting his gaze, he rushed into the kitchen and wrapped his arms around Nicole when he saw that she was about to hurl one of the wrought-iron dining chairs through the patio doors.

'What the hell's going on?' he asked, forcing her to put the chair down.

'Leave me alone,' she roared, twisting free.

'Has something happened to Ryan?' Adam pressed, wondering if his brother-in-law had taken a turn for the worst after the crash. Wes had reported seeing him walking and talking after he got out of the car, and he hadn't heard anything since. But his sister was massively upset about something, and he could only assume – *hope* – that this was the face of grief.

'I *hate* him!' Nicole spat.

Hope deflating, because she wouldn't be saying that if Ryan was dead, Adam guided her to a chair, and said, 'Sit down and tell me what's going on.'

'How did you get in?' Nicole asked, wiping her eyes on the sleeve of her dressing gown.

'I've still got my key,' he told her as he switched the kettle on before picking up the cigarette that was smouldering in the mess of glass and ash in the corner. 'I hope that wasn't Mum's Waterford ashtray? She'll go mental if you've smashed that. It was antique.'

'I don't give a shit!' Nicole glared at him through her tears as he extinguished the cigarette under the tap. 'This is *my* house and I can do whatever I want, so fuck off if you're going to start criticizing me.'

'I'm not having a go,' Adam said, taking two cups out of the cupboard and spooning coffee into them. 'But what the hell's happened to make you flip out like this?'

'None of your business,' Nicole muttered, pulling a tissue out of her pocket and blowing her nose. 'Why are you even here?'

'To see my little sis, obviously,' said Adam. 'I've been meaning to come round for a while, but I've been busy with the club so I haven't had a chance.'

'Busy doing what? Snorting coke and catching diseases off your whores?'

'Wow, harsh.'

'But true.'

'It's not actually,' Adam said piously. 'I haven't used in months, and I've hardly been near the club, 'cos I've been too busy fundraising.'

'Since when have you been interested in charity?' Nicole looked at him with suspicion.

'It's for the club,' Adam said as he carried their drinks to the table. 'It needs a major overhaul, but I've ploughed enough into it.'

'You mean *Dad* has.'

'I haven't used his money, I've been using my share of the family profits. But it needs way more than I'm willing to put in, so now I'm schmoozing investors.'

'Good luck with that,' Nicole snorted. 'It wants blowing up, if you ask me.'

'And that'll be my next step if I don't get the dosh I need,' Adam said. 'I thought it was a good idea at the time, but I want rid, so now I need to do it up so I can offload it at a profit. Speculate to accumulate, an' all that.'

'If you came to ask *me* to invest, forget it,' Nicole said, reaching for her cup.

'Wouldn't dream of it,' said Adam. 'But never mind me and my troubles. What's Ryan's done to get you in such a state? Forgot your anniversary?'

'He's been cheating.'

'You what?' Adam scowled. 'He'd better fuckin' not have been, or he'll have me to deal with.'

'Oh, shut up,' Nicole snapped. 'We both know he'd kick your arse, so don't start acting tough.'

'There's plenty of ways to skin a cat,' Adam said, irritated by her assertion that he wouldn't be able to take Ryan in a fight. In reality, he knew he probably couldn't if it was one on one, no weapons allowed. But he would happily put a bullet through the prick's head.

'I'm dealing with it,' Nicole muttered.

'Looks like it.' Adam cast a pointed glance around the room.

'I am,' she insisted. 'I've already warned Lexi to stay away from him.'

'*Lexi?*' Adam frowned. 'You're not talking about that girl you used to hang around with who accused me of trying to rape her, are you?'

'That's her,' Nicole spat. 'Lying whore! I went through Ryan's phone last night and read a text he'd sent her, but she had the cheek to deny it when I rang her.'

'I thought she left town years ago?'

'She moved back a few months ago. I bumped into her in town and invited her round for dinner.'

'Why? She ruined my life, so why would you even talk to her?'

'I wasn't thinking. I was on my way to a party and I'd had a few drinks. I didn't think Ryan would see her because he was supposed to be working late that night, but he came back early to pick up *your* money. We had a row and he walked out, then I told her to leave as well. That's when I think it started.'

'Don't be blaming me,' Adam said testily. 'You're the one who invited her round, even though you knew she was the reason Dad cut me out of the business. So much for family fuckin' loyalty.'

'I haven't even seen you in months, so don't bother trying to make me feel guilty,' Nicole shot back. 'And I'm the one who should be angry, seeing as it's *my* husband she's been screwing.'

'The way I see it, she's fucked us *both* over,' said Adam. 'Question is, what we gonna do about it?'

Jaw muscles twitching as she visualized Ryan and Lexi together, Nicole snatched her cigarettes up off the table and lit one. 'I want her gone,' she said, squinting at Adam through the smoke. 'And by gone, I mean *permanently*.'

'Now we're talking,' Adam said, grinning slyly.

21

After the shock call from Nicole, Lexi had tried to ring Theo to tell him to warn Ryan that his wife was on the warpath; but his phone had gone to voicemail, and the message she'd sent straight after still hadn't been delivered. Biting her lip, she re-read the text that had caused all the trouble. It had come from an unrecognized number and when she'd seen it, just before Nicole rang, she had wondered if Theo had sent it from Ryan's phone thinking that she'd blocked him because she'd ignored his calls the previous night. Now she knew for sure that it *was* Ryan's number, she decided to ring him direct. Half expecting it to go to voicemail – or, worse, for Nicole to answer it – she was surprised when Ryan picked it up a few seconds later.

'Yo. Who's this?'

'It's Lexi,' she said, her heart beating faster at the sound of his voice.

'*Lexi?*' he repeated. 'You know this is Ryan not Theo, right?'

'Yes, I know,' she said, guessing that, wherever he was, he'd gone outside when she heard the squeal of door hinges in the background, followed by the sound of traffic. 'I've already tried his phone, but it's off, so I thought I'd best speak to you instead.'

'He lost his charger last night and mustn't have found it yet. But I'll be seeing him later if you want me to pass a message on?'

'Actually, I was ringing him to ask him to pass a message on to you.'

'Oh?'

'Nicole rang me five minutes ago. She saw the message your dad sent me on your phone last night and—'

'Thought it was from me. Shit.'

'I tried to tell her it was from your dad, but she was so busy threatening to kill me if I ever went near you again, I'm not sure she—'

'You told her my dad was back in town?' Ryan cut in, alarm in his voice. 'You didn't tell her where he's living, did you?'

'No, we didn't get that far.'

'Thank fuck for that.'

'Sorry?' Lexi frowned. 'Am I missing something here? Only it sounds like you're more concerned about Nicole finding out that you're seeing your dad than about her thinking we're having an affair.'

Ryan didn't reply, and it was only the sound of the traffic in the background that told Lexi he was still on the line. After a moment, he said, 'I can't speak on the phone, but we need to talk. Can we meet somewhere?'

'I don't think that would be a very good idea, do you?' Lexi said. 'Nic already thinks something's going on, and if she finds out we've met up, she's bound to think we were getting our stories straight.'

'I don't give a shit what Nic thinks,' Ryan said, the bitterness in his voice causing Lexi's eyebrows to shoot up in surprise.

'Look, whatever's going on between you two, I really don't want to get involved,' she said. 'Just tell Nic to leave me alone. And you can tell your dad the same, because I really don't need this.'

Lexi cut the call and released a tense breath through her teeth. Hoping that would be an end to all the nonsense, she pushed the lot of them out of her mind, made a cup of tea, and then set about tidying, dusting and sweeping her room before gathering her dirty clothes together to take to the launderette.

Almost ready to leave, she happened to glance out of the window as she was pulling her coat on and saw a flashy car driving slowly by on the road below. Jerking back in horror when the driver suddenly turned his head and looked straight at the house, she dropped to her haunches and peeped over the windowsill. She hadn't seen that face in years – and had hoped never to again. He was older now, heavier, and nowhere near as handsome as he had once been, but there was no mistaking that it was Adam Harvey.

When the car turned the corner at the end of the road, she slowly stood up; her entire body quivering with shock. It was possible that he was in the area to see a friend and had merely glanced out at her house in passing, but her instincts told her otherwise. It was too soon after his sister's threatening phone call for it to be a coincidence, and she guessed that Nicole had sent him round to scare her. If so, it had worked, because she wasn't sure she could face going out now, in case he was lurking somewhere nearby; waiting to pounce on her and finish what he'd started that terrible night.

Still shaking, she sank down onto the armchair by the window and gazed out along the road. In no doubt that Adam *was* looking for her when the same car came back round a few minutes later, she wondered if he'd spotted her when he suddenly put his foot down and drove away at speed. But when her housemate, Six, came into view on the path below, she guessed Adam must have seen him and been spooked by his tough biker appearance.

Turning her head at the sound of another vehicle approaching, she saw a small black car pull into a parking space a couple of houses down, and her stomach dropped through the floor when Ryan climbed out and walked over to Six. After a brief conversation, Six gestured for Ryan to follow him up the path, and seconds later someone tapped on her door.

'All right, love?' Six smiled when she peered out at him. 'Some bloke wants to see you. Says his name's—'

'Ryan. Yeah, I saw him.'

'You know him then?'

'Unfortunately,' Lexi murmured. 'You, um, didn't happen to see the car that went past just before he got here, did you?'

'The Lexus? Yeah, I clocked it when I was putting the rubbish out,' Six said. 'Bit fancy for round here; thought it might have been an undercover. Here, they're not after you, are they?' he teased. 'Always thought you were a mysterious one. *The woman who appeared from nowhere, then disappeared in the night,*' he intoned, affecting an American accent.

Unable to see the funny side, Lexi said, 'It was someone I haven't seen for a long time – and don't particularly want to see again.'

'Hey, I was only joking,' Six said, no longer smiling when he saw her expression. 'If he's giving you shit, say the word and I'll sort it if he shows his face again.'

'Thanks,' Lexi said gratefully. 'But the way he took off when he saw you, I doubt he'll come back in a hurry.'

'He'll be getting my baseball bat wrapped round his head if he does,' said Six. 'What about him downstairs? Want me to get rid?'

'No, it's all right, I'll see him,' Lexi said, curious to know why Ryan was here.

'I'll send him up,' Six said, heading for the stairs.

Still in her doorway when Ryan walked onto the landing a few seconds later, Lexi took a deep breath as he approached her. Now that she knew he was Theo's son, she could see a slight resemblance, but not enough that she would ever have put the two of them together. He was taller than his father and nowhere near as muscular, although he still had a great physique. Their eyes were the exact same unusual shade of hazel, but where Theo's held a glint of humour, Ryan's had the same depth and warmth that had always made her go a little weak at the knees as a girl.

Annoyed with herself for allowing such a thought to enter her head, she folded her arms defensively when he reached her. 'Did Nicole send you?'

'Nicole? No. Why? She hasn't rung again, has she?'

'No, but it's a bit of a coincidence that you've turned up a minute after Adam drove past. *Twice.*'

'You're kidding? How did he know you were here?'

'Nic obviously gave him my address. But I'm guessing she didn't give it to *you*, 'cos there's no way she'd want you coming round here while she thinks we're having an affair.'

'I got it off my dad,' Ryan said, glancing round at the sound of a door opening at the other end of the landing. 'Can I come in for a minute? I don't really want to talk out here.'

'What if Adam drives past again and sees your car?'

'I've got a courtesy car till mine's fixed, so he wouldn't recognize it. Please, Lexi. It's important.'

Lexi hesitated for a moment, then said, 'OK, but make sure it is only a minute, because I need to go out.'

Nodding, Ryan entered the room and looked around. 'Nice place.'

'No it's not,' Lexi said, shoving a pair of panties that were sitting at the top of her laundry further down inside the bag. 'But it's only temporary till I find something better.'

Ryan walked over to the window, leaving a heady trail of aftershave in his wake, and gazed out along the road before taking a seat on the armchair.

'Make yourself comfortable,' Lexi murmured sarcastically, staying on her feet.

'Don't be like that,' Ryan said, resting his elbows on his knees. 'You're treating me like a stranger.'

'You *are* a stranger,' she replied coolly. 'I was a child when you started seeing Nic, and we were never friends, so don't act like you know me. Now what do you want?'

Sighing, Ryan said, 'Nic seeing that text has put us in a dangerous position.'

'She's only angry because she thinks you're cheating,' Lexi said, thinking he meant dangerous for his marriage. 'I'm sure she'll settle down if you tell her the truth.'

'It's not as simple as that. If she finds out I'm in touch with my dad, it'll start a war.'

'What's she going to do? *Ground* you?'

'Like I said, it's complicated. My dad wanted to tell you last night, because he was hoping you'd give him another chance if you knew the truth. I stopped him because I didn't want you getting dragged into this. But now you're on Nic's radar and Adam's sniffing around, it could get really nasty.'

'I know you've got some weird hang-up about her finding out you've been seeing Theo, but come on . . . she's your wife, not your mother.'

'If you'll hear me out, I'll explain.'

'Fine, go ahead,' Lexi said, sighing as she sat on the bed. 'Although, I don't see what it's got to do with me.'

'You're the only one who knows about me and my dad, so you're the only one who can blow us up to Nic.'

'I've got no intention of calling her, if that's what you're worried about.'

'I'm worried about you as well,' said Ryan. 'If Nic and Adam start digging and find out what's going on, they're going to assume you're involved. And, believe me, you don't want Danny Harvey on your case.'

'What's he got to do with it?'

'My dad's probably already told you this, but him and my mum were only kids when she fell pregnant with me,' Ryan said. 'It didn't work out and they split before I was born.'

Confused by the abrupt change of subject, Lexi said, 'Yes, he told me, and it's all very sad, but—'

'Hear me out.' Ryan held up his hand. Continuing when she rolled her eyes, he said, 'He'd started dealing; mainly weed to start with, then coke and smack. My mum didn't want that around me so she took me to live with her family in Leicester. I didn't see much of my dad after that, and he was already inside when we moved back to Manchester when I was thirteen. First time I spoke to him was when he sent me a visiting order on my sixteenth birthday. That's when I found out he'd been charged with murder.'

'*Murder?*' Lexi spluttered.

'Yeah, but he was telling the truth when he told you he was

set up,' Ryan said. 'What you don't know is that Danny Harvey was behind it.' Nodding when Lexi's eyes widened, he said, 'Yep. Nic's dad. They were rival dealers and they'd got into a full-on turf war. My dad was winning, but then a copper got shot and the police received an anonymous tip-off that he'd done it. He had an alibi, but Danny got to his witnesses before the police did and they all denied they'd seen him that night. Then the police found the gun in my dad's car and threw the book at him.'

Horrified to learn that she had spent the last few months being romanced by a man who had been involved in a murder, whether or not he was innocent, Lexi said, 'Let me get this straight . . . you found all this out when you were sixteen, and yet you started going out with Nic when you were seventeen? And then you married her – even though you thought her dad had set yours up for murder?'

'I didn't think he'd done it, I *knew*,' said Ryan. 'I heard him talking about it one time, not long after he took me on; laughing with a couple of his mates about how he'd stitched my dad up and shown every other fucker in Manchester that he wasn't to be messed with.'

'Why would he talk about that in front of you, knowing you're Theo's son?'

'He doesn't know,' said Ryan. 'My mum and dad weren't married, and he wasn't around when she registered my birth, so I've got her surname. I never told anyone about him when I started hanging out on the Kingston, so no one knows we're connected.'

'Nic must know. She's the one who told me he was in prison.'

'No. She thinks my dad is some bloke called Delroy King who went back to Jamaica when he found out my mum was pregnant.'

'Does your mum know you told her that? Only it'd be a bit awkward if Nic ever asks her about him and she tells her the truth.'

'My mum's dead,' Ryan said quietly. 'She'd been diagnosed with ovarian cancer a week before the wedding, but she didn't tell me until a couple of weeks after because she didn't want to ruin the day. She passed away a few days after that.'

'I'm so sorry,' Lexi murmured, saddened to think that the woman in the photo she'd seen had been keeping something as huge as that to herself in order not to cast a cloud over her son's wedding day, unaware that his bride hadn't even wanted her there and had not only callously excluded her from the family photos, but had also thrown away her gift.

'Anyway . . .' Ryan sat up straighter, as if making an effort to shake off the pain of talking about his mum. 'That's why Nic can't find out about my dad: because of the shit it'll stir up.'

'Sorry, but I still don't get it,' Lexi said. 'You had nothing to do with what happened between Theo and Danny, so they can't hold that against you. And Danny obviously trusts you if he's left you in charge of his business, so wouldn't it be better to tell him rather than risk him finding out that you've been lying to him?'

'Believe me, it's safer for everyone this way,' said Ryan.

'Oh well, it's your choice, but I hope you don't live to regret it,' Lexi said. 'You and Nic might be going through a rough patch right now, but if you're going to these lengths to stop her from finding out who you really are, you obviously don't want to lose her. You just need to tell *her* that when you get home, because I'm not having her and Adam harassing me over something I haven't done.'

'He'll get what's coming to him, don't worry about that,' Ryan said. 'I'll make sure of it.'

'And why would I believe that when you're the one who helped him to get away with assaulting me? If you'd told the police what he did, they'd have dealt with him ten years ago.'

'No, they wouldn't,' Ryan said, joining his hands together between his knees. 'I know it's fucked up, but I heard Danny talking to his solicitor after the police called round the last time, and she said they'd already decided to drop it. Apparently, they put it down to you both being drunk; said you'd probably led him on then changed your mind at the last minute.'

'That's not true.'

'I know. And if I'd had any choice, I'd have told them.'

'You *did* have a choice, and you chose to let them think I'd made it all up. And then you asked him to be your best man. Have you any idea how I felt when Nic showed me your wedding photos and I saw you and him having a good old laugh together?'

'That's not the way it was,' Ryan insisted. 'It was Rachel's decision to make him best man, not mine. And what Rachel wants, Rachel gets – and fuck what anyone else thinks.'

Hearing the bitterness in his voice, Lexi believed him. But it still didn't excuse what he'd done.

'If I'd known you weren't the first girl he did it to, I might have done things differently,' Ryan went on guiltily. 'But I only found out a few years later, and you were long gone by then.'

'He did it before?' Lexi gasped, stunned by that revelation, because it had never even crossed her mind that she might not have been Adam's first victim. He had been so good-looking and popular with the girls, it had never occurred to her that he would feel the need to force himself on anyone. But then, rape was about power not sex, so the girls who willingly went there probably hadn't done it for him.

'I don't know for sure, because they're tight-lipped when it comes to family stuff and they've never actually discussed it with me,' Ryan said. 'But I think there was another one after you, as well.'

Shocked, Lexi shook her head. 'I don't believe this. If the police knew he'd done it before, why didn't they believe me?'

'Because the others didn't report him. From what I could gather, Danny paid them off before they went to the police.'

'Bastard! And to think I used to wish my mum had married someone like him instead of Tony.'

'I'm not condoning what he did, but I reckon Rachel's the one who put him up to it. She'd do anything to protect that loser son of hers.'

'She always was a massive bitch,' Lexi spat, remembering the dirty looks and barbed comments the woman had thrown her way over the years.

'Still is,' said Ryan. 'And Nic gets more like her by the day.'

'I can believe that,' Lexi said. 'When we were friends, she always used to put me down and then make out like she was only joking, but I knew she wasn't. And her mum absolutely hated me. She thought they were superior to us because they had money, but my mum was a *million* times better than her.'

'Hey, don't get upset,' Ryan said, going over to her when he saw tears welling in her eyes.

'Losing my mum was the worst thing that ever happened to me,' Lexi sniffed as he gently rubbed her back. 'I had no one to turn to; just a load of strangers deciding what was best for me. I was dreading coming back to Manchester, knowing she wasn't here anymore. I've spent years trying to remember her as she was and not how she looked when . . .' Pausing, she squeezed her eyes shut and swallowed loudly before continuing: 'So when I bumped into Nic at that club and she acted like she was pleased to see me, it felt like I'd reconnected with something solid from my past – you know?'

'Yeah, I do,' Ryan said softly. 'That's exactly how I felt when I saw you.'

'That wasn't the same at all,' Lexi murmured. 'Me and Nic were best mates for years, but I hardly knew you.'

'I always liked you,' Ryan insisted. 'Even before I got with Nic. And that night when I asked you out, I swear I had finished with her.'

'And yet you went straight back there and married her. Funny that.'

'That was never my intention.'

'It's none of my business either way,' Lexi sighed. 'And I'm not really in the mood for a trip down memory lane, seeing as most of my memories from that time are shit.'

'I'm sorry,' Ryan apologized. 'I didn't mean to bring up the past, but it really threw me when I saw you at the house that night. Then when I got to my dad's and realized you were his girl . . .' He paused and blew out a loud breath. 'I'm not gonna lie, I was gutted.'

'I don't see why.'

'Yeah, you do,' Ryan said quietly, giving her a piercing look. 'Just tell me one thing. Do you love him?'

Lexi shook her head. 'No. I did like him, but we hadn't been together long enough for it to get that deep.'

'I'm glad,' Ryan said. 'Sorry, but I am,' he went on when she frowned. 'I know he's my dad, but he's not right for you.'

'Oh really?' she said. 'And I suppose you are?'

'I reckon I could be, yeah.'

'Oh, please. Do I have to remind you—'

Ryan kissed her before she could go on and she felt a bolt of electricity surge through her body at the touch and taste of his lips on hers. Breathless, her heart pounding, she pushed him away after a few seconds and leapt to her feet.

'You need to leave.'

'I'm sorry, I shouldn't have done that,' Ryan apologized. 'But I can't help how I feel. And I think you feel it too.'

'No I don't,' Lexi shot back. 'But even if I did, you're *married*!'

A volley of sharp raps on the door made them both jump, and Lexi squeezed her eyes shut when Six called through asking if everything was all right, followed by Debs asking if she needed them to call the police.

'I'm fine,' she replied. 'I'll see you in a few minutes.'

'We'll be in my room,' Debs said. 'With the door open,' she added loudly.

Turning back to Ryan when she heard them move away from the door, Lexi said, 'You should go. This . . . you and me . . . it's never going to happen.'

Ryan held her gaze for a moment and then nodded his agreement and stood up.

'I'm really sorry you got sucked into this. If I could turn back time, I'd do everything differently.'

'Well you can't, so there's no point dwelling on it,' Lexi said. 'Go home and put things right with your wife before it's too late. And, no offence, but please don't come round here again.'

'I won't,' Ryan said. 'But if anything happens – if you see Adam hanging round, or Nic makes any more threats – you've got my number.'

Nodding, although she knew she would never call him, Lexi opened the door to show him out.

Across the hall, Debs and Six were sitting on the bed facing the open door. When Ryan walked out onto the landing, they both started to get up, but sat back down when Lexi came out behind him and gave a surreptitious shake of her head.

'Take care,' Ryan said.

'You too,' she replied, watching as he walked away.

Shoulders slumping when he'd gone, she blew out a long breath before going over to Debs's room.

22

Pissed off that his plan to check out the address Nicole had given him had been thwarted by the ginger yeti who'd eyeballed him as he drove past, Adam had parked his car a few streets away and gone back on foot. At the corner of the road now, smoking a cigarette and glancing at his watch every few seconds, to make out like he was waiting for someone if anyone clocked him and wondered what he was doing, he narrowed his eyes when he spotted a man coming out of Lexi's house. He couldn't see his face, but the gait was familiar, and he quickly pulled out his phone and zoomed in with the camera, managing to snap several shots before the man climbed into a car that was parked a few houses down.

When the car drew away from the kerb and started heading in his direction, Adam ducked behind a hedge as the vehicle sped past. When it had gone, he scrolled through the photos he'd taken. They weren't very clear, and he'd only managed to catch the back of the man's head in the first few. But the last one, taken as the man opened the car door and turned around, showed his full face, and Adam clenched his teeth when he saw that it was his brother-in-law. His sister had been right: Ryan *was* up to no good. But he needed to be sure that it was definitely Lexi the prick was seeing before he decided what to do about it.

Seconds later, his wish was granted when he spotted a woman looking out through a window on the first floor of the house. He zoomed in with his camera and took a couple of snaps. Again, they were unclear, and the face he'd captured looked older and more beautiful than the one that had haunted his dreams for the last ten years. But it was unmistakably Lexi.

'Has he gone?' Debs asked.

'Yeah.' Sighing, Lexi turned from the window and sat on the sofa.

'So that was the infamous Ryan, eh?' said Debs. 'Doesn't look much like his dad, does he? Not got his muscles.'

'He's got hair, though,' Six, who had only ever seen Theo once in passing, interjected.

'I quite like the bald look,' Debs mused. 'Wouldn't suit you, mind,' she added, eyeing Six's shock of red hair. 'With that beard and no hair, you'd look like a garden gnome.'

'Cheers,' Six mock-huffed.

Nudging him with her elbow to let him know she was joking, Debs turned back to Lexi, and asked, 'So what did he want?'

Aware that she would never hear the end of it if she admitted that she and Ryan had kissed, Lexi gave an extremely watered-down version of the conversation they'd had, excluding the bits which she knew would alarm her friend, like Nic finding that text and threatening her; Adam prowling around; Theo being set up for murder by Nic's dad . . .

It all sounded so dark and messed up, and some of it didn't quite add up to her, but all she could think about right then was that kiss. For the few brief moments it had lasted before she came to her senses and pushed him away, it had felt so right. But it wasn't right; it was wrong on every single level. Ryan was married and, until yesterday, she had been dating his father. That aside, she couldn't ignore the fact that Ryan had asked Nic out all those years ago, despite now claiming that it was Lexi he had really wanted. And, given how desperately he was trying to keep Nic from finding out about his true identity, it was clear that he would choose her all over again if push came to shove. But she was never going to see him again, so she had to let go of the what-ifs and forget about the lot of them.

Still furious with himself for overstepping the mark and kissing Lexi, Ryan eased his foot off the accelerator when he hit the main road and spotted a speed camera up ahead. Lexi had said that she wouldn't tell Nic about his dad, and he could only pray that she wouldn't go back on her word. He didn't think she would, but if living with Nic had taught him anything it was that women could change their minds ten times in as many minutes, and he wasn't ready to deal with the fallout if Lexi betrayed him.

His phone started ringing as he passed the camera and he pressed the button on the steering wheel to answer it. Remembering that it wasn't his car and his phone wasn't paired to the system when nothing happened, he pulled over to answer it manually when he saw the name Django on the screen.

'You found your charger, then?'

'Had to buy a new one,' Theo said. 'Soon as I plugged it in I saw I'd had a missed call and a text off Alexis, but she didn't answer her phone when I tried to call her back. Have you been round there yet?'

'Just left,' Ryan said, his gut clenching at the sound of Lexi's name coming out of his dad's mouth. The way he called her Alexis made him cringe, not only because it sounded pretentious, but also because it was 'their thing'; a reminder that his dad had shared intimacies with Lexi that *he* would never get to share with her. The only consolation was the knowledge that she wasn't in love with his dad, and he held onto that tightly now.

'Was she OK?' Theo asked.

'Not really,' Ryan sighed. 'Nic called her this morning. She must have gone through my phone last night and found that text you sent. Obviously she assumed it was from me and jumped to the conclusion that me and Lexi are having an affair, so she rang her to warn her off.'

'Shit! Alexis didn't tell her about me, did she?'

'No. And she said she won't, so we've just got to hope she means it.'

'Did she say anything else?'

'If you mean did she ask about you, no. She's still pretty mad, so I wouldn't bank on getting back with her anytime soon.'

'Fuck!' Theo muttered. 'I messed up big time, man. Should've been straight with her from the start.'

'To be honest, I don't think it would have worked out, whatever you'd told her,' Ryan said bluntly. 'She might have forgiven you for lying about prison, but finding out that I'm your son was always going to be a massive sticking point. I'm married to the woman whose brother nearly raped her, don't forget. *And* I helped him get off with it by lying to the police.'

'That fucker's a dead man if I ever get my hands on him,' Theo said darkly.

'Yeah, well, he's another problem,' said Ryan. 'Lexi reckons he drove past her place a couple of times before I got there. And Nic's the only one who could have given him the address, so she must have sent him.'

'He didn't see you, did he?'

'No, he'd gone by the time I got there. And I'm in a courtesy car, so he wouldn't have recognized it even if he'd come back. But he's a slippery bastard, and it could get tricky if he starts spying on me.'

'OK, well, go do what you need to do and I'll see you later,' Theo said. 'But keep your wits about you, son. If you think that rapist is following you, don't lead him here. We don't want him sussing things out and alerting his old man.'

Glad to hear that his father sounded like he was back on the ball after the soppy whining over Lexi, Ryan said goodbye and eased back into the traffic. For her own safety, he hadn't told Lexi the full story, so she was now under the impression that he wanted to work on his marriage with Nic. But she didn't know the half of it. Nic wasn't some poor little betrayed wife, she was a Harvey through and through – and the older she got, the more like her mum she became. Both women had used their looks and Danny's reputation to get whatever they wanted out of life; and now Ryan was running things, Nicole would fight tooth and nail to maintain her position as first lady. But as much as she claimed to love him, when the shit hit the fan – which it undoubtedly would – she would be baying for his blood right along with the rest of her family.

23

Adam's head was all over the place as he drove home, and he desperately needed something to help him think straight. After parking in the underground garage, he rode the lift up to his apartment on the seventh floor and scooped up the mail that had been delivered while he was out. He tossed the letters onto the sideboard along with his keys, then poured a glass of neat whisky and swallowed half of it in one before pulling a wrap of coke out of his pocket and tipping a heap onto the glass top of the coffee table. Expertly chopping two lines, he snorted them in quick succession, one up each nostril, and let out an appreciative roar when it set his brain on fire.

As his bitch sister had snidely pointed out that morning, his parents paid his rent, and what little was left subsidized his coke, whisky and loose-women habits. But he was fucked if he was going to thank them for the crumbs they threw him when, in reality, he ought to be running things. For years, they had used the allegations of rape that had been levelled against him as justification for keeping him in his box. But those lying tarts had all been up for it – Lexi James included.

He'd always known Lexi fancied him, right from the first time his sister brought her round to their flat on the Kingston and he'd seen the same longing in her eyes as he saw in the eyes of every other slag who threw themselves at him. He'd seen through her pathetic wallflower act from the start, and had always suspected there was a right little raver hiding behind the lank hair and shapeless clothes; so when she'd gone out of her way to look sexy for him at the party that night, he'd decided to give her what she'd been craving. She had repaid him by trying to get him arrested, and he'd never forgiven her for that, blaming her for his dad later handing over the reins of the business to Ryan instead of him. Now, though, after learning that Ryan was sniffing around her – and might have been doing so for some considerable time – he couldn't help but wonder if his brother-in-law had been behind her sudden change of mind that night.

He'd been high on booze and Ecstasy at the party, so his memory of the actual events had always been a little hazy. What he did remember, *very* clearly, however, was how breathless and weak-kneed Lexi had been after their first kiss; and how she had gone upstairs straight after – a clear invitation to follow her if ever he'd seen one. But just as he'd been about to fuck her, that twat Ryan had charged in like some jealous boyfriend and knocked him out. And then Ryan had finished with Nic and walked out – minutes after Lexi had left. Coincidence? He didn't think so.

With the coke sharpening his mind, Adam could actually see the pieces slotting into place. He'd never liked Ryan and had always suspected that the cocky gutter-rat had only gone after Nic in order to make a name for himself as Danny Harvey's son-in-law. And what better way to make that happen than to manipulate Lexi – who'd been so drunk and upset that night she probably hadn't known right from left – into making that allegation, purely so he could ride to the rescue the following day and worm his way into Danny's good books?

Now he thought about it, his sister had most likely put the idea into Ryan's head in the first place by telling him about the girl who had accused him of assaulting her before Lexi did – a prime example of Nic's complete lack of loyalty to her own blood. Armed with that information, Ryan would have known that Danny would assume Adam was guilty the minute Lexi opened her mouth, thus laying the foundation for what came later: Danny not trusting his own son to run the family business and handing it to that conniving bastard instead.

It was all so obvious he didn't know why he hadn't seen it at the time. But now he *had* seen it, he needed to decide what to do about it.

24

Lexi had fed and watered her old people and dispensed their various medications, and was now tackling the laundry while the residents congregated in the common room for whatever activity had been arranged for them that day. Monday mornings were usually a mixture of armchair yoga and massage therapies, but she could hear somebody sound-checking a PA system as she pushed a cartload of soiled sheets toward the laundry room, and guessed that they were going to be treated to an hour of songs from the crooner who came in once a month to serenade them.

Sheets, duvet covers and pillowcases loaded into the washing machine, she was stocking her trolley with fresh bedding when one of her co-workers popped their head around the door and told her to come to reception.

'I'm a bit busy,' she said. 'Can it wait till I've made the beds?'

'No,' the girl insisted, grinning widely. 'Come on.'

Curious to know what was going on, Lexi abandoned her trolley and followed the girl out. Several of the other women were already gathered around the desk, and Katie, the receptionist, beckoned her over with a wave when she saw her.

'These came for you,' she said, gesturing to a huge bouquet of flowers in a gold box-vase that was sitting on the countertop.

'You're one lucky cow, you,' Julie mock-huffed as she admired the colourful blooms. 'These must have cost someone an arm and a leg.'

'What's going on?' Debs asked, bustling out of the common room.

'Lexi's had a flower shop delivered,' Julie told her. 'All right for some, eh?'

Flashing a secretive smile at Lexi, Debs nudged her, and whispered, 'They're even better than the last lot. He must be *really* desperate to get back into your good books. Let's see what he's saying.'

She reached for the envelope that was sticking up out of the middle of the flowers, but Lexi grabbed it before she got to it and slid the gilt-edged card out. This one wasn't handwritten like the last one, but was printed in gold italics, and she guessed that Theo must have ordered them over the phone.

'*I forgive you, kiss kiss,*' Debs read it out over her shoulder. 'That it?'

Lexi turned the card over and nodded when she saw that it was blank.

'Forgives you for what?' Debs pulled a face.

'I've no idea,' Lexi frowned. 'He's the one in the wrong, not me.'

Ada strode into the reception area and pursed her thin lips when she saw the flowers. 'Who do they belong to?'

'Me,' Debs lied, covering for Lexi because she knew Ada wouldn't be so quick to take the funnies with her.

'Remove them from sight, please,' Ada said, a little less curtly. 'And tell whoever sent them not to do it again. This is your place of work not your home.'

'Will do,' Debs said, lifting the box off the counter and jerking her head at Lexi to follow her when Ada walked away.

'You'd better ring Theo,' she said quietly as they made their way to the staffroom. 'I know you're not ready to talk to him yet, but if you don't and he keeps sending stuff, Ada's going to suss they're for you and get on your case again.'

'I know, and thanks for telling her they were yours,' said Lexi. 'I'll ring him at lunchtime.'

'Do it now, in case he's got anything else up his sleeve,' Debs advised. 'Go in the changing room. I'll distract Ada if she comes in.'

Not looking forward to speaking to Theo, Lexi took her phone out of the locker and went into the changing room. Theo answered after two rings and sounded surprised, delighted and nervous all at the same time.

'Hey, how you doing?'

'I'm OK,' Lexi said, keeping her voice low in case Ada entered the staffroom. 'Thanks for the flowers, they're beautiful, but can you please not send anything else. We're not allowed to get deliveries at work, and—'

'Sorry?' Theo cut in. 'I haven't sent any flowers. I wanted to, but Ry said I needed to give you space.'

'Oh . . .' Lexi felt stupid. 'Sorry, I assumed they were from you.'

'Wasn't there a card with them?'

'Yeah, but it's not signed.'

'What's it say?'

'Nothing much,' Lexi said evasively. 'There's probably been a mix-up at the shop and they're for someone else. Anyway, I'd best go before my supervisor catches me on the phone.'

'Alexis, wait,' Theo said before she could hang up. 'I know you're still upset with me, and I honestly don't blame you – especially after that misunderstanding with Nicole thinking my boy sent you that text. But I've really missed you, and if there's any way I can make it up to you . . .'

Lexi heard the emotion in his voice as he tailed off and knew that he regretted messing things up. But as much as she liked him, she didn't feel strongly enough about him to put herself through the torture of worrying that his son might turn up whenever she was with him. She and Ryan had history, albeit only as friends until he'd turned up at her place and kissed her, and she couldn't deny that she was still attracted to him – more, if she were honest, than she had ever been to Theo.

'I'm sorry, but I think it's best we leave things as they are,' she said. 'You and Ryan have got stuff going on that you don't want me to know about, and I don't want to be with someone who can't be completely honest with me.'

'I understand,' Theo sighed. 'And I respect your decision, so I won't try to persuade you to change your mind. I just hope your next man is worthy of you, because you're a special lady. Don't ever forget that.'

Thanking him, Lexi ended the call and scrolled through her recent calls list. Biting her lip thoughtfully as she stared at the number which she still hadn't assigned a name to, she took a deep breath before ringing it.

'Lexi?' Ryan answered a couple of seconds later. 'Is everything OK?'

'Yeah, everything's fine,' she said. 'I just wanted to ask . . . you didn't send me any flowers, did you?'

'No,' Ryan said, a questioning note in his voice.

'I didn't think so,' she said. 'But your dad said they're not from him, and I couldn't think who else might have sent them, so I thought I'd best check. Only we're not supposed to get stuff delivered at work, so I was going to say please don't do it again – *if* they were you, which, obviously, now I know they're not. Anyway, sorry for bothering you.'

'You're not,' Ryan assured her. 'I've actually been thinking about calling you. To make sure you're OK after – *you* know.'

'I'm absolutely fine,' said Lexi. 'And I, um, hope you got everything sorted with Nic,' she added, more out of politeness than a desire to talk about his wife. 'Bye, then.'

Quickly hanging up, she cursed herself for waffling on at him like a tongue-tied idiot. The sound of his voice had instantly made her feel flustered, and she wafted a hand in front of her face to cool her cheeks before re-joining Debs in the staffroom.

'All done?' Debs asked.

Nodding, Lexi replaced her phone in the locker and locked it.

'Are you OK?'

'I will be.' Lexi forced a smile. 'It wasn't Theo who sent the flowers. He had no clue what I was talking about. And neither did Ryan.'

'Do you think Nic could have sent them?'

Lexi gazed at the flowers, which were now standing in the middle of the table, and shook her head. 'Doubt it. She never gave me a birthday or Christmas card when we were mates, never mind a gift, so I can't see her splashing out on them.'

'Well, whoever it was, I'm sure they'll make themselves known before too long,' Debs said, linking arms with her as they left the room. 'How did you leave it with Theo?'

'I finished it.'

'It's probably for the best, hon. Can you imagine the family get-togethers with Nic as your stepdaughter-in-law?'

'No thanks.' Lexi shuddered at the thought.

'Right, if you're officially done with him, we need to get you back in the saddle before your lady garden starts sprouting weeds,' Debs declared. 'Six has got the night off and some of his mates are coming over for a bevvy. How about we crash the party and see what's on offer?'

'I'll see how I feel later,' Lexi said, already planning a migraine.

Parting ways at the laundry room, Lexi pondered who could

have sent her the flowers as she resumed loading up the trolley. They weren't from Theo or Ryan, and she definitely couldn't see Nic sending them, even if Ryan had somehow managed to persuade her that they weren't having an affair. The only other people who knew she worked here were Debs and their co-workers, but even if they had decided to send them to cheer her up, they weren't stupid enough to send them here knowing that it would get her into trouble. So who the hell *had* sent them?

Stumped for an answer, Lexi put it out of her mind and got on with her work for the rest of the morning; but as soon as lunchtime came around, she rushed to the staffroom and rang the florist whose number was printed on the box. As she'd feared might happen, the woman she spoke to informed her that she couldn't give out clients' confidential information, so she was still none the wiser.

Unwilling to cart the huge bouquet home on the bus, and aware that Ada would probably go on the warpath if it was left in the staffroom, Lexi carried it up to the room of one of her favourite old ladies before finishing her shift.

'Hey, Nessa,' she said, smiling as she entered the room. 'I've got something for you.'

'For me?' Vanessa George's watery eyes widened. 'Is it my birthday?'

'No, love, I just thought you could do with cheering up after your fall the other day,' Lexi said, setting the flowers on the table by the window.

'Oh, you shouldn't have,' Vanessa said, her thin lips quivering in her heavily lined face. 'They must have cost ever so much.'

'I'll let you into a little secret: I didn't buy them,' Lexi said, perching on the chair beside the bed.

'Did you steal them from the cemetery?' Vanessa whispered, a mischievous gleam in her eyes. 'My Frank does that every time he's on the naughty list. Reckons the dead don't appreciate them as much as the living.'

'Sounds like a wise man,' Lexi smiled.

'Oh, he is,' said Vanessa. 'Bugger for the ladies, mind. But . . .' Tailing off, she frowned and stared at the bouquet, confusion in her eyes now, as she asked, 'Who bought me flowers? Is it my birthday?'

25

In his office at DH Deliveries – the initially bogus but now legit courier company Danny Harvey had set up as a front for his drug-and-gun-running business – Ryan was staring at the screen of his laptop, but his mind was no longer on the accounts he'd been working on before Lexi's call came through. Surprised to hear from her, because he'd feared she would never speak to him again, he had hoped that she was calling to say she wanted to see him. But she had quickly put paid to that notion, and now his gut was churning at the thought that some other bloke had probably been hovering on the sidelines while she was dating his dad, waiting for a chance to swoop in and sweep her off her feet. And the minute she was single, he'd made his first move.

Aware that he had absolutely no right to be angry at the thought of Lexi moving on, Ryan released a loud breath. He had blown any chance he might have had with her when he'd misread the signs and kissed her that day, and she couldn't have made it any clearer that she wasn't interested, so he had to respect that and leave her alone.

Slotting his earphones in, he blasted her out of his head with music and concentrated on his work until his alarm sounded at 5 p.m. The office was in near darkness by then, and his shoulders were aching from the hours he'd spent hunched over his laptop. Stretching, he closed down his computer and pulled on his jacket.

Brenda, the company secretary, was also getting ready to leave when he walked into the reception area. A curvaceous lady in her early fifties, she'd been Danny's right-hand woman – and also, Ryan suspected, his mistress. He could totally see the attraction, because she was the polar opposite of Rachel, from her pleasant personality to her undoctored face and natural breasts. But if she was hoping that Danny would ever leave his wife for her, Ryan knew she'd be waiting till the end of time.

'This came for you earlier,' she said, smiling as she handed a small package to him. 'I knocked on, but you didn't answer.'

'Sorry, I was listening to music,' Ryan said, turning the package over to check who it was from and seeing that it had no return address. 'Who dropped it off?'

'Motorbike courier,' Brenda told him, rolling her eyes as she added, 'There should be a rule against them leaving their helmets on when they come inside to deliver stuff. I nearly had a heart attack when I looked up and saw him walking through the door.'

'How many times have I told you to make sure it's locked?' Ryan chided.

'It usually is, but I nipped out for a ciggie and mustn't have pulled it all the way to when I came back in. Fat lot of good *you'd* have been if he'd attacked me, though, eh? Locked away in your office listening to Abba.'

'It was Drake, and it helps me concentrate. Anyway, if you're ready I'll walk you to your car.'

'Thanks, love.' Brenda reached for her handbag.

Waving her out ahead of him, Ryan set the alarm and locked the door. Winter was on its way and the sky was already darker than it had been at the same time a week earlier. The compound, which housed DH Deliveries and three other small companies, was situated on a rundown industrial area and had no car park of its own, so everyone used the vacant lot at the end of the estate. After walking Brenda to her car and waving her off, Ryan climbed into his own car and tossed the package onto the passenger seat before starting the engine and setting off.

Brenda had turned right, but he took a left and headed toward the dual carriageway at the end of the estate road. Stepping on the brake when he spotted the traffic lights up ahead turn to amber, he swore under his breath when the pedal sank straight to the plate. He pumped it several times, but nothing happened, and he broke out into a sweat as he drew ever closer to the now-red light and the heavy cross-traffic on the dual carriageway. Quickly shifting down through the gears, he yanked the hand-brake on as hard as he could and swung the wheel, sending the car into a spin. Bracing himself for the impact of the vehicles he felt sure were going to smash into him when he skidded through the lights before coming to a stop, he sent up a silent prayer of gratitude when several cars swerved around him and those behind him stopped.

'You're leaking petrol, mate,' a lorry driver a couple of vehicles back called out as Ryan climbed shakily out of the car.

Ryan looked down and saw a dark pool forming on the tarmac. 'Sorry, you'll have to go round,' he called out, waving the other drivers on before leaning inside the car to switch the hazards on.

'I'll give you a hand pushing it onto the verge,' the lorry driver said, running over to help after parking behind him and putting on his own hazards to warn the other drivers that there was an obstacle in the road.

'Cheers, mate,' Ryan said gratefully. 'It's not my motor and I think the brakes have gone.'

'If that's brake fluid, you're lucky you stopped when you did,' the man said, gazing down at the rapidly spreading patch. 'Pipe must be fucked.'

'Great,' Ryan muttered, opening the driver's side door and releasing the handbrake before steering the car toward the kerb. Palming the man a couple of twenties when it was safely off the road, he put it into reverse and made sure the handbrake was firmly on again before ringing the garage.

'All right, Bob, it's Ryan King,' he said when his call was answered. 'Sylvester there? Well, when he comes out of the loo, can you tell him I need him to send the tow truck out ASAP. The brakes just went in the courtesy car he lent me and I nearly got fucking creamed.'

After giving his location to the man, Ryan squatted down to take a look at the underside of the car using the torch on his phone. The liquid was now dripping instead of pouring out and he guessed that the reservoir must be almost empty, which told him it had to have been leaking for quite some time between him parking up that morning and setting off this afternoon. Spotting a thin pipe hanging down, he directed the torch beam at it, and muttered, 'What the fuck . . . ?' when he saw that the edges were perfectly even – as if, he immediately thought, it had been cut.

The tow truck arrived fifteen minutes later and Bob, the mechanic Ryan had spoken to, hopped out. Nodding when Ryan showed him the pipe after telling him his suspicions, he said, 'You could be right, cocker. But we won't know for sure till we get it on the ramp.' Then, giving a wry smile, he said, 'Not having much luck with motors lately, are you?'

'No, I'm not,' Ryan agreed.

'If it's any consolation, yours was signed off this avvo and we were going to ring you in the morning to pick it up, so you'll be able to take it when we get back to base,' Bob said, walking round to the front of the car to get it hooked up to the tow bar. 'Don't know if you're superstitious,' he went on jokingly as he worked, 'but I'd be wondering if someone's put a curse on me if I was you. Not pissed off any witches lately, 'ave you?'

'Only the wife,' Ryan muttered, a shiver snaking down his spine when he got the sudden sensation that he was being watched. He did a quick scan of the road, but all he could see was traffic zooming by on both sides and strangers going about their business on foot. But the uneasy feeling was still hovering over him, and he wondered, as he climbed into the passenger seat of the tow truck, if having two near misses in a matter of days wasn't too much of a coincidence to be unrelated.

On the other side of the city, Adam was parked under a tree at the end of a road lined with huge detached houses that made his mum and dad's old gaff look like a shed. He'd been there for almost an hour, his gaze fixed on the gates of the residential home where Nicole had told him Lexi worked, when his phone started ringing. Blood pumping with expectation when he saw that it was Wes Caine, he quickly answered it.

'Is it done?'

'Yes and no,' said Wes.

'What's that supposed to mean?' Adam asked.

'There's a set of lights at the end of the road and he went into a skid before he reached them; slid out onto the dual carriageway. But no one hit him.'

'Cunt's got more lives than a fucking cat.'

'You're telling me,' Wes agreed – sounding almost admiring, Adam thought. 'Anyhow, where should I meet you? Only I'm taking the missus out for a meal tonight, so I could do with picking up my dosh.'

'That'd better be a joke,' Adam replied sharply. 'You fucked it up, so why the hell would I pay you?'

'Yo, don't be taking the piss,' Wes shot back aggressively. 'I did the job, and it ain't my fault he survived, so you'd best fetch the money round or you and me are gonna have a big problem.'

'Threaten me again and *you'll* be the one with a problem,' Adam warned him. 'I took you on when every other fucker turned their backs after you got out, and I've been good to you.'

'All right, man, chill out; I don't wanna fall out with you,' Wes sighed. 'I'm only askin' for what I've earned.'

'And you'll get it,' Adam said, sitting up straighter when two cars pulled in through the gates he'd been watching and a bright security light flared, illuminating a group of women who were walking out. 'I've got to go,' he said, locating Lexi in the middle of them. 'Drop by the club in an hour and I'll sort you out.'

Abruptly cutting the call, he started the engine and crept forward to keep the women in his sights. They stopped at the corner and chatted for a couple of minutes before most of them walked on, leaving Lexi and a fat bird to cross over the road, arm in arm. Frowning when he noticed that she wasn't carrying the flowers he'd sent her, which had cost him almost eighty quid, he drove to the corner and watched as they walked to a bus stop further along the road.

His plan, if she'd been alone, was to pull up alongside her, as if he'd spotted her in passing, and offer her a lift home. He knew from what Nicole had told him that she still blamed him for what had happened at the party, but once he explained that Ryan had manipulated her for his own ends, he was sure she would realize that he wasn't the monster she'd built him up in her mind to be. And when he had her in his arms, his fuckwit brother-in-law would know that the best man had won in the end.

But she wasn't alone, so that plan was out of the window.

Frustrated, but determined to find a way to speak to her, Adam waited until the women had boarded a bus and then pulled into the traffic a couple of cars behind, intending to catch Lexi when she reached her stop if the fat one got off early.

As he followed the bus toward Chorlton, he jabbed his thumb down on the steering wheel button when his phone rang.

'Why haven't you been answering my calls?' his sister demanded. 'I've been trying to get hold of you for days. Haven't you seen my messages?'

'I've been busy. What's up?' he said, slowing down when he saw the bus indicate that it was pulling in to a stop. As he passed, he glanced up at the window near the back beside which Lexi was sitting, and smiled to himself when he saw that she seemed to be lost in her thoughts; maybe wondering who had sent her the flowers and wishing she could thank them. Well, she'd get her chance soon enough.

'You said you were going to let me know if you'd seen Ryan at that bitch's house,' Nicole went on, the whine in her voice irritating him.

'And if I had I would have,' he said, pulling over a short distance ahead of the bus.

'So he wasn't there?'

'I just told you that.'

'No, you said—'

'Nic, I haven't got time for this,' Adam interrupted, easing back into the traffic when the bus trundled past. 'I've got an important meeting, so if that's all you wanted, I'm getting off.'

'I just need to know if you're still watching her place,' Nicole said. ''Cos if you're not, I'll do it myself. Ryan's acting weird, and I need to know if he's still seeing her.'

'Stay away from her!' Adam said sharply, afraid that she would fuck up his plans if she did anything before he'd had a chance to speak to Lexi. 'I said I'll take care of it, and I will. Now have some bloody patience and let me do this my way.'

He cut the call before Nicole could reply and continued following the bus. When it pulled in to a stop around the corner from Lexi's house ten minutes later, he drove quickly past and took the next left to approach her road from the opposite end. Parking up, he watched as she and the fat woman made their way into the house. Seconds later, lights came on behind two windows on the first floor and both sets of curtains were drawn. He knew the window on the left was Lexi's, because that was where he'd seen her after Ryan left that day, so he guessed the other woman must live in the room next to hers.

After sitting there for twenty minutes and seeing no further movement from the house, Adam remembered that he'd told Wes to meet him at the club and turned the car around to head over there. It pissed him off that he still had to pay the man even though the job had been messed up, but he was going to need all the help he could get if he was to stand any chance of ousting Ryan from his dad's business, so he had no choice but to keep the man sweet.

At the garage, Ryan watched as Bob and his boss, Sylvester Campbell, examined the underside of the courtesy car. The father of one of Ryan's old schoolmates, Shamar, Sylvester treated him like family, only ever charging mates' rates and making sure he got top-notch service whenever he brought a motor in.

'Definitely cut,' Sylvester said, wiping his hands on a filthy towel. 'You're lucky you managed to stop when you did, Ry, or me and Sham'd be carrying your coffin into the crem in a couple of weeks. Any idea who could've done it?'

'No.' Ryan shook his head. 'But my secretary had her tyres slashed a few weeks back, and a security guard at one of the other units saw a gang of young lads hanging around earlier that day, so it could have been them.'

'Yout' dem got no respek,' Sylvester said, slipping easily into the patois of his own youth. 'Dey need licks, man.'

'They'll get more than licks if I catch any of them near my motor,' Ryan said, sliding his wallet out of his pocket. 'How much do I owe you?'

After settling the bill, Ryan thanked the men and hopped into his newly repaired Range Rover. Bob was lowering the ramp as he reversed out onto the forecourt, and he saw Sylvester's Rottweiler, Satan, run over to the courtesy car and start sniffing around the passenger-side door. About to drive away, he heard a whistle and rolled his window down when Bob hurried toward him, parcel in hand, Satan on his heel.

'You left this in the car,' Bob said, chucking the package through the window as Satan made a jump for it. 'If it's what I think it is, you'd best hurry up and get it stashed, 'cos if this 'un can smell it, them drug squad dogs will be all over it in a flash.'

'It's definitely not that,' Ryan laughed, amused by the notion that anybody he knew would be stupid enough to send drugs through the post. Jerking back from the window when Satan jumped up and shoved his massive head inside, so close to his face Ryan could feel the heat of its funky breath on his cheek, he decided to see what had got the dog so hyped up and ripped open the parcel. His brain didn't immediately compute that he was looking at a dead rat wrapped in cling film. Sickened and horrified when it did, he chucked the parcel out in disgust and shuddered when the dog snatched the rat up into its mouth.

'Sly, Satan's got a rat!' Bob yelled, the disgust on his face matching that on Ryan's as they watched the dog trot away to enjoy its find in peace.

'What the *fuck* . . . ?' Sylvester said, running out from the office and skidding to a stop when he saw the mess Satan was making. 'Where'd he get that?' he demanded.

'Someone sent it to me,' Ryan said. 'Sorry, I freaked and chucked it out the window.'

Shaking his head, Sylvester pulled on a pair of heavy-duty gloves and prised the disgusting article out of the growling dog's mouth. After dropping it into a bin and slamming the lid down on it, he walked over to Ryan, his expression grim, and rested his hand on the roof of the car.

'Looks like someone's got it in for you, son. First the motors, now this. You sure you don't know who's behind it?'

Still feeling nauseous, Ryan thought about who he could have pissed off enough to make them want to kill him. Danny Harvey's reputation as a ruthless bastard had kept most of the chancers who dabbled in their line of work from making any serious attempt to muscle in on their established territory, but some new faces had recently appeared on the scene, so it was possible that one of them was trying to take him out of the game. But why send him a rat? That type of message was usually reserved for grasses or dirty dealers, neither of which applied to Ryan. He knew Adam hated him, but if Adam wanted revenge he'd have done something when Danny cut him out of the business, not three years down the line. And he definitely couldn't see Nic doing something like this. Not only would she die if she saw a rat – alive *or* dead – she was still pressurizing him to have a baby, so killing him would deprive her of that.

Unless she was already pregnant and just wanted him out of the way?

He dismissed that thought as fast as it had come to him. As cold-blooded as Nic could be, she enjoyed the prestige of being first lady in her dad's business too much to relegate herself to the position of first daughter, forced to watch from the sidelines as her mother reclaimed the top-bitch role when Danny took back control – which he would if Ryan was off the scene.

But if it wasn't Nic or Adam, maybe he needed to start looking at his crew. Most of the men had been with Danny from the start and had proved themselves to be loyal and trustworthy, but there were a few new additions who hadn't yet been tested to any great degree, so it was possible that one of them had designs on taking over. Danny would be all over it like a rash if he heard what was going on, but Ryan wasn't about to involve him and have the men think he was incapable of handling his shit without his father-in-law to hold his hand.

Aware that he needed to be extra cautious until he found out what was going on and who was behind it, he rang his dad as he drove away from the garage and told him he was on his way over.

26

Lexi had tried to wriggle out of going to Six's room that evening, but Debs was having none of it, so she eventually caved in and agreed to go for one drink. It was the first time she'd been in his room on the top floor, and she was surprised that not only was it almost double the size of hers, it also had a tiny balcony and a fire escape that led down into the backyard. His bed was curtained off, giving the impression of a separate living room; and his sofa was big and comfortable – the kind she could imagine herself curling up on with a book and a glass of wine at the end of a shift. The floor lamps that were dotted around gave off a cosy glow, and soft rock music was drifting out through four tall, thin speakers that were standing in the corners of the room.

Feeling light-headed within seconds of arriving, thanks to the smoke coming from the spliffs Six and his mates were passing around, Lexi smiled when one of the men handed her a can of beer. She took a seat on the sofa between Debs and a biker type called Eddie, who had a bald head with a skull tattooed onto it, and one of the longest beards she had ever seen, and listened as the men, who all seemed to have been roadies like Six, chatted about the good old days when the *real* gods of rock and roll and punk ruled the stages and airwaves.

The chilled atmosphere reminded her of Hebden Bridge, where everyone had prided themselves on being a free spirit and a little bit eccentric, and which had felt more like a commune than a community, and she felt herself relaxing more and more as the night wore on. Debs was clearly enjoying herself too, and Lexi noticed that she and Six seemed to be chatting more to each other than to anyone else, and making good-natured jokes at each other's expense. She wished the woman would stop thinking of him as a brother, because she was convinced they could be happy together – far happier than Debs would ever be with any of the fuck-buddies she brought home from the club on Saturday nights. But Debs either couldn't see the chemistry that was so blatantly obvious to everyone else, or she was choosing to ignore it because she was scared of getting hurt again. Either way, she was missing out, because Six was a really nice guy.

Wiped out by midnight, and worried that she would sleep through her alarm in the morning if she didn't get going, Lexi said her goodbyes and headed back to her own room. Falling asleep as soon as her head hit the pillow, she was woken by her phone ringing on the bedside table half an hour later.

'Hello?' she croaked, answering it with her eyes still closed.

'Hey there beautiful,' a man replied, his voice a soft drawl. 'How did you like the flowers?'

Eyes snapping open, Lexi sat up and looked at the screen, but the number was withheld. 'Who is this?' she demanded.

'Don't you recognize my voice?' he asked.

'No, I don't,' she said, only certain that it wasn't Theo or Ryan.

'Oh, come on, you're not even trying,' he chuckled. 'Shall I give you a clue?'

'I'm too tired for games, so just tell me or get lost,' she said, not caring if she sounded rude.

'Why didn't you take your flowers home?' the man asked. 'Didn't you like them?'

Skin crawling at the thought that, whoever he was, he must have been watching her when she came out of work – or, worse, when she got home – Lexi tried her hardest to place his voice, but it wasn't ringing any bells at all. Two males worked the day shift at the home, but they were both older than this man sounded, and one was Scottish. She hadn't given her number to any men apart from Theo since moving back to Manchester, and it definitely wasn't her ex, Kyle, because she'd have known his fake-posh accent anywhere.

'Still trying to figure out who I am?' the man said. 'Let me give you that clue . . . *party*.'

Relaxing when she realized it must be one of Six's friends, and that Debs had probably told them about the flowers and got them to ring her to wind her up, Lexi said, 'Nice try, Eddie, or Luke, or whichever one of you it is; you nearly had me there. Now thanks for a great night, but I'm in bed, so, bye.'

Lying down after cutting the call, she switched her phone to silent when it immediately started ringing again, then sent a quick text to Debs asking her to tell the guys to stop because she was trying to get to sleep.

Less than a minute later, a tap came at her door, and Debs called, 'Lexi? Are you OK, hon? I just got a weird message off you. Lexi . . . ?'

When another knock came, Lexi reluctantly got up and opened her door. Debs and Six were on the landing, and she gave a mock-exasperated sigh at the sight of them.

'*Seriously?* I told Eddie, or whoever it was, that I was in bed, so if you've come to get me to go back to the party, forget it.'

'I don't know what you're talking about,' Debs said, confusion on her face. 'The guys left about ten minutes ago.'

'Yeah, right.' Lexi gave a disbelieving smile.

'It's true,' said Six.

'You must have given them my number then,' Lexi said, still convinced it was a joke.

'I wouldn't do that,' Debs insisted. 'Why? Has one of them called you?'

'I thought they did,' Lexi frowned, less certain now. 'He asked if I liked the flowers and why I hadn't brought them home, and you're the only one who knew about them, so I assumed you'd put them up to it. I know how funny you think you are when you've had a drink.'

'Hon, I'm nowhere near drunk enough to do something daft like that,' Debs said. 'Didn't you recognize his voice?'

'No. He wanted me to guess, but it didn't sound familiar at all.'

As soon as the words had left her mouth, her phone lit up on the bedside table. Picking it up and seeing the withheld number, she said, 'I think it's him again.'

'Answer it,' Debs said, walking in and sitting on the edge of the bed.

'I don't want to,' Lexi said, flopping down beside her. 'If he knows about the flowers, it must be the guy who sent them.'

'Don't start worrying,' Debs said, squeezing her hand. 'It's probably Theo messing about.'

'No, it wasn't him, and it wasn't Ryan either,' Lexi said with certainty. 'But it must be someone I know – or *used* to know.' Face paling as soon as she said that, she muttered, 'Oh my God, what if it was Adam? Nic's brother,' she elaborated when they both looked at her blankly. Then, to Six, she said, 'Remember when Ryan turned up the other day and I asked you if you'd seen that other car?'

'The flashy undercover one? Yeah, I remember. You said it was someone you hadn't seen in years.'

'*That* was Adam.'

'What's this?' Debs looked at each of them in turn.

Remembering that she hadn't told Debs or Six the full story on the day Ryan called round, Lexi told them now about Nic's threatening phone call and Adam driving past an hour or so later. And then, keeping the details to a bare minimum because it still filled her with shame to think about it, she told them about the night of Adam's party.

'Bloody hell, no wonder you're so freaked out,' Debs said. 'What a pair of nasty bastards. She wants a good slap, and *he* wants locking up, the dirty pervert.'

'Why don't you ring that Ryan bloke and ask him to have a word,' Six suggested.

'No.' Lexi shook her head. 'I don't want Nic thinking I've been contacting him behind her back. She'll make his life hell.'

'He's married to her, so I'm sure it already *is* hell,' Debs snorted. 'But seriously, hon, this isn't funny. If I was you, I'd call the police. They must still have the assault on record, and they'll warn him off if he's harassing you.'

'He never got charged so I doubt they kept it on file,' said Lexi. 'And sending me expensive flowers is hardly going to look like harassment, is it?'

'OK, but if he sends anything else or tries to contact you again, please think about it,' Debs urged. 'I don't want to scare you, but he's got to be a bit deranged if he actually thinks you'd be interested in talking to him after he tried to rape you.'

'That *is* a bit fucked up,' Six agreed.

'This is Nic's fault,' Lexi said bitterly. 'I always knew she was a vindictive bitch, but giving him my address and number is low even for her.'

'Well don't give them the satisfaction of knowing they've

got to you,' Debs counselled. 'Ignore any calls from withheld numbers until they get the message that you're not interested.'

'Yeah, I will,' Lexi agreed. 'Anyway, it looks like he's given up for now, so I'm going to try to get some sleep.'

'She's kicking us out,' Six said, nudging Debs.

'No shit, Sherlock.' She rolled her eyes and got up.

Saying goodnight, Lexi locked the door and climbed back into bed. Convinced now that it was Adam who had sent the flowers, she felt sick to her stomach when she remembered the message on the attached note. *I forgive you* . . . as if *she* was the one who had done *him* wrong, the twisted bastard. As for Nic, she was equally as despicable for sending him here. Even if she'd never experienced it herself, she had to know how disturbing it would be for a woman to suddenly be confronted by her would-be rapist.

Angry, she decided she would ring Nic in the morning and have it out with her. She didn't really want to involve the police, because she doubted they would do anything since nothing had actually happened, but maybe the threat of it would be enough to make Nic and her vile brother see sense and quit with the stupid games.

27

Adam was furious. Hearing Lexi's voice after all those years had given him a massive buzz, but then she'd gone and ruined it by mentioning the names of men she had obviously been with a short time before he rang her. That had pissed him off big time, and the two glasses of whisky he'd knocked back after she hung up on him had ignited a raging fire inside his gut.

In need of someone to vent his anger on, he got up from behind his desk and yanked the office door open. Head pounding along with the distorted music that was blasting out through the club's crappy speakers, he glanced over to the table where he'd left Dave, Loz and Jonesy – the three fuckwits who made up his crew, along with Wes, who hadn't come back after picking up his money earlier. Clenching his teeth when he saw two fresh bottles of house champagne sitting on the table, which he guessed they must have ordered as soon as he left them to go and make his call, it took every ounce of willpower he possessed to keep from marching over and smashing the bottles into their greedy, piss-taking faces.

As high as he was, he knew the men would fuck him up if he tried anything stupid like that, so he snapped his gaze off them and looked around the crowded room for someone else to target. Most of the girls were occupied, some on the stage, others on punters' laps; but when he spotted one sitting alone in a corner, he made a beeline for her.

'What d'you think you're doing?' he demanded, snatching the glass she was holding out of her hand before grabbing her arm and pulling her to her feet. 'Since when do I pay you to sit on your arse and drink my profits?'

'I'm on a break, and it's only lemonade,' she said, fear and pain flaring in her tired eyes as his fingers dug into her bony arm. 'Sue said it was OK.'

'Is Sue the boss?'

'No, but—'

'*No* was the right answer,' Adam hissed. 'There's only one boss here, and that's me. Now get your arse into my office while I decide what to do with you.'

He pushed her ahead of him through the club and into the office. Closing and locking the door, he slipped the key into his pocket and then walked to his seat behind the desk and sat down.

'Give me a good reason why I shouldn't sack you?' he said, staring at the girl who was visibly quivering in front of him.

'Please don't,' she pleaded. 'I really need this job.'

'How much do you need it?' he asked.

'I *really* need it,' she said, nervously licking her dry lips.

'I – I've got a little boy, and his dad doesn't help me out at all. No one does.'

'Don't bore me with your domestic shit, I ain't your therapist,' Adam sneered. 'I said how *much* do you want this job?'

The penny dropped, and the girl put on the sexy smile she used on her punters as she walked round the desk and straddled him.

'Not like that,' Adam said, roughly pushing her off and twisting her round. 'Lean over the desk.'

Unzipping his fly when she'd done as he said, he threw her short skirt up over her hips and ripped her G-string to one side.

Going limp after several thrusts, he pulled out with a roar of frustration.

The girl straightened up and tugged her skirt back down before stumbling around the desk.

'If you tell anyone about this, I'll ring social services and report you for leaving your kid alone while you fuck strangers for money,' Adam warned before she reached the door. 'And I've got the CCTV tapes to prove it.'

Turning, her face drained of colour, she whimpered, 'Please don't report me, Mr Harvey. If they take my boy away I'll—'

'What?' Adam sneered. 'Kill yourself? Go ahead, love, you'll probably be doing him a favour. Now keep your mouth shut and I might do the same – yeah?'

She nodded and scuttled out, and Adam sank down onto his chair and slammed his fist down on the desktop. He was confident that she wouldn't dare tell anyone what he'd done, but he could have landed himself in deep shit if he hadn't had the threat of reporting her to social services to hold over her. And it wouldn't matter that she was a prostitute. If she'd cried rape, like those other tarts had, his dad would disown him and cut him out of the business for good. And without the money he got from that, he'd be destitute within a week.

Nerves jangling, stomach churning, Adam took a wrap of coke out of the drawer and snorted it straight off the grimy desktop. Grimacing when it burned his nose and exploded in his brain before racing through his bloodstream, he wiped his streaming eyes on his shirt sleeve and breathed in and out several times to slow his pounding heart.

In control again, he pondered what to do about Lexi. Every bad thing that had happened to him over the last ten years was a direct result of her making that accusation, and now it was time for payback.

28

Ada Briggs had always been a light sleeper – which was just as well now her ageing pug, Walter, was becoming increasingly incontinent. Up and out of bed as soon as she heard his claws clipping across the laminate flooring – no doubt leaving a trail of urine in his wake – she pulled on her dressing gown and let him out into the front garden. At 2.30 a.m., the silence on the usually noisy road was blissful, and she lit a cigarette – one of her guilty night-time pleasures – as she waited for Walter to do his business.

When ten minutes had passed and Walter was still squatting in the same place, but hadn't yet done anything, which told her he was probably bunged up again, Ada released a sad sigh as she stubbed out the cigarette and dropped the dimp into the paper bin. His bowel movements were becoming worrisome, because he seemed to have diarrhoea one day and constipation the next. The vet had put it down to age the last time she'd taken Walter in, but she suspected something more sinister was going on, and the thought of losing him filled her with dread.

Unable to bear watching him struggle now, she walked over and gently picked him up, saying, 'Come on, old fella; let's get you back in the warm, shall we?'

As she stepped over the threshold, something hit her hard in the back and sent her flying. Losing her grip on the dog as she went down, she cried out when he skidded across the floor before smashing into one of the bicycle frames that were propped against the wall. Unsure what had happened, she was scrambling to get up and go to him when a foot came out of nowhere and connected with her jaw, and the pain made her feel as if her head had exploded before everything, mercifully, went black.

The lower half of his face concealed behind a scarf, his distinctive blond hair covered by a beanie hat, Adam closed the front door and, stepping over the skinny old woman, grabbed the now-yapping dog. Hurling it through the open door of the woman's room when it started snarling and trying to bite him, he dragged the woman in after it and pushed the door shut with his foot.

The woman's eyes were open and her jaw was hanging at a disgusting angle, making it look, Adam thought, as if she'd had a stroke and coughed up a load of blood. He hadn't intended to kill her, or the dog, but after hearing her talk to it like it was a baby when he crept up behind her, he figured he'd probably done her a favour, because she'd have been gutted if she'd woken up to find it dead.

Conscience salved, he did a quick search of the room and pocketed the woman's keys and a few other bits and pieces. Then, in a flash of inspiration, he slid something out of his inside pocket and pushed it under the woman's bloody cheek before creeping out of her room and up the stairs.

More worried about the flowers and the weird phone call than she'd admitted, Lexi had struggled to get back to sleep after Debs and Six had left her. In a light doze now, she woke when she heard a floorboard creak outside her room. It was pitch-dark and there were no noises coming from anywhere else in the house, so she reached for her phone to check the time and frowned when she saw that it was 2.40 a.m. Sitting up when she heard a scraping sound, followed by a dull thud and the whine of hinges that she recognized as Debs's door opening, she wondered if her friend had gone back up to Six's place earlier and was now creeping back to bed.

About to lie down again, she jerked upright when she heard what sounded like a muffled cry coming from across the landing. Quietly sliding out of bed, she tiptoed to the door and pressed her ear to the wood before slowly opening it and peeping out. Debs's door was shut, but she could hear faint noises coming from inside. She didn't want to knock in case Debs had invited a man over, but her instincts were telling her that something wasn't right, so she crept down the landing and up the stairs to Six's room. After tapping on his door a couple of times and getting no answer, she tried the handle and was surprised when it opened.

'Six?' she whispered, feeling her way over to the curtained off area in the dark. 'Are you awake?'

Bedsprings groaned on the other side of the curtain, and Six grunted, 'Who's that?'

'It's Lexi. Look, I'm probably imagining things 'cos of what happened earlier, but I think someone might be in Debs's room.'

'What?' Six yanked the curtain aside and squinted at her through bleary eyes.

'I thought it was her creeping back in at first, but then I thought I heard her crying out. Like I said, I could be imagining it, but—'

'Stay here,' Six cut her off, already pulling his jeans on.

Lexi nodded and hugged herself when he grabbed a metal baseball bat that was standing against the wall next to the bed and rushed out. Hoping to God that she'd got it wrong, but dreading the thought of facing Debs if Six stormed into her room and caught her and some man mid-shag, she almost jumped out of her skin when she heard Six yell, '*GET THE FUCK OFF HER!*' followed by the sound of a scuffle and an ear-piercing scream.

Panicking when she remembered she'd left her phone in her room, Lexi ran to the back door that led to the small balcony and unlocked it using the key that was in the lock. As she carefully made her way down the slippery metal fire escape into the pitch-dark backyard, she noticed the kitchen light coming on in the house next door and raced out through the gate. Blinded by a security light that came on when she approached the back door of the neighbouring house, she threw her arm up to protect her face when her silver-toothed neighbour, Billy, lurched out wielding a large knife.

'Fuck ya doing, creepin' round out here, ya daft cow?' he spluttered, lowering the knife when he saw who it was. 'You nearly got yourself sliced an' diced, man.'

'Someone's in my house,' she babbled. 'He was in my friend's room and I sent one of our housemates down to make sure she was all right, and now he's shouting and she's screaming and—'

'Whoa, slow down,' Billy said, putting his hand on her shoulder. 'Fuck me, you're freezing, come in here,' he said, pulling her arm until she followed him into the house.

At the sound of another faint scream coming through the wall from next door, Billy rushed back to the door.

'Don't go in there,' Lexi pleaded. 'Call the police!'

Billy hesitated, then nodded and pulled a phone out of his back pocket, saying, 'You'd best do it. I've just got in and I'm a bit wrecked, and they always respond faster to birds. I'll go check out front.'

Hands shaking violently, Lexi made the call as Billy went out into the hall. The operator had just answered and asked which service she required when she heard shouting and running footsteps outside.

'Police!' she yelped, going to the front door in time to see Billy chasing a man dressed all in black down the road.

Still on the phone to the operator, Lexi ran to her own house, the front door of which was wide open, and raced up the stairs.

'What's going on?' a man in a dressing gown asked, peeping out from behind door number two.

Ignoring him, Lexi continued on to Debs's room. The door was open and the light was on, and the scene that greeted her dragged her right back to that terrible morning when she had gone home to find her mum covered in blood behind the sofa.

'Help him!' Debs cried, looking up at her with a tear-streaked face as she held a blood-soaked towel to Six's throat. 'I think he's dying!'

'The p-police are coming,' Lexi stammered, frozen to the spot.

'He got away,' Billy gasped, running in at that moment. 'Oh, fuck!' he muttered when he saw Six. Then, leaping into action, he gently moved Lexi out of the way and knelt down next to Debs, asking, 'Are you hurt, love?' as he checked Six's pulse.

'No.' She shook her head. 'Is – is he . . .'

'Not if I can help it,' he said, placing his hands on Six's chest and pumping rhythmically. Looking up at Lexi, he said, 'They still on the line? Tell 'em we need an ambulance quick as.'

'*LEXI!*' Debs yelled when Lexi didn't move.

Jumping, Lexi raised the phone to her ear, and said, 'My – my housemate's been stabbed in the neck! No, I don't think he's breathing. My friend's got a towel on the wound and my neighbour's doing that chest thing . . . compressions, yeah.'

The man from room two appeared in the doorway behind Lexi, and his face visibly paled when he saw what was happening. 'Is there anything I can do?' he asked.

'Take over from her.' Billy nodded at Debs, who was still sobbing hysterically.

As the man took Debs's place, the operator told Lexi that an ambulance was on its way.

'Please tell them to hurry,' Lexi said, her gaze riveted to Six's lifeless face. 'He looks really bad.'

'They're coming,' Billy said, looking up when he heard the blare of sirens in the near distance.

A few seconds later, tyres screeched to a halt outside and blue lights strobed the wall through the gaps in the curtains.

'Police!' someone yelled, followed by the sound of footsteps entering the house.

'Up here!' Billy called out.

Five uniformed officers rushed up the stairs. Rapidly assessing the scene, one of them ordered everyone out onto the landing as his colleagues took over attending to Six.

'Is the assailant still in the property?' he asked.

'No, I chased him down the road,' Billy said. 'Fucker was fast, man.'

'Was he known to any of you?'

'No.' They all shook their heads.

'He had a scarf over his f-face,' Debs sobbed. 'And a hat and gloves.'

'Can we go into my room so she can sit down?' Lexi asked, putting her arm around her friend. 'That's her room, and he attacked her as well.'

Nodding his agreement, the officer followed them all into

Lexi's room and pushed the door shut to block their view when two paramedics rushed along the landing and into Debs's room. After taking everyone's details, he asked what had happened. But as Lexi started to explain, a shout rose up from the floor below, and he quickly excused himself and rushed out, telling them all to stay there.

As Lexi comforted Debs, Billy walked over to the window and watched as more vehicles pulled up outside. When he saw a Rapid Response Unit among them he knew something serious was going on and, guessing that the bloke who'd been stabbed in the other room must have pegged it, he flashed a look back at the sobbing woman, who he assumed to be the man's girl-friend.

'What is it?' Lexi asked, gazing over at him.

He gave a little shake of his head, and then pulled a pack of tobacco out of his pocket, asking, 'Anyone mind if I smoke? Looks like we could be stuck in here for a while.'

'I'd rather you didn't,' the man from room two said stiffly.

'It's fine,' Lexi countered.

'He thought I was *you*,' Debs mumbled.

'What?' Wondering if she'd misheard, Lexi peered at her.

'The man . . . he thought I was you,' Debs repeated. 'He said your name.'

'Oh my God.' Lexi felt as if she'd been punched in the gut.

'I couldn't see his face, but I'm sure he was white,' Debs went on. 'I saw his wrist when him and Six started fighting, before . . .'

She tailed off and Lexi hugged her when her face crumpled

again. 'He's going to be fine,' she said, even though she had a horrible feeling that he wouldn't be.

The officer came back into the room, and said, 'You all need to come with me.'

'He's not dead, is he, mate?' Billy asked, squinting at him through the smoke from his cigarette.

'I can't give out any details,' the officer replied. 'But the house is now a crime scene and we need to clear everyone out.'

Sure that Six must be dead, Lexi put her arm around her sobbing friend as the officer herded them out of the room and down the stairs. In the hallway, two more officers were standing outside Ada's room, the door of which was open.

'Stay close to the wall and don't touch anything,' one of them ordered.

With the lights now on, Lexi's stomach dropped when she spotted a congealing pool of blood on the floor that she hadn't noticed in the dark. A smear of it led into Ada's room, and her legs almost gave way as her eyes followed it and she saw the woman's body inside.

'Don't look,' Billy said, putting an arm around her waist to hold her up as he helped her outside.

29

After shaking off the have-a-go hero who'd chased him, Adam
had run hell for leather to where he'd parked his car a few streets
away, and had then driven to The Danski, avoiding the roads
which he knew had cameras on them. As he let himself in, he
thanked God that he hadn't bothered to get the CCTV system
fixed when it broke down some months earlier; because there
would be no record of him being there out of hours if the police
checked. Hurrying straight to his office, he put on the clothes
he kept there for those times when he couldn't be bothered to
go home and get changed before opening up.

After bagging the blood-soaked clothes he'd taken off, along
with his jacket, shoes, scarf and gloves, he paced the floor and
thought about ringing his dad. He didn't want to, because his
old man would go apeshit if he admitted that he'd fucked up
again. But he didn't know what else to do.

Remembering the threat he'd made to that girl earlier, when
he'd lied and told her that he had CCTV footage of her, a plan
began to form in his mind, and he rushed over to the filing

cabinet in which there was a folder containing the phone numbers and addresses of everyone who worked for him. Barely able to remember any of the girls' names, because they were nothing more than walking pussies to him, he sifted through the file several times before finding the one he wanted. After taking a screenshot of her address, he opened the safe and took out the wad of emergency money he kept in there. Then, grabbing the bag of clothes that needed getting rid of, he left the office and took a bottle of Jack Daniel's from behind the bar before heading back to his car.

Tina Klein lived in a tiny two-bed end-of-terrace house a couple of miles away from the club where she'd been working until Adam Harvey had sacked her earlier that night. She despised the customers who groped and ogled her each night – but she despised herself even more, for leaving her beautiful four-year-old son, Caleb, alone in the house while she sold her soul. Each time she came home, her heart was filled with dread at the prospect that one of the neighbours might have been keeping tabs on her comings and goings and had the police take him away. And every time she saw that the padlock on his door was still intact and she opened it to see him sleeping, she cried tears of relief – and guilt.

She'd have given anything to have a normal, respectable job, but there was nothing going in her area that she was qualified for with child-friendly hours; and without the extra money she earned at the club to top up her Universal Credit, she couldn't afford to feed and clothe Caleb, never mind pay her bills.

With no help from her family, who had turned their backs on her when she'd decided to give Patrick another chance the previous year, only for him to walk out on her again and set up home with his new bitch, Fran, she'd been left with no option but to take the job at the club. But now, because she hadn't been able to satisfy her creepy boss, she was out of a job, and she'd been lying awake worrying about it for the last couple of hours.

When the doorbell rang at 4 a.m., she immediately thought that the man had followed through on his threat and reported her to social services. Shaking violently, convinced that she was about to lose her child and be charged with neglect, she pulled on her dressing gown and went to the door to face the inevitable. Shocked to find Adam Harvey on the step, and not the police or social services, she blinked at him in confusion.

'All right, Toni?' He grinned. 'Not disturbing you, am I?'

'It's Tina,' she murmured.

'I knew that.' He winked, turning on the charm that had always got him what he wanted in his earlier years. 'I brought you a present.' He held up the bottle of Jack Daniel's.

'Why?' she asked, wrapping the dressing gown tighter around herself when the icy early morning air bit into her flesh.

'I felt bad about what happened and wanted to apologize,' he lied. 'I shouldn't have sacked you.'

'Are you saying I can have my job back?'

'Yeah, course. Now can I come in, only it's fuckin' freezing out here?'

Still wary of him after the way he'd treated her earlier, but scared that he might sack her again if she refused to let him in, Tina stepped aside.

'Where's the kid?' Adam asked, closing the door behind him.

Eyeing him nervously as he slid the bolt into place, Tina said, 'He's sleeping. But he always wakes up really early, so he could get up anytime. And his dad usually calls round to see him before he goes to school,' she added, hoping that would put Adam off staying too long.

'Yeah, whatever,' Adam said, brushing past her and poking his head into the small sitting room before looking around the tiny kitchen. 'Anyone else here?' Smiling when she shook her head, he waved her into the kitchen, saying, 'Go get us some glasses then.'

'I can't drink,' Tina said, handing him a plastic cup off the draining board. 'If they smell it on me when I take my son to school, I'll get in trouble.'

'Suit yourself,' Adam said, sloshing a measure of booze into the cup and downing it in one before wiping his mouth on the back of his hand.

'You're bleeding.' Tina pointed out a red smear on his wrist.

'Cut myself when I was cooking,' Adam lied, pulling the cuff of his shirt down over it. 'Anyway, never mind that. I need a favour.'

'Oh?' Tina gave him a questioning look, wondering what on earth she could possibly have that he would need.

'If anyone asks, I need you to say I've been here with you all night,' Adam said, pouring another shot into the cup.

'Why?' Tina frowned, not liking the sound of that.

'You don't have to worry about the whys,' Adam said dismissively. 'I just need to know you'll do it.'

'I don't know,' Tina said cautiously. 'I can't afford to get into anything dodgy. If I lose my son—'

'You ain't gonna lose him,' Adam assured her. 'And I'm not asking you to do it for nothing.' He pulled a wad of money out of his pocket. 'There's a grand here,' he said, licking his finger to count off some of the notes. 'I'll give you two hundred upfront if you agree to do it, and the rest if you need to give me an alibi.'

Tina stared at the money and swallowed loudly. The club was cash-in-hand and paid way below the legal minimum wage, and the girls had to hand over any tips they made at the end of the night. Christmas was only a couple of months away, and she could only usually afford cheap second-hand toys from the charity shops for Caleb, but with that money she'd be able to buy him something new. And if she got the rest of the money he was promising on top, she'd be able to pay all her bills *and* do a proper food shop.

'OK, I'll do it,' she said, half expecting Adam to snatch the money back and tell her he'd been joking.

'Good girl,' he said, smiling as he handed the money over. Holding onto it when she reached for it, he warned, 'Don't even think about fucking me over or I *will* come after you. Understood?'

Tina's instincts were screaming at her to tell him to take his money and get out, but the thought of Caleb opening his presents on Christmas morning overrode her misgivings and she nodded her agreement.

'I knew I could rely on you,' Adam grinned, watching as she stashed the money inside her bra. 'Now hows about you and me head upstairs for a bit of fun, eh? And who knows . . . if you do it properly this time, I might think about making it a regular thing.'

Tina's heart sank. He was younger and far better looking than most of the revolting men who came to the club, but something just wasn't right about him. It wasn't only that he had as good as raped her in his office, it was the way he looked at and spoke to her and the other girls in general, like they were less than human. But if keeping him happy secured her job and benefitted her son, she didn't have much choice.

30

Ryan was up and getting ready for work when the doorbell rang, followed by several heavy raps on the knocker.

'Who the hell's that?' Nicole complained, squinting at him over the top of the duvet.

'Police,' Ryan said when he looked out of the window and saw a police van and an unmarked car parked outside.

'You what?' She sat up. 'What do they want?'

'How am I supposed to know?' Ryan said, heading out of the door. 'Stay there while I find out.'

Jumping out of bed when he'd gone, Nicole pulled on her dressing gown and crept out onto the landing to listen as Ryan opened the front door.

'Can I help you?' Ryan asked, eyeing the four uniformed coppers and the two in plain clothes – one male, one female – who were standing on the step.

'Are you Ryan King?' one of the uniforms asked, stepping forward.

'Yeah,' Ryan replied, immediately wondering if something had happened to his dad.

'I'm arresting you on suspicion of the murder of Ada Briggs and the attempted murder of James Stanley,' the copper said, slapping handcuffs on his wrists. 'You do not have to say anything, but anything you do say—'

'What's going on?' Nicole squawked, rushing down the stairs and out through the door. 'Why are you arresting my husband?'

The female detective took out her badge. 'Detective Inspector Benson, CID,' she introduced herself. 'You need to vacate the house while we conduct a search, Mrs King. But I'll need to ask you a few questions before you go.'

'Go to hell,' Nicole spat. 'I'm calling my solicitor.'

'Good idea,' Benson said, waving two of the officers inside while the others walked Ryan to the van.

31

Lexi and Billy had both been interviewed and were now sitting in the police station's busy reception area waiting for Debs. Still in her pyjamas, with the smelly jumper Billy had insisted on lending her on top, Lexi shivered every time the door opened and a blast of icy air blew in. Exhausted from lack of sleep, and still traumatized by the memory of Six's horrific injury and Ada's dead body, she prayed that the detectives who had interviewed her would take seriously her suspicion that Adam was behind both attacks. She might not have seen him, but if the man had said her name when he woke Debs, it had to be him. His drive-by after the threatening call from Nicole the other day, followed by the flowers with the weird message and the phone calls earlier that morning all pointed to him, and she hoped they would catch him and throw him in jail for the rest of his rotten life.

Glancing round when the door opened again, Lexi blinked in confusion when she saw two uniformed officers bringing Ryan inside in handcuffs. He looked over at her as he was booked in, and her heart fluttered when he locked eyes with her for the briefest of moments before being whisked through an internal door.

'What's up?' Billy asked.

'I know that man who was just brought in,' she replied quietly, conscious of the other people who were sitting close by. 'I hope it's got nothing to do with what happened.'

'If it is, he ain't the dude I chased,' Billy said. 'He's too tall, for starters. And didn't your mate say the bloke was white?'

'Yeah, but it was dark, so the police might not take her word for that,' Lexi said, looking round when the door opened again and a slim brunette wearing a smart grey trouser suit and heels swept in and walked over to the reception desk.

'Faye Dunlop for Ryan King,' the woman said.

'That must be his solicitor,' Lexi whispered.

'Looks like a ball-breaker,' said Billy. 'And he must have some serious dosh to hire her. She's got them red soles on her shoes.'

Lexi watched as the woman was buzzed in through the internal door. Seconds after it had closed behind her, it opened again, and Debs came out, wearing the grey tracksuit she'd been issued after her nightclothes were taken as evidence.

'Are you OK?' Lexi jumped up and rushed over to her.

Shoulders slumped, her eyes red and puffy from all the crying she'd done in the last few hours, Debs said, 'I will be. Did you ring work to let them know what's happened?'

'I haven't got my phone, but I'll do it when we get home.'

'Any word on Six?'

'They said they'd let us know when they get any news, but we haven't heard anything yet.'

Sighing, Debs sank down onto a chair.

'Shall I ask if someone can take us home?' Lexi asked, perching beside her.

'My sister's coming to pick me up,' Debs said. 'I can't face going back there today. Poor Ada,' she went on sadly. 'I know she was a witch, but she didn't deserve that. And he killed her dog, as well, you know? There was no need for that at all.'

'I know.' Lexi squeezed her hand. Then, lowering her voice, she said, 'Ryan was brought in just before you came out.'

'Theo's son?' Debs frowned. 'Why?'

'No idea. But he was in cuffs, so it must be serious. And then his solicitor turned up.'

'I doubt it's got anything to do with this,' Debs said.

'Bit of a coincidence if it isn't,' Lexi countered worriedly. 'I'll ring Theo when I get back; see if he's heard anything.'

'Debs?'

Looking round at the sound of the voice, Lexi was momentarily confused when she saw a woman who looked exactly like her friend approaching them.

'We're twins,' Debs explained as she stood up to greet her sister. 'Megs, this is my friend, Lexi.'

'Pleased to meet you.' Megs flashed a distracted smile at Lexi before turning back to her sister. 'John and the kids are outside in the car. Are you ready to get going?'

'Yeah, won't be a sec,' Debs said. Then, turning back to Lexi, she hugged her, saying, 'Look after yourself, hon.'

'You're coming back, aren't you?' Lexi asked, picking up on a note of finality in her friend's voice.

'I can't face it right now,' Debs admitted. 'I'll ring you when I'm feeling a bit stronger.'

Sad to think that she might not see her again for a while, that there would be no more shared dinners after work, or gossipy nights on the wine, Lexi said goodbye and watched as Debs and her sister walked out.

'You all right, love?' Billy asked, coming over and touching her shoulder. 'Wanna get out of here?'

'Yes please,' Lexi said, blinking back the tears that were stinging her eyes.

'It don't look like we're getting a lift off these fuckers, so I'll ring a cab,' he said. 'On me,' he added when she opened her mouth to tell him that she had no money on her.

'Thanks,' Lexi murmured, smiling gratefully as they made their way outside.

As they stood at the foot of the steps waiting for the taxi, a silver Mercedes pulled into the car park, and Lexi's stomach clenched when Nicole climbed out.

'What the fuck are *you* doing here?' Nicole spat when she reached them. 'It'd better not have anything to do with my Ryan, 'cos if I find out you've been sniffing around him again, I'll—'

'You'll what?' Lexi interrupted, in no mood for her nonsense. 'Send your rapist brother round to harass me again?'

'Shut that filthy mouth before I shut it for you!' Nicole hissed, jabbing a nail into Lexi's chest. 'No one believed your lies back in the day, and they definitely won't believe you now. But that doesn't mean I'm going to stand by and let you slander his good name.'

'Oi, that's enough,' Billy said, stepping between them.

'What's *this*?' Nicole sneered, looking him up and down in disgust before turning back to Lexi. 'Don't tell me you've sunk so low you're shagging tramps now?'

'Hey, I might be a tramp, love, but at least I ain't made of plastic,' Billy said. 'Now jog on, Barbie.'

'Do you know who I am?' Nicole asked, raising her chin. 'I'm Nicole Harvey, and my dad *owns* Manchester, so you'd best watch your mouth before he gets your disgusting teeth welded together!'

'Bring it on, sweetheart,' he laughed.

'It's OK, Billy, I've got this,' Lexi said, touching his arm.

'You've got *nothing*,' Nicole scoffed. 'Never did have, never will. Look at the state of you. And my *God* you stink,' she added, wafting a hand in front of her nose. 'You're just like your pathetic mother – and if you stop with this loser long enough, you'll end up in the same place as her, an' all.'

Eyes blazing, Lexi clenched her fists and pushed her face into Nicole's, hissing, 'You're lucky we're outside the police station or I'd make you pay for that. Now fuck off out of my face before I change my mind and rip those rats-tails right out of your ugly, blown-up head!'

Nicole's mouth flapped open, but the taxi Billy had ordered had just pulled in, so Lexi pushed past her and climbed into the back of it before she could think up a suitable comeback.

'I take it Ryan's the bloke you saw getting brought in?' Billy asked when he slid in beside her.

Lexi nodded and closed her eyes. It had been a horrendous night and morning, and her head was banging, so the last thing she'd needed was a screaming match with Nicole. She just hoped the bitch would leave her alone now, because she never wanted to clap eyes on her sneering, entitled face again.

32

Surprised to find the main door open when she arrived at work that morning, because Ryan was forever telling her to make sure it was locked, Brenda cautiously entered the reception area.

'Ryan, is that you?' she called out when she heard noises coming from the office.

'Morning, Bren,' Adam greeted her brightly as he strolled out.

'Morning,' she replied warily, glancing past him. 'Is Ryan in there?'

'Nope. Only me.'

'How did you get in?'

'With a key, obviously. Now if you've finished with the Spanish inquisition, make yourself useful and go get me a latte from Costa.'

'That's not my job,' Brenda said, walking behind the desk and slipping her coat off.

'It is now,' Adam countered. 'Oh, sorry, didn't my dad tell you he'd put me in charge?' he went on gloatingly. 'Oh well, you know now, so off you go, there's a good girl.' He flapped his hand in the direction of the door.

Furious, but unsure what was going on, Brenda decided she'd better do as he'd asked and pulled her coat back on.

'*Good girl my fucking arse*,' she muttered as she marched out, slamming the main door shut behind her. She was old enough to be his mother, and it would be a cold day in hell before she'd take orders from that arrogant little shit.

Ringing Danny as she walked back to her car, she said, 'What the hell's going on? Why is Adam at the office claiming you've put him in charge?'

'Sorry, I was going to tell you, but things have been a bit hectic,' Danny apologized. 'Don't worry, it's only temporary till I know what's happening with Ryan.'

'Why, what's wrong with him? He's not ill, is he?'

'He's been arrested on suspicion of murder.'

'*Murder?*' Brenda stopped walking. 'No way.'

'I don't know the ins and outs yet, but Faye'll bring me up to speed when she's finished at the station,' Danny said. 'Soon as I know what's what, I'll bell you.'

'You'd better hope he does get out,' Brenda huffed. 'You know I'd do anything for you, Danny, but I will *not* have that boy of yours treat me like a glorified coffee girl.'

'Don't let him get to you, darlin',' Danny soothed. 'Like I say, it's only temporary. If worst comes to worst and Ryan doesn't get out, I'll be coming back.'

'Are you sure that's a good idea?' Brenda asked. 'We don't want you getting arrested the second you step off the plane.'

'I'm not on the run, I've been lying low,' Danny reminded her. 'And I'd have come back ages ago if Rachel hadn't insisted on staying, so this might be the kick up the arse I needed.'

'It'll be good to see you if you do,' Brenda said as she unlocked her car and climbed in.

'Ditto,' Danny said. 'Speak to you later.'

Smiling at the thought of the real boss coming back, Brenda turned the key in the ignition and set off to do the devil's bidding.

Back at the unit, Adam had chucked Ryan's shit out of the office that now he considered to be his, and was sitting with his feet up on the desk. This day had been a long time coming, and he was ecstatic that it had all panned out so smoothly. He'd been wasting his time trying to kill Ryan, because the fucker had a charmed life – or, at least, he *had* until this morning. Not only had the bastard been arrested, meaning that the police probably wouldn't bother looking for anyone else and Adam wouldn't need the alibi he'd paid Tina for, but big daddy had personally asked him to look after the business. It might only be a convenience thing in his dad's mind, but it had opened the door for Adam to prove his worth, and he intended to start putting some long-held plans into action to do just that.

As smart as his dad and Ryan thought they were, neither had his vision or ambition. They were happy to continue supplying the mid-level dealers in the ghetto, but they had never even considered branching out into the goldmine that was the city centre, where the Armani-suited men and women who occupied the office blocks and penthouse apartments snorted coke for breakfast, lunch and dinner. Adam had seen the potential of infiltrating that market many years ago, but it would take serious money to secure the amount of gear he'd need to get started, so he'd never stood a chance on his own. But now he had ousted Ryan, he was in prime position to make his dreams a reality.

33

Ryan had been shocked to see Lexi at the station when he was brought in – and even more shocked to hear that the murder and attempted murder he'd been arrested for had occurred at her house. With no clue as to why he'd been linked to the crimes, his head had been all over the place as he and Faye waited for the detectives to start their interview. Nic still hadn't tackled him about the text she'd read on his phone, but she had warned Lexi that she would kill her if Lexi didn't stay away from him, and he wondered if she had somehow found out about him going round there the next day and had sent someone to attack Lexi, only they'd got it wrong and killed the other woman instead. She definitely had the ability to do that, because all she'd have to do was ring Daddy and get him to arrange it for her. But why would she try to implicate him in it if she was that desperate to keep him? It didn't make sense.

When, at last, DI Benson and her colleague, DC Lynes, arrived and the interview began, the first question they asked was where Ryan had been between the hours of two and three a.m. that morning.

'I was in Stockport from midnight till around half two,' he said. 'I think I got home at about ten to three.'

'And who were you with?'

'A friend,' Ryan said evasively, reluctant to give his father's name in front of the solicitor in case she recognized it and told Danny. 'I can give you the address. I'm sure they've got cameras inside and outside the block.'

Benson made a note of the address and handed it to the uniformed officer who was standing in, asking him to take it to someone on her team to get it checked out. Turning back to Ryan when the man had gone, she said, 'What can you tell me about your relationship with Alexis James?'

'What?' Ryan frowned. 'Nothing. We haven't got a relation-ship.'

'But you *are* friends?'

'Yeah. Well, kind of. She was my wife's best mate when we were kids.'

'We have information that you recently visited Ms James at her home address. Is that correct?'

'I did call round there a few days ago, yeah.'

'And what was the purpose of that visit?'

Acutely aware of the solicitor sitting beside him taking everything in, Ryan shifted in his seat. 'Lexi and my wife had an argument, and Nic got it into her head that me and Lexi are having an affair.'

'And are you?'

'No.'

'So why did you go round there?'

'Because Lexi rang me. She was upset about them falling out, and she'd just seen Nic's brother driving past. They've got history, so she was a bit freaked out.'

'And you went to comfort her?'

'It wasn't like that,' Ryan murmured, conscious that it probably sounded *exactly* like that.

'Did you enter Ada Briggs's room on that occasion?'

'I didn't go into any room apart from Lexi's. You can ask her housemates, 'cos two of them saw me there. I don't know their names, but they were in the room opposite hers and they had the door open when I came out, so they both saw me leave.'

'Are you referring to Deborah McKinley and James Stanley?'

'No idea. The bloke's the one who let me in: big guy with red hair and a beard. I only caught a glimpse of the woman when I was leaving, so all I can tell you is she's got short dark hair.'

'When you say they saw you leave, I assume you mean from Ms James's room on the first floor, not the actual house?' said Benson. 'In which case they wouldn't have known if you had any communication with Ms Briggs.'

'I didn't see or speak to anyone else in there. I went straight out after I left Lexi's room.'

Benson had brought a small plastic evidence bag into the room. She pushed it across the table now, saying, 'Can you explain how this came to be in Ada Briggs's room? For the record, I'm showing the suspect a credit card bearing the names *DH Deliveries* and *Mr Ryan King.*'

'That's my company credit card,' Ryan said, his frown deepening when he leaned forward to look at it and saw that it was caked in blood. 'But I keep it in the safe at work, so I've got no idea how it could have got there.'

'This same card was used to purchase a bouquet of flowers from a florist's shop called Occasions,' Benson went on. 'The transaction was made over the phone by a man who gave your name. The flowers were delivered to a Ms Lexi James at Daisy Nook Residential Care Home in Didsbury at ten fifteen a.m. yesterday. Can you explain that?'

'No, but it definitely wasn't me,' Ryan insisted. 'I knew nothing about the flowers till Lexi rang and asked if I'd sent them.'

'I need to consult with my client,' Faye interjected.

Nodding, Benson paused the recording, and she and DC Lynes left the room.

Alone, Faye turned to Ryan, and said, 'If you sent those flowers you need to tell me right now. And why is the name Lexi James familiar to me?'

'When I first met you, you were getting set to defend Adam in a rape case,' said Ryan. 'She was the girl who'd accused him, and I was the witness. And, *no,* I didn't send her the flowers.'

'So why would she think that you had? Is something going on between you?'

'No. She didn't know who they were from, so I presume she rang all her friends.'

Faye studied him through narrowed eyes for a moment, before saying, 'If you're having an affair with her and you're worried about Nicole finding out, I can assure you she won't hear it from me. I'm more concerned about who could have used that card to send flowers to a woman you've already admitted to visiting in the house where the murder was committed. And, more importantly, how it ended up in the victim's room covered in her blood.'

'I've got no idea,' Ryan said truthfully. 'It's for company expenses, but I've got an app on my phone so I don't need the actual card. That's why I keep it in the safe.'

'Who has access to the safe?'

'Only me and Danny.'

'What about the secretary?'

'No.'

'Nicole?'

'Definitely not. Danny told me not to even write the code down in case she gets her hands on it, 'cos he knew she'd be helping herself to money out of it left, right and centre.'

'Adam, then?'

'No.' Ryan shook his head. 'Even if he knew the code, Brenda wouldn't let him anywhere near the office if I wasn't there.'

'Well, if you say you didn't take the card out, somebody else obviously knows the code,' said Faye. 'Maybe we should get the CTTV recordings checked; see if anyone went into the office when you weren't there.'

'We don't have CCTV,' Ryan told her. 'Danny had the system dismantled when he opened the company. He reckons they're too easy to hack, and he didn't want anyone being able to listen in on what gets discussed in there.'

'Sounds about right.' Faye rolled her eyes.

'It's not looking good, is it?' Ryan asked.

'No,' Faye said bluntly. 'The card being there doesn't prove that you'd been in that room, but if you add in the fact that those flowers were bought with it in *your* name, for the woman your own wife thinks you're having an affair with, well . . .' She tailed off and shrugged. 'You've got to admit that does look suspicious.'

'Yeah, it does, but it wasn't me,' Ryan said quietly.

Faye had no more questions, so they sat in silence waiting for the detectives to return. Thinking over everything he'd heard, Ryan began to lean toward Adam as the culprit. A man had called the flower shop claiming to be him, so it definitely hadn't been Nic – although she could have put him up to it. She also had access to the keys to the office, so she could have given him a spare. Neither of them knew the code to the safe, as far as he knew, but one of them could easily have seen their dad entering it when he was still in charge. It would certainly explain those times when Ryan had felt sure that things had been moved in there in the past. At the time he'd assumed that it must be Brenda, that maybe she'd gone in to get a pen or do a little tidying up, but what if it had been Adam all along?

The more he thought about it, the more likely it seemed that Adam might be behind all of this – in which case, it was entirely possible that he was also responsible for his brakes failing and the dead rat that had been sent to him. Adam had made no secret of the fact that he hated him, and he was twisted with jealousy about his dad handing the thriving family business over to him – especially so since his club appeared to be haemorrhaging money. But was he capable of cold-blooded murder?

A tap came at the door, and Ryan sat up a little straighter when the detectives re-entered the room.

'About time,' Faye said frostily. 'I was starting to think you'd forgotten we were here.'

'I apologize for the delay,' DI Benson replied coolly. Then, to Ryan, she said, 'You're free to go, Mr King. One of my colleagues attended the address you gave in Stockport and spoke to your father, who confirmed that you were with him last night. The CCTV footage of you arriving and leaving at the times you stated verified your statement, so no further action will be taken.'

Relieved that the detective hadn't named his father, and hoping that Faye wasn't aware that he wasn't supposed to be in contact with him, Ryan stood up.

'So I'm free to go?'

'For now,' said Benson. 'But we might need to speak to you again at some point, because we still need to ascertain how your credit card found its way to the murder scene – *and* who used it to purchase those flowers, if you're insisting it wasn't you.'

'It wasn't, and I'm happy to talk to you anytime,' Ryan agreed. 'Can I get my clothes back now?'

'I'm afraid they've already been sent to the lab, along with those taken from your home,' Benson said. 'But I'll arrange to have them brought back to you when they're released.'

Thanking her, Ryan turned to Faye. 'Ready?'

'I'll be out in a minute,' she said. 'I need a quick word with DI Benson first.'

Nodding, Ryan left the room and made his way to the reception area.

Nicole was sitting by the door. Jumping up when she saw him, she rushed over. 'What's happening? Have they let you go? Why are you wearing that horrible tracksuit? They're not keeping you in, are they? Where's Faye, and—'

'Nic, please stop talking,' he pleaded, his head already banging from the hours of waiting for the interview to start, followed by the tension of realizing he'd been set up.

'Can we get out of here?' Nicole asked, pulling a face as she added, 'I been sat here for hours, and the stench of BO and poor people is killing me.'

Flashing an apologetic look at a scruffy man who was glaring at them, Ryan pushed the door open and waved Nicole outside, saying, 'Why don't you go and wait in the car? Faye'll be out in a minute and I need to speak to her.'

'About what?' Nicole frowned. 'I thought they'd let you go?'

'They have, but that doesn't mean it's over,' said Ryan. 'I'll explain later. OK?'

'Whatever,' Nicole huffed. 'But hurry up, 'cos I've got an appointment to get my extensions done in an hour and I don't want to be late.'

'I'll get a lift off Faye if you need to get going,' Ryan said. 'I'm only going home to pick up my car, then I'm going to the office.'

'Adam's there, so there's no rush,' Nicole said.

'You what?' Ryan scowled.

'My dad sent him to look after things when I told him you'd been arrested,' Nicole explained. 'We didn't know how long you were going to be in here, so he had to do *something*.'

'Did you give him the key?'

'No, he's got his own,' Nicole said, confirming what Ryan had suspected. 'But he wouldn't have been there long anyway, 'cos my dad'll be taking over when he gets back.'

'And when will that be?' Ryan asked.

'He hasn't given me an exact date, but I reckon it'll be soon,' said Nicole. 'And that reminds me,' she went on. 'We need to find a place of our own ASAP, 'cos there's no way I'm living with my mum again. I've already rung an estate agent and asked them to put together a list of apartments in the Northern Quarter, so I'll pick the brochures up while I'm in town. That'll be so much better for us than a house, won't it?'

'Yeah, whatever,' Ryan muttered, his mind on more important things. 'Anyway, get yourself off to your appointment. I'll see you later.'

Behind the door, Faye had been watching Ryan and Nicole through the reinforced glass as she waited for an answer to the call she had placed after speaking to DI Benson. She liked Ryan and had always thought him to be a decent man. He was also extraordinarily handsome, and if she were twenty years younger she most definitely wouldn't say no. His wife, on the other hand, was her mother's daughter through and through, and Faye couldn't abide either of them. But she and Danny Harvey went way back, and he was the one who paid her, so her loyalties would always lie with him.

'It's Faye,' she said, when at last her call was answered. 'His alibi checked out so they've let him go, but there's something I think you should know . . .'

34

Worried after the visit from the detective, who had told him that Ryan had been arrested but not why, Theo had driven over to Stretford police station, where he'd been told his son was being held. Parked across the road now, from where he had a good view of the entrance without being too conspicuous in case someone he knew was in there, he was about to wind his window down and whistle when he spotted Ryan coming out, but changed his mind when he saw that he was with a blonde woman. Guessing that it must be the infamous daughter-in-law he had heard so much about but never met, he watched as she and Ryan talked for a minute before she walked down the steps and climbed into a Mercedes. Almost immediately, another woman – an older, attractive brunette in an expensive-looking suit – came out and joined Ryan.

Theo slid down in his seat when the Mercedes pulled out of the station parking lot and drove past him. Seconds later, a black Audi A7 being driven by the brunette went past, and Theo started his engine and set off after it when he clocked Ryan in the passenger seat.

Ryan had spotted his dad's car as Faye drove out of the car park, and he could see him now, in the side mirror, tailing them a few cars behind.

Eager to get away from Faye, who had been acting cagey since leaving the station, Ryan jumped out of the car as soon as she pulled up outside his house and he saw that Nicole's car wasn't there.

'Thanks for the lift. But I won't invite you in, if you don't mind. I'm just gonna get changed and head over to the office.'

'No problem.' Faye smiled. 'Speak soon.'

Nodding, Ryan tapped the roof of her car and watched as she drove away. When she'd turned the corner at the end of the road, he looked the other way and held up his hands, indicating that he would be ten minutes, when he spotted his dad's car. A flash of headlights told him that his dad had got the message, so he ran up the path and, taking the spare key that Nicole had insisted – against his advice – on hiding under a plant pot, entered the house.

The police had trashed the place, but he wasn't concerned about that. Rushing upstairs, he hurriedly changed out of the tracksuit he'd been given at the station and then chucked a load of his clothes into the large sports bag he kept in the back of the wardrobe before looking for his phone. Unable to find it after searching all over the house, he guessed the police must have taken it along with his other clothes. But his dad had all the numbers he needed, so he took one last look around to make sure he hadn't forgotten anything important and then left the house.

Unable to take the Range Rover, because it was registered to the company and he knew Danny would report it as stolen as soon as he realized what was happening, he walked down the road and climbed into his dad's car.

'What's happening?' Theo asked as he set off. 'Why did they arrest you? They wouldn't tell me nothing.'

'Someone tried to set me up for murder,' Ryan told him.

'Say *what?*' Alarmed, Theo swerved the car, almost hitting a stationary van.

'I'll explain everything later,' Ryan said, throwing his hand out to right the steering wheel. 'But we need to wrap things up ASAP. Danny's solicitor was there when the detective told me they'd been to see you. They didn't say your name, but she stayed behind for a few minutes after I left the room, and I think she might have asked for it, 'cos she was acting weird when she came out.'

'Damn,' Theo muttered. 'Is everything moved over?'

'Near enough, yeah. I was going to do the last lot today, but the police came to the house before I left for work, so I didn't get the chance. Nic told me that Danny sent Adam in to look after the place while I was away, so there's no way I can go back there now. She also said Danny's coming back soon to take over, but if Faye's told him about you, he's probably already on his way, so we need to disappear.'

'Right, OK,' Theo said. 'I'll call my guy when we get back to the flat; see if he can take that last batch early.'

'Let's hope he can, or we'll have to leave it,' Ryan said. 'Have you got your phone on you?' he asked then. 'The police took mine and I forgot to ask for it back before I left the station.'

'Yeah, here . . .' Theo slid it out of his back pocket and opened it with his thumbprint before handing it over. 'Who you ringing?'

'Lexi. I need to warn her.'

'About what?'

'The woman I was accused of murdering was her housemate.'

'Not Debs?'

'No, her name was Ada something. And some bloke got stabbed in the neck, as well.'

'Jeez, that's bad, man. Alexis wasn't involved, was she?'

Ryan gritted his teeth as the usual irritation rippled through him at the sound of his dad calling Lexi by that name. Swallowing it, he said, 'She was at the station when I got there. She looked tired, but she didn't seem injured, as far as I could tell.'

'Thank fuck for that.' Theo released a tense breath. 'So what do you need to warn her about?'

'I think it might have been Adam,' Ryan said. 'Remember she saw him driving past just before I got there the other day? And then she got flowers and asked if you'd sent them? Well, guess what . . . they were bought with my company credit card and the bloke who ordered them gave my name. And that's not the worst of it,' he went on. 'I keep the card in the office safe, but it was found in the dead woman's room, so it was obviously planted there by whoever bought the flowers. It's got to be him.'

'Fucker!' Theo snarled. 'I bet he's been following you and seen you with me, and now he's trying to stitch you up like his old man did to me.'

'I wouldn't put it past him,' Ryan said. 'But if he'd sussed us, I reckon he'd have told Danny by now.'

'Maybe he wanted to fuck you over first, to prove he's got what it takes to get back into the business.'

'Maybe. But we can't stick around to find out, 'cos Danny'll come after us all guns blazing once he knows.'

'Shame I can't be here to welcome the cunt home,' Theo spat. 'But this is gonna hurt him way more than me giving him the beating he deserves.'

'Yeah, it is,' Ryan agreed, allowing himself a bitter smile at the thought of the Harveys having to start over from scratch. 'But he's another reason I need to warn Lexi. The detective asked why I'd gone to hers that day, and I told her about Nic accusing us of having an affair. I don't think she believed me when I said we weren't, and the solicitor didn't either. If she tells Danny about it, he'll immediately assume Lexi was in on this.'

'Fuck,' Theo muttered. 'I didn't think of that. Hurry up and ring her then.'

Ryan brought up her number and pressed *Call*. It rang several times and then switched to voicemail.

'She's not picking up,' he said. 'She'd gone when I got out, so I'm assuming she went home. Do you think we should go round there? We're not that far away, are we?'

Theo didn't need asking twice and immediately detoured to Chamberlain Road. He stopped at the corner when they arrived a few minutes later and saw two police officers standing guard outside.

'It's still taped off, so they won't have let her in,' he said. 'She's probably gone to stay with a friend.'

'I hope so,' Ryan said. 'But I'll leave a message asking her to ring us before she goes back in, just in case.'

35

Lexi's dig about her extensions looking like rats-tails had stung, and Nicole had booked an appointment with her stylist while she was waiting for Ryan at the station. Home now and feeling on top of the world with her freshly done hair and her skin still tingling from the facial she'd had while she was there, she was surprised to see Ryan's car parked in the driveway. Hoping that he'd decided to come back early so they could spend some quality time together after their ordeal, she rushed inside and called his name. No reply came, and she realized that he mustn't be home after all when she saw that all the lights were off.

Disappointed, because she'd been looking forward to the two of them going through the brochures she'd picked up from the estate agent, she put her bag down on the table and pulled out her phone. She always switched it off when she had a long session at the salon or the clinic, because she liked to be pampered in peace. When she switched it back on now, she saw that she'd missed a load of calls off her dad. Assuming that he'd been ringing to find out what was happening, and that Faye would probably have filled him in by now, she rang Ryan and tutted when it went straight to voicemail.

Leaving a message asking him to ring her when he was on his way home, she walked into the kitchen and poured a large glass of wine before heading upstairs. Running a bath and pouring in some of her favourite scented oil, she went into the bedroom to get undressed. The police had pulled the contents out of every drawer, and she muttered a curse under her breath as she scooped up a pile of her bras and panties off the floor and dropped them onto the bed. As she turned to get more, something struck her as odd, and she pursed her swollen lips as she tried to figure out what it was. A sickly feeling washed over her when it came to her that, apart from a couple of pairs of Ryan's boxers and a few pairs of socks, the underwear was all hers. Rushing to the wardrobe, the feeling of dread intensified when she saw that his sports bag was gone, along with most of his jeans and T-shirts.

Jumping when her phone started to ring on the bedside table, she dived across the bed and grabbed it.

'Where the fuck have you been?' her dad barked when she answered. 'I've been trying to get hold of you all day.'

'Sorry, I was at the salon so my phone was off.'

'Where's that fucking husband of yours? Put him on.'

'He's not here,' Nicole said miserably. 'I just got home and some of his stuff is missing. I think he might have left me, Dad. What am I gonna do?'

'Quit whingeing for starters, and tell me what you know about Theo Walker,' Danny snapped. 'And I'd better not find out you knew about them and didn't tell me, or I'll—'

'What you shouting at *me* for?' Nicole cut in. 'And who the hell's Theo Walker?'

'Your fucking *father-in-law*, that's who,' spat Danny. 'The one Ryan was with last night who gave him the alibi that got him released.'

'What?' Nicole was confused. 'But his dad's locked up in Jamaica, so how could he have been with him? And his name's Delroy, not Theo.'

'No it ain't, he's been lying from the off,' said Danny. 'Our Adam always said he only got with you to get to me, and he was fuckin' right.'

'What are you talking about?' Nicole frowned.

'He's ripped me off,' Danny said angrily. 'I checked the accounts after Faye rang me, and they're all empty. And I'll bet my life it was him who had away with those shipments that went missing, an' all.'

'He wouldn't do that,' Nicole insisted, refusing to believe that Ryan would rip off her dad, because that meant he'd ripped *her* off too. 'It could be a glitch at the bank, for all you know. At least give him a chance to explain before you start gunning for him.'

'Too late,' spat Danny. 'And you'd best get your head out of the clouds, 'cos if we don't get that money back, we're fucked. And by fucked, I mean the house'll be getting sold, and the motors, and all them expensive bags and shoes you and your mam are obsessed with.'

Horrified by the thought of losing her lovely things, Nicole jumped up when she heard the front door opening down below. 'Dad I've got to go,' she said. 'I, er, left the bath running and I think it's overflowing.'

'Well, you'd best get it sorted before we get back, or your mam'll go apeshit,' said Danny. 'And make sure our room's ready.'

'Why? When are you coming?' Nicole asked as she rushed out onto the landing.

'We'll be there in about half an hour by my reckoning,' Danny replied.

'What?' Her mouth fell open. 'You *are* joking?'

'No I ain't. We just got off the plane, so I'll see you in a bit.'

Muttering, '*Shit!*' when the line went dead, Nicole raced down the stairs, yelling, 'Ryan, my dad's gonna be here in half an hour and he's going to kill you, so you need to—'

She abruptly stopped speaking when she entered the kitchen and saw her brother leaning back against the counter with a glass of whisky in his hand and a sly smile on his lips.

'Surprise,' he drawled, raising the glass to her.

'What are you doing here?' she asked.

'Dad rang and said they're on their way home, so I thought it'd be nice if we were both here to welcome them,' said Adam. 'Not sure it'll be a happy reunion once Mum clocks the state of this place, though,' he added, looking pointedly at the mess.

'The police did it,' Nicole said, making a half-hearted effort to pick up some of the stuff off the floor.

'Mum would have had it cleaned up the minute they left, like she used to all those times we got raided back in the day,' Adam reminded her.

'I've got bigger things to worry about than fucking *cleaning*,' Nicole yelled, hurling a tea towel at him. 'Ryan's gone, and Dad wants to kill him!'

'And so he should, seeing as the cunt's had away with every fucking penny we've got.'

'No he hasn't! He wouldn't do that to me.'

'You ain't stupid so quit acting it,' Adam said. Tutting when she let out a howl and buried her face in her hands, he walked over and put his arms around her, saying, 'I know me and you haven't always got on, but you're my little sister and I've been trying to warn you about him for years. You couldn't see it 'cos you're not a bloke, but I could tell he wasn't really into you from the start. And you know who his old man is, don't you?'

'Delroy King,' Nicole sniffed, pulling away from him and grabbing a piece of kitchen roll to blow her nose.

'No, it's Theo Walker – the bloke who got sent down for murdering that copper when we were kids,' Adam told her. 'Remember that?'

'Vaguely.'

'Yeah, well, what you *won't* know is him and Dad used to be best mates. They were working together and had started to make a load of money, then he tried to cut Dad out and frame him for the shooting. Only it backfired on him, 'cos he got caught red-handed with the gun before he could plant it on Dad.'

'Even if that's true, it's got nothing to do with Ryan.'

'You don't think it's a coincidence that he got with you a few years after Theo went down?' Adam asked. 'He knew exactly who you were, and he used you to get in with Dad.'

'If that was all he wanted, he wouldn't have married me and stayed with me this long.'

'He's been playing you like a fiddle from the off,' Adam sneered. 'And he played Lexi, an' all.'

'Do not mention that bitch in my house,' Nicole spat.

'I know you hate her, but this is all his doing,' Adam went on. 'I don't know how, but it was him who persuaded her to try to get me done for rape. It all fell into place when I saw him leaving hers the other day when you sent me round there.'

'He was there?' Nicole's face fell. 'You told me you hadn't seen him.'

'I said that to protect you,' Adam lied, reaching for the bottle of whisky to pour another shot. 'But it's not like she's the first.'

'What?'

'Ah . . .' Adam gave a fake-remorseful grimace. 'Soz. I assumed you and him had the same shit going on as Mum and Dad. All that *the man can fuck whoever he wants so long as she ain't family shizz.*'

'Who else has he been with?' Nicole demanded, her eyes now blazing.

'Don't shoot the messenger,' Adam said, holding up his hands. 'But you know how you always have a go at me for making him come to the club to drop off my money? Well, let's just say *he's* the one who set that up. And once he was in, he had a habit of staying till the end – know what I mean?'

'You're lying,' Nicole hissed, glaring at him as she sank onto a chair. 'He'd never go near one of those skanky bitches. Why would he when he's got *me*?'

'Don't ask me.' Adam shrugged. 'But those bitches let men do shit their wives would *never* let 'em do.'

'I've never stopped Ryan doing anything,' Nicole argued. 'We've got a great sex life.'

'Whoa!' Adam screwed up his face. 'T M I, Sis, T M fuckin' I. Anyway, I'm only telling you this so you'll stop fantasizing about your perfect marriage, 'cos it's a sham – like him. If Dad had put me in charge in the first place, none of this would have happened,' he went on self-righteously. 'But now he knows what a mistake that was, we'll get the company back on track in no time – you watch.'

'I don't see how, if Ryan's stolen all the money,' Nicole muttered.

'Don't you worry your little head about that,' Adam said, winking at her. 'I've got big plans. And now that idiot's out of the way, Dad's bound to give me the go-ahead to start putting them into action.'

Nicole narrowed her eyes when she saw his smug grin. 'It was *you*, wasn't it?' she said. 'You shifted all the money into another account when you got in there today, didn't you?'

'What's this?' Danny asked, walking in before Adam could answer and dropping the holdall he was carrying onto the table.

Almost jumping out of her skin because she hadn't heard him come in, Nicole turned to him, and pointed at Adam, saying, 'He did it, Dad. He moved the money out of the accounts so you'd blame Ryan.'

'Fuck off,' Adam snapped, quickly pouring a whisky for his dad. 'I'd never rip my own family off. What d'you take me for?'

'I'm not saying you were going to *keep* it,' Nicole argued. 'But Ryan's been running things for years and nothing's ever gone missing, and the minute *you* go in, the accounts get emptied. Bit of a coincidence, don't you think?'

'Don't be blaming your brother to get that fucker off the hook,' Danny barked.

'Come on, Dad, it's obvious,' Nicole persisted. 'He's always hated Ryan, and this is his way of getting rid of him and getting back in with you.'

'Too right I hate him,' Adam said. 'He's a parasite and he's been leeching off us for years – *and* I got pushed out of my own family because of him. He's the one who made Lexi tell the police that bullshit story about me trying to rape her, an' all. He was obviously fucking her the whole time – and still *is*!'

'No he isn't!' Nicole cried.

'So why did you tell me they were having an affair and beg

me to go round to her place to see if he was there?' Adam shot back. 'Which he *was*, by the way,' he went on, speaking to his father now. 'And I've got the pictures on my phone to—'

'*NICOOOOOLE* . . . !' Rachel's furious screech echoed around the hallway, silencing Adam and making even Danny wince. Then, marching into the kitchen, she glared at Nicole. 'What the *fuck* have you done to my house?'

36

Exhausted, concerned about her friends, and worried that she might have dropped Ryan in it when she'd mentioned him after the police had asked for the names of any recent visitors to the house, Lexi gave Billy a wan smile when he handed a cup of tea to her. He'd invited her into his room after arriving home from the police station to find her house taped off, and she felt guilty for the way she had dismissed him on sight as someone to be avoided on her first day there. There weren't many people who would have leapt into action the way he had last night; not only putting himself in danger by chasing the man who'd broken into her house, but also potentially saving Six's life. And then he'd paid for a cab home and had told her that she could stay at his place for as long as she needed to – all above and beyond anything she could have hoped for, considering she was a virtual stranger to him.

'Mind if I smoke?' Billy asked, holding up the spliff he'd just rolled. 'I'll go outside if it's gonna bother you.'

'Don't be daft,' Lexi said. 'If my head wasn't so mashed already, I'd probably have a bit with you.'

'Serious?' He gave a questioning grin.

'Why do you look so surprised?' she asked.

''Cos you're posh, like,' he said.

'Oh my God, you've got to be joking,' Lexi laughed. 'I grew up on the Kingston and I've lived hand to mouth my entire life. Didn't you hear what my *friend* said back at the station?'

'To be honest, her lips were distracting me too much to pay any mind to what she was saying,' Billy snorted. 'What's with birds who do that shit to themselves?'

'Don't ask me.' Lexi shrugged. 'She was stunning when we were younger, so I've got no idea why she went down that road. Actually, no, that's not true,' she corrected herself. 'Her mum was the Botox queen of Manchester, so I guess it was obvious she'd follow suit.'

'Give me a natural girl any day,' Billy said, shaking his head as he lit his spliff and opened the window. 'Shit,' he muttered, quickly closing it again when he leaned out and saw one of the coppers outside Lexi's house look up. 'I forgot them fuckers was out there.'

'Just sit down and smoke it,' Lexi said. 'I honestly don't mind.'

Doing as she'd said, Billy flopped onto his shabby sofa and took a drag. Squinting at her as he exhaled the smoke, he said, 'I hope you don't think I'm being nosy – and tell me to mind me own if you don't want to answer – but what did the blow-up doll mean about you ending up in the same place as your mam?'

Grip tightening on her cup, Lexi took a deep breath, before saying, 'My mum was murdered by my stepdad when I was fifteen.'

'Shit, I'm sorry,' Billy said. 'No wonder you looked like you wanted to kill her. What a fuckin' troll for throwin' that in your face. That's low, man.'

'Nothing she says could surprise me anymore,' Lexi murmured, sipping her tea.

Billy took another drag on his smoke. Then, noticing her eyes starting to droop, he said, 'Why don't you lie down for a bit, love? I need to nip out, so you'll have the place to yourself. And I usually kip on the sofa, so you're welcome to the bed.'

'Are you sure?' Lexi asked, concerned that she might be putting him out. 'I don't mind taking the sofa.'

'I'm positive,' he said, getting up and pulling his jacket on. 'And if you want owt to eat, my stuff's on the top shelf of the fridge. Help yourself.'

'Thanks,' Lexi said gratefully. 'I'll pay you back when this is over.'

'Like fuck you will,' he snorted. 'Mates don't do shit to *get* shit.'

'You're a good man.' She smiled.

'You're not so bad yourself, kidda,' he said with a wink.

Finishing her tea when he'd gone, Lexi looked around as she made her way over to the bed. The room was an absolute mess of empty food cartons and beer cans; the walls were covered in dark posters of punk and heavy metal bands, and a Union Jack flag was tacked to the top of the window in place of curtains. It smelled pretty bad, too, and the cheap air freshener Billy had sprayed around the place when they first came in had only added a weird chemical smell to the stale air. But she didn't care about any of that; she was just grateful not to be out on the street.

Over on the Riverside estate, Nicole had finished cleaning – under orders from her mother, who was in the foulest mood ever – and had just carted her stuff and what was left of Ryan's into her old room. Chucking it down on the floor, she threw herself onto the bed and screamed into the pillow. This was supposed to be *her* house now, but her mum had told her in no uncertain terms that it had only ever been on loan to her. The bitch had also gone off her head about all the changes Nicole had made, raging about the furniture she'd replaced, and making out like her old grandma-style decor had been better than the classy paper Nicole had chosen.

Nicole had never hated anyone as much as she hated her mother right then, and she cursed God under her breath for allowing their plane to land safely instead of crashing into the sea. Sitting up, fresh tears welled in her eyes when her gaze landed on the brochures she'd picked up from the estate agent, detailing the plush city-centre apartments she had planned on viewing with Ryan. She had been so excited at the prospect of moving up in the world, but now Ryan had gone missing, and her dad had called his old mates together to hunt him down, her dreams were in tatters.

Gritting her teeth when she heard her name being called, Nicole tossed the brochures aside and stomped down the stairs. Her dad was sitting at the head of the kitchen table, as if he'd never been away, with her mum on his right and Adam on his left, while the three men from his original crew – who all looked like ancient boxers to her, with their scarred faces, beady eyes and tattooed hands – were sitting side by side opposite them.

'What?' She stopped in the doorway and folded her arms.

'Get that look off your face before I slap it off,' her mother warned. 'And sit down.'

Flouncing over to the table, arms still folded, Nicole flopped down onto a vacant chair next to one of the bruisers, whose name she vaguely remembered was Mash, short for Machete.

'Put the password in,' Danny said, shoving a laptop across the table to her.

Glancing at the screen and seeing that it was open on the Lloyds online banking page, she said, 'I don't know your password. You never gave it to me.'

'Not mine, *yours*,' said Danny.

'Why?' Nicole frowned. 'That's mine and Ryan's personal account. You can't just help yourselves to our money 'cos you've lost yours. That's not fair.'

'Whatever you've got in there it came from *us*, so quit being cagey and do as you're fucking told,' Rachel ordered, slapping her hand down hard on the tabletop.

'I'm not being cagey,' Nicole muttered, tears of humiliation smarting her eyes when the men all stared at her. 'But I don't want everyone seeing what we've got.'

'We ain't gonna take your fucking money,' Danny assured her. 'We just want to see if he's used any of his cards since he's been gone, so we know where he's been.'

As Nicole reluctantly tapped in the password, Danny's phone started ringing, and all eyes turned on him when he said, 'Well?' Hanging up after a few seconds, he said, 'Theo Walker's place has been cleared out.'

'Already?' Rachel asked. 'They'd have needed a van for that, surely.'

'I'm talking about his personal shit, not the furniture,' said Danny. 'You sure you didn't tell Ryan I was on my way back?' This he aimed at Nicole.

'She *would* have, given half a chance,' Adam piped up. 'She heard me coming in and thought I was him; ran down the stairs like her arse was on fire to warn him.'

'I couldn't have spoken to him even if I'd wanted to,' Nicole said, shooting daggers at her brother. 'His phone's off.'

'We need to find Lexi,' Rachel said, pouring herself a fresh glass of wine. 'If they've been at it, she'll know where he is. It'll take me two seconds to get the truth out of the tramp.'

'I need to go over and check on the club, so I can drive past her place and see if the pigs have gone yet,' Adam offered.

'Yeah, do that,' Danny said. 'But don't be getting pulled, 'cos you've necked half a bottle of my fuckin' whisky since we got back.'

'I've only had a couple,' Adam lied, grinning as he got up and pulled his jacket on. This was the first time he had ever been allowed into his dad's inner circle, and he intended to hold onto his new-found position of trust with both hands.

Lexi woke to the sound of a door slamming followed by the squeal of gate hinges. Disorientated when she opened her eyes and found herself in a strange room, it took her a moment to remember where she was. Shoving the grubby duvet off her legs, she stumbled over to the window. It was dark outside and she quickly pushed the window open when she saw two police officers walking to a squad car that was parked across the road.

'Excuse me,' she called out. 'Are you leaving?'

'Yeah, all done,' one of the officers replied as his colleague climbed into a car and started the engine.

'Have you closed the front door?' she asked.

'All secured,' he assured her.

Muttering, '*Damn!*' when he got into the car and it pulled away, Lexi bit her lip, wondering what to do since she didn't have her keys. If Billy had been there, she would have asked if she could use his phone to ring Debs. Then she remembered that Debs hadn't had her phone or her keys on her when they had left the house, so she still wouldn't be able to get in even if she could get hold of her.

Unsure what time it was, because there didn't seem to be

any clocks in the room when she turned the light on, Lexi decided to go round to the back of her house and check if Six's fire-escape door was still unlocked. She didn't really fancy the idea of going into the house on her own, but she had no idea when Billy might be back, and she desperately wanted to take a shower and put on some clean clothes.

Billy's door clicked shut behind her, and so did the back door when she let herself out. Aware that she wouldn't be able to get back in, and wishing she had waited for Billy, she hugged herself as she walked round to her own backyard. The metal fire escape steps were steep and slippery, and she gripped the handrail as she carefully made her way up.

Relieved to find that Six's door wasn't locked, she let herself in and turned the key before making her way out onto the landing. Unnerved by the deathly silence in the house, she peeked over the banister rail to make sure no one was lurking below before setting off down the stairs.

The door to her room was wide open, as was Debs's. The overhead light was also on in there, and she felt sick when she glanced inside and saw the blood on the floor and the mess of medical packagings the paramedics had left behind. Rushing into her own room, she locked and bolted the door before going over to the window to close the curtains Billy had opened to have his smoke.

More jumpy than she had ever felt in her life before, she decided she couldn't face taking a shower and got changed instead. Initially thinking that the police must have taken her phone when she saw that it wasn't where she had left it, she let out a little cry of relief when she saw the corner of it sticking out from behind her bedside cabinet and realized she must have knocked it off when she'd got up after hearing the man break into Debs's room.

Numerous missed call, text and voicemail notifications appeared on the screen, and her uneasiness intensified when she saw that the majority were from Nicole. They were mostly threats of what Nicole was going to do to her if she found out Ryan was with her, so she only read a few before deleting the rest.

The first voicemail was from Ryan.

Lexi, it's me. I'm with my dad and we're on our way to his place. Ring us as soon as you get this, and please don't go back to your place till we've talked.

The second was also from him, and sounded even grimmer than the first.

I don't know if you got my first message, but you need to ring me back as soon as you get this, Lexi. Danny Harvey's back. Ring me, it's urgent!

Listening to the third message, her stomach clenched when she heard Nicole's voice.

I tried to warn you but you left it too late you stupid bitch, and now my dad's coming after you both. I don't give a fuck about you, but if you care about Ryan at all, tell him to get away while he still can!

Hands shaking, Lexi plugged the charger into her phone

when she saw that the battery was almost dead. Afraid that Danny must already have caught up with Theo and Ryan when she tried to ring them and neither answered, she felt the walls closing in on her. She needed to get out of there, but where was she supposed to go? Billy was out, she had no clue where Debs's sister lived, and she didn't have enough money to catch a train to Hebden Bridge and throw herself on the mercy of one of her old friends there. The only other person she knew in Manchester whose number she had was Julie, but she'd already spoken to her when she had used Billy's phone earlier to make sure that work had been informed about what was happening, and knew that she had volunteered to do a double shift to cover for Six that night.

At the sound of footsteps outside, Lexi jumped up off the bed and rushed over to the window, hoping that Debs had decided to come back, or that the police had forgotten something. Deflated when she peeped round the edge of the curtain and saw a random man walking past, she was about to move away from the window when she caught him flick a hooded glance up at the house before crossing the road and heading toward a car that was parked at the end. Recognizing it as the car Adam had driven past in that day, her legs almost buckled beneath her.

Sure that he was after her, she grabbed her bag and her coat and yanked the charger cable out of her phone before running out of the room. Hesitating at the top of the stairs when she saw a shadowy figure through the glass of the front door, followed by the sound of a key slotting into the lock, she ran up the other stairs to Six's room. Unlocking the fire escape door, she took the key and, slipping outside, locked it behind her to prevent Adam – or whoever had entered the house – from coming after her.

Praying that Adam hadn't sent someone round to the back, she descended the slippery steps as fast as her shaking legs would allow and rushed out into the alley. No lights were on in Billy's place still, so she ran to the gate opposite hers and let out a little cry of relief when it opened. Inside the backyard, she saw someone moving around in the kitchen and, ducking down, ran to the window and tapped on it.

'Who's that?' an elderly woman asked, looking out.

Popping her head up, Lexi mouthed, 'Help me! *Please!*'

Seconds later, she heard a bolt being slid back on the door to her right, and then light spilled out. Still crouched over, she ran to the woman, and whispered, 'Please can I come in? I live at the back of you and—'

'In *that* house?' The woman's eyes widened.

Guessing that news of the murder had already spread, Lexi said, 'Yes, and I think the man who did it is in there now!'

'Oh my lord!' The woman clutched her dressing gown to her throat and stared over at the house.

'Please can I come in?' Lexi begged. 'I don't want to stay; I just need to escape before he comes after me.'

'Yes, of course,' the woman said, stepping back. 'Oh dear, how terrible.'

Thanking her, Lexi said, 'Phone the police and lock the door!' as she ran through the kitchen and out into the hallway. After peeping through the spyhole in the front door to make sure no one was out on the road, she let herself out and ran for her life.

In the car, Adam tipped a little heap of coke onto the back of his hand and snorted it. He'd got the rooms the wrong way round last night and had ended up on top of the fat bird instead of Lexi. Now he knew that the room on the other side was hers – *and* that she was definitely in, because her curtains had been open the first time he drove past but were now closed – he was ready to get the job done properly. But first, he needed Wes to give him the all-clear that no other fucker was in there as well, because he could do without getting another baseball bat aimed at him. Luckily he'd had a knife in his hand when the ginger yeti went for him, so he'd got out relatively unhurt, but he wasn't taking any chances.

Hyped up, his anticipation turned to irritation when he saw Wes come out of the house, and hurry back to the car.

'What you doing?' he asked when Wes climbed in.

'Place is empty,' Wes said, handing back the keys Adam had given him to let himself into the house. 'Must've been some fuckin' beast who killed the old bird and did the bloke in, though,' he went on as he lit a fag. 'Shoulda seen how much blood there was, man.'

Ego swelling at hearing himself being described in a way that was usually reserved for his father, Adam wished he could tell

319

Wes that he *was* that beast. But the coke had sharpened his mind enough to know that it would be foolhardy to expose himself when he'd already got away with it. He trusted Wes, but if the man got pissed and let something slip to one of the other guys, they'd grass him up in a heartbeat if they thought there might be a reward in it. So, keeping his mouth shut, he rang his dad to update him.

'The pigs have gone so I checked the place out,' he lied, aware that his dad would flip out if he told him he'd actually sent Wes in to do his dirty work. 'Someone was definitely in there when I drove past, but they must have left before I turned back, so what do you want me to do?'

'Nothing,' Danny said dismissively. 'I've had word the cunt's set up a meet in London, so I'll take it from here. You go play with your dollies – or whatever it is you do at that shithole you call a club.'

Fuming when the line went dead, Adam slammed his fist down on the steering wheel.

'Fuck's up with you?' Wes frowned at him.

'Shut your mouth,' Adam hissed, starting the engine.

'Yo, don't be acting like a bad man just 'cos your dad's back in town,' Wes warned him. 'And why'd you tell him it was you who went in?'

'Would you rather I told him it was you and let him shut your mouth *permanently*?' Adam asked. ''Cos that's what'd happen if I told him I'd brought you in on this. You're *my* soldier, not his, so he ain't gonna trust you like I do.'

320

'Fair enough.' Wes shrugged and took another drag on his cigarette. 'So who's the bird your dad's lookin' for? Only I heard he's old school and only goes after blokes.'

'Been doing your homework, have you?' Adam sniped, flashing him an angry side-glance. 'Don't be getting your hopes up about working for him, 'cos I'll be taking over soon, and any fucker who didn't have my back on the way up can take a hike.'

'Yo, I've had your back from time, so don't be treatin' me like some kind of dickhead,' Wes replied coolly.

Still stewing over his dad's *go play with your dollies* jibe, Adam decided he couldn't be bothered arguing with Wes and drove on in silence. He'd thought he had regained his old man's trust after he'd been tasked with looking after the business in Ryan's absence, but he clearly hadn't earned his respect yet, and that pissed him off big time. He'd been treated like a joke and a liability by his family for long enough, and if things didn't change – and *quick*! – they would only have themselves to blame when he showed them who they were dealing with.

37

With her hood pulled over her head and her chin tucked down inside her collar, Lexi scanned the road through her eyelashes as she walked. Relieved to arrive at the Kingston without encountering any familiar faces, she took a deep breath before trying the handle of the communal door at the end of the block where she used to live. Surprised when it opened, because she had expected that she would have to start ringing bells and hope that somebody would release the door, she slipped inside and quickly made her way into the lift and jabbed the button for the sixth floor.

The lift was even clankier and slower than she remembered, but at last it stopped and she stepped out onto the landing. Dipping her head again when she saw a group of youths standing at the end passing a very strong smelling spliff between themselves, she walked along, looking at the doors, trying to remember which one the mad yoga woman had lived in.

'Who you after?' one of the youths called out when they spotted her.

Flicking a glance at them and seeing that they only looked around fourteen or fifteen, which – she hoped – was too young to have been recruited as street sellers by Danny Harvey yet, she said, 'Jamie.'

'Six ten,' the lad said.

Muttering a thank you when he turned back to his mates, Lexi knocked on the door of the flat he'd directed her to and almost cried with relief when Jamie opened the door a few seconds later.

'Hey!' His face lit up at the sight of her. 'What are you doing here? Jen . . . come see who it is!'

The living room door opened and a tiny doll of a young woman with bright pink hair came out.

'Hello?' she said, joining Jamie in the doorway and smiling at Lexi with no recognition in her eyes.

'It's Lexi,' Jamie told her.

'Oh!' Her blue eyes widened, as did her smile. 'Wow, it's really great to meet you at last.' Then, to Jamie, she said, 'Why've you got her standing outside in the cold? Move out of the way and let her in, you big lump.'

'Sorry,' Jamie apologized, still grinning as he waved Lexi inside. 'I thought you must have lost my number when you didn't call,' he said as he showed her into the living room.

'I, um, did,' she lied. 'Sorry. I've been meaning to call round for ages, but . . . work, and stuff. You know how it is.'

'Stop making her feel awkward and go put the kettle on,' Jen said, rolling her eyes at Lexi.

'Soz,' Jamie apologized. 'I'm just made up to see you, Lex.'

'Was he as daft as this when you were kids?' Jen asked, smiling fondly as he rushed out to the kitchen.

'He was only ten when I knew him, but he was a good lad,' Lexi said. 'I used to feel really sorry for him because he got picked on a lot, and his mum wasn't the best. But he never felt sorry for himself, and I really admired that about him.'

'The less said about his mum the better,' Jen said quietly. Then, smiling again, she said, 'Anyway, take your coat off and make yourself comfortable.'

Thanking her, Lexi slid her coat off and laid it over the back of the sofa.

'You're really beautiful,' Jen said, peering at her when they were both seated. 'I thought Jamie was exaggerating when he said you looked like a film star, but you really do.'

'Bless you, but you both need glasses,' Lexi said, smiling at her. Then, looking round, she said, 'You've got a lovely home.'

'Thanks,' Jen beamed. 'It's mostly second-hand, but it's amazing what you can find if you look in the right places.'

'You've got a good eye,' said Lexi. 'And the paintings are incredible,' she added, looking at the one that was hanging on the wall above the fire, which was of an angelic-looking white-blonde child surrounded by ethereal-looking fairies.

'That's me,' Jen said. 'My mum painted it. She had a thing about fairies and angels.'

'Sorry, forgot to ask – tea or coffee?' Jamie said, popping his head round the door.

'Whichever's easiest,' said Lexi. 'White, one sugar, please.'

'So Jamie tells me you've only recently moved back to Manchester?' Jen said, settling back against the cushions.

Surprised by how well-spoken she was, considering she'd grown up on the same estate as Lexi and her friends, who had all been as rough as anything, Lexi nodded.

'I don't know how much Jamie's told you, but I went into care when I was fifteen, and I've been living in Hebden Bridge for the last eight or nine years.'

'I heard about your mum,' Jen said. 'It was hard enough losing mine to cancer, but I can't begin to imagine how difficult it must have been for you to lose yours like that.'

'It was, but you find a way to live with it,' Lexi said. Then, changing the subject, she said, 'I saw your daughter when I bumped into Jamie that night. I can see where she gets her looks from. She's the image of you.'

'My little mini me,' Jen said, her eyes shining with pride.

'Here we go . . .' Jamie came back carrying a tray containing three cups of tea and a plate of biscuits. 'I wasn't sure if you'd prefer bourbons or custard creams, so I've put some of both out.'

'Thanks,' Lexi said, blushing when her stomach rumbled at the sight of them. 'Sorry, I haven't eaten today. It's been a bit of a weird one.'

'Oh no,' Jen said, concern on her pretty face. 'Is everything all right?'

'Not really,' Lexi sighed. 'That's kind of why I came,' she went on guiltily. 'I was meaning to at some point, anyway, but . . . well, I'm in a bit of trouble and I didn't have anywhere else to go.'

'What can we do to help?' Jamie asked without hesitation.

'I need somewhere to stay for a couple of days,' Lexi said.

'What kind of trouble are you in?' Jen asked, searching Lexi's face with her eyes.

Unsure where to start – or how much to tell them, Lexi said, 'Did you hear about the woman who got murdered in Chorlton yesterday?'

'Yeah, I saw something on the news about it earlier,' Jen said. 'Did you know her?'

'She was my housemate.'

'Fuck, Lex,' Jamie murmured. 'I'm so sorry.'

'We weren't close,' Lexi told him. 'In fact, I don't think she liked me very much. We kind of got off on the wrong foot when I moved in. And then I found out she was my supervisor at work, so it was a bit awkward between us.'

'Still, it must have been an awful shock,' Jen said. 'Were you there when it happened?'

'Jen,' Jamie said quietly.

'It's OK,' Lexi said. 'And, yes, I was there. Not in her room, but in the house. He attacked two of my friends straight after, so I escaped and called the police. My neighbour chased him, but he got away.'

'Bloody hell, that must have been terrifying,' Jen said. 'No wonder you don't want to go back there.'

'Well you can stop here as long as you like,' Jamie said. 'You can have Poppy's room and she can come in with us. And I can borrow my mate's van if you want a hand picking up your stuff.'

'Thank you, that's really kind, but I don't want to put you out,' Lexi said. 'I just need to keep my head down for a couple of days while I work out where to go.'

'You're not putting us out at all,' Jen assured her, reaching across and squeezing her hand. 'Now I'm going to make you something decent to eat while Jamie moves Poppy into our room, then we'll take it from there.'

'The biscuits will be fine,' Lexi insisted, touched by the younger woman's compassion, considering it was the first time they had ever met.

'No point arguing with her when she's made up her mind about something,' Jamie said, grinning when Jen got up and headed out to the kitchen. Lowering his voice when she'd gone, his expression more serious, he said, 'I know you probably don't want to talk about it, but are you OK, Lex? You look wiped, and you've been shaking like a leaf since you got here. That bloke didn't do anything to you, did he?'

Lexi dipped her gaze and bit her lip. She didn't want to alarm Jamie and his wife by telling them the truth, but what if she was putting them in danger by keeping them in the dark? What if Adam found out she was here, or one of those youths outside worked for Danny and told him?

'I'm really sorry, I shouldn't have come,' she murmured. 'You've got your family to think about, and if anyone finds out I'm here . . .'

'Is someone after you?' Jamie asked, sitting forward when she tailed off.

'Do you remember my old friend, Nicole?' Lexi asked. 'Her dad's Danny Harvey and they used to live on this block.'

'I know who they are. Harvey roped our Mark into running drugs for him when he was fourteen. That's how he ended up inside.'

'Do you remember his son, Adam, as well?'

'Unfortunately,' Jamie said bitterly. 'The bastard used to kick my head in every time he saw me.'

'I'm so sorry,' Lexi said. 'I had no idea.'

'It's all right.' Jamie shrugged. 'I got worse at home off me mam and her fuck-buddies, so I was used to it.'

'I think Adam might have had something to do with what happened at my place,' Lexi said.

'You're joking!'

'Wish I was. When I bumped into you that night, I'd just come from Nicole's. We'd had a row 'cos she got it into her head that something was going on between me and Ryan.'

'Ryan King?' Jamie asked. 'Yeah, I heard he'd married her. I was a bit surprised, to be honest. He always seemed all right; didn't peg him for the type to get involved with that lot.'

'Well, he did,' said Lexi. 'Anyway, long story short, I started seeing someone a few months ago, but then I found out he was Ryan's dad and finished it.'

'Seriously?' Jamie said. 'You and Ryan's dad?'

Lexi nodded, then continued with the story, telling him

everything that had happened up to her going back into the house earlier that night and being forced to flee when she heard somebody coming in.

'Jeezus,' Jamie said, raking a hand through his hair. 'I always knew Adam Harvey wasn't right in the head, but I never dreamed he was capable of doing something like this. Have you told the police?'

'I told them about the stuff that happened before the break-in, but I don't think they thought it was connected,' Lexi sighed. 'They actually arrested Ryan this morning, but my friend had already told them the man who attacked her was white, so I don't know what that was about. I really need to speak to him, but I need to keep my head down till I find out what's going on.'

'Take all the time you need,' Jen said, coming back into the room and handing Lexi a plated bacon sandwich. 'We won't tell anyone you're here – will we, Jay?'

'Absolutely not,' he agreed. 'And if you need anything while you're here, you only have to ask.'

Thanking them, Lexi bit into the sandwich and gave Jen the thumbs up when she asked if it was OK.

38

After stopping off at the flat to grab Theo's clothes and personal items, and also the money Ryan had spent the last few months incrementally transferring into different accounts before withdrawing it and storing it in a hole in the wall behind Theo's bed, father and son tied up a few loose ends before driving over to Liverpool, where Theo's old friend, Lee Wilkinson, had a spare room waiting for them. It would only be a temporary stay, just long enough for them to withdraw the rest of the money from the various accounts they'd set up before closing them all down, and then they intended to lie low for a bit while Danny Harvey exhausted every avenue in his quest to track them down.

They had leaked word to an untrustworthy acquaintance that they were heading to London to pull off a big deal, and they had every confidence that this info would already have found its way into Danny's ears, sending him on a wild goose chase while they set up the real deal to offload the last shipment of coke Lee had hijacked for them a couple of weeks earlier.

RUNNING SCARED

This was the culmination of many years of plotting and planning; Ryan working his way into the heart of the Harvey family and the business while his dad served out his time, in order to take Danny Harvey for everything he owned the minute Theo was out. And Ryan had played it by the book, right up until his dad's release a few months earlier, gaining Danny's trust to the extent that the man had relaxed into his new life in Spain, not bothering to check the accounts as long as there was enough dosh to cover his daily expenses and nightly bar bills.

There had only been one transfer left to make, which Ryan would have done that morning if he hadn't been arrested. But it wasn't a life-changing amount of money – certainly not enough to make it easy for Danny to get back on his feet, so they weren't too concerned about being forced to abandon it.

Ryan, however, *was* concerned about abandoning Lexi, who still hadn't responded to the two voice messages he'd left. Unsure if she was deliberately ignoring them because she'd seen him at the station and thought he was involved in the murder, or if she simply hadn't received them yet, he was relieved when, after reaching Lee's place later that night, he asked his dad to check his phone and they saw that she had tried to call several times, but they hadn't heard them because Theo had accidentally knocked his phone into silent mode when he'd shoved it into his back pocket.

It was almost 1 a.m. by then, and Ryan was hesitant to call her in case she was sleeping. But his dad and Lee, who had been mates since high school, were hitting the Wray and Nephew rum like it had gone out of style, and he was fed up of listening to them talk about days gone by and people he hadn't known, so he decided to get some shut-eye and ring her in the morning.

Back in Manchester, Adam and Wes had arrived at The Danski. The bar manager, Sue, had opened up, and the usual crowd of middle-aged leerers were supping cheap, watered-down beers and spirits and ogling the lacklustre dancers who were going through the motions on the centre stage. As Wes headed over to their usual table in the corner, where their mates were already seated – and on, Adam noticed with irritation, at least their second bottle of house champagne – Adam made his way to the bar.

'Didn't think you were coming in tonight,' Sue said, walking over when she spotted him.

'I'm not stopping long,' he said, looking around as he spoke. 'Where's that girl?'

'You'll have to be a bit more specific than that,' Sue said, pouring him a glass of Jack Daniel's.

'I think her name's Toni,' he said, snatching the glass up and swallowing it in one.

'We haven't got any girls called Toni,' Sue said, refilling the glass when he slammed it down on the counter. 'You're not talking about Tina, are you? Skinny bitch, scraggly hair?'

'Yeah, that's the one. Where is she?'

'No idea.' Sue shrugged. 'I haven't seen her tonight. Paris is over there, though.' She nodded toward the back tables where a tiny dark-haired girl was sitting on the lap of an elderly man. 'If you're after a bit, I can go get her for you.'

'Who the *fuck* do you think you're talking to?' Adam glared at her.

Taken aback, Sue's eyes widened. 'Sorry, I didn't mean any offence. I just thought—'

'Well you thought wrong,' Adam spat. 'And don't ever talk to me like you and me are mates, 'cos we ain't. I'm your boss, so speak to me with respect in future, or fuck off.'

He downed the second drink at that and, pushing his way through the customers, went into the office, slamming the door behind him, and tipped what was left of the wrap in his pocket onto the tabletop. Quickly snorting it and not getting anywhere near the buzz he'd hoped for, he opened his desk drawer and took out the plastic bag containing his stash. There were only two wraps left in it, and he didn't have enough money to ring his dealer and ask him to fetch another batch over. Under normal circumstances, he'd have nipped over to DH Deliveries and helped himself to a bit of dosh from the safe. But that fucker Ryan had emptied it along with the bank accounts, so he would have to raid the till instead.

After snorting another wrap, he pocketed the last one and headed back into the clubroom, where Wes and the lads were busy getting lap dances off a couple of his girls. Still smarting from his dad's put-down comment and in no mood for the lads' shit, he walked behind the bar and emptied the notes out of the till before heading back out to his car.

* * *

Woken by the sound of someone continually jabbing their finger on the doorbell, Tina's heart sank when she looked out of her bedroom window and saw Adam Harvey on the step below. Rushing into her little boy's room when she heard him start to moan, she quickly settled him before heading down the stairs.

'Why the fuck are you not in work?' Adam demanded, pushing past her when she opened the door.

'I'm not well,' she said, her voice a hoarse whisper. 'And please keep it down,' she urged. 'The doorbell nearly woke my son.'

'What's up with you?' Adam asked, peering at her in the darkness of the hallway.

'I think it's a virus,' she said, hugging her aching, shivering body. 'I rang the club and told Sue I wouldn't be able to make it tonight. But I'm hoping my doctor will give me antibiotics in the morning.'

'Sue never said you'd rung.' Adam frowned. Then, shrugging, he said, 'Oh well, just keep your face turned so you don't pass it on to me. Last thing I need is a fuckin' virus wiping me out.'

'*Excuse* me?' Tina stared at him in disbelief as he started making his way up the stairs, taking his jacket off as he went. 'What are you doing?'

Hesitating, Adam looked down at her over the banister rail. 'What's it look like?'

'But I'm ill.'

'Yeah, and I said keep your face turned so I don't catch it. Or are you deaf, an' all?'

RUNNING SCARED

Shocked when he shook his head in a gesture of irritation before continuing on up the stairs, Tina stayed where she was for a few moments. She wasn't lying about being ill; she'd felt like death all day and the thought of having sex with her boss again made her feel physically sick. But she had no idea what he might do if she didn't follow him up to bed, and she really didn't want Caleb to get woken up again. So, hauling herself up the stairs, she slipped the padlock into place on her son's door before going to her room.

39

Danny Harvey hadn't slept a wink. He had trusted Ryan, and now he felt like a prize twat for giving him free rein over the company accounts. And it wasn't only the business side of things that the bastard had screwed him over on; he'd also somehow managed to remortgage the house in Danny's name, and had pocketed a large sum of money which he'd borrowed on it for imaginary repairs. With that, an almost empty bank account, and his supplier demanding payment for the three shipments of coke that had gone missing before he would hand over any more gear, Danny was in debt to the tune of tens of thousands. His only hope of climbing out of the deep dark hole he'd been chucked into was to find Ryan and Theo and get his money back. But the cunts had pulled the mother of all disappearing acts, and nobody he'd asked had admitted to knowing where they were.

Waiting to hear back from the men he'd sent to London, following the one tip-off he had been given, Danny had just poured a glass of whisky when the doorbell rang at 8 a.m. Glass in hand, he looked through the spyhole in the front door and saw an attractive young woman and a slightly older man, both wearing nondescript suits, standing on the step. Instantly pegging them as detectives and guessing it was something to do with the murder case, he put the glass down on a ledge before opening the door.

'Morning.' The woman flashed her badge. 'Detective Inspector Benson. Is Mr King available?'

'You just missed him,' Danny lied. 'Can I pass on a message?'

'I came to return these.' She held out a plastic bag containing Ryan's confiscated clothes. 'Also, I was wondering if Adam Harvey might be here?'

'Adam?' Danny pulled a face as he reached for the bag. 'He doesn't live here, love. Hasn't for a long time.'

'This is the address we were given for him,' Benson said. 'I don't suppose you have his new one?'

'Sorry, I've never been there, so I couldn't tell you.' Danny shrugged.

'And may I ask who you are?' Benson asked.

'And may I ask why you want to know?' Danny shot back smoothly. 'Not being funny, love, but I only came back into the country yesterday, so if this is about that stuff you arrested Ryan over, I can't help you.'

Benson held his gaze for a moment, then said, 'Thanks for your time.'

'No problem.' He smiled and closed the door.

'What did they want?' Rachel came down the stairs as he turned to go back to the kitchen after retrieving his drink.

'They brought that fucker's shit back.'

'I thought I heard her mention Adam?' she said, following him into the kitchen.

'Yeah, she asked if he was here and I told her he wasn't,' Danny said, chucking the bag down on the table and flopping onto a chair. 'Nosy bint tried asking who *I* was, an' all.'

'Why did she want to speak to Adam?' Rachel asked, frowning as she carried the kettle to the sink.

'How the fuck should I know?' Danny muttered, reaching for his phone.

'I don't like it.' Rachel folded her arms and leaned back against the counter after switching the kettle on. 'If they're digging into the family because of Ryan, they might have seen the report that bitch Lexi made against Adam.'

'That was years ago. And it was dropped, so it wouldn't mean nothing even if they had seen it,' Danny said dismissively.

'It's a link between her and Adam,' said Rachel. 'And it was *her* house where the murder happened, don't forget. They've already ruled Ryan out, so they're going to start looking into anyone else who's got history with her, aren't they?'

'She's not the only one who lives there,' Danny pointed out. 'And it wasn't her who got murdered, so why are they going to look into her past any more than they'll look into the others'?'

'They must think it had something to do with her or they wouldn't have arrested Ryan,' Rachel argued. 'She's the only link *he's* got to the place.'

'Ray, belt up, you're giving me earache,' Danny complained.

'Whoever did it, that's for them to find out. As long as we know it wasn't Adam, there's nowt for you to worry about.'

Irritated by his blasé attitude, Rachel pursed her lips and turned her back to him to make her coffee. He was so wrapped up in trying to find Ryan and his father, he couldn't see the warning signs that were staring them right in the face. They knew Adam wasn't involved, because he'd already told them he had stayed late at the club on the night of the murder and had then slept at his girlfriend's place. But the police sniffing around *any* member of the family was a concern. And these weren't run-of-the-mill street coppers, they were detectives, so God only knew what they might stumble across if they dug deeply enough.

'Who was at the door?' Nicole asked, wiping sleep from her eyes as she came into the kitchen still wearing her nightclothes.

'The police,' Rachel told her, giving her a disapproving look as she stirred the coffee. 'You look a bloody mess. When was the last time you had your hair done?'

'Yesterday,' Nicole replied, self-consciously smoothing her messy extensions. 'Hey, is that Ryan's stuff?' she asked, spotting the bag.

'The pigs just dropped it off,' Danny said, taking a swig of whisky.

'His phone's in it,' Nicole said, reaching for it.

'Do you know the password?' Rachel asked, carrying her drink to the table and sitting down.

'As long as he hasn't changed it again, yeah,' Nicole said, tearing the plastic bag open.

'Why are you women so obsessed with seeing what's on a bloke's phone?' Danny grumbled. 'And you wonder why we don't fuckin' trust youse.'

'If we could trust you, we wouldn't need to keep tabs on you,' Rachel replied spikily.

'It's open,' Nicole said after tapping in the number.

'Who are all those messages from?' Rachel asked, leaning over to look.

'Some of the guys on his crew,' Nicole said, scrolling through them. Then, jaw clenching, she said, 'And *her*.'

'Lexi?' Rachel frowned.

'Fucking two-faced bitch,' Nicole spat. 'Acted like she didn't know what I was talking about when I confronted her about seeing Ryan, but they've obviously been talking. Listen to this message she sent him last night,' she went on furiously. '*Sorry I missed your calls, my phone was in the house and I couldn't get it till the police left,*' she mimicked. '*I tried to call you back on Theo's phone, but he's not answering, so I thought I'd best try yours instead.* Just wait till I get my hands on her. And as for *him* . . . I'm gonna kill him!'

'I told you she was trash from day one, and I never trusted him,' Rachel said.

'Morning,' Adam drawled, strolling in and shrugging his jacket off. 'Wha'pp'nin', fam?'

'*Seriously?*' Nicole gave him a withering look.

'Chill, Sis; you'll get wrinkles,' he teased, ruffling her hair as he passed, then wiping his hand on her shoulder. 'Anything for brekkers, Ma?' He gave Rachel a hopeful look as he sat down. 'I could murder one of your famous fry-ups.'

'Fat chance of that when your sister's got the fridge full of stupid power drinks and frozen shite,' Rachel sniffed.

'Pardon me for trying to stay healthy,' Nicole muttered, aware that it was another dig to add to the ones her mum had already made about her furniture and the decor.

'You just missed the police,' Rachel went on, ignoring Nicole. 'They were asking for you.'

'You what?' Adam's smile slipped. 'Why?'

'You tell us,' Danny said, instantly suspicious when he clocked his son's expression. He knew him inside out, and the guilt was seeping out of his pores like sewage water.

'Don't look at me like that. I haven't done anything, I swear,' Adam blustered. 'That bastard's probably said something to try and drop me in it.'

'Like what?' Danny asked.

'It won't be Ryan, it'll be this bitch,' Nicole said, holding up Ryan's phone. 'Listen to this voice message she sent him last night after that text.'

She pressed play and put it on loudspeaker.

Ryan, where are you? Lexi's voice was hushed, as if she didn't want whoever she was with to hear her. *I'm getting really worried now. I saw Adam and some man outside my house earlier, and I heard someone coming in, so I had to run. I don't know what to do. Please ring me. I'm scared.*

'So she *was* in the house when you went round there, but

she spotted you, dickhead,' Danny said, giving his son an accusing look. 'And who's the bloke she said you were with?'

'No one, I went on my own,' Adam lied. 'I did see someone walking down the road when I pulled up, so she must have seen him and thought we were together.'

Unsure if he believed him, Danny said, 'Well, thanks to you she's gone into hiding, so what we gonna do now?'

Adam dipped his gaze. He'd been on a high when he first came round, not only because he'd managed to score some really pure gear that had given him the old rush he'd been craving, but also because he'd fucked Tina into a near coma – visualizing Lexi James's face with every thrust. On top of the world when he'd left her place, he had decided to forgive his dad for that dolly jibe and start over. But, yet again, he was in his dad's bad books – and all because of that fucking whore, Lexi!

The doorbell rang.

'I'll get it,' Rachel said, walking out into the hall.

'Sorry to disturb you,' DI Benson said, flashing her badge. 'We called round a few minutes ago.'

'Yes, I know. You spoke to my husband.' Rachel gave her a frosty look. 'What do you want now?'

'We were driving past on our way back to the station and noticed the Lexus,' Benson said, gesturing to Adam's car, which was now parked alongside the Range Rover. 'We did a quick check and it's registered to Adam Harvey.'

'And?' Rachel folded her arms.

'If he's here, we need to speak to him,' said Benson. 'It shouldn't take long.'

Tutting, Rachel turned her head and yelled, 'Adam, the police are here again. They want to speak to you.'

In the kitchen, Danny leaned across the table and grabbed Adam's arm as he made to stand up.

'Whatever's going on, you tell them fuckers nothing – do you understand?'

Swallowing the sickly taste in his mouth, Adam nodded. Then, straightening up, he faked a nonchalant smile and went out into the hall.

'Mr Harvey?' Benson asked when he joined his mother at the door.

'Yeah. Can I help you?' Adam said, looping an arm around his mother's shoulders. 'If it's about Ryan, I'm afraid he's already left for work.'

'So I believe,' Benson said. 'Could you tell us where you were between the hours of two and three a.m. yesterday morning?'

'At the club,' Adam said. 'I own The Danski in Cheetham Hill,' he elaborated when Benson gave him a questioning look. 'I'm there every night; usually lock up around three.'

'And were you there until three yesterday?'

'I went to my girlfriend's straight from there, so it was probably more like quarter to, to be honest.'

'Was anyone with you who could verify that?'

'No, my employees leave before me, and I cash up before locking up,' Adam said. Then, frowning, he asked, 'Do you mind telling me what this is about, only this is starting to sound like I'm being accused of something?'

'Just routine,' Benson assured him. 'This girlfriend you mentioned . . . could you tell me her name and address?'

'Yeah, sure,' Adam said. 'It's Toni – sorry, *Tina* Klein. I call her Toni as a joke,' he added, thinking on his feet when he saw the detective's eyebrow twitch. 'I used to date a girl called Toni before her, and I called her that by mistake one time when we were . . .' He paused and flashed a hooded glance at his mother, before saying, 'Not the kind of convo I really want to be having in front of my mum, but I'm sure you get the gist.'

'Address?' Benson asked.

When Adam and Rachel returned to the kitchen a couple of minutes later, Danny was on the phone.

'What did they want?' Nicole asked quietly.

'To know where he was when that woman was murdered,' said Rachel, refilling the kettle to make a fresh brew. 'But it's OK, 'cos he was with his girlfriend – weren't you, son?'

'Really?' Nicole gave Adam a funny look. 'Since when have you had a girlfriend?'

'I don't tell you everything,' he replied, avoiding her eye as he lit a cigarette.

'That was Mash,' Danny said, his expression dark as he came back to the table after finishing his call. 'They've been staking out the place where the deal was supposed to be going down, but no fucker turned up.'

'I told you it was bullshit,' Rachel said. 'You shouldn't have sent them.'

'And what else was I supposed to do?' Danny shot back angrily. 'If we don't catch them, the money'll be gone – along with this house and every other fucking thing we own.'

'I've got an idea,' Nicole said. 'Lexi doesn't know we've got Ryan's phone,' she went on when they all looked at her. 'If we message her pretending to be him, we'll be able to flush her out.'

'She'll know it's not his voice, idiot,' Adam sneered.

'I'm talking about a text not a voice message, dumb shit,' Nicole retorted icily.

'Saying what?' Rachel asked, carrying four cups of coffee to the table and handing them out before sitting down.

'I don't know.' Nicole shrugged. 'But if she thinks he's going to come and save her, she'll have to tell him where she is.'

'But she clearly doesn't know where *he* is, or she wouldn't be begging him to ring her, so what's the point?' Adam asked. 'She's got his dad's number, an' all, don't forget, so as soon as she realizes it wasn't him, she'll warn them. And she left him that message hours ago, so she might have already spoken to them by now and found out that Ryan's not got his phone.'

'It's worth a try,' Danny said thoughtfully. 'If she doesn't answer, it's a fair bet she knows it's not him. But if she does and we play smart, we can find out where she is and go get her.'

'Then use *her* phone to trick Ryan into coming to meet her,' said Rachel.

Pleased that her parents were taking her idea seriously, Nicole flashed Adam a smug smile. She had tried to warn Ryan, but he obviously thought more of that bitch than he did of her, and she was starting to realize just how bad life was going to be if her dad didn't get his money back, so it was Ryan's tough luck if he got what was coming to him. Let Lexi mop up the blood and cry at his funeral. Nicole was done with the lying, cheating bastard!

40

Lexi had slept fitfully in the single bed in Poppy's room; her dreams plagued by images of Adam and other men whose faces she couldn't see chasing her around her house. Grateful to Jamie and Jen for allowing her to stay, but desperate to get out of there before she brought harm to their door, she checked her phone when she woke up to see if Ryan had replied to the message she'd sent before going to sleep, asking him to call her. Heart leaping when she saw that he'd sent her a text message a few minutes earlier, she sat up to read it.

Sorry I didn't get back to you last night, only just got my phone back. Can't talk right now, but things have gone a bit weird with my dad. I think him and Danny have done a deal, so don't call him and don't answer if he tries to call you, 'cos I think he's trying to find out where you are to send Danny after you. He might even pretend to be me to get you to open up, so be careful! I'll text you when I've found somewhere safe to meet up xx

Alarmed, and upset to think that Theo would turn on her like that when he claimed to care so much about her, Lexi's hand was shaking as she typed out a quick reply, telling Ryan that she wouldn't contact Theo again and would, instead, wait for Ryan to contact her.

Ryan sent a text straight back, and she frowned when she read it.

I'll call you tonight darling. Love you xx

The intimacy of the words made her wonder if he'd actually meant to send that message to Nicole and had sent it to her by mistake; and that, in turn, made her wonder if he was really trying to help her, or if *he* was the one she ought to be wary of. He was married to Danny Harvey's daughter, after all; and he'd shown that his loyalty lay with them in the past, when he'd denied all knowledge of Adam attacking her, making it look like she'd made the whole thing up. But the way he'd opened up to her when he'd called round at her place that day had felt sincere, and her instincts told her that he genuinely did like her, so would he really conspire to put her in danger after sending her those voice messages warning her not to go back to the house?

Confused, and filled with dread about what might happen next, Lexi got dressed and made her way into the living room, where Jen was playing on the carpet with Poppy.

'Hey, you're awake,' Jen smiled, jumping up. 'Did you sleep OK? I know that bed's a bit lumpy.'

'It was fine,' Lexi assured her. 'And thank you so much for letting me stay.'

'It's our pleasure,' Jen said, reaching down to lift up her

daughter. 'Say hello to Auntie Lexi,' she said when the child stared at her guest.

'Hello, Poppy.' Lexi smiled. 'Aren't you the prettiest little girl in the whole world?'

'Aw, look,' Jen said when Poppy grinned and held out her arms. 'She wants to come to you.'

Awkwardly, because she hadn't held a small child in many years, Lexi took her, and was surprised when the child planted a kiss on her cheek.

'Wow, you're honoured,' Jen said. 'She's usually really shy around strangers.'

'It's probably because she's in her own home and feels safe,' Lexi said, picking up the sweet scent of apples from the child's silky hair.

'Come through to the kitchen and I'll make you a brew and some toast,' Jen said, already heading for the door.

'Tea will be fine,' Lexi said, carrying the child, who was now playing with her hair, after her.

'Stop acting like you're putting us out,' Jen chided softly. 'Jamie's absolutely made up to have you here – and so am I. You obviously don't realize what an impact you had on him when he was a kid,' she went on, waving for Lexi to take a seat at the table as she bustled around the small clean kitchen. 'He told me you were the only one who ever spoke to him like he wasn't a piece of S-H-I-T.'

Smiling at the way Jen had spelled out the word instead of swearing in front of her child, Lexi said, 'He had something about him, even back then. And now look at him; all grown up, with a beautiful family. You're a lucky woman.'

'I know,' Jen agreed, the light in her eyes whenever she spoke about Jamie a clear indication that she considered herself blessed.

'Where is he?' Lexi asked, cuddling Poppy when the child rested against her and put a thumb into her mouth.

'At work,' Jen said, placing a cup of tea on the table before going back to butter the toast. 'He's an outreach worker for at-risk kids; those who've got troubled home lives, or have been excluded from school, and what have you.'

'Wow.' Lexi was impressed.

'He's so good with them,' Jen went on proudly. 'He's only been doing it for a year, but he's really helped some of the kids round here. It helps that he was once in their shoes, because they sense he's one of them and not some stuck-up social worker who's learned everything from a book but knows nothing about the realities of trying to survive abuse and neglect.'

'Sounds like you should be doing it yourself,' said Lexi.

'I'm happy just being a mum, for now,' said Jen. 'But when Poppy's old enough for school, I'm thinking about training to be a yoga teacher.'

'Ah . . .' Lexi smiled knowingly. 'Like your mum?'

'She wasn't a teacher, but she really should have been,' Jen said. 'I know people round here thought she was cuckoo, but she had pure magic going on in here.' She tapped her temple.

'I'm sorry I never got to meet her,' Lexi said. 'I used to see her out back in the rain, and I've got to admit I was one of the ones who thought she was cuckoo. But she'd have seemed perfectly normal in Hebden Bridge.'

'Is that where you were living before you came back?' Jen asked, scooping an almost asleep Poppy out of her arms after placing her plated toast on the table.

'Yeah. My last foster placement was there, and I liked it so much I decided to stay.'

'Do you miss it?'

Feeling a sudden longing for the simple way of life there compared to the stresses she'd encountered after coming back to Manchester, Lexi nodded. 'Yeah, I do. But there's no work there, and you can only kip on friends' couches for so long before they get sick of you, so . . .' She tailed off and shrugged.

'That won't happen with us,' Jen assured her. 'When we said you can stay as long as you like, we meant it.'

Dipping her gaze when she felt the sting of tears in her eyes, Lexi murmured, 'Thank you.'

'I'm just going to put Pops down for her nap and let you eat your breakfast in peace,' Jen said, touching her shoulder softly before heading out.

Alone, Lexi sighed as she bit into a slice of toast. She envied Jen and Jamie. They lived in this place she herself had considered a shithole when she was growing up, but she'd have given anything, right then, to go back in time and be back in that draughty flat with her mum.

'I heard your phone ringing,' Jen said, coming back a short

time later with the phone Lexi had left in the bedroom. 'Sorry I didn't get to it in time.'

'It's OK,' Lexi said, drying her hands on a tea towel after washing her plate and cup. 'It won't be anything important.'

Opening the screen, she saw she'd had two missed calls off Theo and bit her lip as she contemplated calling him back. Still unsure who to trust, she decided to wait until Ryan rang her later and let her instincts guide her once she'd heard his voice.

41

Theo had still been sleeping – and snoring – when Ryan woke up at just gone 9 a.m. Guessing that his dad and Lee must have carried on reminiscing into the early hours when he headed into the living room and saw the empty bottles on the coffee table and the numerous spliff-dimps in the ashtray, he shook his head as he made his way into the kitchen to make a brew. Now more than ever his dad needed to be on the ball, but the man would be lucky if he could think straight after knocking back that much overproof rum. Still, they weren't going anywhere just yet, so he supposed one blowout wasn't going to hurt.

Coffee in hand, he pulled his dad's phone out of his pocket as he made his way back into the living room and took a seat on the sofa. Lexi hadn't sent any messages or tried to call during the night, and she hadn't picked up when he'd tried to call her twice while waiting for the kettle to boil. Remembering that she'd been wearing pyjamas when he'd seen her at the police station, and figuring that she probably hadn't had a chance to grab her phone before leaving the house, he tried not to worry too much about the ongoing silence from her end. It was entirely likely, given that it was a murder investigation, that the police would still be at the house, so he had to assume that she was safe for now. But he would try her again later, just to make sure.

Looking round when the door opened behind him, he said, 'Morning,' when Lee walked in.

'*Jeezus!*' the man squawked, almost jumping out of his skin. 'I totally forgot youse were here.'

'Sorry,' Ryan apologized. 'Want me to make you a brew? You look rough as fuck.'

'Blame your old man,' Lee said, yawning as he scratched his bald head with both hands before wandering over to the window and plucking a half-smoked spliff out of the ashtray on the sill. 'I forgot how much the brother can put away without feelin' klish. I was so wasted by the time I hit the hay, thought I was on a fuckin' yacht in the Caribbean. Still can't feel my legs proper.'

'Here, take this,' Ryan said, getting up and handing his cup to him. 'I'll make myself another.'

'Cheers, kidda,' Lee said, sinking down onto an armchair. 'Any word from Theo's lady yet?' he asked as Ryan went back into the small kitchen. 'He was telling me about her last night; sounds like a beaut.'

'She is,' Ryan said, keeping his back turned so Lee wouldn't see his expression. When he'd left the pair last night they had been discussing the multitude of birds they had pulled when they were young studs, and he hadn't been impressed to hear that they'd had some kind of system where they passed conquests on to each other after getting what they wanted. He knew it had been a different world back then, but still . . .

'So what's the story with you and your missus?' Lee went on, interrupting his thoughts. 'She gonna join you when you and T are settled?'

'Definitely not,' said Ryan. 'Didn't my dad tell you she's Danny Harvey's daughter?'

'Seriously? Fuck, man!' Lee shook his head. 'You Walkers like playin' with fire, innit? I remember when T met your ma; the shit they got off her folks 'cos of him being black.'

'I never knew that,' Ryan said, coming back with his brew and sitting down.

'To be fair, they got it from both sides,' said Lee. 'But he was a stubborn bastard, so it only made him more determined to be with her. He did love her, though, so it's a shame it didn't work out. Thought the world of you, an' all. Used to show me all the pics your ma sent him when you was a nipper. Proper proud, he was.'

Ryan hadn't been aware of any of that. All he'd known growing up was his mum's side of the family, and his dad's name had rarely been mentioned – and not in a particularly good way when it was. His grandparents had always treated him the same as his white cousins, so it had never occurred to him that they might have disliked his dad because he was black. He'd always assumed it was because of the lifestyle Theo had chosen, and the fact that he'd abandoned their daughter and left her to bring up his child on her own. It was good to hear that Theo had cared about him, though, because he had often wondered if his dad had only contacted him on his sixteenth birthday in order to use him as a tool to eventually take revenge on Danny Harvey.

'Any idea where you're gonna go after you've offloaded that last batch of gear?' Lee asked, squinting at Ryan as he pulled on the spliff. 'Your da was talking about Jamaica.'

'It's an option,' Ryan said, wondering just how much his dad had told the man. They might have been best mates when they were kids, but they hadn't seen each other in at least the fourteen years that Theo had been inside, because his dad had told him he'd only had female visitors – one of whom had been Ryan's mum, which had been news to him, considering she had never once mentioned it. Theo trusted Lee with his life, but Ryan had only recently met him so his judgement was reserved.

'Well I'll be booking myself a flight to come over for some R and R soon as the dust settles and I can start spending the lovely dosh youse are giving me for setting you up with my guy,' Lee grinned. 'It's been pure time since I've had the chance to visit the motherland.'

'You're from Jamaica?' Ryan asked, sipping his brew.

'Nah, born and bred in Gorton,' Lee said. 'I moved over here after all that shit went down with your dad and Harvey, but I've got family in Montego Bay, so it feels like home whenever I go over there.'

'Nice.'

'It's paradise, man,' Lee said wistfully. 'Shit, I might even move in with you if you settle there,' he added with a grin. 'Then I can introduce you to all the fine gal dem.'

Ryan smiled as if he liked the sound of that, but girls were the last thing on his mind – apart from Lexi, of course. At the thought of her, he took another look at the phone, but there was still nothing from her, so he laid the phone on the table and told himself to stop thinking about her and concentrate on his and his dad's next step.

42

Nicole's emotions had been up and down all morning; yearning for her husband one minute, then hating his guts the next. She genuinely hadn't believed that Ryan could have done what her father had accused him of, but it was beginning to sink in that he really had taken their money and done a runner. Even so, she wasn't happy about the wording her mum had used in those texts she'd sent this morning.

'I still don't see why you had to put *"love you"*,' she complained as the family sat around the table eating the breakfast her mum had thrown together from the freezer she rarely stocked up.

'You want her to believe it's him, don't you?' Rachel said, pulling a face at the skinny noodles and scrambled egg on her plate.

'It's time you admitted he wants her more than he ever wanted you,' Adam chipped in, twisting the knife. 'I can see why,' he went on as he shovelled food into his mouth. 'She's hot as fuck now she's filled out.'

'I think you mean *fat*,' Nicole shot back sulkily, still

bewildered as to why Ryan would choose Lexi over her when she made such an effort with her appearance and that tramp clearly made none.

'Jealousy always did look good on you, Sis,' Adam chuckled. 'Gives you a bit of colour in your cheeks and makes your eyes look less dead.'

'Quit with the childish digs,' Rachel scolded, sticking up for her daughter for a change. 'Your sister's a beautiful woman who takes care of herself, and that little bastard ought to have been grateful she gave him the time of day, never mind fucking her best friend.'

'Yeah, that's totally out of order,' Adam agreed, looking over at Danny as he added, slyly, 'Blokes shouldn't go near family, friends, or the help – ain't that right, Pops? I was only saying to Brenda yesterday—'

'Shut the fuck up and eat your breakfast,' Danny said, giving him a warning look. 'I'm trying to think.'

'Why did you say you'd find a place to meet up with her later?' Nicole asked her mum. 'I thought you wanted to find out where she is now?'

'She's probably hiding out at a friend's place, and they're likely to call the police if they realize she's in danger, so we need to get her on her own,' Rachel explained. 'And it has to be at night, so there'll be less chance of anyone seeing us.'

'Stroke of genius telling her that Theo might pretend to be him, so not to answer her phone if he rang her,' Adam grinned. 'Her head'll be so fucked, she won't know if she's coming or going.'

'It'll be even more fucked when I get my hands on her,' Nicole muttered.

'Right, I'm going to get a shower,' Danny said, pushing his plate away and standing up. 'Then I'm calling the boys in to make plans for later, so you lot had best make yourselves decent.'

'Can I be the one to do it?' Adam asked. 'No offence, Pops, but you and your guys look like fucking Mafia OGs, and she'll spot you in a second.'

'She spotted you fast enough last night,' Nicole reminded him.

'Yeah, but I can blend into the background when I need to,' Adam insisted. 'Please, Dad. This is personal, so let me do it. I promise I won't fuck it up.'

Looking down at him, Danny sighed and then nodded. 'Fine. You get her, and we'll take it from there.'

'*Yes!*' Adam crowed, already excited.

43

As hard as she'd tried to relax in Jen and Poppy's company, Lexi had been on a knife's edge all day. The text from Ryan telling her not to trust his dad had unnerved her, and she had phoned Debs when Jen had nipped out to the shops earlier, hoping that her friend might be able to help her to make sense of it. Debs had met both of them, but she knew Theo far better than she knew Ryan, and had made no secret of the fact that she fancied him, so Lexi had been surprised when Debs had said that she sensed Ryan was telling the truth.

'I know Theo really liked you, but I always got the feeling he was more in lust than love,' she'd said. 'And that's no reflection on you, 'cos you're beautiful and any man would be lucky to have you. But there's a huge difference between the way he used to look at you and the way I saw Ryan looking at you when he was leaving yours that day. Trust me, that boy's feelings are deep.'

Lexi had sensed the same thing herself and knew exactly where Debs was coming from. But her instincts were still warning her that something wasn't right, and knowing that Danny Harvey was back in town and potentially looking for her made it all the more vital that she didn't place her trust in the wrong person.

Unable to discuss any of this with Jamie and Jen, because she didn't want to worry them, she took herself off into their daughter's bedroom when a message from Ryan popped up on her phone at just gone 9 p.m. that night.

Sorry this is so late, but I've been hiding out and wanted to wait till it was safe to contact you, he'd written. My dad's gone out and I'm sure he's meeting up with Danny, so this is probably the best time for us to get together without them finding out. Can you meet me at the arches behind Oxford Road station at ten? We'll be able to talk there without anyone seeing us xx

Still nervous, Lexi typed out a quick reply.

I'd rather meet somewhere more public, if you don't mind? There must be somewhere where no one will recognize you?

She thought about adding a kiss, but changed her mind and sent it as was.

No problem, Ryan replied a few seconds later. I get that you're nervous – I am too. But you can trust me, I promise. I just want to make sure you'll be OK before I leave town. There's a bar not far from the arches called Dillons. Meet me there xx

Feeling better now he'd agreed to meet in public, Lexi went back into the living room, where Jamie and Jen were cuddled up on the sofa watching a film.

'I just spoke to my friend Debs and she's asked me to meet her at the house so we can check up on things,' she lied, thinking it best not to tell them where she was really going. 'I might be a couple of hours, but she said I can stay at her sister's, if that's too late for you?'

'Course it's not too late,' Jamie said, sliding his arm out from behind Jen and sitting up. 'I'll come with you.'

'No, you stay here with Jen,' Lexi insisted. 'Debs's sister is going to pick me up in five minutes, and she'll drop me back at the door, so I'll be fine. If anything changes, I've got your number.'

'If you're sure?' Jamie asked, his expression concerned.

'Positive.' Lexi forced a smile.

'Take this, then you don't have to worry if you get back later,' Jen suggested, leaning over to get her handbag and taking out a key.

'Thanks,' Lexi said, slipping it into her pocket. 'And I'll try not to disturb you if you're already in bed when I get back.'

Letting herself out of the flat, Lexi saw the same group of youths at the end of the landing who'd been there when she arrived. Aware now that some of them were kids who Jamie had been working with, and that they definitely *weren't* working for Danny Harvey, she smiled when they spotted her and nodded hello. She still couldn't get over what a great man her little mate Jamie had become, and she felt the kind of pride she imagined a mother – a decent one, at least – would feel for their child. Smiling about that, she took the lift down to the ground floor and, pausing to pull up her hood before pushing out through the door, set off to meet Ryan.

44

Dillons wine bar was situated in a row of arches a couple of hundred feet from the row of derelict ones where Ryan had originally suggested meeting. As she approached the door, Lexi heard music, chatter and laughter coming from inside and decided that she'd made the right call asking to meet there instead.

It was a cold night, but the air inside the packed bar was stiflingly hot, and she felt it settle over her like a damp blanket as she pushed through the door. Standing just inside, she looked around for Ryan and guessed he mustn't have arrived yet when she saw no sign of him.

Reaching into her bag for her phone, to text him and let him know she was there, time seemed to grind to a halt when her gaze landed on Adam on the other side of the room. He turned around at that exact moment and she knew he'd seen her when he fixed his gaze on her. The sound of her own heartbeat pounding in her ears drowned out the chatter in the bar, and the revellers disappeared from her vision, leaving just the two of them in the room; him smiling, her shivering uncontrollably as her legs threatened to give way.

Adrenaline burst through her veins when he started moving, and she forced her way through the bodies that were blocking her path to the door and lurched outside. Throat on fire, eyes streaming, she ran without looking back; racing around corner after corner until she found herself on an unfamiliar road lined on both sides with dark-windowed factories and office blocks.

Above the howling wind and the echo of her heels bouncing between the buildings, she picked up on a second, faster set of footsteps, and a sob escaped her lips when she realized he was gaining on her. The head start she'd had on him hadn't been enough, and when he caught her he would—

Unwilling to think about that, she veered into the mouth of a narrow alleyway between two of the buildings. It was pitch-dark in there, and she pressed her back against the wall and held her breath. Seconds later, Adam ran past, and she waited until his footsteps had faded before blindly groping her way along the alleyway, praying with every step that she would find a doorway or alcove to hide in before he realized where she'd gone and came after her.

A pile of rubble halfway along brought her to her knees, and she bit down hard on her lip to keep from crying out when something sharp sliced through the material of her trousers and pierced her flesh. Bleeding now, tears streaming, she got up and forced herself on toward the thin sliver of grey light she'd glimpsed up ahead.

The sliver widened as she got closer, and a wave of relief washed over her when she heard male voices on the street beyond. As bad as Adam was, she doubted he would risk doing anything to her in front of witnesses, so she would be safe if she could reach those people before he reached her.

Two men were standing by a Transit van a few feet from the alleyway, their faces bathed in the blue light emanating from the screen of the phone they were both looking at. They snapped their heads round and stared at her when she lurched out onto the pavement, and she staggered toward them, crying, 'Help me! Someone's chasing me, and he's going to—'

The words froze on her tongue when she saw the glint in the eyes of the man who was closest to her, and she took a stumbling step back. But it was too late.

'Gotcha!' he said, grinning as he pushed her up against the wall and pinned her there with his forearm across her throat.

Behind him, the other man gave a thin, high-pitched whistle. Seconds later, Adam ran up to them, and Lexi whimpered in fear when he loomed over her, his hot breath scorching her icy cheeks.

'Well, well,' he drawled, grinning as he peered into her eyes. 'It's been a long time. Have you missed me?'

'Adam, please let me go,' she croaked, twisting her head round when he pressed himself up against her.

'And why would I do that when I've waited so long for this?' he whispered, stroking her hair off her face before grasping her chin and forcing her to face him. 'I was willing to forgive you,' he said, his eyes glittering brightly as he stared into hers. 'But you betrayed me again, so now you've got to be punished.'

'I didn't do anything,' she sobbed. 'You attacked me.'

'Shut your mouth,' he hissed, his fingers clamping down harder on her flesh and distorting her features. 'You wanted me, and then you stabbed me in the back for that fucker, Ryan. Thought he cared about you, didn't you?' he sneered. 'But he used you just like he used our Nic. All he ever wanted was a way in with my dad, and you gave it to him, so well done you.'

'I – I don't know what you're talking about,' Lexi said, trying not to move her head in case he increased the pressure of his grip again. 'There was never anything between me and Ryan.'

'Tut, tut, tut,' Adam said, shaking his head. 'You always were a terrible liar, weren't you? You obviously thought no one knew about him popping round to your place for a crafty shag, but I saw him – and I've got the pictures to prove it.'

'Please, Adam, you've got it all wrong,' Lexi argued. 'He's only ever been to my place once, and he only came because Nic thought we were having an affair and I was asking him to set her straight and stop her threatening me. That's all it was, I swear. It was his dad I was seeing, not him. Ask him, he'll tell you.'

'I wouldn't believe a word that cunt said any more than I believe you,' spat Adam. 'You've both fucked with the wrong family, and you're gonna pay for it. But, hey . . .' He grinned again. 'You've gone through all this so you can be together, so at least you'll have the comfort of knowing you'll be *dying* together. And if you behave yourself, I might not make you suffer like your mum did. She made the mistake of trying to fight me, but we both know that's not a good idea, don't we?'

'*What?*' Lexi's head was spinning and she felt as if she was about to faint.

'Oh yeah, that's right . . . you still think your stepdaddy did it, don't you?' Adam grinned. 'That's how fucking smart I am,' he went on proudly. 'I didn't even have to break in, because you left your keys at mine when Nic kicked you out. It was so fucking easy, it gave me a proper hard-on, I can tell you. But don't worry, I didn't interfere with your old woman before I sent her on her way. Not like your stepdaddy interfered with you, eh?'

'Mate, someone's coming,' Wes said quietly, touching Adam's shoulder.

Turning his head and seeing a couple staggering in their direction from the far end of the road, Adam hissed, 'Get the doors open and let's get out of here.'

Too shocked by what she'd heard to resist when Adam grabbed one of her arms and his mate grabbed the other and threw her in through the open side-door of the van, Lexi cried out when her head smashed against the corner of a metal toolbox before the door was slammed shut and darkness descended.

45

After a day spent in front of Lee's TV, listening as his dad and his buddy indulged in another nostalgia trip while getting high, Ryan's nerves were jangling when his dad's phone started ringing. Seeing Lexi's name on the screen – or, rather, *Lady Alexis*, which was how Theo had saved it – he leaned forward and snatched it up off the coffee table.

'Lexi? Are you OK?' he asked when he answered it. 'I've been trying to call you for—'

'Hello, son,' an all-too familiar voice drawled into his ear. 'You've got some explaining to do, you thieving little fucker.'

'Who dat?' Theo asked from the other side of the room.

Shushing him with a wave of his hand, Ryan said, 'Where's Lexi? If you've hurt her, I'll—'

'You'll *what*?' spat Danny. 'Pull your Superman cape on and fly to her rescue? Too late, dick-face.'

'What d'you mean, too late?' Ryan asked, the blood draining from his face. 'Where is she? What have you done with her?'

'I ain't killed her, if that's what you're whingeing about,'

Danny sneered. 'But I *will* if I don't get my money back – and that's a promise you can bank with interest, son. Now be a good boy and put your father on the line.'

Turning to Theo, Ryan put his hand over the phone, and said, 'It's Danny. They've got Lexi and he wants to talk to you.'

Sobering up faster than Ryan had ever seen anyone sober up before, Theo got up and snatched the phone out of his hand.

'What've you done to my girl, Danny? 'Cos I swear to God I'll finish this once and for all if you've touched one hair on her head.'

'Oh, that's right, Adam said she'd told him it was you she was seeing, not Ryan,' Danny laughed nastily. 'That's just gonna make it all the sweeter when I do what I've got to do. But tell me, Theo, how did it feel to know you were dipping your wick in your son's sloppy seconds?'

'Don't fuck with me, Danny,' Theo warned, the suppressed rage in his voice sending a shiver down Ryan's spine. 'And leave my boy out of this. You fuckin' owe me.'

'The way I see it, you're the one who's sitting on my cash and gear, so I think you'll find it's the other way round.'

'I served fourteen years because of you, and you'd better believe I'll happily see out the rest of my life behind bars if anything happens to Alexis. Only this time I *will* be guilty.'

'Yeah, yeah, yadda, yadda,' Danny drawled. 'You fuckin' deserved everything you got, and you know it, so quit with the threats and remember that none of this would've happened if you hadn't fucked my girl and tried to run me off the estate.'

'Ain't my fault your girl was beggin' for it,' Theo shot back. 'If you'd been man enough to keep her satisfied, she wouldn't have come sniffing round the brothers.'

'Dad, shut it!' Ryan hissed. 'You're just winding him up.'

'Better listen to your little lapdog,' Danny jeered. 'He might not have your brawn, but he's sure as hell got the brains you missed out on. Subject of, put him back on.'

'You and me ain't done by a long shot,' Theo hissed. 'See when I get my hands on you—'

Snatching the phone out of his hand before he could finish his sentence, Ryan said, 'Just tell us what you want, Danny.'

'You know what I want,' Danny replied icily. 'And you know where I'll be when you fetch it. And make sure you've got every last penny and every last grain of snow you stole from me, or she'll be getting the first bullet, and you'll be watching.'

'*Fuck!*' Ryan yelled, hurling the phone down on the couch when the line went dead. 'We've gotta take it back.'

'Over my dead fuckin' body!' Theo argued. 'That cunt owes me for fourteen fucking years of my life.'

'He's got Lexi,' Ryan reminded him. 'He'll *kill* her.'

'Then I'll kill him,' said Theo. 'And he still ain't getting the money.'

'I thought you were supposed to love her?' Ryan said accusingly.

'Man, we're sitting on nearly two mill,' Theo fired back. 'And she ain't interested in me, so—'

'So you'd let her die?' Ryan cut in angrily. 'That's fuckin' sick!'

371

'Guys, guys, chill out,' Lee interjected, getting up and pushing them apart. 'Youse are reacting instead of acting, and you need to cool it and start thinking how to get around this.'

'You don't know Danny like I do,' Ryan said, raking his fingers through his hair as he paced the floor. 'He's already got Lexi, and as soon as *we* show up, we're all dead.'

'Not necessarily,' countered Lee. 'And you're forgetting we knew Danny back in the day, young blud, so we seen how he operated from time. Done the right way, we can take this fucker down so he *never* gets back up.'

'I'm pretty sure he's changed his methods since you two ran in those circles,' Ryan argued. 'He's got a twenty-strong crew, and a ton of street kids who think he's some kind of god 'cos he gives them the opportunity to earn a few quid. How the fuck are we supposed to take him on with those odds stacked against us?'

'Stealth,' said Lee. 'And who says there's only three of us? Me and T have got nuff brothers who'll step up for us if we give the word.'

'So, what you saying?' Ryan asked. 'We get a crew together and go in there all guns blazing. Because you do know that's how it'll end up, don't you? A gunfight bloodbath.'

'Let's sit down and talk this through calmly,' Lee said, heading back to his chair. 'I'll make some calls and call some trusted brothers over, then we'll make our move.'

46

Lexi had been knocked unconscious after hitting her head on the toolbox in the van. Awake now, and terrified to find herself tied to a chair in what appeared to be a damp, dimly lit cellar, she blinked to clear her vision as she looked around. She could hear faint music coming from up above, and there were shapes in the corner which she recognized from her mum's time in the pub as beer barrels and stacked crates containing bottles. There didn't seem to be anybody in there with her, so she strained against the cable ties that were binding her wrists together behind her back and her ankles to the chair legs, trying her hardest to snap them. Giving up when she felt the plastic digging into her flesh and getting tighter, she used her tongue to try and dislodge the thick tape covering her mouth, but all she got for her trouble was the sickening taste of glue. Next, she started rocking the chair, figuring that if she could tip it over and get the feet off the floor, she could try to slide the cable ties down and free her legs. But she hadn't managed to make it topple when a door opened, spilling light down a flight of stairs in the right corner of the room.

'Awake, are we?' Danny asked, smiling at her when he'd trotted down with Adam and two huge men behind him. 'Let me guess . . .' he went on, walking behind her and leaning down to examine the cable ties. 'You've been trying to snap them, but all you've done is nearly cut your wrists? That was a bit silly, wasn't it?'

Unnerved by his genial tone as he got up and walked round to the front again, Lexi eyed him warily when he squatted down and rested his arms on her lap.

'I remember you when you were a girl,' he said. 'You were a pretty little thing, but you've grown into a real beauty, haven't you? No wonder you've got all the men acting loopy over you. Even my boy here.' He jerked his head back at Adam. 'I hear he's been sending you flowers and trying to get you to talk to him, but you wouldn't give him the time of day. Shame, that. He could use a nice girl like you to get him on the straight and narrow.'

Barely able to breathe as her heart pounded in her chest, Lexi forced herself to hold his gaze. She hadn't seen much of him when she and Nicole were friends, but he'd always been nice to her on the few occasions their paths had crossed, and he still had the same twinkle in his eyes that had made her envy Nicole for having him as a dad back then. She was only glad that his bitch wife and daughter weren't here, because she was sure she wouldn't still be in one piece. But she had no idea what he planned for her, so it was still a possibility.

'Your men are on their way,' Danny told her now, pulling up

another chair and sitting in front of her before lighting a cigarette. 'Shouldn't be too long, so try to relax, eh?'

Unable to speak with the tape over her mouth, Lexi stared
at him; pleading with her eyes for him to let her go.

47

Tina Klein had already been ill, but after Adam had turned up and subjected her to several hours of violent sex – all from behind so he didn't have to see her face or risk catching whatever she had – she'd been in agony. The pain in her backside was excruciating, her stomach felt like it was filled with acid that was burning her alive from the inside out, and her head was pounding worse than any migraine she had ever experienced in her life before. Terrified when she tried to get up in the middle of the night and found she couldn't move her legs, she screamed out in pain as she rolled over and groped for her phone on the bedside table. With Caleb sleeping in the next room, she couldn't ring an ambulance, so, instead, she rang his father, Patrick.

It took three attempts before he answered, and he sounded as angry as he always did when she called him out of the blue.

'Why are you ringing at this time of the night? You know I've got work in the morning.'

'Help me, Pat,' she sobbed. 'I – I think I'm dying.'

'Yeah, whatever,' he scoffed. 'Been on the booze again, have ya? Well, serves you fuckin' ri—'

'Pat, I'm *bleeding*,' she cried. 'And C-Caleb's sleeping so I can't . . . I can't get an ambulance. Please, Pat, I need you.'

'Tina, what's going on?' Patrick asked, concerned now. 'Where are you?'

'At home,' she said, her voice weakening. 'But I don't think I . . .'

'Tina?' Patrick said when she tailed off. '*TINA?*'

Jumping out of bed, Patrick Kelly grabbed his jeans off the chair and yanked them on.

'What's going on?' his girlfriend, Fran, gazed blearily up at him over the duvet. 'Was that Tina on the phone? Is something wrong?'

'I think she's in some kind of trouble,' Patrick said, yanking his T-shirt over his head. 'I need to go round there. She sounded bad, babe; like *really* bad. Reckons she's bleeding, and my boy's in bed. And then she just stopped talking.'

'I'll drive you,' Fran said, getting up and reaching for her own jeans.

'Thanks, babe,' he said gratefully as he shoved his feet into his trainers and set off down the stairs.

When Fran pulled up outside Tina's house fifteen minutes later, Patrick leapt out of the car and banged on the front door with his fist. Getting no answer after several attempts, he stepped back and yelled her name.

'Is that Caleb?' Fran asked, nodding to one of the bedroom windows, where a small face was just about visible behind the net curtain.

'Stand back,' Patrick said, moving her out of the way before taking a run at the door and smashing into it with his shoulder.

Running inside when the door flew open, he tore up the stairs, yelling, 'Tina . . . are you up there?'

The door of the house next door opened, and a woman peeped out. 'What's all the noise?' she asked, giving Fran a suspicious look.

'I'm not sure,' Fran said. 'We think Tina might be ill.'

'Maybe she wants to stop going out at all hours and leaving that kiddie on his own,' the woman sniped. 'And as for them men she's been fetching home, she ought to be ashamed of herself. Had me awake for hours the other night, the racket she was making.'

Fran had only met Tina a couple of times, but she definitely hadn't struck her as the kind of woman her neighbour was making her out to be. Leaving the self-righteous bitch muttering to herself on the step, she walked inside Tina's house and pushed the splintered door shut.

'Fran, call an ambulance!' Patrick yelled.

Pulling her phone out of her pocket, Fran ran up the stairs. Stopping at the top when she saw a small boy rubbing his eyes in the doorway of the room next to the one in which she could hear Patrick trying to rouse his ex, she smiled, and said, 'Hello, lovely. You must be Caleb. Shall we get you back to bed?'

'Have you called them?' Patrick yelled, twisting his head as she passed the door.

'Just give me a second to put your boy to bed,' she hissed.

'Oh fuck, come on, Tina,' Patrick said, putting his ear to his ex's mouth before touching her throat to feel for a pulse.

'Ambulance,' Fran said, speaking into the phone as she came into the room behind him. Looking at Tina on the bed, her face deathly white, blood all over the sheet, she said, 'I don't know . . . Is she breathing, Pat?'

'I think so,' he said. 'But it's really shallow, like, so tell 'em to hurry.'

'My boyfriend says she is breathing,' Fran told the operator. 'But there's a lot of blood, so please send someone fast. No, I have no idea what's happened. She rang and said she needed help, so we came as fast as we could.'

'Adam . . .'

'What?' Patrick leaned his ear closer to Tina's mouth when she spoke. 'What did you say, love?'

'Adam,' she repeated, her voice little more than a whisper. 'He said he killed a woman . . . and . . .'

'And what?' Patrick pressed when her voice faded. 'Tina? And *what*?'

'He said he'll kill me and Caleb if I tell,' she croaked. 'And he . . .'

Her voice faded again, and Fran said, 'I'm sure she said he raped her.'

48

Amy Benson was sleeping when her mobile started ringing on the bedside table. Groping for it, she pulled it under the duvet.

'DI Benson.'

Eyes snapping open when she heard what the caller was saying, she sat up and shoved the quilt off her legs.

'Which hospital? I'm on my way.'

The duty doctor had just come out of Tina Klein's cubicle when Benson arrived at the A & E department of Wythenshawe hospital half an hour later.

'How is she?' she asked, after introducing herself.

'Not good,' he said quietly, ushering her to an office out of earshot of the cubicles. 'We're taking her into theatre as soon as the surgeon and anaesthesiologist get here. From my preliminary examination it appears she has sepsis as a result of a torn rectum, and possible internal damage.'

'Sexual assault?'

'I certainly wouldn't imagine it could have been consensual, given the size of the wound. She'd have been in considerable pain.'

'Is she conscious?'

'In and out.'

'Can I speak with her?'

'You can try, but keep it brief. Her partner's in the family room if you'd also like to speak to him. I believe he's the one who found her.'

Nodding, Benson gestured to the uniform who had met her outside, and they both followed the doctor into the cubicle. In the bed, covered in wires and attached to various monitors and drips, Tina Klein looked – and smelled – like death. She had looked unwell when Benson had called round at her house earlier that day, at which time she had verified Adam Harvey's claim that he had been with her at the time of the murder. She'd said she had been trying to get an appointment with her GP to see if he could give her some antibiotics, but the sepsis must already have begun to take hold by then to cause such a rapid deterioration.

'Tina?' she said quietly, perching on a chair beside the bed. 'It's Detective Inspector Benson. We spoke earlier. Can you hear me?'

Tina made a noise and her eyes flickered open.

'Adam,' she whispered. 'He wasn't . . . with me. He murder . . .'

'Are you saying Adam Harvey wasn't with you at the time I asked you about earlier?'

Tina gave the tiniest of nods, then added, 'He gave me . . . money . . . Said he kill . . . me and Caleb. Hurt me . . .'

'Did he do this to you?' Benson asked, glancing up at the uniformed officer who had just entered the cubicle.

Tina gave another tiny nod.

'Did he tell you he murdered someone?' Benson pressed.

'Yes.'

'And he gave you money to provide him with an alibi?'

Nod.

'And he also threatened to kill you and your son if you told anyone?'

Another nod, and then Tina's eyes closed and her head drooped to one side.

Jumping up when an alarm rang out and medical staff rushed in, Benson left the cubicle.

'Did you catch all that?' she asked the uniform.

'I did, ma'am,' he confirmed.

'I need to speak to her partner,' she said, heading for the family room.

A worried-looking man was sitting in the otherwise empty room; his elbows on his jiggling knees, his head in his hands.

'Are you Tina Klein's partner?' Benson asked.

'Yeah.' He looked up. 'Well, ex, actually. We split up last year.'

She showed him her badge and introduced herself, then asked, 'Could I take your name?'

'Patrick Kelly.'

Sitting beside him while the uniformed copper stood guard

by the door, Benson said, 'I spoke to Ms Klein earlier in relation to a murder I'm investigating. Did she mention it to you?'

'No.' Patrick shook his head. 'Not about talking to you, anyhow. We don't really . . . well, I'm with someone else now, so we don't talk much any more. That's why I was surprised when she rang me tonight. I thought she was gonna have a go – about child support, or whatever, you know? But when I heard the state of her voice, I knew summat bad must have happened, so we rushed over there.'

'It's a good job you did, by the look of things,' Benson said.

'She's gonna be all right, isn't she?'

'I believe they'll be taking her into theatre soon, so the doctor will keep you updated.'

'How the fuck could someone do that to her?' Patrick muttered, shaking his head. 'Me and her didn't have the best relationship, and I've done stuff I proper regret now. But I *never* hurt her like that.'

'When you got to the house tonight, did Tina tell you what had happened?' Benson asked.

'She wasn't really making much sense, to be honest, so me and Fran – my girlfriend – thought she might be delirious, and that. She said the name Adam, though – we both heard that. And Fran reckoned she said rape, so it's pretty fuckin' obvious what she meant, isn't it?' He looked at Benson with haunted eyes.

'Don't worry, we'll find out what happened,' Benson assured him. 'Before I go, do you recall anything else she said?'

'Yeah, she said this Adam, whoever he is, said he'd killed someone and would kill her and Caleb if she said anything,' said Patrick. 'But I swear to God, if the bastard goes anywhere near my boy . . .'

He didn't finish the sentence, but Benson knew exactly what he meant – and she didn't blame him one bit.

49

Carrying his sports bag in which he had packed his clothes the previous day, Ryan walked across the parking lot of The Danski and rapped on the metal door. A small grille in the centre opened and a pair of eyes peered out at him before the door clicked open.

Stepping inside, Ryan touched fists with the doorman, Piotr, and then handed him an envelope, saying, 'We've had a tip-off that immigration are on their way to check for illegals, so clear everyone out and get yourself off home. That should keep you going till you find something else.'

A Polish man whose work visa had long ago run out, Piotr shook Ryan's hand and then followed him into the clubroom and watched as he made his way behind the bar before disappearing through an internal door which led to the back door and the door to the cellar.

'What the fuck is going on in here tonight?' Sue, the bar manager, asked, placing her hands on her hips. 'It's like Piccadilly fucking Circus.'

'Immigration are coming to check for illegals,' Piotr told her.

'You're kidding?' she spluttered. 'Fuck that shit, I'm out of here!'

Turning a blind eye when she grabbed her handbag from under the counter before opening the till and helping herself to a wad of notes which she stuffed down her bra before rushing out, Piotr pulled the plug on the music system and turned the main lights on.

'Everybody out,' he shouted when all eyes turned his way. 'We're about to be raided.'

Instant chaos ensued as customers, worried about getting collared, named and shamed, rushed for the door; and the girls, most of whom were Eastern European, scrambled to get to the changing room to grab their clothes and bags before fleeing.

Sue had left the till drawer open and there was still a stack of notes in it. Walking over, Piotr lifted them out and stuffed them into his pocket along with the envelope Ryan had given him. If it had been Ryan's place, he'd have closed the drawer without taking a penny. But it was Adam's place, and he despised the man, so he felt no shame about stealing from him.

Down in the cellar, Danny was circling Ryan as Mash and the other bruiser, a man called Franko, stood in the shadows pointing sawn-off shotguns at him.

'Where's Theo?' Danny demanded. 'Fucker might be a shithouse, but there's no way he'd have sent you on your own.'

'It was my decision,' Ryan replied coolly, holding his father-in-law's gaze. 'He's already done time for you, so you and him are quits. This is between you and me. Here's your money and your gear . . .' He held out the bag. 'Everything's there, so you don't need to count it. But no doubt you will anyway.'

'Too fuckin' right we will,' Adam piped up, aiming a punch at Ryan's face.

Forcing himself not to flinch, Ryan kept his gaze on Danny. 'Like I say, it's all there. And I'm the one who set it all up, so let her go.'

'Who? Your little girlfriend?' Danny raised an eyebrow. 'I don't think so, matey. See, in my world, shagging your wife's best mate is a no-no – especially when your wife also happens to be my *daughter*, fuckwad!' he added through gritted teeth as he drove his fist into Ryan's gut.

Doubling over, Ryan clutched at his stomach and gasped, 'Do the right thing, Danny. This has got nothing to do with her.'

'*Wrong!*' Adam spat, booting him hard in the back and sending him sprawling to his knees. 'It's got *everything* to do with her, considering you and her have been taking the piss out of us for years.'

'I didn't believe my boy when he tried to tell me what you were up to,' Danny said, putting his foot on Ryan's head and grinding his face into the concrete. 'For years I've been holding him back and treating *you* like my son instead of him; punishing him for the lies that bitch told the cops about him. But now I know you're the one who set that up to get to me, I think it's time I made amends. So here's what I'm gonna do.'

He squatted down now, and yanked Ryan's head up so he could look him in the eye. 'I'm gonna let him beat the shit out of you,' he hissed. 'And when you can't take any more, but you're still just a *little* bit alive, me and my guys are gonna leave him to take care of your girlfriend – while you watch. How does that sound?'

'Don't you fuckin' touch her, or I swear to God I'll kill you all,' Ryan spat, blood trickling out of his mouth and down his chin.

'Ah, such loyalty,' Danny said. Then, slamming Ryan's face down into the concrete again, he said, 'Pity you couldn't give it to the people who've been carrying your sorry arse for the past ten fuckin' years, though, you backstabbing fuckin' bastard!'

Parked out of sight behind a derelict warehouse some way down the road from The Danski, Theo, Lee, and five of their old mates watched as a load of men streamed out of the club, some climbing into cars, others running; followed a few minutes later by twenty or so women in various states of undress.

When the last of them had disappeared and the road was quiet again, the men pulled up their hoods and made their way over.

Piotr, carrying a bag stuffed with bottles of brandy and whisky he'd lifted on his way out, had just stepped out through the door when he saw the men heading his way. Scared that they were immigration officials, he was about to drop the bag and run, when a muscular black man at the front of the group said, 'Stay cool, brother; we're with Ry. Where are they?'

Unsure what was going on, but not fool enough to interfere, Piotr said, 'Cellar.' Then, pushing the door open again to allow them entry, he walked quickly away without looking back.

Ryan had told them the layout of the club, and also that the CCTV system had been out of order for months. Locking the door after they had all quietly entered, Theo pointed the way to the bar, behind which he knew one of the doors led to the cellar.

Sitting on the chair again, watching as Adam booted Ryan repeatedly in the ribs and head, Danny sucked on the cigarette he'd lit and chuckled softly to himself.

'That's ma boy,' he said proudly to Mash and Franko. 'And to think we all thought he was gonna turn out gay, eh? Proper little animal, ain't he? Right chip off the old block.'

He twisted in his seat now, and looked back at Lexi. Frowning when he saw that she had her eyes squeezed shut and tears were streaming down her cheeks, he said, 'You not watchin', darlin'? Oi!' He booted her leg. 'I'm talkin' to you.'

A loud click brought his head back around, and he smiled when he saw Theo coming down the stairs holding a semi-automatic.

'Well, well, you decided to join us, at last,' he drawled, tapping Adam's shoulder to stop him.

Panting, Adam spun round, and swallowed nervously when

he got his first look at his father's old rival. Unnerved by the sheer size of the man, and more so by the evil look in his dark eyes, he edged behind his dad.

'It's been a long time,' Danny went on, taking another drag on his cigarette. 'You're looking good, T. Amazing what a spell inside can do for ya, eh? All that free gym time to build yourself up. No wonder your little girl over here wanted a piece of you. These young bitches love a nice bit of muscle, don't they?'

'You're a funny man,' Theo said, a cold smile on his lips as he walked toward the man who had set him up.

'Not too close,' Danny said, nodding toward Mash and Franko who had stepped out of the shadows with their sawn-offs, both of which were now aimed at Theo. 'You know how delicate the triggers on these old things can be.'

'If I was you, I'd be telling them to back off,' Theo said, jerking his head toward the stairs as Lee and the others came down. Grinning when he saw Danny clock their weapons, he said, 'Recognize them, do ya? Yeah, that's right – they're yours. Cheers for that, bud. So much faster off the mark than the relics your guys have got. So much more *accurate*.'

'So what now?' Danny asked. 'We all gonna shoot the fuck out of each other so no one gets out alive?'

'Well, I ain't going down for you again, so I guess so.' Theo shrugged. 'Either that or you admit you set me up and pay your dues like the boss man you pretend to be.'

'You're the one who tried to set *him* up,' Adam protested,

still hiding behind his dad. 'Ain't his fault it backfired and you got caught.'

'That what you've been telling him, is it?' Theo asked, his dark gaze still fixed on Danny. 'That it was me who killed that copper and tried to pin it on you? Tell your mates that, an' all, did you?'

'What's this?' Mash said, frowning as he lowered his gun.

'Oh, didn't you know?' Theo looked back at the old bruiser. 'Yeah, it was him. I was nowhere fuckin' near. Knew nothing about it till I got nicked.'

'This right, Dan?' Franko asked.

'Is it fuck,' Danny scoffed. 'He's talking shit to get himself off the hook.'

'No he ain't,' Ryan wheezed, clutching his ribs as he hauled himself into a sitting position. 'Ask Leroy and Fletch. I heard them and Danny laughing about it when I first got on the crew. They were there that night; they saw him do it and helped him set my dad up.'

'And I'm not the only one he's stitched up,' Theo said. 'I met two guys in Wakefield who are serving time for this spineless cunt. Like to make out you're the big man with the big heart, don't you, Danny boy? Set those kids up with nice trainers and phones, then send them off to deliver your gear and guns – and fuck 'em when it goes wrong.'

'I'm good to them kids,' Danny shot back. 'Done more for 'em them *you've* ever done, you cocky twat.'

'Not much I *could* do from a cell, was there?' Theo retorted angrily, standing nose to nose with his old adversary. 'And all the time I was stuck in there, you was out here livin' it large; playing daddy to my boy and treating him like the son you *wish* that rapist you spawned coulda been.'

'Your boy's a cunt, like you,' Danny replied coolly. 'But at least he had the sense to fetch back what you stole, so we'll leave it at that this time.'

'Fuck you!' Theo snarled, headbutting him. 'This ain't over till I *say* it's over!'

'I'm outta here,' Mash said, laying the sawn-off on top of a beer barrel. 'We've got no beef, Theo,' he added respectfully. 'I didn't know you'd been screwed.'

'Same,' said Franko, shooting a look of disgust at Danny, who had dropped to his knees and was cradling his broken nose in his hands as blood dripped onto the concrete beneath him.

'We're cool,' Theo said, nodding for the other guys to let them go.

'Not you,' Lee said, blocking Adam's path when he tried to follow the men.

Face as white as a sheet, trembling from head to toe, Adam backed away and looked over at Ryan, who was helping Lexi to her feet after cutting the cable ties with a knife he'd spotted on the ledge behind her.

'Come on, Ry . . . this has gone far enough,' he spluttered. 'We're family, bro. You're m-married to my sister. I was your best *man*.'

'Just because I *used* to fuck your sister, that don't make us bros,' Ryan said icily as he held Lexi to him. 'Ain't that what you said at your party that night, after I stopped you from trying to rape her?'

'Get on the chair,' Theo snarled, smashing Adam in the face with the butt of the gun.

Crying hysterically, Adam staggered to the chair and sat down.

'Not like that.' Theo dragged him up by the back of his jacket and flipped him onto his front.

'Wh-what you gonna do?' Adam wailed. 'Please don't hurt me! Please, I'm begging you. *Please . . .*'

As Theo was tugging Adam's belt out of his trousers to tie his wrists together, the door at the top of the stairs opened and Mash and Franko lumbered back down.

'A shitload of pigs are pulling up outside,' Mash hissed.

'Fuck,' Theo muttered.

'Fire exit,' Ryan said, indicating a door in the far corner. 'The building's blocked off at both sides so you'll have time to get to the canal at the back before they get round there. *Go!*'

Nodding, Theo told Mash and Franko to grab their discarded guns. Then, ramming his fist into Adam's face, knocking him out, he booted Danny in the head before grabbing the sports bag and following the others. At the exact same time he pushed the fire door shut, the boom of metal slamming into metal came from above.

'No one was here except me, you and them two,' Ryan whispered to Lexi as he held her.

Lexi nodded and buried her face in his chest. 'I'm so sorry,' she whimpered. 'This is all my fault. They tricked me. I – I thought it was you texting me or I'd never have agreed to meet him.'

'None of this is down to you,' Ryan insisted. 'And you just tell the police what happened, OK? They kidnapped you and brought you here, then lured me over so they could try to kill us because they think we're having an affair. The rest is irrelevant, so we stick to that – right?'

'Yes,' Lexi whispered, gazing up into his eyes.

Hugging her gently, Ryan heard footsteps and the call of *'Police!'* overhead, and yelled, 'Down here!'

Epilogue

The Lord Rodney pub, a ten-minute walk from Manchester Crown Court, was busier than it had been in years, and the landlady was beaming as she and her staff ran around, catering to the group who had taken over one side of the place.

It was nine months since the stand-off in the cellar of The Danski, and Danny had been sentenced three months earlier to twenty-five years for charges ranging from kidnapping and unlawful imprisonment, to possession with intent to supply class-A drugs and illegal firearms. DI Benson and her team had uncovered a treasure trove of coke, heroin, guns and ammunition in a private lock-up in Danny's name during their investigation, but it had been determined that Ryan wasn't involved in that side of things, as he had been running the legitimate business, so he'd been cleared, despite Danny trying to implicate him.

Adam's trial had taken longer to reach a conclusion, as he'd had more charges levelled against him than his father – several of which were accusations of rape by women who came forward after he was arrested. There had been no proof to connect him to the murder of Lexi's mum, so he hadn't been charged with that; and he also couldn't be held to account for Tina Klein's death after she passed away on the operating table, because she hadn't been able to give a formal statement to confirm what she'd told DI Benson and her ex. Those cases aside, he had been sentenced to two life sentences for the murder of Ada Briggs, the attempted murder of James Stanley, and three charges of rape.

The group of people whose lives had been the most badly damaged by the men were in a celebratory mood now, and the atmosphere was buzzing as they all swigged the champagne Theo and Ryan had ordered.

Sitting beside Lexi on a curved bench seat under the window, Ryan looped his arm around the back of it and stroked her hair.

'You OK, beautiful?'

'I'm fine,' she said. 'You?'

'Over the fucking moon,' he grinned.

'Let's have a toast,' Theo said, getting up and grabbing the champagne bottle that was standing in the middle of the table to refill all their glasses. 'To the Harveys . . .' He raised his into the air. 'May the pair of them rot in their cells for the rest of their miserable lives.'

'Hear hear,' the others chorused, raising their glasses.

Sitting back down, Theo gazed at his son and Lexi over the rim of his glass as he sipped his drink. Along with Lee and the other guys, Theo had gone straight to his flat in Stockport after running out of the club, and Ryan and Lexi had joined them there later after giving their statements to the police and getting checked over in hospital. As soon as he'd seen the way they looked at each other, and how gently his son treated her, he had known they had feelings for each other. It had been quite a shock at the time, because it had never even occurred to him that there might be anything between them. But once he'd got his head around it, he was fine with it; and it had actually worked out for the best, because he'd since found a woman who looked at him the way Lexi looked at Ryan – and the sex was mind-blowing.

'No regrets?' Debs asked quietly.

Snapping his gaze off his son and Lexi, Theo grinned as he put his arm around her and pulled her to him. 'None whatsoever, darlin',' he said truthfully before planting a soft kiss on her lips.

'Pack it in,' she chided, pulling away. 'You're getting me all worked up.'

'Save it for later.' He winked. 'I've booked us a table at Giuseppe's for nine, then we're gonna go back to the hotel and get wasted.'

'As long as you can still get up in the morning,' Debs said. 'The flight's at eight, but we need to check in by six. Which reminds me, I've got to nip over and say bye to Six before we go.'

'Poor fucker.' Theo shook his head. 'Who'd have thought getting stabbed in the neck could paralyse you?'

'Hey, don't be feeling sorry for him,' said Debs. 'He's a fighter, so there's every chance he'll beat the odds and walk again. And, in the meantime, he's quite happy being pampered by his biker ladies – especially Lydia. You should see the way his eyes light up when she walks into the room. She's definitely the one that got away, and now they're back in touch, I've got a feeling I'll be needing to buy a hat before too long.'

'Sack the hat, get them to fly over and get hitched on the beach near our place,' Theo said.

'Our place?' Debs gave him a questioning look.

'Yep.' Theo grinned. 'Got the call this morning while you were in the shower. Deal's done. We can pick the keys up when we land.'

'Oh my God,' Debs squealed, throwing her arms around his neck.

'What's this?' Ryan called over. 'Not proposed already, have you, Dad?'

'Hey, don't be giving her ideas,' Theo laughed. 'I'm just telling her my offer was accepted on the house.'

'Brilliant,' Ryan said. 'I'm really happy for you.'

'Fuck, yeah!' Lee crowed, coming up behind Theo and Debs and wrapping his arms around their necks. 'When do we move in?'

'*We* move in tomorrow,' Debs said, giving him a mock-stern look. '*You* can sleep on the decking – if you behave.'

'My idea of heaven,' he grinned.

'What about you two?' Theo asked his son. 'You gonna join us?'

'Try and stop us,' Ryan said, winking at Lexi.

* * *

Across town, wearing sunglasses and scarves in an effort to conceal their identities, Rachel and Nicole climbed out of the back of the tatty Transit van that had brought what was left of their possessions to their new flat on the Kingston estate. They had pleaded to be moved further out, but there had been nothing else available; and now their house had been repossessed and the bailiffs had removed everything of any value from it, they'd had no choice but to accept it. The villa in Marbella was also gone, seized under the Proceeds of Crime Act, so they had pretty much lost everything apart from their clothes and the bits and pieces of furniture they'd had stored in the garage.

'I'm going to kill myself,' Nicole said, the tears in her eyes hidden behind the glasses as she stared up at the depressing block of flats.

'Shut up and get inside,' Rachel hissed, pushing her toward the communal door as the van driver and his mate climbed out and started unloading the boxes. 'Third floor,' she called to them before scuttling after her daughter.

As they reached the door, a woman pushed it open from the other side. Stopping in her tracks when she saw them, she smiled nastily.

'Well, well . . . if it ain't Queen and Princess Harvey. What are you bitches doing round here? Thought you was too good for this place?'

Refusing to be cowed, Rachel raised her chin and said, 'Can we get past, please?'

'Oh, you have *got* to be joking?' the woman said when she clocked the van and the heap of boxes the men had unloaded. 'No way are you moving back here!'

'Mind your own business,' Nicole snapped. 'And stop blocking the door.'

'Or what?' the woman challenged. 'Your daddy ain't here to protect you now, love, so I wouldn't be copping attitude if I was you. In fact, you'd be better off getting back in that van and fucking off while you've still got a chance, 'cos you ain't welcome round here.'

She brushed past them at that, and Rachel twisted her head when she heard the Transit doors slamming shut.

'Hey, where are you going?' she called out when the driver and his mate opened the front doors. 'You can't just leave all those boxes there. I've paid you to bring them up to the flat.'

'Nah, love, you only paid us to fetch 'em over,' the driver said. 'And think yourself lucky I didn't charge extra for fetching youse two, an' all,' he added, before climbing into the van.

'You wait till my husband hears about this!' Rachel yelled.

Grinning, he started the engine and pulled away, sticking two fingers up as he went.

It was late afternoon by the time the van transporting Adam and several other prisoners who'd been sentenced that day arrived at the prison. Inside, he was signed in and ordered to strip, and was then searched before being escorted to the cell he'd been allocated at the far end of the first-floor landing.

RUNNING SCARED

Terrified by the evil looks being aimed his way as he was forced to walk through the middle of the other prisoners who were standing around in groups, Adam kept his head down and his gaze on the floor.

'Can you lock me in, please?' he begged the guard when they reached his cell.

'I don't think your room-mate would be too pleased if he came back and couldn't get in, do you?' the guard said, giving a sly smile before walking out.

Sinking down onto the edge of the bottom bunk when he was alone, Adam swiped at a tear that was trickling down his cheek.

'What you cryin' for, batty boy?' a gruff voice asked.

Looking up, Adam's stomach fell through the floor when he saw three men in the doorway, and his eyes widened in fear when the one at the front, a mixed-race man with huge biceps and a tattoo of a dragon on his neck, walked slowly in.

'Welcome to Wakefield,' the man said, grinning down at him as the others entered the cell and the door was slammed shut. 'Theo sends his regards . . .'

OUT NOW

RUN

Mandasue Heller

When there's nothing left, and no escape . . .

After being cheated on by her ex, Leanne Riley is trying her hardest to get her life back on track, which isn't easy without a job and living in a bedsit surrounded by a junkie and a madwoman.

On a night out with her best friend, she meets Jake, a face from her past who has changed beyond all recognition. Jake is charming, handsome and loaded, a far cry from the gawky teenager he used to be. Weary of men, Leanne isn't easy to please, but Jake tries his best to break through the wall she's built around herself.

But good looks and money can hide a multitude of sins. Is that good-looking face just a mask? And what's more, what will it take to make it slip, and who will die in the process . . . ?

PRAISE FOR MANDASUE HELLER

'Mandasue has played a real blinder with this fantastic novel'
Martina Cole on *Forget Me Not*

'Captivating from first page to last'
Jeffery Deaver on *Lost Angel*

OUT NOW

SAVE ME

Mandasue Heller

When Ellie Fisher misses her train home one night, she has no idea that being in the right place at the wrong time will change her life forever.

That night she comes across Gareth, a young man about to take his own life, because as far as he's concerned there is nothing left to live for. Putting her own life in danger, Ellie convinces Gareth that there is always something left. Her own life is no bed of roses, she explains, but she always pushes on.

However, good deeds aren't always repaid the way we want. Has Ellie unwittingly put her life in danger, or is the real danger a lot closer to home?

PRAISE FOR MANDASUE HELLER

'One of the bad girls of gritty crime,
Heller has written a blinder'
Daily Mirror

'Thoroughly gripping'
Guardian on *Two-Faced*

BRUTAL

Mandasue Heller

When Frank Peters' wife Maureen dies, he feels that his once-idyllic life on the Yorkshire Moors is over. And with a daughter emigrating to Australia and a son who has his own marital problems, Frank feels resigned to a life of loneliness. Then one night he finds a frightened young woman hiding at the back of his farmhouse. She explains that her name is Irena and she was brought to this country by a man who promised her the world and then forced her into prostitution.

Frank offers her a bed for the night but it's the middle of winter, and when heavy snowfall prevents her from leaving the next day, he's forced to extend the invitation. But the longer Irena stays, the easier it gets for the men she's trying to escape from to find her.

People-trafficking could just be the tip of the iceberg, and Frank has no idea what these people are really capable of.

WITNESS

Mandasue Heller

She saw too much. She knows too much.

Holly Evans and her over-protective mother, Josie, are living a hand-to-mouth existence, moving constantly from one squalid dump to the next. When they move into an illegally sub-let council flat in Manchester, Holly feels settled for the first time in her life – even if she is forbidden to go out, or even open the front door to callers when her mum's at work. What exactly are they hiding from?

Then Holly has a falling out with her best friend, and suddenly finds herself becoming increasingly isolated and alone in the world. But she is about to make a new friend in Suzie – the glamorous woman who lives directly across the road, who Holly witnesses being beaten up by her violent boyfriend. When it happens a second time it's Holly who Suzie turns to for help, and a bond is quickly formed between the pair. But whoever Holly and Josie have been running from is about to find them, and nothing will ever be the same again . . .

You can only run for so long, and some will kill for your silence . . .

TURN OVER TO READ A
BRAND-NEW SHORT STORY BY

Mandasue Heller

A SHOT IN
THE DARK

1

'One love . . .' Jaynie's voice floated out of her tiny amp as morning shoppers rushed past her on Market Street. 'One he-a-art . . .' A couple of heads turned. 'Let's get together and feel all right . . .' A fifty-pence piece landed on the scrap of blanket she'd placed on the floor.

More coins were dropped as the song progressed, and a couple of people stopped to listen before moving on again. Smiling when she saw a few pound coins among the silver and copper, Jaynie strummed the opening chord of her next song.

'There's a fi-re, starting in my heart . . . rea-ching a fever pitch, it's bringing me out the dar—'

The word froze on her tongue when she spotted her ex, Carl Davies, on the other side of the precinct. He'd been released from prison a few days earlier; she'd known he would come after her, so she had packed up and left her flat in Liverpool as soon as the liaison officer told her he was on his way out. But how the hell had he found her here, in Manchester, when she hadn't told anyone where she was going?

Anyone apart from Annie, that was. Her best mate ... her sister from another mister ... the girl she had thought she could trust with her life.

God, why had she ever thought she could rely on Annie to keep her mouth shut? The girl had always fancied Carl, and he'd known it, so it had probably taken him all of two seconds to seduce the information out of her.

Jolted into action when Carl locked eyes with her and gave a sinister little smile, Jaynie snatched a handful of coins off the blanket, grabbed her rucksack and legged it, leaving her amp, microphone and stand behind.

'Watch it,' a man barked when she ploughed into him at the corner, dislodging the lid of the coffee cup he was holding.

'Sorry,' she gasped, glancing back over her shoulder and swallowing loudly when she spied Carl weaving his way through the crowd behind her.

She barged past the complaining man and ran out into the road, oblivious to the screeching tyres and angry curses from the drivers who narrowly avoided hitting her. Up ahead, a bus was idling at a stop. Reaching it as the doors were beginning to close, she forced her way on, and yelped at the startled driver: 'Please go! He's going to kill me!'

Staring out through the back window as she spoke, she almost wet herself with fear when she saw Carl running hell for leather up the road. But just as she thought the driver was going to kick her off, the doors swished shut and the bus lurched forward.

'Are you OK, love?' a woman asked.

Jaynie snapped her head round and felt her cheeks redden when she saw the curious looks on the faces of the other passengers.

'Sorry,' she mumbled. 'My– my ex was chasing me, and I was scared he'd catch up.'

'You're safe now,' the driver assured her. 'Go sit down and catch your breath.'

Jaynie made her way to an empty seat across the aisle from the woman.

'Men, eh?' The woman rolled her eyes.

Jaynie replied with a weak smile and, propping the guitar on the seat beside her, took out the money she'd managed to grab. Dismayed to see that she'd left the pound coins behind, she chewed on her thumbnail and stared out through the window as the bus headed out of town. She had no idea where it was going – or what she would do when it got there – but Carl turning up at her busking spot had been no accident. And if he'd tracked her down to there, she had no doubt that he would also know about the hostel where she'd been staying.

The other passengers had all got off the bus by the time the driver pulled into a stop and twisted round in his seat to tell Jaynie that he was heading back to the depot from there.

'You're welcome to stay on if you want to go back to town,' he offered.

Afraid to go back and risk running into Carl again, Jaynie shook her head and gathered her things together.

'How much do I owe you?' she asked.

'It's on me,' he said, waving her hand away when she held out the coins.

Jaynie thanked him and stepped down onto the pavement. Unsure where she was, she looked around when the bus moved off. It was a run-down area, with an estate of old terraced houses on one side and a row of scruffy shops on the other. Hoping that one of the shop workers might be able to direct her back to the hostel so could nip in and grab her stuff, she waited for a set of traffic lights further down the road to change so she could cross over. But as the lights turned red and the traffic stopped, her blood ran cold when she spotted Carl climbing out of a taxi in the queue.

Aware that he must have seen her getting off the bus, she turned and ran into the estate. Throat on fire, she raced past the houses until she spotted a narrow passageway between two blocks. She swerved into it and continued on to the alleyway that ran behind the houses. The ground there was cobbled and jagged shards of glass and coils of barbed-wire topped the walls on both sides. Most of the gates were closed, but one, halfway along, was slightly ajar. Desperate to get out of sight before Carl caught up with her, she used her shoulder to force her way in and then pushed the gate shut behind her.

The small garden she found herself in was a jungle of thigh-high weeds and nettles. Three overflowing wheelie bins stood behind the gate, and a heap of stinking bin-bags were piled in the doorway of a brick outhouse. Clambering over the bags when she heard footsteps in the alleyway, her heart leapt into her throat when she accidentally plucked the guitar strings as she squatted in the shadows at the side of an ancient toilet. The footsteps abruptly stopped, and the hairs on the back of her neck stood on end when she heard Carl's voice croon: 'Oh, Jaynie . . . Come out, come out, wherever you are . . .'

A door at the back of the house suddenly opened, and Jaynie held her breath when she heard shuffling footsteps heading her way. A few seconds later, an elderly woman appeared in the outhouse doorway carrying a bag of rubbish.

About to deposit the bag with the others, the woman hesitated when she spotted Jaynie squatting in the shadows. Before she could ask what the hell she was doing there, the gate hinges squealed behind her, and when she saw the terror in the girl's eyes she quickly placed the bag on top of the pile to conceal her before turning to face the young man who had just entered her garden.

'Who are you and what do you want?' she demanded. 'There's nothing here for you to steal, so get off my property!'

'Chill out, love, I'm only looking for my girlfriend,' Carl replied smoothly. 'Haven't seen her, have you? She's mixed-race, with long curly hair and a guitar?'

'Get away from me!' the woman barked.

'That's not very nice, now, is it, love?' Carl drawled as he took a step toward her. 'And there was me being all polite.'

'*HELP!*' the woman screeched. '*SOMEBODY HELP ME! I'M BEING ATTACKED!*'

'What's going on?' a gruff voice called out from a neigh-bouring house.

Heart pounding, Jaynie heard Carl mutter '*Shit!*', then foot-steps as he ran away – followed by more footsteps as the neighbour came out to see what was going on.

'You all right?' the man asked. 'He didn't touch you, did he?'

'He was about to,' the old woman replied. 'But I think you scared him off.'

'Did you know him?

'No. Never seen him before in my life.'

'Well, get yourself inside while I do a quick scout around,' the man said. 'And make sure all your doors and windows are locked.'

'Thanks, pet, I will,' the old woman agreed, her voice quivering.

Still squatting in the outhouse, Jaynie heard the man leave the garden, followed by the sound of the gate being pushed shut. Then the old woman lifted the bag of rubbish off the pile and peered down at her.

'You can come out now,' she said, no trace of the weak little voice she'd used on the man.

Climbing over the foul-smelling bags, Jaynie said, 'Thanks for not giving me away.'

'You stink,' the woman said bluntly as she looked her up and down. 'And you look like a vagrant.'

Cheeks blazing, Jaynie said, 'I've been living in a hostel, and it's a bit of a tip, so . . .'

'Why were you hiding from your boyfriend?' the woman interrupted, folding her arms.

'He's not my boyfriend,' Jaynie muttered.

'A mark, then?' The woman raised an eyebrow.

'Sorry?' Jaynie was confused, then offended when she realized what the woman meant. 'Absolutely not! I'm no thief.'

'Why was he so desperate to find you, then?'

'Because . . .' Jaynie tailed off and sighed. 'It's a long story, but it's not your problem so I won't bore you with it. If I could just wait here for a couple of minutes to make sure he's gone, I'll get out of your hair.'

The woman peered at her for a few seconds. Then, jerking her head toward the house, she said, 'Come inside. I've just brewed a pot of tea and you look like you could do with a cup.'

'Thanks, but I don't want to put you to any trouble,' Jaynie said, hitching her rucksack higher onto her shoulder.

'If it was any trouble I wouldn't have offered,' the woman said, already heading back to the house.

Jaynie hesitated and bit her lip. She wasn't sure she wanted to spend any more time with the rude old woman, but it had to be better than going back out into the alley and running into Carl. It was also freezing, and she hadn't made enough money that morning to buy a cup of tea, so the offer was too tempting to refuse.

Decided, she followed the woman inside and looked around the small kitchen as the door was locked and bolted. It was a throwback to the 1950s with its yellow cupboards and peeling lino, and there was even an old tin bath standing in the corner.

'Here you go, Dolly Daydream,' the woman said, handing Jaynie one of the two cups of tea she'd poured before walking into the next room.

Jaynie followed and found herself in a tiny, stiflingly hot parlour that was crammed full of old, grubby-looking furniture and dusty ornaments of animals and dancing girls.

'Take your coat off and sit down,' the woman ordered as she took a seat on a sagging armchair beside the open fire.

Jaynie unhooked the strap of her guitar from around her neck and stood it in the corner, then dropped her rucksack next to it. She draped her jacket over the bag and then perched on the two-seater settee.

'Biscuit?' The woman pulled a pack of Digestives from down the side of her cushion.

'Er, no, I'm OK, thanks,' Jaynie said politely.

'Watching your figure, eh?' The woman sniffed and stuffed them back where they'd come from. 'I'm Phyllis. And you are?'

'Jaynie.'

'So, Jaynie, where are you from? I've been trying to place your accent.'

'Liverpool.'

'Ah . . . a *scouser*.' Phyllis smiled. 'A gentleman from your neck of the woods used to court me in my younger days, so I really ought to have recognized it. And what brings you over here?'

'That man you just met is my ex,' Jaynie said. 'He's been in prison, but they let him out early so I had to leave town.'

'What was he in prison for?'

'Like I said, it's a long story,' Jaynie said, her stiff shoulders beginning to relax as the heat from the fire seeped into her bones.

'I'm in no hurry.' Phyllis settled back in her seat.

Sensing that she wasn't the type to take no for an answer, Jaynie said, 'OK... long story short, I was seeing him for a few months, but he started to get really controlling; telling me who I could and couldn't talk to, and checking my phone to see if I'd been messaging any men.'

'Ah, one of *those*,' Phyllis said knowingly.

'I tried to tell him I wasn't like that, and I made a real effort to prove he could trust me,' Jaynie went on. 'But nothing I did made any difference. And then he hit me, so that was it.'

'Is that why he went to prison?'

'No. He apologized and promised it'd never happen again, so I didn't report him that time.'

'That old chestnut,' Phyllis snorted. 'And I suppose you forgave him?'

'Definitely not; I'm not stupid,' Jaynie replied indignantly.

'And yet you put up with the other stuff before it got to that,' Phyllis shot back before taking a noisy swig of tea.

'Yeah, well, I don't like to give up on people without trying to sort things out first,' Jaynie muttered. 'But once I realized he wasn't going to change, I put an end to it.'

'I take it that didn't go down too well?'

'He left me alone for a couple of weeks so I thought he'd accepted it,' Jaynie said. 'But then I started getting weird phone calls at all hours, and I felt like someone was following me whenever I went out. Then, one night, I got up to use the loo and saw him standing across the road. He was staring at my window with this really weird look on his face, and it freaked me out so I called the police. They spoke to him, but he convinced them we'd just had an argument and he was waiting for me to calm down, so they let him go. But a few nights later . . .'

'A few nights later?' Phyllis prompted when Jaynie stopped talking and blew out a tense breath.

Blinking back the tears that were welling in her eyes, Jaynie said, 'He broke into my flat when I was sleeping, and he . . .' Unable to say out loud what he'd done, because the shame she'd felt ever since still burned deeply, she swallowed before continuing: 'He kept me prisoner for three days. I genuinely thought he was going to kill me, and I think he would have if my neighbour hadn't spotted him through the window and got suspicious. She knew I was terrified of him, so when I didn't answer my door or phone, she guessed something was wrong and called the police.'

'Sounds like a smart girl.'

'She saved my life,' said Jaynie. 'I was in a pretty bad way when the police got there, so I couldn't tell them he was lying when he said we were still seeing each other and he'd come home and found me like that. They didn't believe him and he was arrested, then it came out in court that he'd done the same thing to two previous girlfriends. He got four years, but he only served two.'

'And now he's out and seeking revenge?'

'Yep.' Jaynie wiped her nose on the back of her hand. 'My so-called best mate must have told him I was here, 'cos she's the only one who knows. I always knew she fancied him, but I never thought she'd betray me like that.'

'Women often show their true colours at the whiff of penis,' Phyllis said sagely. Then, chuckling when she saw Jaynie's eyebrows shoot up, she said, 'Don't look so shocked, dear; I was young and beautiful once, and I've met my fair share of alley-cats, believe you me. All sweetness and light until a good-looking fellow makes an appearance, then the claws come out and it's every bitch for herself. Anyway, I digress ...' She flapped her hand. 'What's the plan now he's on your trail?'

'I've no idea,' Jaynie admitted. 'I've left a few bits at the hostel, but I can't risk going back there in case he's waiting for me. And I can't stay in Manchester now he knows I'm here, so I'll have to try and sell my guitar and buy a ticket to somewhere else.'

'I wouldn't imagine you'd get much for that,' Phyllis said, pulling a face as she glanced at the guitar. 'It's as filthy as you.'

Blushing, Jaynie said, 'It's all I've got, so I haven't got much choice. I had to abandon my amp and mic when I spotted Carl, so it's not much use to me now, anyway.'

'Can't your parents help?'

'No. They're both addicts, and I haven't seen them in years.'

'Friends, then?'

'Carl knows them all so I wouldn't trust any of them.'

Phyllis pursed her lips thoughtfully for a moment. Then, swallowing the last of her tea, she leaned forward and put the cup on the table, saying, 'You're welcome to stay here tonight, if it'll help?'

'Thanks, but I couldn't expect you to do that,' Jaynie said. 'You don't even know me.'

'My instincts have served me pretty well for eighty-five years, and I don't get the feeling that you're the type who'd cut a good Samaritan's throat while they're sleeping,' said Phyllis. 'Or *are* you?' she added, her pale eyes twinkling with amusement.

'Absolutely not.' Jaynie smiled. 'But, honestly, you've done enough already by letting me come in and get warm.'

'I'm not completely heartless – although some may say different,' Phyllis replied. 'And, to be honest, this has been the longest conversation I've had with anyone other than my doctor in years – and he's a boring old bugger, so that's never from choice. I also have a spare room that hasn't been used in decades, so you wouldn't be putting me out in the slightest.'

Touched that this woman, who she'd initially written off as a rude cow, was willing to let her, a complete stranger, stay the night, Jaynie said, 'Are you sure?'

'Positive,' said Phyllis. 'Although you'll probably be desperate to escape once I start chewing your ear off. I might be as old as God's teeth and prone to forgetting what I did two minutes ago, but my memory's as clear as a bell where the past is concerned, and I have a *lot* of stories to tell. Now how about we get ourselves another cuppa, then I'll tell you about the time I worked as a chambermaid in a swanky hotel and chanced upon a Hollywood legend being pleasured by his male co-star while his wife was zonked out in the next room . . .'

2

It was almost midnight before Phyllis announced that she was ready for bed, and Jaynie had never felt more exhausted in her entire life. The woman hadn't been joking when she'd said she had a lot of stories to tell, and her voice was still ringing in Jaynie's ears as they made their way up the narrow staircase.

When they reached the tiny landing, Phyllis turned and said, 'Thank you for a wonderful day, my dear. You've made a lonely old woman very happy.'

'I've had a great time, and thank *you*,' Jaynie replied sincerely. 'You've no idea how grateful I am that you invited me in. It's the first time I've been able to relax in weeks, and that shepherd's pie was amazing.'

'You can take the leftovers with you when you leave,' said Phyllis. 'You'll need something to keep you going on that long journey. Although why you decided on Scotland as your destination, I do not know. The weather is horrendous at this time of year.'

'That's exactly why I chose it,' Jaynie grinned. 'Because Carl will never think to look for me there.'

'Well, get a good sleep and try not to think about him any more,' said Phyllis. 'I imagine he's hot-footed it back to Liverpool by now.'

'Hope so,' said Jaynie.

Still smiling as she made her way into the musty-smelling spare room after saying goodnight, she stripped down to her T-shirt and knickers, climbed into bed, and fell asleep as soon as her head hit the pillow.

On the other side of the alleyway, in the back bedroom of the vacant house where he'd been holed up since being forced to flee the old woman's garden, Carl saw the lights go out in her house and slid his cigarettes out of his pocket. The temperature had plummeted, and his hands were shaking so badly it took him three attempts to light up. Taking a deep drag when he finally managed it, he checked the time on his phone and smiled when he saw that it was just gone midnight. Not much longer and he'd be able to do what he came to do and then go home to his nice warm bed at his mam's flat. And if that cunt she'd shacked up with while he was inside kicked off about him waking them up to get in, he'd slice his throat and shove him out of the window.

Grinning at the vision of the fat bastard free-falling fourteen storeys and landing on the concrete below, Carl took another drag on his cigarette and scanned the windows of the houses across the way. He hadn't realized the alleyway was blocked off at the far end until he'd started running in that direction, so when the old woman's neighbour had come out he'd been forced to clamber over a wall and hide in a garden. From there, he'd heard the man tell the woman to lock her doors and windows. And then he'd heard Jaynie's unmistakeable voice, which told him he'd have had her if only he'd got there a few seconds earlier.

Too scared to break cover after glimpsing the have-a-go-hero and seeing that he was built like a brick shithouse, he'd waited until all had gone quiet and then crept through the gardens until he reached the boarded-up house he'd spotted at the end of the row. He'd easily forced the rotten back door open and made his way up the stairs. Able to see in through the old woman's parlour window, he'd been surprised to see Jaynie sitting on the sofa with a brew in her hand. Her loose-knickered mate, Annie the fanny, had told him she was living in some grotty hostel, so he guessed she must have moved out when she heard he'd been released and was now renting a room off the biddy. It would explain why she'd gone straight there after getting off the bus – *and* why the old bitch had covered for her when he asked if she'd seen her.

Determined to punish them both for fucking him over and forcing him to freeze his balls off in this dump all day, he checked out the windows of the houses on either side of hers. The burly neighbour had gone out a few hours earlier, wearing an orange jacket with a 'SECURITY' logo emblazoned across the back. His house had been in darkness ever since, which told Carl he probably lived alone, and there had been no signs of life in the house on the other side.

A SHOT IN THE DARK

Deciding that he would give the pair an hour or so to make sure they were properly asleep before he made his move, Carl sat down on the floor to finish his cigarette.

3

Woken by a dull thudding sound, Jaynie prised a sleepy eye open and squinted at the silhouettes of unfamiliar furniture. Both eyes popping open when she heard what sounded like a glass or a cup shattering, she remembered where she was and sat up, wondering if Phyllis had gone downstairs to make a pot of tea. The room was pitch dark and she felt like she'd only slept for a few minutes; but now she was awake, she figured she might as well get up.

Stretching her arms above her head, she frowned when she heard the door at the bottom of the stairs slowly opening. A stair creaked, then silence for several seconds, and then another creak. Instincts bristling, because she couldn't imagine Phyllis creeping around in her own house, she held her breath and strained to listen for more noises.

Phyllis's bedroom door suddenly opened, and she heard the woman call: 'Is that you, Jaynie?'

Heart pounding when she heard a man's voice – *Carl's* voice – hiss, 'Shut your fuckin' mouth!' Jaynie slid out of the bed and looked for somewhere to hide. Biting down on her hand to keep from crying out when a piercing scream filtered through the door, only to be instantly muffled, she knew she had to do something and looked for a weapon instead. Her guitar was the only thing close to hand, so she grabbed it and took a deep breath before yanking the door open.

The landing was dark, but Phyllis's door, directly opposite, was open, and in the faint glow coming from the streetlamp outside the window Jaynie made out the shadowy figure of Carl holding Phyllis down on the bed with his hands around her throat. Adrenaline surging, she raised the guitar above her head and ran at him, yelling, 'Get the fuck off her!'

Carl leapt to his feet before she reached him and threw his arm up to deflect the blow from the guitar before punching her square in the face, sending her sprawling out onto the landing carpet as blood sprayed out of her nose. Marching after her, he grabbed the front of her T-shirt and hauled her to her feet, hissing, 'Here she is . . . the bitch who tried to ruin my life.'

Tears streaming from her eyes, Jaynie screamed at the top of her voice, but doubled over when Carl punched her in the stomach.

Grabbing her hair to force her to straighten up, he said, 'The goon's out for the night, so you're wasting your breath if you think he's going to come to your rescue again. And there's no one in on the other side, neither, so it looks like you're fucked, don't it, darlin'?'

'Carl, please don't do anything stupid,' she whimpered.

'Bit late for that,' he scoffed, giving a backward jerk of his head to indicate that he was talking about the old woman. 'That's your fault, that. All you had to do was stand up and take your punishment like a big girl, but *no* . . . you had to go and drag that wrinkly fucker into it, didn't you? But don't worry, you won't have to live with her death on your conscience for long, 'cos you'll be joining her once I've had my fun,' he went on coldly. 'Then again, you don't give a shit about anyone but yourself, so it probably doesn't bother you that she's dead, does it? Just like it didn't bother you when I got sent down because of your lies!'

'I didn't lie,' Jaynie croaked, taking a step back in an attempt to draw him away from Phyllis's room when she saw the woman move behind him. 'You're the one who kept me prisoner in my own flat and raped me.'

'I'd fucked you thousands of times, so how was that rape?' Carl spat, his eyes blazing as he stepped forward and tightened his grip. 'And you asked for everything you got; treating me like some divvy cunt while you were putting it out for all me mates.'

'I never went near your mates,' Jaynie argued. 'You kicked off so bad whenever they came round, I didn't dare speak to them, never mind *that*.'

A noise made Carl snap his head round, and Jaynie grabbed his arm when she saw Phyllis on her feet in the doorway.

'Carl, don't!' she yelled. 'Just leave her alone and go! I won't tell the police you were here, I promise.'

'Shut your mouth,' he snarled, yanking his arm free. 'She's seen me; she's got to go.'

'She's got dementia so she'll have forgotten what you look like in a minute,' Jaynie lied, hanging onto the back of his jacket. 'And it's me you're after, not her, so please don't hurt her, I'm begging you.'

'Have you heard yourself, you pathetic bitch?' Carl sneered, turning and grasping her by the throat. 'Do you seriously think I give a flying fuck what you want after you betrayed me? I *hate* you and I'm gonna kill her and then finish what I started at your place before that nosy bitch called the po—'

The word caught in the back of his throat and confusion flared in his eyes as he let go of Jaynie and threw both hands up to his neck. Seconds later, his eyes rolled back in their sockets and he fell forward like a sack of coal, landing face-down on the carpet.

Jumping back, Jaynie gaped at Phyllis. 'What did you do?'

'Double dose of insulin,' Phyllis wheezed, holding up two empty syringes. 'My late husband was diabetic, so I always kept a few shots in my drawer in case he needed one during the night. Kept meaning to throw them away, but never got around to it.'

'Is– is he dead?' Jaynie asked.

Phyllis shuffled out onto the landing and poked Carl with her toe before carefully lowering herself to her knees and putting her ear to his lips.

'Still breathing, but only just,' she said, rifling through his pockets and taking out his wallet before straightening up again. 'What we do next depends on how badly you want rid of him.'

'I– I don't know what you mean,' Jaynie stuttered.

'Yes you do,' Phyllis said quietly. 'He almost killed you once before, don't forget. And I don't think he was joking when he said he was going to do away with the pair of us.'

Jaynie bit her lip and stared down at Carl. When they had first met he'd been charming and affectionate, and he'd made her feel like the most beautiful woman in the world. The speed with which he'd changed after they slept together had been alarming, and she'd been convinced she was going to die when he broke into her flat after she finished with him. Even after he'd been sent down, the campaign of terror had continued. He might not have been able to get to her personally, but chilling voicemails from withheld numbers had been left on her phone, and hand-delivered letters had been pushed under her door warning her that she could be taken out any time he gave the order. She'd lived on a knife-edge the whole time he was inside, and now he'd found her and had told her in no uncertain terms that he intended to kill her, she didn't know what to do.

'Do you want this to end?' Phyllis asked, her soft voice penetrating Jaynie's thoughts. 'All it would take is one more shot.'

'Of course I want it to end, but not like this,' Jaynie replied shakily. 'If . . . if we call an ambulance and get him taken to hospital, I'd be able to get away before they let him out, wouldn't I?'

Phyllis held her gaze for several long moments. Then,

nodding, she said, 'As you wish, dear. But I suggest you take your leave before they get here. I have no connection to him, so I can easily play the feeble old lady defending herself against the nasty burglar card. But you and he have history, which might make this look intentional.'

'Yeah, you're right,' Jaynie agreed. 'But please call them quickly, because I don't want you to be on your own with him if he starts coming round.'

'Don't you concern yourself about that,' Phyllis said calmly. 'Now take this,' she said, withdrawing the notes from the wallet and holding them out.

'No, I can't,' Jaynie protested. 'It wouldn't be right.'

'He *owes* you,' Phyllis insisted, forcing them into her hand. 'Go and find the happiness you deserve and let me get this mess cleaned up.'

Nodding, Jaynie gave Phyllis a hug, whispering, 'Thank you so much. I'll never forget how kind you've been.'

'Nor me you,' said Phyllis. 'Now go.'

Swiping the tears off her cheeks, Jaynie rushed into the spare room and quickly got dressed. Then, grabbing her rucksack, she came back out onto the landing and stepped over Carl to retrieve her guitar.

Phyllis was sitting on her bed with the landline telephone in her hand. 'Oh, hello,' she said, nodding goodbye to Jaynie as she spoke. 'I need an ambulance, please . . .'

Taking one last look at Carl, Jaynie walked quickly down the stairs and let herself out of the house.

With the phone's dial-tone buzzing in her ear, Phyllis waited until she'd heard the front door click shut before dropping the handset into its cradle. Then, taking another syringe out of her drawer, she walked back out onto the landing and gazed down at Carl for a moment before calmly plunging the needle into his neck.